THE ACTOR

MHARLYN MERRITT

Copyright © 2020 Mharlyn Merritt.

All rights reserved. No part of this book may be reproduced, stored, or transmitted by any means—whether auditory, graphic, mechanical, or electronic—without written permission of the author, except in the case of brief excerpts used in critical articles and reviews. Unauthorized reproduction of any part of this work is illegal and is punishable by law.

This is a work of fiction. All of the characters, names, incidents, organizations, and dialogue in this novel are either the products of the author's imagination or are used fictitiously.

ISBN: 978-1-7169-6043-7 (sc)
ISBN: 978-1-7169-6042-0 (e)

Because of the dynamic nature of the Internet, any web addresses or links contained in this book may have changed since publication and may no longer be valid. The views expressed in this work are solely those of the author and do not necessarily reflect the views of the publisher, and the publisher hereby disclaims any responsibility for them.

Any people depicted in stock imagery provided by Getty Images are models, and such images are being used for illustrative purposes only. Certain stock imagery © Getty Images.

Lulu Publishing Services rev. date: 08/18/2020

DEDICATION

To my late, great parents, Dorothy Merritt and Jymie Merritt,
who gave me an enduring love of movies
and the need to escape into them.

ACKNOWLEDGMENTS

My deepest thanks to Randall, Justine, Bernard, Mona, Ave, and the rest of the Smedley Writers Group for encouraging me to take my writing seriously.

I am so very grateful to Prof. Walter Cummins and Director Rene Steinke of the MFA Program in Creative Writing at Fairleigh Dickinson University whose guidance, instruction and faith in me contributed to the completion of this novel.

There are no words big enough to completely express my appreciation for the care and expertise of Maura Grace Harrington Logue, The Graceful Grammarian whose editing and formatting skills added the sparkle and shine that made everything better.

A great big thanks to everyone at Lulu Publishing.

INTRODUCTION

I'm a Southerner by birth. I like to drag things out: my words, hot baths and love affairs. You may have heard of me. I am a writer of science fiction, speculative fiction, cyberpunk — whatever they're calling it today. Most of my fans are fiercely loyal and rather pathetic; they live in their parents' basements, have long, greasy hair and no interest in sex or making a living; they will, however, sit for hours in front of a computer screen communing with the like-minded about the esoteric minutiae of my work, I mean stuff I can't even remember writing for God's sake. I tell you it just boggles the mind. Who knew when I started out in Hot Coffee, Mississippi, that it would come to this?

    I had a definite feeling my life was destined for greater things than Hot Coffee, and I knew I was different from the moment the doctor pulled me kicking and screaming from my mother's womb. My parents must have known, too, because they let me and my sister Della do whatever we damn well pleased. Consider the time they let me wear a tutu and twirl a flaming baton for the talent show at Dalton Elementary School or another time when Della and I decided we wanted to be each other for a day and went to school dressed accordingly. Of course, the principal sent us home with a suspension note, requesting our parents' immediate presence. We had, they said, disrupted the school by attending each other's class taking on the appropriate persona and refusing to step out of character when confronted by our totally flummoxed teachers. Our parents were so upset by what my dear mother called "a tempest in a teapot" that they took us out of school altogether. We returned to formal education in high school, having been tutored at home by mother and father, and I am proud to say we were leaps and bounds ahead of the other students.

    Flora and Eldridge Pickles were unique, and Grandmother Pickles was the light of my life. My father had been a classical pianist until rheumatoid arthritis robbed him of his career; he had played at Carnegie Hall and toured Europe. My mother was a seamstress and had worked for several successful Broadway musicals. Flora and Eldridge met in New York and bonded instantly when my mother's accent revealed she was from Oxford, Mississippi.

Both my parents wanted a life outside of that poorest of States, but finances — or lack thereof — and the death of Grandfather Pickles hastened their return. In the end, they were happy to be back. My father taught music at Hot Coffee High and my mother continued her trade as a seamstress doing alterations and making prom dresses and the like. They've both passed on now, along with Grandmother Pickles. There was so much love among our little tribe in Hot Coffee I can hardly bear to think of it, my heart aches so. I can see my parents' faces, beaming with pride, when I graduated high school. I smeared those proud faces with lipstick kisses and my mascara ran with tears of joy.

No matter what you may have gone through during your adolescent years, you cannot imagine the trauma of being a fag in Hot Coffee, Mississippi. I don't know what I would have done if it wasn't for my family. I felt as lonely and dejected as a whipped dog when I was at Stanford; then Della, who had won the local beauty pageant and was crowned "The Cream of Hot Coffee," got a free trip to Hollywood and started working in a soap opera.

It was Della who met and became friends with Academy Award-winning production designer Gordon Burdett.

One fateful night Della kidnapped me and forced me to be her escort to one of Gordon parties; that's when I met and fell in love with Gordon's second wife, the bronze bombshell herself: Felicia Lake. I dubbed her Babe after Paul Bunyan's Blue Ox, because Felicia was what you call zaftig. Not fat, but big where it counts, tall and all woman: tough on the outside and even tougher on the inside, but warm and sweet with it, you know?

I had not felt so unconditionally loved since my childhood days in Hot Coffee. It was Babe who gave me the money to get to London and live for a while when I got accepted, on full scholarship, to pursue my master's degree at London University, which is where I met The Actor and fell hopelessly in love with him, but that's another story altogether.

Gordon Burdett died and so did my baby sister Della. Babe went on to husband number three, but she was more precious to me than ever. We were cohorts.

Since those early days, shrouded in a mist of nostalgia and Jack Daniel's, I have travelled many a rugged highway with Babe. I love her, I love her company.

I was all too familiar with her tendencies to prevaricate, exaggerate and recall moments in her personal history from an extremely biased point of view, so when she asked me to help her write about her encounter with the man I call "Thespian" I was honored. Babe, Thespian and myself have remained the most devoted of friends.

The following discourse is in Babe's voice. I acted merely as an amplifier and arbiter. After all, I was the one who introduced them, although I do believe that they had already met on some metaphysical level long before I became an intermediary.

I don't believe Thespian has ever read the manuscript, although it was offered to him to read and edit as he saw fit. Babe, on the other hand, has gone through this with a fine-tooth comb, so you can blame her for any inaccuracies. I suggested the title **The Actor** *because it covers so many elements in their lives: conscious versus subconscious, tragedy versus comedy, professionalism versus predilection. In the end it's all show business, honey.*

— Raymond T. Pickles

CHAPTER 1

Dear World: I am leaving because I'm bored.

— from actor George Sanders' suicide note

There is a line in the film *All About Eve* that makes me howl with laughter. No, it's not the famous seat-belt line. It's when Addison Dewitt, portrayed with such icky precision by the masterful British actor George Sanders confronts Eve Harrington in a hotel room after she's trampled on the souls of all those who have befriended her, in her ruthless climb to the top; most especially her benefactress, Margo Channing (Bette Davis at the height of her powers).

DeWitt says something that infuriates Eve Harrington (Anne Baxter at her scene-chewing best), or maybe she's just pretending to be infuriated, as she whirls over to the door and basically tells DeWitt to let the doorknob hit him where the good Lord split him. DeWitt smiles and with all the charm of a rattlesnake says, "You're too short for that gesture." Ah, George Sanders: viciousness with class. George Sanders has a lifetime pass to my heart. He was married to Zsa Zsa Gabor, the Hungarian H-bomb, enough to make any man commit suicide, which is what George Sanders did, poor baby.

I was meditating on George Sanders over a large glass of whiskey at Bridgewater's Bar and Grille. It was the anniversary of my mother's suicide and I was depressed. I was also angry as hell, because my tenure had been denied and I was asked to resign from a second rate university that was little more than a glorified vocational training school and this, this crummy watering hole in the middle of a train station, was the scene of my fall from grace.

It was on a Wednesday: Dan Fesman, professor of comparative

literature was sitting at one of the tables with his teaching assistant. It was no secret he was conjugating her verbs as an extra-curricular activity. His voice held weight within the committee that was evaluating my bid for tenure, and he had used this as leverage to try to blackmail me into sleeping with him. When I refused and outed him through formal channels as a sexual harasser, the university closed ranks around him and made my life a living hell. So, on that Wednesday night when I spied him, with his little piece of heaven, I was ready for him.

As I sat at the bar Fesman, being true to the slimy thing he is, approached me on his way to the men's room. He leaned in close and whispered that if I had only played the game things would have turned out so much better for me. Even as a child I was never good at playing games; I let him know in no uncertain terms. He adjusted his tie and strolled off towards the men's room, him and his Men's Warehouse suits. It was a shame he looked so much like Robert Taylor in *Johnny Eager*; I would have slept with him without the blackmail. Just goes to show you how insecure Professor Fesman is, the asshole.

I was thinking about how much of an asshole he truly was when I tripped him, as he walked past me. He fell flat on his face and broke his nose. There was blood everywhere. His little TA was crying as she held a wad of napkins to his face. I was laughing so hard, I cried, too.

Recalling the joy of hearing Professor Fesman screaming, "My nose is broken!" did nothing to set aside my depression. I had been drinking too much and thinking too little. On my way home, the streets were wet with rain, the headlights made reflecting pools out of puddles and sinister shadows loomed in the angles between tall buildings — all classic visual signatures of film noir. I ought to know, I wrote the book on it, a book called *Rebels, Dames and Misfits* about the heroes and heroines of film noir, required reading for the class I taught.

Sitting in the back of that cab I felt like Robert Ryan in *On Dangerous Ground*. I wanted the cab driver to drive me all night, drive me into a new life. I was tired, so very tired. That was what was written on the crumpled piece of paper found in my mother's hand: "I'm just so very tired."

THE ACTOR

The cab pulled up to the door of my little rented house on my little dreary street and all I could think of was, Bette Davis curling her lip and spitting out, "What a dump." I paid the cabbie, unlocked the door and walked into the darkness. I had run out of husbands, or was it that I simply could not stomach the idea of a fourth, despite the fact that I hated sleeping alone?

I found the light switch, which only served to illuminate the detritus of a lifetime. The crap I convinced myself I couldn't live without: a faux Louis XIV chaise lounge upholstered in red brocade and framed in gold, once a prop in the movie *Dangerous Liaisons*; stacks of *Women's Wear Daily* magazines, way too heavy to throw out; shelves and shelves of books; a Turkish rug which I probably hadn't vacuumed since I bought it — things once meaningful, now meaningless.

The best thing I could do for mankind would be to burn the goddamned house to the ground with me in it. Hadn't I always wanted to be cremated? Then I remembered: I really, really didn't like pain and I was very, very drunk.

This same night forty years ago my mother had locked herself in the bathroom and swallowed a handful of pills. What had she been thinking, I wondered? It was so long ago, and I still wondered. When I thought about my mother's death, I always thought about George Sanders as Addison Dewitt, because he reminded me of my mother. Raymond T. Pickles saved me from certain disaster that night, when I was at the crossroad: forced to resign, tenure-less and husband-less, thinking about suicide — my mother's, George Sanders' and possibly my own. I didn't want to return to California. My daughter and her husband would have welcomed me back with open arms, as would my third husband Nick Ravelli. California held so much for me, but it also held so much against me. Nashville was calling, and Pickles needed me to go to London. Writers never have any money. His publisher had refused any more advances because of some typically prurient Pickles activity, which had left his publisher less than confident in Raymond's promises.

I was to bankroll this adventure and Pickles would repay me "in-kind." This was arts-grant-speak for not in money but something of equal value; to me there is nothing of equal value to cold hard cash, but this was classic Pickles. I was always a sucker and willing accomplice for whatever half-baked schemes he had in mind; however, I had made other plans which had sprung from questions I had about my mother's death.

My father, T. Laurence Lake the sculptor, had been an indulgent, supportive, kind and loving man, but on the subject of Catherine Bannister-Lake he was always acidic and now unintelligible, reduced to almost Brussels sprout status because of a stroke. So, I decided to use my unforeseen free time to track down my older brother, TL Jr., in hopes of getting a few questions answered. I was determined, and not even Pickles could talk me out of it.

I would rendezvous with Pickles at the Camden Locke Hotel, because it was cheap and central to everything in Camdentown, where Pickles' publisher was.

"Perfection, sugar, but let me warn you, you will not like Nashville no matter how much you like country music. You will not be able to get a decent latte to save your life. Remember you heard it from me." I hate to admit this, but Pickles was generally right about fashion, men and food. I had toyed with the idea of living in Nashville, thought better of it, and thank God I did because it was a schizoid city now, bouncing back and forth between two cultural identities. There was the Nashville of legend with the Confederate flag flapping in the wind, pulled pork, Jack Daniel's, NASCAR and the Country Music Hall of Fame (where I got a really cool laminated copy of a 21-year-old Elvis' driver's license).

Then there were the refugees from 5th Avenue, with cell phones glued to their ears, ordering watery Cosmopolitans before they ran off to see Kanye West at the Ryman Auditorium, original home of the Grand Ole Opry. I liked the old Nashville better.

It was 102 degrees Fahrenheit when I visited TL Jr. in the gated community outside of Nashville where he lived with his wife of ten years, Mary Constable. Mary had been a country singer once, fairly well known, but a drug habit had cut her career short and been responsible for a fight that resulted in the business end of a stiletto heel blinding her in one eye.

She and TL Jr. didn't have any children. They had one of those mysterious relationships that worked but it was anybody's guess why. TL Jr. is about six foot two, thin with long hands and long fingers. He has fierce grey eyes with yellow flecks in them and his complexion is the color of walnuts, like mine. If you took a picture of Frederick Douglass, the former slave, abolitionist and writer when he was a young man, put it beside a picture of my father when he was young man and a recent picture of TL Jr. you'd be hard pressed to tell who's who.

It was TL Jr. who broke down the bathroom door and found my mother. He was seventeen at the time. I don't think he ever got over it. None of us has, really. The day after I arrived in Nashville, TL Jr. took me to a Mexican restaurant on Vanderbilt's campus.

My brother TL Jr. is a man of few words. Most of the talking I did with him on the phone was to ask if he was still on the line. He had not changed. He was as taciturn as ever, at first.

Later I would come to realize how much he hated our father and how much he loved our mother. It never occurred to me that all that stoic silence was the mask of a shy, sensitive man who was deeply hurt and hurting. I knew very little about what he did for a living. I knew he did research in cell and developmental biology at Vanderbilt University School of Medicine. I only knew that because I Googled him.

TL Jr. might not be the happiest of men, but he had made his peace with life. I wanted some of that. He looked up from his burrito and broke the silence:

"Mary asked me if you'd come out to poker night tomorrow. I told her everything you feel shows on your face."

"Is she any better?"

"She's dying and that's all I'm saying on the subject."

We continued eating our super burritos and drinking our Coronas in silence. I felt sad. I wasn't close to Mary, but I did like her. She'd had a rough life and now this. I stared at TL for the longest trying to figure out how to let him know how sorry I was. He raised his left eyebrow and gave me that "don't even go there" look, and I backed off. I was not, however, going to back off of the subject of Catherine Bannister Lawrence, our mother.

"TL, why do you think Mom killed herself?"

"You just can't leave it alone, can you? Always, picking at a scab until it starts to bleed."

"I just think you know something you're not telling me."

"Felicia, I know a shit load of things. I'm a smart man, respected in my field; knowing something and being able to change that something are two different things. What I'm saying is: what I know is not going to make a difference. I got to go to work. Let me know if you're coming to poker night. I'll pick you up at the motel."

With that, TL Jr. got up, threw some money on the table, even though he had already paid for our meals, kissed me on the forehead and left. As I stuffed the money into my purse, I realized that this was the longest conversation I had ever had with my brother in my life. What I couldn't figure was whether he had been talking about our mother or his wife.

Well, I had kicked the sleeping dog and he was wide awake and growling, like my stomach. I lay in one of two double beds in my motel room at the Days Inn, wishing I had gone to poker night. I had come here for answers and all I got for my trouble were more questions. I finally fell into a stress-induced sleep and dreamt a strange dream about a man I was destined to meet a week later. The man who would change my life forever: The Actor.

I'm in the kitchen of a small restaurant. Judging by the clothes, furnishings and utensils it's the 1950s. Amid the hustle and bustle of the kitchen, where meals are being prepared and waiters whirl in and out through swinging doors, my father sits quietly at a table in the corner. He looks dignified in his tuxedo, but older and more worn out than in life. The table where my father sits happens to be near a little cubbyhole that houses the dish-washing station. Even though it's steamy hot in the kitchen, the green chiffon dress I'm wearing is cool against my skin. My hair is bobbed, it feels foreign. This is me, but inside someone else's body.

I ask one of the prep staff: "Where's Pop's meal? He has to go back on in twenty minutes." As another waiter rushes out with another order, I see a shiny black grand piano through the swinging door.

There's a commotion between the busboy and the dishwasher. The chef quells it before it gets out of control. Still irritated, the dishwasher, who has his back to us, shouts that my father and I should get out of the kitchen and that he's sick of "that old man."

"That old man was famous before you were born," I shout back. Then the dishwasher whirls around and stares at me with such hate I almost lose my balance. He's a skinny blond kid about 25 or so, with deep-set blue eyes that are full of anger and pain. He's twitching like he's high on something or needs to get high on something. His eyes are wild and red-rimmed. He hasn't shaved. His blond hair, damp with sweat, is plastered to his head. The dirty, threadbare white shirt he wears, sleeves rolled up, collar unbuttoned at the neck, is rendered transparent by perspiration. His food-encrusted black pants are shiny from dirty dishwater. He looks crazed and dangerous. As he moves slowly towards me, I gather my father up, saying, "Come on, Pop, let's go. You'll eat out front tonight." Just then, the maître d' comes in wanting to know what the shouting is about, says the customers can hear it.

When he sees the state of the dishwasher, the maître d' takes my father out into the club with instructions for one of the waiters to bring Pop his meal. The maître d' and Pop disappear through the door and all at once the dishwasher's in my face. He's trembling like an exposed nerve end. He's so close I can feel the heat of his breath. I can't tell if he wants to hurt me or he wants me to help him. "What do you know about it? Huh?" he asks through clenched teeth. He reaches inside his pants pocket for something.

He moves closer but loses his balance, trips and falls onto the chair where my Pop had been sitting. He begins to cry. He gestures to me like he wants me to come to him, as if he has something to tell me. I hear voices all around: "Don't go near him", "What's the matter with him, anyway?" "The kid's got rabies or something."

Despite the chorus of protests, I move towards him, compelled by pity. As I lean forward, he grabs a cake knife with a pale green glass handle from the counter and points it at me. There is a collective gasp in the little kitchen. I see the chef circling behind the dishwasher.

"It's all right," I say holding out my hand, "Everything's going to be OK. You can give it to me." He calms down and hands it over. Then, in an instant, he's a wild man again screaming: "You were never there when I needed you". That's when I realize he's delirious with some kind of fever and has superimposed some hurtful person from the past onto me, but why me? He's sobbing now.

The chef, who has managed to circle behind him, begins to close in. The maître d' bursts in again, angry about the noise. It's at this instant the dishwasher pulls out a pearl-handled revolver from his pants pocket. Someone shouts: "He's got a gun!"

The dishwasher jerks to his left and then to his right waving the gun unsteadily as people duck and pans and dishes clatter and crash to the floor. The dishwasher calms down for a moment, shakes his head like a wet dog then raises the gun as if he is going to give it to me like the cake knife; there is a flash of white light and then everything goes black.

I woke up terrified. I didn't like this. I didn't want to know what it meant, because I didn't like the way it made me feel. I didn't like being shot in my own goddamned dream.

CHAPTER 2

I will continue with my eccentricity.

— Tennessee Williams

I arrived at Heathrow in one piece; however, my luggage was nowhere to be found — neither was that rascal Pickles. But what else was new? I learned that during my two-hour layover in Toronto, my luggage had been diverted to God knows where. Thank you, Air Canada. At this point I was so fucking tired that I stood in front of the baggage carousel, tranced-out in a jet-lag induced Zen coma. Somehow, I noticed this whacky dame out of the corner of my right eye.

I have an antenna for and aversion to crazy women because my mother was one. I had developed staying out of my mother's way into an art form. This woman I spied out of the corner of my eye could well have been my mother: squat with blonde-tipped, brown rooted hair, that stood straight up on her head. She wore tinted wrap-around sunglasses, a yellow short-sleeved shirt, Capri jeans and the obligatory flip-flops. I turned to get a better look, which was a big mistake, because she whipped her head around like a velociraptor and stared at me intently over the rim of her glasses.

I put my head down and stared at the floor for a few seconds, frightened at how familiar this woman was to me, despite the fact that I'd never seen her before. When I looked up again, she was slumped over her luggage cart like Markham's "The Man with the Hoe": "Bowed by the weight of centuries he leans…"

Her face was contorted by an angry, tortured, grimace as if some violent storm were raging inside her head. She reminded me of Judi

Dench in *Notes on a Scandal*: utilitarian, blunt and taxing. I moved as far away from her as I could, and of course, she followed me. I am a magnet for crazy people.

Slow dissolve to mark the passage of time. Maybe I'd fallen asleep, I can't remember. The luggage cart was still jerking round, and still no luggage. I felt a chilly presence on my left; sure enough, there was the whacky dame. This time she spoke. "I don't think we're getting our luggage," she hissed through clenched teeth. "It's been an hour — one hour."

She looked American, but her accent was English — not totally unexpected. I was too tripped-out on the faux-high of total fatigue and hunger to carry on a conversation.

Holding on to my luggage cart for support and comfort, I carefully maneuvered my weary body across the great expanse before me, towards the Air Canada baggage desk looming in the distance like some shimmering mirage, and there she was. I couldn't figure out, for the life of me, how she had gotten herself over there without me seeing her pass by, and yet there she was, Ms. Whacky, at the Air Canada baggage desk having it out with this poor red-headed guy, who just backed up and disappeared through a doorway.

Ms. Whacky turned on her heels gave me a desultory look, expelled air through her clenched teeth like a vent releasing steam and shot off in a huff.

As I stepped up to the Air Canada baggage counter, an older woman with a pleasant face and helmet-hair mysteriously appeared like the good witch Glinda. She was so sweet, that I really didn't give a shit about the missing luggage anymore.

She insisted I take an Air Canada goodie bag with stuff for the luggage-less in it: toothpaste, toothbrush, giant white T-shirt.

Operating on some semi-conscious level with my carry-on bag in tow and my Air Canada goodie bag clutched in hand, I tried to find my way out of Heathrow. Every door seemed to have a sign that read, "Emergency Exit Only." I saw two Sikh worker-dudes, bearded with red turbans, dressed in brown overalls chilling on a flatbed cart. "How do I get out of here?"

They just stared at me as if I had two heads. By this time, I had a headache that was big enough for two heads. One of the Sikhs said, "Go" and the other one said, "Out there," as he pointed to the emergency exit. "And what do I do then?" The Sikh bookends looked at each other and then at me and said in unison, "Just go."

I couldn't tell if they were annoyed with me or if they were being helpful. I exited into the glare of a London sun, shining on happily. Bah-humbug! I wanted dark roiling skies churning up fog as thick as pea soup. I wanted damp streets and the elements to be as foul as my mood. I wanted film noir to go with my headache and the precarious nature of my future.

Two generation-nexters were handling the cab queue. Why do these people look the same all over the world, regardless of race, creed or national origin? Like the real person fell asleep and this is the giant pod re-creation pretending to be human while plotting a takeover. And why did their aesthetics hearken back to the seriously square period of the early 60s? Why didn't they have any body fat? "Let's be thankful they haven't brought madras back," my brain said to me, in consolation. One of them was speaking: "Where ya headed?" They couldn't fool me, these pod-creatures. They had brought madras back.

"Camden," I said without looking at him. The other one chimed in.

"Oh, Camden is it?"

If they only knew how much I was spoiling for a fight. "Just get me a fucking cab."

If there's one thing I've learned in my travels, it's that fear of an angry Black woman is universal. The two pod-droids receded as a totally chill cobalt blue cab rolled up in front of me — slow-motion, cue music. The door opened by some invisible hand. I stepped inside with the grace and dignity of the Royals, whisked away to Camdentown, bidding farewell to the little pod-droid assholes with a majestic swivel of my hand.

I'll never forget my cab ride. Not even my forays into the minds of the ghetto-fabulous had yielded such a breakdown in communications. The cabbie was sweet but barely intelligible. Conversing with someone who, for all intents and purposes, speaks the same language and not being able to understand what the fuck they're talking about is frustrating and exhausting, and I already had a headache. To make matters worse, the cabbie couldn't understand me either. Let's face it, they speak English; we speak American.

Fifteen minutes into the ride we settled on some form of the language we both could understand. I suppose our ears had gotten attuned to each other's accents. I liked this guy. He was no-frills: early 50s, stocky with hair the color of gunmetal, hairy forearms, round, red, pock-marked face with generous features; wearing a Hawaiian shirt and smelling of tobacco.

He began to fret over my plight: all alone in the big, bad city, a woman such as yourself. This innocent face of mine has gotten some poor man or other into trouble most of my life. Now, the cabbie was telling me how to save money. I should eat in the pubs. Good basic food at a fair price. I shouldn't eat the fish and chips if they were greasy. "They shouldn't be greasy, luv." I should try to find another area to stay. Camden was too expensive.

As we pulled up to the Camden Locke Hotel, there were two punk-girls standing at the entrance. One girl was on the chubby side. She was wearing a Ramones T-shirt that had been ventilated by razor blades. Her hair was dyed jet black and looked as though she had cut it with a rusty spoon. Short fleshy legs swathed in black fishnets extended from cut-off jeans with the de rigueur motorcycle boots. She had face metal and tattoo panoramas running down both arms.

The woman she was talking to was a little more subdued, what I like to call "conservative out-there": pixie haircut, black roots purple tips, slim but not cadaverous. She wore a purple and black striped blouse over a chartreuse miniskirt, her legs covered in black leather hip-boots.

The outside of the hotel was a flat, boring slab of white with yellow-framed windows and a cheap box sign above the doorway that read "Camden Locke Hotel" in black letters.

"All you need," the cabbie said, "beer drinkers on the step." As I got out of the cab, the cabbie was there to close the door behind me. I paid him and tipped him. He looked hurt and surprised. He gave me back a couple bills and his card.

"Too much; this isn't America. Don't go tipping like that or you'll go broke. Wrote my home number on the back of the card. If you get into any trouble just call me."

I kissed him on the cheek and told him I would. His name was Fred. I watched Fred drive away with a slight pang in my heart. He was a nice guy, so I showed him some mercy: I never called him.

THE ACTOR

I headed towards the hotel with my one piece of carry-on and my Air Canada goodie-bag. The two punk-girls were still deep in conversation at the entrance, only they weren't drinking beer, they were drinking Red-Bull and the one with the purple-singed hair was the concierge.

Once inside, at the front desk, I told her about my luggage and that the airline was supposed to deliver it. She was a pretty girl with a sullen face and dark circles under her eyes.

"I have people waiting weeks for luggage," she said in a thick Greek accent. "Join a club. Here is key. Room 201. Your friend already in room."

"Which way is the elevator?"

"Stairs on left."

No elevator. I was kind of happy I didn't have any luggage. I would have just curled up right there on the floor in the lobby rather than drag suitcases up stairs. As I trudged up the two British flights, which translate into three American, I began to think about George Sanders.

I could hear water running as I approached the open door to Room 201. As I stepped into the room, Pickles emerged from the bathroom just to the left of the open door. He was wrapped and turbaned in white towels. I gestured towards the open door with incredulity. "I knew you were on your way up," he said as he pressed a damp cheek against mine, "That Cossack bitch at the desk called."

"She's Greek," I said, walking past him to check out the room.

"Big whatever. Give me a minute to get myself together and I'll get your bags."

I whirled around and displayed my rectangular black canvas Calvin Klein shoulder tote with the white and green piping, as I held out my plastic Air Canada clutch, "These are my bags."

"That's it? That Calvin Klein fragrance give-away bag and that dollar store thing. That's all you crossed the Atlantic with? Child, how the mighty have fallen. You should turn in your subscription to W and be drummed out of the corps."

"The airline misplaced my luggage."

"Well, thank God. I thought you'd turned into a hippie. I like that black dress, though. Neiman Marcus?"

"I am a hippie, and yes, it is."

"I saw it in the catalog and those silk rainbow espadrilles, definitely Gucci. What do you mean misplaced? You don't seem worried. Why, the old Babe would have the Queen on the phone by now."

"Deepak Chopra says worrying is putting negative energy into the air. Where's my bed?"

Pickles dropped his towel and began to dress. This was purposeful. He knew it made me uncomfortable being exposed to his pudgy cadaver-white nakedness, but Pickles had no shame.

"We're in here together," Pickles said patting the bed with glee.

"What do you mean, we're in here together? In the same bed? Are you crazy?"

"Now sugar, you know I am. I'm just economizing, trying to save us some money, honey. You know you don't have to worry about Mr. Pickles' pickle."

"I hate it when you talk like that."

I plopped down on the bed, too beat to argue. Save me money, hah! I knew the Pickle man. He was saving me money so he could borrow it to go off and do God only knew what, with God only knew who. Quietly I resigned myself to my fate. Collapsing on the bed with the Calvin Klein tote still on my shoulder and the Air Canada bag clutched in my hand, I fell asleep.

When I awoke the room was in semi-darkness, illuminated eerily by the streetlight outside the window. I was scared for a minute, disoriented. I sat up, and there he was in the chair in the corner underneath the wall-mounted TV: the dishwasher who had killed me in my dream.

He was wearing a long black cashmere coat, very stylish. The streetlight outside the window cast a yellow glow. I could see that he had aged into a ruggedly handsome man, his face tough but tender, still something wild about those blue eyes. His damp blunt-cut blond hair glowed in the dark, his sunken blue eyes still pleading, his knuckles white as he gripped the arms of the chair:

"Where are you?" he snarled, "Where are you?" I hit the overhead light switch and he was gone. I couldn't catch my breath. I went to the open window hoping the air would fortify me.

It was barely dark, yet in the street below the overflow of trendies from the pub on the corner was already clogging the road.

THE ACTOR

I wondered how much real fucking was going on among the young these days, amid the texting, the posturing, the smoking of the big ganja weed and the dosings of Special K and E. It was better to think of this — it was better to think of anything — than the blond man in the chair. I wondered where Raymond T. Pickles was, because I was afraid the blond one would return.

Then, as if directed by magic, the door opened, revealing a shadowy figure on the threshold, outlined in a glowing halo from the hall light, like the Virgin of Guadalupe. The glowing shadow figure stepped into the room. It was Raymond T. Pickles, who informed me in no uncertain terms that we were going to eat at Nardo's, around the corner and then we were going to The Jazz Café to hear Diesler and his band, all on my dime mind you, the big deadbeat. I was never so happy to see anyone in my whole life.

I couldn't tell if Nardo's was Spanish or Portuguese. I heard both being spoken behind the counter in a weird, mixed-up way that made it sound like neither. A grilled chicken meal came in at around six pounds. The wine was red, coarse and equally economical. The smell of the chicken, a tangy perfume of secret spices with overtones of sage and rosemary, was sensual and reassuring. The rough-hewn wooden tables gave us the perfect platform for serious eating. It was all about the eating in this place. Alas, my romantic notions about Nardo's were destroyed when Pickles informed me that it was a franchise.

I amused myself as I ate by trying to figure out exactly what the hell Pickles was wearing. For years he had worn these ensembles reminiscent of the Mad Hatter, but within the last year or so he had toned it down to a more subdued insanity: the hushed and controlled madman.

Tonight he was wearing huge baggy red pants and a white X-Files T-shirt, all wrapped up in a black patent leather trench-coat; his jaw-length curly black hair stuffed into a black knit Rasta cap, low- cut classic black suede Pumas on his sock-less feet, white Jackie-O sunglasses on his nose and a red and black striped scarf which he was using as a napkin. I kept trying to remove bits of chicken caught in his mustache, but he flicked my hand away.

"I am not your child, woman."

"What do you call that? I mean it's not really a mustache is it? There's that big space in the middle of it."

"Honey, there's a big space in the middle of everything." With that, Pickles threw off the Rasta cap and shook his hair out.

"Pickles, you cheat. You've dyed your hair."

"Black hair to go with my black heart . . . Well, you dye yours, don't you?"

"I'm cutting this conversation short."

We stepped out onto the high street and were immediately caught up in the flow of humanity, as we headed towards The Jazz Café. I would have preferred a cab, but Pickles wanted to walk, and walk we did, amid tall German hippies, high on Special K; Arab women all garbed up, pushing double-barreled baby-strollers; and families of molasses-colored Africans with blank looks on their faces.

We were at Ferdinand Street now, with the big pink store on the corner with the big pink chair hanging from the second story, just a couple doors down from the original home of the original Doc Martens'. As we approached the bridge over the Grand Union Canal, to our right loomed one of the many tentacles of the Starbucks beast. We walked on past more commerce, more people moving slowly leaving wakes of un-bathed aromas. We floated through the Camden Market like visiting dignitaries surveying the provinces.

"You see," Pickles began, "energetically, we're travelling on another plane. We can see them, but they can't see us."

"Yeah, well they're staring pretty hard for people who can't see us."

What a nerve they had, these people — only seconds away from being arrested by the fashion police, and they were staring at us.

We came to the nexus of Camdentown where the high street crosses Parkway at the Camden Tube Station: a thick clot of humans and traffic. Pickles said this is where the locals rub elbows with the tourists and the day trippers, the panhandlers with the Paris Hilton wannabes, the junkies with the backpackers, while the luvies dash out of the tube station, running like their pants are on fire towards the safety of Primrose Hill.

I learned that past this point, walking south towards the Mornington Crescent Tube Station, only the hard-core tourists will venture, usually the hostel dwellers looking for drugs.

As we crossed the intersection past the T-Mobile store, the street vendor selling produce, and a newsstand — there, looming above us, was this white building like an iceberg, with a blue neon sign: "London's World Famous Jazz Venue."

Two security guys were planted on the front step, both in black suits with purple shirts and black ties. One checked a goofy American college girl's backpack (she was stoned and couldn't stop giggling) while the other security guy remained expressionless. Pickles thought these guys were Russians. I thought they were Greek. The unoccupied security guy nodded us in. Once inside I paid for Pickles and myself — $60 fucking USD (but it's only 30 pounds, luv). Kiss my ass.

Two guys dressed exactly like the two guys on the step were stationed by the "ticket booth" looking like they just couldn't wait to beat the shit out of somebody, anybody (as long as it wasn't us, Lord Jesus).

A split bar, serving the lounge and the main room, faced us as we made our way into the main room where the band was playing on a raised stage. In front of the stage, which was about 10 feet off the floor, a tribe of lost children jumped up and down to the beat. Drunk, high on Special K and Ecstasy, they'd taken that throbbing pulse into their nervous systems and for the moment it had replaced the beat of their hearts.

The grey walls were throbbing as the sound filled the cavernous space and made me move in spite of myself. The horn section (trumpet, trombone and tenor sax) was killer. They had this lock-step-bob thing going that just made me nuts. Even Pickles was squirming to the music with his snaky movements.

The trombone player caught my eye: tall, navy blue sharkskin suit, spiked platinum blond hair. As the drummer and the bass player laid it down in the pocket with vicious precision, the singer took center stage.

She was a giraffe-like goofy brunette with the body and features of a bargain basement model. Her low-riders kept riding lower as she danced this goofy digging-for-clams dance with this goofy spaced-out expression on her stupid face. She was either mentally deficient or stoned or both. The music got the crowd crazed, jumping up and down like Maasai warriors. The drummer, a compact, bald, rough dude, who looked like he could satisfy any woman — or man, for that matter — had Pickles hypnotized.

I ordered two, surprisingly cheap Jack Daniel's — handed one to Pickles who grabbed it without taking his eyes off the drummer:

"Doesn't he look just like Grant on the *EastEnders*?"

"Pickles, I've seen that so-called singer before."

"Oh, to hell with her. Get your ass up there and show her how it's done."

Just then the singer stepped up to the mic with her white sleeveless tank top hanging off one shoulder marked with sweat, tangled in a necklace of white enamel O's and gold chains — the epitome of trendy-sexy-cool — then she opened her mouth. What came out was like the sound of a cat being strangled by a yodeling cowboy, and it went on and on and on.

I just stared at her in utter disbelief. She must have felt the vibe, because she looked at me and instantly lost her cool, but only for a moment. With one maniacal flip of her hair she was back in there making sounds that would kill a dog.

I turned my back on the whole thing and ordered another drink. I guess this was what was passing for singing these days. I was glad I was out of that game. I mean Christ, this was the reason I'd stopped singing in the first place. What was the point? This crap just reminded me of how fucked up the world was in these terroristic times: kicks without quality because it's the fricking apocalypse-goddamned morons.

Thankfully, the set was over. Diesler, looking a little sheepish, thanked the crowd and the band left the stage, ascending the stairway to the Valhalla of the dressing rooms. I followed the trombone player with my eyes, plotting on him. All the while Pickles was checking me out:

"He's not the man for you, Babe. I've got the man for you."

"Isn't that chick, the alleged singer, the Stretch Armstrong chick, isn't she an actress on that Brit Com? You know the one."

"I don't know what in God's name you're talking about, but that woman sure as hell could not sing to save her life."

Pickles was so drunk now he was drawling like a Confederate Army colonel from *Gone with the Wind*. I was pretty plastered, having managed to position one butt cheek on a bar stool to steady myself, when the drummer from Diesler's band appeared on the floor.

THE ACTOR

Pickles was about to snap into predatory mode when the inevitable happened: fans.

There was a tall, portly, moon-faced, unshaven youth with long, dark, greasy hair parted in the middle tugging at Pickles' sleeve. The kid was dressed in the uniform of the faithful: all black and way too many pockets.

"Are y-y-ou D-D-Dr. P-P-P..."

"PICKLES!" Raymond T. shouted so loud that heads turned.

His identity confirmed, the kid motioned and three of his buddies who were hanging back emerged from the shadows. They began talking in rapid fire succession:

"You are the best..."

"I've read everything..."

"I think *New* Genesis is the seminal cyber–punk work of the decade..."

"The bible," they all *said* in unison.

As much as Pickles said he hated this crap, he was beaming. He nodded in affirmation not saying a word; "let them salivate and worship at the throne" was written all over his face. He slurped down the remainder of his double Jack Daniel's, absently handing me the glass as he motioned for more like he was the King of freaking France or some shit.

It was easy for me to forget Pickles had a PhD, was one of the world's foremost authorities on science fiction, and one of the founding fathers of cyber-punk.

He had taught the novel *Necromancer* as a graduate course. These kids would keep him here all night.

"Pickles, time to go!"

"My handler. OK, fellas, Thursday night at Oxford Arms, High Street, nineteen hundred. Be there or be square."

With that we were out on the street headed toward a Noodle House where I ate something that made me sick.

The next morning, I was awoken by Pickles flopping over on me and wriggling like a flounder on the deck of a fishing boat. I was already rest-broken and cranky, having had my sleep interrupted by the noise of early morning rubbish removal in the street below. Nothing seemed to disturb the distinguished Dr. R. T. Pickles. I learned later that he used earplugs, the big cheat.

He looked so peaceful now, just like a mentally deficient child. I was sure the jammies he wore were relics from his late grandfather. I thought the paisley-print sleep mask was a bit Norma Desmond, but who am I to judge? I had no clothes, no pajamas — just a pair of undies and a big-ass white T-shirt courtesy of Air Canada. It was half past seven in the a.m. and I was not going to get any more sleep, so I got up, showered, and put on the same dress I had been wearing since I arrived.

Downstairs the little lobby was deserted except for the night-man, a middle-aged unshaven Greek, who was still on duty. He eyed me suspiciously, as I headed for the lounge where a spartan breakfast had been laid out. I settled for a Styrofoam cup of instant coffee and nodded at the Greek: "See, friendly American" as I walked out to Chalk Farm Road. I had no idea where anything was except Nardo's, which I remembered was around the corner. I knew it wouldn't be open this early.

Then a strange thing happened. I felt something tugging at my left arm and I just followed it down the Chalk Farm Road past the tube station until I got to Adelaide Street. This force kept pulling me to my left. I had no idea where I was going, which pretty much describes the story of my life, when wham-o! I found myself walking up a path into a beautiful little park.

As I trudged onwards and upwards, I could see from my vantage point that all paths led to the summit. This little park was comforting in the compact and logical way it was laid out. There was an elderly man walking his terrier, but aside from the two of them and me the park was empty. I felt so safe, as if I had been here many times before as part of a comfortable routine. I was a little winded, my legs a little wobbly when I got to the top of the hill, but the view of central London was worth it. I sat down on a bench to soak it all in: the muted sounds of gulls crying, a distant titwillow chirping, the old man's terrier yapping, the perfume of morning dew on the grass and I thought if I died right in this moment I wouldn't give a shit. Truth be told I *didn't* give a shit. I was living, but my heart wasn't in it. Somehow, this place made me feel something, gave me hope. Whoa! What was I doing? Was I becoming self-aware? Is this what happens when you're having a nervous breakdown? Oh, this crap would never do. This is precisely why I needed another husband: to distract me from such thoughts, such feelings. This place had allowed me to feel, to reflect — and I felt better afterwards: better, but scared shitless. Weird.

I returned to the Camden Locke Hotel to find Pickles on his way out.

"My god, Babe, you look absolutely radiant. Who was he?" "Not a 'he' an 'it,' a place."

Pickles put his arm around my shoulders and pulled me close enough to smell the patchouli on his neck:

"You're not on E, are you?"

"No! Goddammit. Pickles, I've been energetically transformed or something."

"Well, like Robert De Niro said in *The Godfather Part II*: 'Si tu contento, mi contento.' If you're happy, I'm happy. Don't you just love your Uncle Pickles?"

"What's not to love?"

"Why can't the world see me through your eyes? Look, I've got to meet Roger, the publisher from hell. Are you going to be OK on your own?"

"Yeah, but we've got to get out of this place…"

"…if it's the last thing we ever do. I love that song. C'mon let's sing it right here street corner doo-wop style."

"Earth to Pickles, come back you're drifting. This is serious. I hate this place. I want my own bed. No offense."

"None taken, honey bunch. I wanted to save this for later, but since we're on the subject, I have a friend an actor who lives close by. He owes me a solid. We can stay at his place. Only thing is he's hung up in Italy, but he'll be back day after tomorrow. So, if her highness can stick it out for say 48 hours tops, we can be in new and fabulous digs at no cost, hah!"

"OK, you know what? This sounds like another one of your half-baked… An actor? C'mon."

"He's a friend from way back, a good guy, and he has this really cool crib. I know I've made some big promises in the past…"

"Uh-huh. I'm in no mood for another sure thing that fell through."

"Babe, I promise."

And with a kiss on the forehead, Pickles turned and disappeared around the corner. I stumbled into the hotel dazed, confused and pissed off, when I remembered my missing luggage. The sullen punk-girl with the purple-tipped hair was at the desk now — and no, my luggage had not turned up — big surprise. I returned to Room 201 and collapsed on the bed.

This actor business was bugging me. I had lived in Hollywood for several years when my third husband Gordon Burdett was still working as a production designer. I didn't like it. The writer Rod Serling, creator of *The Twilight Zone*, once said, "Hollywood is a great place to live if you're a grapefruit."

I didn't like actors. It's like this: my father is a sculptor, I know when he's not sculpting; my third husband is a musician, I know when he's not making music; Pickles is a writer, I know when he's not writing; with an actor, you never know when he's not acting. As a woman, I find this extremely disturbing. Don't get me wrong, I've had some great sex with actors. I'm just saying actors, as far as I can tell, are always acting. This did not lead me to have faith in the Pickles proposition. All this actor business was making me way too stressed out. I decided to do some Dosha Yoga and then start looking for a flat to rent, but I fell asleep instead and had a dream about the blond one again:

I am in the little park walking up the path to the top of a hill. It's dark and I can barely find my way. It starts to rain. My legs are so heavy, every step is an effort. Then, the whacky dame from Heathrow is at my side. "You'll never make it", she snarls; then just as suddenly, she's gone. Crawling on my hands and knees, I make it to the top. Ahead in the darkness, I can make out the silhouette of a man in a long dark coat. He steps towards me and lifts me from the ground into his arms. It's him, the blond one. He searches my eyes. Even though it's raining, I can tell he's been crying. He pulls me close to him. I can feel his breath on my cheek, feel his heart-beat against my breast. He smells like lemons and whiskey. He whispers into my ear: "It never really got freaky enough for me," and then... I woke up. It was now 13:30 and no sign of Pickles. I went down to the desk because I felt uneasy and because I didn't know what else to do; lo and behold my luggage had arrived. The little punk-chick was still on duty:

"I knock on door. Loo-gage come three hours, but no answer from you."

"I was asleep."

She rolled her eyes. "OK. So you take, no?"

"I take, yes."

CHAPTER 3

He wasn't a man. He was a way of life.

— final line from *Ruthless*, starring Zachary Scott

"Money was his god," I think that's one of the lines from the trailer for the 1948 movie *Ruthless*. Zachary Scott is so underrated, the way he called out, "Mildred" with his dying breath at the beginning of *Mildred Pierce,* with such sex and agony, I mean c'mon. Money might have been multimillionaire Horace Woodruff-Vendig's god in the movie, but the man who portrayed him, Zachary Scott, allegedly died penniless. Sometimes life chooses not to imitate art.

By the time of Pickles' return I was vegetating in front of the telly watching the craziest game show I'd ever seen in my life. It was kind of like *Sabado Gigante* with David Gest as Don Francisco. I did feel for David Gest when one of the game show questions was about his marriage to the diminutive and allegedly abusive diva Liza Minnelli. Is it me or has she just channeled all of her mother's bad parts?

When the camera cut to David Gest's face after the Liza Minnelli question; he looked as if Liza might be waiting for him in the wings with a hatchet or that he'd just lost control of his bowels at the thought, but no amount of humiliation, fear or shame can trump the almighty euro. At this touching moment, fraught with the kind of extreme public degradation that only TV can provide, Pickles entered the room. I had told him I never watched television.

"You're busted, sugar. I knew you were lying about TV. Turn that off. I've got news."

"C'mon it's David Gest's game show. It's so cheesy and pathetic it's brilliant."

"Only you would think so," Pickles said as he tore the remote from my hand and made the TV go black.

I hadn't noticed before, but Pickles was as clean as the Board of Health. He was wearing a light-weight grey suit like the one Cary Grant wore in *North by Northwest*, sans belt and tie. Instead of a crisp white shirt he wore a black Robot from *Forbidden Planet* T-shirt. His hair was pulled back under an Orvis Stetson Lido-Vented Panama hat with a brown center-braided leather hatband. He had exchanged the white Jackie-O sunglasses for a pair of black super huge Lew Wassermans.

"Such a great outfit and you're wearing flip-flops?"

"What can I say? I've got to be me." He plopped down on the bed, bouncing up and down like a kid. He had an orange plastic Sainsbury's bag in his hand, and he smelled of gin.

"I've got news," he said as he produced what was left of two six-packs of Greenall's London Dry Gin and Tonic.

He handed me a can, popped the tab on another and commenced guzzling. Draining the can in one gulp, he smacked his lips, belched and said: "Man, that's coffee," and proceeded to open another can.

"You are such a fucking throw-back. Thank God I'm hip to all your esoteric references. By the way, that's from a TV commercial, Mr. Snobby."

"I watched TV. Never said I didn't. I just stopped watching after they took Star Trek off the air on June 3, 1969."

"You were a child!"

"Children can't have taste? Anyway, this is off the subject. I've got news. Roger, the publisher from heaven, has got me some book signings lined up and if I'm a good boy, his words, he'll give me an advance on The Madman of Nogales. Isn't that delicious? Aren't you happy for your Uncle Pickles?"

"The question, as I see it, is not can you be a good boy but will you be a good boy?"

"I may not behave myself at all times, but I am good, Babe." "Good for nothing. This is me you're talking to, not Roger." "I swear on the grave of Colonel Beauregard Pickles..." "There is no such person." "I beg to differ, darling..."

THE ACTOR

"OK, OK. No history lessons now, Professor, if you please. So, what's our itinerary?"

"Well, I'm meeting some of the boys tonight down at the Oxford Arms at 19:00, 7 p.m. normal time. Roger wasn't too thrilled about it, but he's arranged for some Press coverage so it shouldn't be a total freebie. Wednesday, I'll read from the galleys for *Madman* and sign some books at the Congress Centre and the same again on Saturday at Forbidden Planet. Wake me up in an hour."

With that he fell backwards onto the bed and began snoring loudly. I intercepted a half-full can of Greenall's from his hand as he descended. I hadn't even opened mine.

Damn, that Pickles. I wanted to tell him about my last hypnagogic experience while it was still fresh in my mind. I wanted to discuss this actor business and what I should wear to the Oxford Arms that night. I took a swig from Pickles' unfinished Greenall's and clicked the remote to see if David Gest was still on.

That night the Oxford Arms and about 25 die-hard cyberpunk fans embraced Dr. Pickles. Tables were pulled together, well-worn books were offered for autograph, pints were pulled, questions asked and answered. Even I fielded a few ridiculous questions after Pickles introduced me as his inspiration for Dr. Destiny Monique Jones: biochemist/immunologist/former lingerie model and a key character in Pickles' forthcoming tome *The Madman of Nogales*.

Someone in the crowd asked, "How exactly did you come up with the antidote for the Blow Plague?" as if I *were* Dr. Destiny Monique Jones herself. I deferred to Pickles and made a hasty retreat to the bar.

I had to squeeze past this big guy wearing an Arsenal T-shirt, whose head looked like it had a five o' clock shadow. It felt kind of nice, our bodies mashed together momentarily like that. I could see he was thinking the same thing. God, he was so tall and so good-looking in a thug kind of way. Then the moment was over and he was absorbed by the crowd.

From the bar, Jack Daniel's in hand, I watched Pickles with the observing eye of a movie camera. By now, he was looking a little crumpled since he had slept in his beautifully tailored grey suit. He was sweating profusely, but he didn't remove his suit jacket. He did remove his Panama hat for a moment to mop his brow with a cocktail napkin. He shook out his hair, put his hat back on his head and was refreshed. God knows how he did it. He must have had at least one six pack of Greenall's, three pints and two whiskies, yet he was composed, articulate and engaging. He was almost inhuman in this respect. I mean the man never even got a hangover.

"Are you a Sci-Fi fan?"

I looked to my left and there stood this thin, handsome young man with auburn hair sporting a neatly manicured beard and mustache. He was dressed simply, but a little too elegantly for the Oxford Arms: black silk shirt, True Religion Ricky Short Fuse Straight Leg Jeans all wrapped in a dark chocolate colored knee-length retro leather jacket that looked as if it had been snatched off the body of a pimp in the 1970s. I was about to comment on his classic low-cut black suede Pumas when he said: "Not many women come in here dressed like you."

I had waited all evening for Pickles to comment on my teal green Glamour Pants and Navy Blue Swan Blouse from J. Peterman, but a compliment from a stranger was better than no compliment at all. The stranger's eyes drifted down to my toes, nails all red and shiny peeking through the Salvatore Ferragamo gold bow slide-on sandals with the little kitten heel. He laughed when I said:

"I'd say we win the best dressed prize for tonight, and probably any other night."

"You're American?"

"Every day, all day including Sunday. What about you? You've got an accent I can't quite place."

"Guess."

"Germany's my first guess."

He took a sip from his pint.

"Good guess. I lived in Germany for many years after we left our country. I'm from Croatia."

Croatia: something new. When a man tells me what country he's from, my first thought is whether or not he's circumcised. Of course, if he's Jewish this becomes a moot point, which is why I've always had a fondness for Jewish men and the Jewish people in general. I mean circumcision is right up there with the invention of the Internet in my book.

I examined his face across the rim of my whiskey glass: the very things he hoped would mask his youth gave him away-- there was a baby face lurking beneath all that facial hair. The lowered eyebrows, the careful pose, the arrogant yet unsure playfulness were all dead giveaways. He chose his words the way I chose apples at the produce stand; then again, this could be the language thing: he spoke three of them.

We began to chat about stuff. He was casual about serious things and serious about casual things. I couldn't tell if he knew the difference. He was young enough to be my son. Christ, my own daughter would probably think he was too young for her.

The young ones always seemed to gravitate to me. I had spent considerable time in tutorial mode because of this and it was tiring, to say the least. But what were my options? The men my age were either married or dead or both.

I did like this young Croatian man, named Ivan: a clean, strong, plain, simple name. However, time and several husbands had left me with the increasingly annoying habit of stopping to think, weighing the pros and cons of sex with the proper stranger. Don't even get me started on all the machinations that went into determining whether or not I should get involved with someone.

The Croatian and I were pretty drunk at this point. We began trading vital stats. He lived near Piccadilly; not far, but far enough.

"Your hotel is close?"

"Yes. But there's a problem."

"Is it that man there, signing books. Is he your husband?" "No. He's what you might call my travelling companion." "Sounds so old-fashioned."

Ivan got the attention of the cute, petite female bartender with the short, curly black hair and the huge breasts that were determined to fight their way out of her tight red tank top.

I told Ivan maybe some other time, and by the time I'd said that, I was just a memory. Ivan's Croatian life-force was totally focused on the female bartender. I was so upset I ordered another Jack Daniel's and took out a *NY Times* crossword puzzle book from my Boudicca magenta, grey and yellow linen flower tote bag. I looked up to find Pickles standing over me with a concerned look on his face: "He's not the man for you, Babe. I've got the man for you, and you are meeting him tomorrow." I was so moved, I went back to my crossword.

The next day the sun rose with a vengeance and crushed the crisp cool early morning air into a dream. By the time I got up the sky wore a blank blue stare and the day was sweltering. I felt content to spend the day in an air-conditioned room, alone. Pickles had other plans. I had forgotten. This was *the* day Pickles was to introduce me to, " . . . the man for me,"

The Actor.

Pickles practically dragged me across the road to the Chalk Farm Tube Station. He set me straight; it was not the subway. It was the Tube. What did I know of London? I'd been here once with my third husband, Nick Ravelli. It was the first leg of his last European concert tour. All I can remember, aside from the champagne and coke, was the inside of limousines and room service.

In retrospect, I think my first ride on the Tube triggered an anxiety attack. I remember being sandwiched between Pickles and a fat woman in a sleeveless shirt-waist dress. The sweat from her arm left damp spots on my white 100% Mediterranean cotton shirt. I was unconscious of the fact that I had begun to rock back and forth and hum to myself. Pickles' elbow in my ribs jolted me back to sanity. Then, I remembered I was somewhat hungover from the night before. Maybe that's the reason I felt as if my knees were practically touching the knees of the boy with the green hair, torn Clash T-shirt and graffiti-riddled leather pants, sitting across the aisle from me. I was beginning to feel the real panic of a claustrophobic. I knew just how toothpaste felt inside the tube.

"You think that's why?" I asked Pickles.

"Why what? Child, look at that one over there."

Pickles motioned to the door across the aisle to his right. A young man with sandy hair in a dirty white suit had dried vomit caked all over his nice blue shirt. He was unsteady, trying desperately to find something or someone to hold on to (aren't we all?). Looks like it had been quite a night. He moved over to where an older Asian woman was standing and leaned against her. He was quite charming, despite his appearance; friendly and chatty. The Asian woman was nodding and smiling as he spoke, until she noticed the can of Forster's beer in his hand and the general state of him. She quickly walked to the end of the car, leaving the poor slob still jabbering on as if she were still standing there. Pickles whispered,

"This ongoing display of public drunkenness the Brits seem to be engaged in is just downright disgusting." Well, wasn't that the pot calling the kettle?

"Pickles, I was formulating a theory. Do you think this feeling of being like toothpaste is why they call this the Tube?" He refused to speak to me until we were in Waterloo Station.

Standing in the center of Waterloo Station was like standing in the middle of a giant beating heart, the rush of humanity like the blood flowing in and out of the various arteries of transit.

Pickles was practically dragging me to the far end of the station. I wrenched myself from his grip and almost made it to the Eurostar, with hopes of reaching Paris and avoiding the impending encounter with this actor guy. But that Pickles was fast; once again he had me in his clutches, pulling me along like a wayward child who doesn't want to go to school.

Up steps, down steps, down some more steps, through a long tunnel, past the Imax, up some more steps and across a street, down some cobblestones, past some beautiful modern glass and steel buildings to the South Bank on the Thames river to more throngs of people. Different tourists from the ones in Camden. These were mostly families and couples dressed from a J. C. Penney's catalog. Whatever happened to zero population control?

Pickles was giving me the Cook's tour: "Over here is the National Theatre, and there's the British Film Institute," like I gave a shit at this point. I was looking for some rocks to throw at the goddamned seagulls, who I just knew were talking about me, when off in a corner I spied with my little eye a barefoot woman who looked like the British comedic actress Dawn French, sitting on a large red pillow.

I wandered off from Pickles towards her. She was shuffling a deck of tarot cards. She looked up and saw me staring: "Read your cards for a pound?" By this time Pickles was at my elbow:

"Babe, we haven't got time for this. My God, you're turning into Shirley MacLaine."

The tarot card woman looked at me as if she knew my deepest, most disgusting secret, and was cool with it. She turned a single card over on the black felt cloth she had laid out in front of her: The Lovers.

"There's more to it than you think," she said.

Pickles gave her a pound. "Honey, there always is," he said as he whisked me away.

When we reached the Tate Modern Museum, I realized this was our destination. Pickles refused to drop any money into the donation box, because he'd given the tarot reader a pound, the cheap bastard. Again, I was footing the bill. "Is five pounds enough, do you think?" Pickles ignored me. He had my arm in a vise-like grip and was dragging me through the museum to an elevator.

We got out on the 5th floor — of course it was really the 6th floor — and Pickles was flat out igging me. He would not respond to my protests. This was a museum, for god's sake — not a sprint race. We finally ended up in front of a wall-sized painting that looked like Walter Velez had collided with Peter Max in the middle of an African military coup.

"What time is it?" Pickles asked, gasping for air.

"You know I don't wear a watch, you freaking lunatic. What's going on?"

"It must be about two, I mean 14:00, don't you think?"

"Why are we here? What's going on? Look, I'm out of here if you don't tell me what you're up to."

Then Pickles grabbed me and hugged me, and not with affection. He was immobilizing me to prevent my escape. He whispered in my ear:

"This painting's from Kinshasa. That's in South America, I think, maybe."

"Do I look like I give a shit? Let me go."

By this time people were watching us and doing some whispering of their own. Off in the corner by the entrance there was this lone guy: slim, medium height in a starched white cotton dress shirt, and Levi's, low-cut classic Chuck Taylors on his feet, no socks. On his head a New York Yankees baseball cap, his face obscured by Ray-Ban wraparounds. He was laughing his ass off.

He looked like a DEA agent. I prayed – yes prayed – that Pickles wasn't holding. Then, Mr. Ray Ban wraparounds started walking towards us. Was this going to be yet another sad, embarrassing chapter in the annals of Babe and Professor Pickles? If it was, goddammit, Pickles would pay.

THE ACTOR

All at once, Pickles released his grip on me, whirled around and bear-hugged this guy with a little too much enthusiasm for a public place; the guy responded in kind and winked at me over Pickles' shoulder. I was captivated. Pickles cried out: "Thespian" and the thespian cried out, "Lesbian"; it was a Kodak moment. Some kids walking through casually remarked to each other, "Homos." I certainly felt like a third wheel, maybe because, at this point, I was one.

They slowly untangled, squared-off and looked at each other, just grinning. I cleared my throat theatrically. Pickles took my cue: "Thespian, this is my sister from another mother, Babe. Babe, meet The Actor."

The Actor took my right hand between his two warm, soft hands then he pulled me in close for an even warmer hug. His body felt good. We melted into each other for a sensuous moment. He smelled so familiar. He released me slowly, then abruptly turned to Pickles and said, "Let's check out the Steve McQueen exhibit."

I felt like an idiot, as I sat on the aisle seat of the little screening room, waiting for the iconic blond actor from the 70s to appear on screen. Instead, there was an experimental video, entitled *Bear*, by the conceptual artist Steve McQueen who was naked and Black. Pickles and The Actor tittered like teenage girls.

After being wedged between Pickles and The Actor in the back of a cab, for what seemed like an eternity, we arrived at a vegetarian restaurant called Manna. The two of them talked across, but not to me. The Actor's voice was a mellow, raspy baritone — as warm as his hug. He paid no attention to me at all, chatting on and on with Pickles.

As we sat down to table, Pickles asked The Actor if he planned to keep his hat and glasses on through the meal. The Actor laughed and said he'd quite forgotten he was wearing his "disguise." With a flourish he removed them both, which caused an immediate stir in the restaurant. Then, we were besieged by wait-staff and the object of stares, and discussion at the other tables.

The Actor cocked his blond head to the side, stared straight into my eyes, with his baby blues, smiled so sweetly I went hot and cold all over, promptly falling sideways off my chair onto the floor. My butt hurt, but my pride hurt even more. I couldn't move. My head was swimming. I faintly heard someone ask: "Is she all right?"

Pickles, The Actor, and a frightened waiter hoisted me to my feet. I was disoriented and gasping for air. The Actor said: "How are you, luv?" Then he turned to Pickles, lowered his voice and said, "Maybe we should get her to hospital." The waiter kept saying, "Oh, my God", until I wanted to smack him. Pickles intervened: "Poor thing's exhausted. Can you walk, Babe? Let's get you to the ladies', splash some cold water on that gorgeous face." He turned to The Actor and said:

"She'll be fine. Order something for us. Some food will do us all good." Then he turned on the waiter: "You paralyzed, honey? Get our table some menus and some water."

As Pickles whisked me off to the ladies' room, I heard The Actor say calmly to a woman who looked like the manager: "No one's fault really." She said whatever we ordered was on the house, then she asked if he would pose with her for a selfie.

Pickles ushered me into a stall, lowered the seat on the toilet and sat me down: "Put your head between your knees and breathe deep. I'll get a damp paper towel for your neck. You scared the living daylights out of me, woman." I sat there and listened to running water from the cold tap drown out whatever Pickles was saying.

"Pickles," I moaned, "I'm so embarrassed."

"I know sugar, but look at it this way, so is everyone else."

I felt the cool, damp paper on the back of my neck, and Pickles' thigh providing a nice resting post for my head. I began to feel better.

"Why didn't you tell me? I thought he was just an actor."

"He is just an actor. Did you hit your head when you fell off the chair?"

"You know goddamned well what I'm talking about. This guy is famous."

"He's also infamous. So what? So's your ex-husband Nick."

How could I explain to Pickles that it wasn't just him being famous? This man, The Actor, had been haunting me for months. How could I explain to Pickles, The Actor was the man from my dreams?

I returned to our table with as much dignity as I could muster, under the circumstances. The Actor was diplomatic and comforting all through our meal. He was gracious to the room, above and beyond the call, signing autographs and posing for selfies.

THE ACTOR

When we left the restaurant there was a black sedan waiting. We got in. The Actor gave the driver directions and we sped off. The Actor grinned and pulled out a joint, which he lit, toked and passed to me. This reminded him of an episode from the old days, when he and Pickles used to work at a dodgy restaurant owned by a philandering Turk and his wife:

"We used to go into the kitchen, turn on the radio and dance; drove the poor chef crazy. What was his name? Always had to have his nerve medicine, which was really vodka poured into a medicine bottle. Remember, Pickles? One night we got into his nerve medicine and I ended up spilling a plate of food in a man's lap. Thank God, it was the owner, or I would have been sacked on the spot."

"I'll never forget the look on his face," Pickles chortled. "It was just like the look on Babe's when her ass hit the floor."

Pickles and The Actor were laughing so hard they started to cry. "Make me piss me self," The Actor said. As the laughter subsided, The Actor turned to me and searched my face, as if he were looking for something he'd lost. He whispered something that I couldn't make out. Then everything began to slow down: Pickles chattering in the background, the taxi, our movements, our breathing. I could hear my pulse. I felt The Actor's hand enclose mine as he moved closer. His blond hair, like fresh cut grass, brushed my cheek softly, as he nuzzled my neck. I could feel the heat of his breath, the moistness of his lips and teeth on my throat, as he squeezed my right hand so tight it hurt — all the while, his right arm pulling me closer and closer until my face was buried in his chest. I gasped for air and the smell of lemons filled me. His body was now draped across mine, pressing down hard, pinning my left arm to my side. I felt as though I was being absorbed into the marrow of him. His right knee burrowed between my thighs. Then, abruptly he drew back and settled into his place between Pickles and me. All at once, everything snapped back into real time: Pickles still laughing, the cab still moving, the joint still being passed around. The Actor said, quietly and to no one in particular, "Sometimes he goes too far." The cab pulled up in front of the Camden Locke Hotel. The Actor, like a child on the first day of school, reluctantly let go of my hand. I felt a rush of sadness. I didn't want him to go.

"Don't worry. I'll see you tomorrow. I'm sending a car 'round to collect you and the gherkin, early," The Actor said softly.

We stepped out of the cab and he was gone. I was left in the middle of the Chalk Farm Road wondering what on Earth had just happened.

"Quite a spectacle, you two in the cab; thought I was in the middle of a porno," Pickles said, as he rotated the tip of a joint, now a roach, between his index finger and thumb. He deposited the roach in his pants pocket.

"What did Uncle Pickles tell you?" he went on as we climbed the stairs to Room 201. "Can I pick 'em or can I pick 'em?"

I was in no mood. There was so much Pickles didn't understand, or did he?

"Child, you were on each other like white on rice." "My ass hurts."

"I bet it does," Pickles jibed, as we entered the room.

He turned on the light and a look of horror passed over his face. He approached me slowly, reached out and stroked my neck.

"You're bleeding, honey."

"Bleeding? Come on, now. This is not funny."

"No, no. It's not. I'm sorry. I should have told you he likes it rough."

That's when I remembered The Actor biting my neck. I rubbed the side of my neck. It was beginning to hurt; sure enough, there was blood. I ran into the bathroom and started to wash the wound. I heard Pickles in the other room frantically rummaging through his bags. "I've got peroxide and a Band-Aid," he hollered. I looked up and he was there dabbing peroxide on the side of my neck and covering the wound, which had stopped bleeding, with a Band-Aid. "I want to know is this guy going all Marat Sade on me or was biting me on the neck like a vampire the extent of it? Just when were you going to tell me he's a big fucking freak? Or did that just slip your mind when you were making this love connection?"

Pickles looked down at his shoes and without lifting his head said, in a trembling whisper, "Nobody's perfect, Babe." What could I say? He was right. Everybody's got a little freak in them. Let's face it: if The Actor were a normal guy, would I be the least bit interested in him? Pickles knew the answer and I hated that he knew.

Later that evening, I was snuggled in bed watching the BBC News. Pickles was down at the corner pub, comforting his hurt feelings. Apparently, Big Ben would not be chiming for a while due to much needed repairs and a Tube strike by maintenance workers was looming. Even though I was exhausted, I was afraid to go to sleep. I regretted not going with Pickles. I just couldn't cope with another metaphysical communication with you know who. I had to tell Pickles about the dreams. I wondered whether Pickles had hooked me up with Thespian on his own or at Thespian's request. Either way, there was no point in trying to reason it out. Yes, I knew better, but I was falling for the guy.

The next morning at the crack I awoke from a dreamless sleep to find Pickles gone and his bags packed. I called downstairs. The surly Greek night concierge was still on duty.

"Your boyfriend saying you check out today. Saying you pay bill." "Yes. I pay bill. Is he down there?"

"He say to tell you, 'back in a minute.'"

The thought of trying to explain to the Greek guy, yet again, that Pickles was not my boyfriend, gave me a headache. I hung up. Although I was sure Pickles would look back on our time together here with nostalgia, I couldn't wait to leave this dump.

And where was Pickles? He was up early and apparently organized. This was highly irregular; definitely cause for concern. I decided to shower, dress, pack and worry later. Maybe I'd have enough time to clean my chakras. No such luck. While I was brushing my teeth, Pickles arrived with coffee and croissants, a copy of the *Camden New Journal* and a distressed look on his face.

I praised the delivery of breakfast, to which Pickles absently replied, "Sainsbury's," as he removed a half pint of whiskey from his jacket pocket and topped up both our coffees.

He gulped the coffee, then took a long swig from the whiskey bottle. He wiped the back of one hand across his mouth, ran his fingers through his hair and that's when I noticed how badly his hand was trembling. He threw the paper at me and in a raspy voice said: "Page three."

I opened to page three spread across the top of the page were the words: "Father of Cyber-Punk Says Bush Worships Satan." I began reading the article, but was distracted by the headline on the opposite page: "Pop Star Wants A Sober Twist For Noisy Pub." Pickles was sitting on the edge of the bed, wringing his hands and rocking back and forth: "Roger wanted publicity — well, he got it."

"Nice photo of you, Raymond."

"I was drunk for Christ's sake. You know me when I'm drunk. I'm liable to say anything. What does it say I said?"

"You got all worked up over this, and you haven't even read it?"

"I got distracted by the pop star wanting the pub to keep the noise down."

"Yeah, it says: ' . . . presently the people already spill into the street leaving used cigarette butts, food and . . . '"

"Please, will you read what they say about me? Please?"

I perused the article, which went into way too much detail. I decided to twist the knife a little, so I could watch Pickles squirm.

"This is from the event at the Oxford Arms . . . "

"I know that!"

"It says you were the guest of The Camden Friends of Cyber-Punk . . ."

Pickles fell onto the floor and buried his face into the dirty carpet. He lifted his head and moaned, "Go on, get to it. This is agony." A small thrill shot through me.

"Apparently you announced to the room, that George W. Bush is Damien from Omen3 and that he, Tony Blair and Vladimir Putin have a regular three-way going."

"This is why I need you with me, at all times. I'm not responsible."

"Oh, no you did not say this. Now, this is the kind of shit that'll land your ass in the Hotel Guantanamo."

"Lord! What did I say? As God is my witness I don't remember. I plead the fifth."

"Drank a fifth is more like it. Well, according to this you said Bush and, I'm quoting, 'other members of the unholy alliance, he calls his cabinet, conduct satanic rituals in the White House using babies' blood.'"

Pickles crawled over to the bed. All the color had drained out of him. I felt bad that I had exploited this disturbing news simply to amuse myself. The feeling soon passed. Pickles crawled onto the bed and curled into a fetal ball. When he finally found his voice it was a strangled version of its true self.

"I should demand a retraction. My God, I should sue. I said babies' blood? I should call for a public apology. I should . . ."

"Go into hiding?"

"This is no laughing matter. It's a paranoid, narrow-minded, buttoned-down, cold-war mentality out there with no room for irony. We live in a world where people don't have a sense of humor about these things."

"I think it's funny as hell."

I wanted to finish the pop-star and the pub article, thought better of it and retreated into supportive silence as Pickles uncurled himself, leapt to the floor, and began to pace back and forth like Bette Davis. And who said the theatre was dead?

"You know, now that I think about it, I could swear someone was following me."

"From Sainsbury's? Now, who's being paranoid? Look, it's the *Camden Journal*, not the BBC News of the World. I'm telling you, this too shall pass. Besides, in 100 years who'll give a shit?"

My attempt at reassurance fell on deaf ears. Pickles had collapsed onto the bed, fast asleep before his head even hit the pillow. Amid the low rumble of his snores, I attempted to finish reading the paper. Just when I was about to find out "What did happen to Dot's antiques?" the phone rang. The getaway car had arrived. I woke Pickles.

Two minutes later our driver, extremely handsome in a crisp baby blue cotton dress shirt and starched, sharply creased khaki pants, was at our door. He was dark brown-skinned, solidly built, with the most perfectly shaped bald head I had ever seen.

Pickles' mood had shifted. He shot this guy such a flirty smile. The driver gave back a sly wink, and without a word began taking our luggage down to the car. Things were getting even more interesting, as if that were possible.

I paid the bill. Goodbye, three flights masquerading as two. Goodbye, smelly toilet and surly Greeks. Goodbye, raucous rubbish collectors and pub overflow in the Chalk Farm Road. I will miss you. I will miss you all. And I did, for about ten seconds.

Our chariot, a sleek black sedan awaited. Although I did appreciate Pickles' attempt to make a socialist out of me, I had made my peace with being shallow, a long time ago.

As I ensconced myself in the back seat, I took in a deep breath:

the smell of luxury, my favorite perfume. I had no idea where we were going, only that I'd be glad to get there.

I felt the trunk (or I should say boot) of the sedan slam shut and then nothing, no Pickles, no driver. I looked into the rear-view mirror to see what was going on. There, in the broad light of day, for the world to behold, were Pickles and the driver locked in an embrace to rival John Garfield and Lana Turner in the original film version of *The Postman Always Rings Twice*. I mean you'd have to peel these two off each other, and I'm sure tongues were involved. Somehow the Beatles' "Why Don't We Do It in the Road?" sprang to mind.

A car had pulled up behind them. God knows how long it had been there taking in the show. A middle-aged woman with a face like a hawk and wild red hair rolled down the driver's side window, stuck her head out and sighed in a weary voice:

"Really. Can we move it along?" At the same time, her look-alike teen-aged daughter, in the passenger seat, rolled down her window and shouted: "My brother came out and my parents think he needs an exorcism or something. Well, you do, Mum — you may as well admit it." Pickles and the driver hastily disengaged and scurried into the front seat of our car, without giving me a passing glance. We sped off in silence across the A502 onto Adelaide Road, past the Chalk Farm Tube Station towards Primrose Hill. My hand sprung involuntarily to my mouth. Something contracted inside me and tears began to pour. For a moment, I couldn't breathe. I sucked in the air through my mouth with such force it made Pickles jump and turn round.

"Is she all right?" I heard the driver whisper.

"Babe, you're crying," Pickles said with alarm.

He reached back and wiped away my tears. I was sobbing like a ninny now, as the unthinkable happened: I was rendered speechless. "Is it about the rough stuff? Are you scared? Because, I promise you he's not crazy. Well, not in a bad way . . . " Pickles turned to the driver.

"Hey, honey isn't this, the place?" The driver kept on driving.

"Yes, but we're being followed." Pickles looked at me in the rear-view mirror and said. "See, I told you."

After maneuvering around north London for what seemed like

hours, the driver was satisfied that he'd shaken the tail and we finally arrived at our intended destination. I had managed to calm down. Intrigue was such a wonderful mood enhancer.

The house rose up from the trees and the brick wall that obscured it to three gleaming white stories with all the eves and angles of Victorian England. The doors and window frames were painted shiny black, and the second floor front was rimmed by a small roof terrace, which I presumed The Actor never used.

The driver pulled up to a black livery gate, removed a remote from the glove compartment, pushed a few buttons and the gate slowly opened onto a graveled driveway, to the left of which was a lovely garden that wrapped around the side of the house. Pickles helped me out, while the driver retrieved our luggage. Pickles held on to me tight. "Did you have a premonition? That's what got you so upset? You saw the Stasi closing in on us. Didn't I tell you? Didn't I just tell you?"

I grimaced and tried to pull away.

"Babe, are you seeing something? Is something bad going to happen?"

"You're standing on my foot, you moron."

I felt someone's eyes on me. There, to our left in the doorway, stood The Actor dressed in just his Sloggi boxers and a smile. He was pale and unshaven, his blue eyes red-rimmed. The driver gave The Actor a saucy look, as he brushed by him with the luggage. My curiosity was peaking.

"Well, get in here you lot, before I catch my death."

Pickles led me into the foyer, then scurried after the driver. The Actor gently closed the front door, turned and stood staring at me for the better part of a minute, then he grabbed my hand.

"Let me show you to your room."

"What about Pickles?"

"Oh, Mario can take care of Pickles."

Mario. That was the driver's name. Who was this Mario?

"Mario is my gift to Pickles," The Actor said.

We were half-way up the stairs when,

"Stop, just stop, please." I was feeling light-headed.

"You don't look so good." "I don't feel so good."

We sat down on the stairs and The Actor began stroking my

hand, as if it were a pet. He offered to get me a glass of water, but I didn't want one. I had other concerns.

"Who is Mario?"

"Remember the story about the restaurant, the one where I worked with Pickles, back in the dark ages? And remember the nervous chef, with the medicine bottle filled with vodka? That's Mario, Mario Lightbourne: Pickles' unrequited love. Mario owns a car service now."

"Why you're a regular yenta aren't you?"

"Well, if Pickles can play matchmaker, so can I."

"Are we a match?"

He paused, "Let me show you to your room."

Upstairs there was a dressing room, family bathroom and three bedrooms with en-suite bathrooms. There was a small, winding staircase to the third floor, at the opposite end of the hallway. I was to learn later that this was the Forbidden Zone, as it led to The Actor's walk-in closet on one side and his exercise room on the other. Apparently, The Actor was very protective when it came to his clothing.

The Actor flung open the door to a room as we passed: "This is for his lordship . . . " It was a pink and lavender room, decked out with all the necessary accoutrements of a tween girl. " . . . my daughter's room, when she's allowed to visit," The Actor said.

"I'm sure Ms. Pickles will love it."

"I thought so," The Actor, said absently as he drifted away in thought for a moment.

We walked farther down the hall to an open door. He pushed me inside. "This is my room," he said, so close to me I could feel the heat of his body and the moisture of his breath.

The curtains were drawn. The damp aromas of lemons, whiskey and sweat mingled in the air. I could make out the silhouette of an unmade bed over which hung a painting, partially illuminated by the light streaming in from the hallway. I was trying to get a better look when The Actor pulled back a curtain to let the sunlight into the room. I could see it now.

It was a canvas of a man with his back to us. A man possibly of noble birth, or one of the Romantic poets maybe, standing on a rocky plateau, his hair wind tossed, as he leans on a walking stick looking out over an enveloping fog, rising from a jagged outgrowth of rock above the angry, feral presence of the invisible sea below. It was hypnotic. I could hear it, as well as see it.

"It does that to me too. It's Caspar David Friedrich's *Wanderer above the Sea of Fog*. From the mid-1800s, I think. Sometimes, I stare at it for hours. I'm usually stoned when that happens."

"Must have cost a fortune."

"Philippe gave it to me, said he inherited it, probably a copy, sorry about the mess."

Still in his Sloggi boxers and nothing else (there is a God), he led me over to a doorknob in the opposite wall, which I thought was some sort of contemporary art thing; it was actually attached to a door that looked as though it were part of the wall. The Actor opened the door with a flourish: "This is your room."

It was a big and airy, all yellow and white, with a crystal chandelier and painted blue birds flying across the ceiling. There was a big brass bed that took up much of the room. The windows were open. Soft curtains billowed on the breeze. I felt him close in behind me. He pulled my arms behind my back and held my wrist together, a little too tightly, as if he were going to handcuff me. He buried his face in my hair. I could feel his chest rise and fall as he breathed in and out slowly. He yanked my wrists downward. I let out a short, sharp cry. Without lifting his face from my hair he said: "Am I hurting you?" He didn't wait for an answer. He simply released his grip, freeing my arms, and pulled me back against his body so tightly I could practically feel his corpuscles. He was hard and I was intoxicated. He whispered:

"You can smack me if you want. I plan on being a very bad boy. You don't mind if it hurts do you?" "Must there be pain?" I asked. "Pain can be very informative, Babe."

Then he just let go of me, like a toy he'd become bored with and gave me a little push. I lost my balance for a moment, stumbled forward a few steps and recovered. I turned to find him leaving the room mumbling, "I'm sorry, luv. I didn't get much sleep."

CHAPTER 4

We've been wrong a lot and unlucky a long time.

— Jane Greer as Kathie Moffat in *Out of The Past*

I stumbled over to the bed, sat down and stared out the window trying to figure out what had just happened. The more I tried, the more I wanted him. I began to think about Robert Mitchum as Jeff Bailey in *Out of The Past*. Mitchum, that baddest of the film noir bad-asses, not because he was so hard-boiled, but because you knew he had a heart and he knew it too, but he just didn't give a shit. The way that Kathie Moffat played him. The way he let her. The erotic sado/masochism of it all, like fucking on an elevator to hell. It doesn't get much sexier than that.

Then there was Jane Greer as Kathie Moffat, that implacable baby face, courtesy of childhood facial paralysis, betraying neither emotion nor purpose: the sweet helpless scorpion. If I had to re-cast this movie I would be Jeff Bailey and The Actor would be Kathie Moffat.

I must have fallen asleep; however, I dreamt no dreams that I could recall. I felt as if I'd been drugged. Maybe I was still sleeping, because my eyes were open and it was dark.

In the distance, I thought I heard Flora Purim singing, men laughing and glasses tinkling. I had no idea where I was. I looked out the window and saw my little park across the street, bathed in moonlight, and then I remembered.

There was a lamp on the nightstand. I switched it on; nothing happened, so I got up and felt around the wall until I found a light switch. The little chandelier was illuminated. It looked like a waterfall of teardrops. The bedroom door was open. The dark hallway was lit only by the light coming from my room.

As I walked to the stairs, drifting towards the sound of music and men laughing, I really couldn't tell if I was asleep or awake. The stairway was dark, as was the foyer and the living room. I almost tripped more than once. Beyond the living room there was a light coming from the dining room, where Pickles, Mario and The Actor sat around the table, eating omelets and drinking Krug's champagne.

"Sleeping Beauty has arisen," Pickles said as he poured me a glass.

Mario pulled a chair out for me, while The Actor, still barefoot, now dressed in a tight black T-shirt and even tighter jeans, winked at me from across the table and said, "Better get some food in you before you start boozing." Mario volunteered to rustle up an omelet for me.

The Actor leaned back in his chair, a drink in one hand, a cigar in the other, looking every bit the famous naughty boy he was. He blew a puff of smoke in my face then grinned at me like Steve McQueen, the iconic actor from the 70s. Pickles, who, up to this point, had been preoccupied with eating and drinking, dropped his fork and waited. It was a visceral reaction on my part, practically involuntary. I said: "If you blow smoke in my face again, I'll Tase your ass, and I'm not even kidding."

At the stove in the kitchen, I heard Mario drop something. By now Pickles' breathing was audible. The Actor leaned across the table, still grinning like McQueen: "You are such a big fucking tease." He dropped his cigar in his champagne glass.

"This is how much I love you. This is how much I fear you." Pickles exhaled.

"My God," he said, "That was like Gunfight at the O.K. Corral."

Mario gingerly put a plate full of perfectly delicious-looking omelet in front of me, sat down and with hands shaking pulled out a joint. The Actor reached over and lit it for him. Pickles opened another bottle of champagne.

"Babe, did you see that beautiful baby grand Bosendorfer in the living room?"

"It was dark, Pickles I didn't see anything, let alone a piano." I was puzzled. I looked at The Actor.

"No luv, I don't play the piano. Well, not in any real sense. My daughter does, though, when she's allowed to visit."

All of a sudden he jumped up and started looking around anxiously. "Wait a minute, I thought I . . . I had them here just so I could . . . Where the hell did I put them?"

The Actor ran into the living room and began rummaging around in the dark. Pickles looked at me and shrugged his shoulders. Mario said, "Don't ask me" Then the sound of breaking glass and a frantic cry from the living room got Pickles, Mario and me on our feet.

When we reached the living room The Actor was standing in the darkness, cradling something in his arms. Pickles found a light switch. "Look!" The Actor shouted, "I've got the vinyl!" He was cradling a stack of my records, everything I had recorded in the 80s. He was so proud he had tears in his eyes, at least that's what I thought the tears were for until Mario shouted, "You've cut your foot, mate. You're bleeding." The Actor looked at the sole of his right foot, "It would appear so," he said flatly.

In his haste, he had knocked over a lamp, then stepped on one of the shattered bits in the dark. Pickles asked him if it hurt and The Actor said he thought it must. You have to understand we were all pretty high from the weed and the champagne by this time. Eventually, we got organized: Mario found the first aid kit and tweezers, Pickles found a basin and filled it with water, I removed the glass from The Actor's foot, cleaned and dressed the wound while Mario and Pickles cleared away the shattered lamp and cleaned up the blood. Our jobs done, we all plopped down in an exhausted heap on the The Actor's plush pillow back sofa. "Thank God, I'm high. I don't think I could have handled this otherwise," Pickles said. We all were in agreement about the benefit of our individual states of inebriation.

"If you lot weren't here . . . " The Actor cried out, "Philippe usually cleans up my messes. Philippe keeps me sorted. I don't know what I'd do," he sobbed. "I don't know what I'd do." He was weeping now, like a heartbroken teen girl, with his head buried in my lap.

"Oh my, he's really drunk," Pickles sighed, "Fun's over. He'll go on all night about Philippe, if we let him."

"Too right," concurred Mario, "Better get him to bed straight away."

THE ACTOR

While Pickles and Mario struggled to get The Actor to his room, I began tidying the kitchen. It was quite masterful, the manner in which Pickles sort of hypnotized The Actor with his voice: "You are just too tired to go on, sweetness. I know all you want is to lie down in that big old bed of yours," and so forth until The Actor collapsed like a wet noodle — must be that Southern accent.

Mario, who was in a lot better shape than Pickles – a lot better – hoisted The Actor over his shoulder, fireman style, climbed the stairs to The Actor's room with Pickles running behind stage whispering, "Watch his head."

This is what Ozzie and Harriet must have gone through with Ricky in his teenage years, only it was probably Ricky carrying Ozzie. And where was David? We'll never know.

I was a whiz at washing up, but don't ask me to cook a meal — only if you enjoy having your stomach pumped. Mario and Pickles made their way into the dining room just as I finished. They were huffing and puffing, as if they had been laboring like migrant farm workers. Pickles sat himself down in a big comfy seat at the table and declared, "I need a drink Mario, honey."

Mario was in the kitchen digging into the refrigerator's freezer. He mumbled over his shoulder, "You're on your own, mate."

I poured Pickles a glass of what was left of the champagne; that's when I noticed there was a small gash on his forehead, and that the pocket of his shirt was torn and dangling by a thread. Mario came in from the kitchen holding a bag of frozen peas to his mouth. There was a trickle of blood on his chin. I tilted the champagne bottle. There was a smidgen left. I offered the bottle to Mario. He shook his head, so I finished it off.

"This is going to require more alcohol," I declared. Mario pointed to a cabinet in the far corner. The liquor cabinet, which among other delights, contained a bottle of Jack. I uncapped it and took a healthy swig.

"Bring that bottle over here, Missy," Pickles commanded. I handed the bottle to him.

"Well, what happened?" I asked, "This silence is killing me."

Pickles drank from the bottle and retorted, "Me and Mario almost got ourselves killed, thank you very much Miss-where-were-you."

Apparently, just as Mario was depositing the Actor in his bed, The Actor came to and started swinging. Pickles got clipped on the forehead and gashed by The Actor's pinky ring. Mario, in an attempt to protect Pickles, was punched in the mouth for his effort. In the end, Mario had to sock The Actor in the jaw rendering the "crazed bastard," as Pickles referred to him, unconscious.

"No matter how much things change, they somehow manage to remain the same," Mario said quietly.

"Ain't that the truth," Pickles said, "but you know, despite it all, he's still a great guy."

"Loaned me the readies to start my business, couldn't ask for a better mate," Mario agreed.

"OK, OK before you two start singing 'Feelings' what is the four-one-one on Philippe?"

Pickles started fanning himself with his hand, like he was in a Southern Baptist church.

"Oh Babe, please. Philippe? Girl, that's the Forbidden Zone. You listen to Dr. Zaius."

"She'll find out anyway. May as well tell her now," Mario said as he reached for the whiskey.

"Well," Pickles started, "you remember on The West Wing when the President had his 'body man', the guy who followed him around, kept him sane, kept him organized?"

"And kept other people off The President's back . . . " Mario chimed in.

"Right, well Philippe Noiret is The Actor's body man, figuratively and literally, if you get my drift."

"Yes," Mario said, taking up the thread, "only unlike the President's body man . . ."

"Philippe Noiret walked off the set of that movie The Actor was filming in Italy three weeks ago . . . " Pickles added.

"And he hasn't been heard from since," Mario said in a hushed tone.

"You remember Rocco, Nick's drummer?" I asked Pickles. "God, do I remember Rocco," Pickles said as he turned to Mario and licked his lips.

"Rocco was straight, Mario. Pickles is just remembering some fantasy he had. Anyway, Rocco disappeared for two weeks once, only to be found in a motel room in Fresno, with some chick he met at the supermarket. It happens."

THE ACTOR

"You said 'was straight,'" Mario shot back.

"He died in 2002, heart attack. Anyway, we're off the point as usual. What I'm saying is that men walk off to do whatever a man's got to do, all the time. It's no biggie. This guy Philippe, he'll turn up." Mario and Pickles gave each other the "girlfriend is clueless" look and proceeded to enlighten me. Philippe had entered The Actor's life in the same manner he had left it: abruptly and mysteriously. Mario and Pickles were convinced that Philippe had managed to strike up a friendship with The Actor's mum, who was, as Pickles put it, "nutty as a fruitcake," in order to get to The Actor.

When The Actor's mum finally introduced Philippe to The Actor it was as if she had introduced her son to crack cocaine. Philippe took immediate possession of The Actor, body and soul. The Actor's emotional and physical dependence was practically pathological. This unholy thing between The Actor and Philippe had been going on for almost three years. Mario and Pickles were convinced that as tight as Philippe had embraced The Actor he had embraced The Actor's checkbook even tighter.

Philippe had also tapped into The Actor's inner freak, taking what had been, up to that point, mild sado/maso sexual behavior to a dangerous level, bordering on torture. In fact, Mario thought that was part of the way they got off, seeing who could take the most pain. But the real disturbing element, to Professor Pickles anyway, was how much The Actor relied on Philippe for his everyday existence.

Philippe organized everything from The Actor's daily schedule to his clothes closet. He answered all The Actor's emails and other correspondence, dealt with The Actor's ex-wife, brought The Actor's daughter birthday presents, fielded phone calls, arranged for female companionship when The Actor needed it, copped his drugs, all while riding The Actor's emotional roller-coaster with him. To me, it just sounded like the job description for a wife.

"Welcome to the world of the heterosexual female, boys."

"Look, Babe, Mario and I know Thespian, and we know he is kind of eccentric, but the way he behaved tonight, and earlier with you in the car, not sleeping for days on end — well it's a little strange, even for him. He's usually good for one seriously out-there episode per day, especially if he's been drinking, but two or three in a row . . . "

"Something's amiss," Mario said, "and I put it down to Philippe."

"Well, where does he come from, this Philippe?" I asked. "France?" Mario said.

"OK, smarty-pants. Maybe he had a personal emergency and went home. Maybe he got hit by a car, and he's in a hospital somewhere. Maybe he has amnesia."

Pickles said wearily, "That's a lot of maybes, baby. Anyway, I'm pooped. See if you can get any more info, Babe. Inquiring minds want to know."

Pickles motioned to Mario and they both drifted off to Pickles' room. As they were leaving, Pickles blew me a kiss over his shoulder and said: "After the events of this evening, I'd sleep with the door locked, sugar."

I was left all alone with the remainder of the Jack. If I had been in my right mind, I would have used the opportunity to give my situation some thought. I decided to finish the whiskey instead. I left the downstairs lights on, so I could find my way up the stairs without killing myself. I looked for the door to my bedroom, which should have been at the end of the hall near The Actor's room, but there was no door. Then, I realized the only way to get to my room was through his. Strangely, this did not surprise me.

I went back to The Actor's room, the door was ajar. I could hear him mumbling in his sleep as I tip-toed in. The curtain was still open, allowing light from the street to partially illuminate the room. It was an alarming sight: a floor lamp was turned over, its shade crushed, the bed sheets had been torn from the bed and were lying in a heap on the floor; a black Hermes leather Camargue travel bag (even in my inebriated state the bag caught my eye) was lying on the floor, its contents strewn about as if the bag had exploded. The dresser had been shoved out of place with such force it left a big scrape mark on the wall. There were several small, dark blotches on the carpet, which I assumed were blood stains, and there on his sheet-less bed, barefoot and fully clothed, The Actor slept like a big tormented baby. He grimaced and spat out unintelligible profanities. I tried, but couldn't make out what he was saying. I sat there on the edge of the bed watching him for some time. Even asleep, in the throes of subconscious turmoil, he was a sexy motherfucker.

THE ACTOR

I threw one of the sheets from the floor over him, then I stumbled to my room and my bed. I couldn't sleep. There were far too many questions rolling around in my head, the Philippe situation, the daughter who wasn't allowed to visit, the violent outbursts, the way I couldn't stop thinking about The Actor, the way he had invaded my dreams. Outside, lightning flashed without thunder.

In an instant, rain was coming down in buckets.

There was no way of telling how much time had passed. Normally, I would have just rolled over and gone to sleep in my street clothes, but I felt clammy so I peeled everything off and got under the covers. I was listening to the rain, when I heard the door to my room open slowly, then I remembered what Pickles had said about locking my door. While I may have forgotten to lock the door, I had remembered to put my stun-gun under my pillow, fully charged.

I knew it was The Actor. He stood next to the bed without moving or saying a word for almost a full minute. Then he began to undress. I could hear him unzip his jeans and strip them off, then his undies. He was breathing slow and heavy, as if he were sleeping. He laughed softly and said in a raspy voice: "I had this horrible dream, a nightmare really. We had a fight and I killed you." He crawled under the covers with me. I could smell his sweat. He jerked me so close to him and with such force it knocked the wind out of me. He was kissing my neck, my ear, my shoulder. I could feel him getting stiff. I was too weak to resist, when out of nowhere he almost bends me in half and starts to go hard-core anal penetration on me; not something I am remotely into as first-time fucking with a man I barely knew. So, I Tased him, and I think the big weirdo liked it, up until the point he passed out. I must say, it certainly gave me a thrill.

The next morning, or maybe it was early afternoon by then, the rain had stopped, the sun was shining and my head was pounding. Something about the room was off, but I couldn't quite put my finger on it. Oh yeah, The Actor. Where the hell was he? I couldn't be bothered with thoughts of him now. I needed to pee and find some aspirin. Anyway, he'd probably gone back to his room. All this was rolling around in my aching head as I stepped out of bed. My foot never touched the floor. Someone grabbed my ankle. "Don't think I'm going to let you walk all over me," The Actor said.

He was lying on the floor, naked and bruised. The cut on his foot was bleeding through the bandage. There was a tattoo of a scorpion that went from the middle of his back, over his butt cheek and down to the middle of his thigh. Gee, I must have been really out of it, because I hadn't noticed it before.

"What are you doing in Philippe's bed?" The Actor asked. He was clearly bewildered. He let go of my ankle and began taking inventory of his body. I stepped over him, to make my way to the bathroom. I was peeing, as his questions continued, each one mounting in anxiety: "What the fuck happened? My foot is bleeding, and what are these marks on my chest? Why am I on the floor?" I looked up as I wiped myself and there he was, standing in the doorway. I don't think he had any idea who I was or what I was doing there, then a ripple of recognition rolled across his face.

"Babe, that is you, isn't it?"

"All day every day, and twice a day on Sunday. You got any aspirin?"

He pointed to a chest of drawers near the sink and whispered, "You're not wearing any clothes. I thought I was dreaming." I found aspirin and bandages, everything to tend his wounds and my own. I also found about a million condoms, two dozen tubes of Astroglide lubricant and, "What are these things?"

"They're anal beads, the unholy rosary ... " The Actor answered impatiently, as he peed for what seemed like the better part of two minutes. A very inspiring pee, which brought to my throbbing mind a website called monstercocks.com. I swallowed three aspirin without the benefit of water: one for my headache the other two for the thought of what damage he could have done to me, with that lovely, monstrous thing, if I had let him jam it in the undefiled pathway of my anus.

The Actor flushed, lowered the toilet seat lid, sat down and looked at the sole of his foot. "How did this happen?"

I didn't answer him. I just set about cleaning and redressing the wound, as he rubbed the Taser marks on his chest in disbelief.

"Well, that's the best I can do. You might need some stitches."

"You Tased me. You did, didn't you?" he laughed.

I looked up and I was staring directly at his giant stiffy, just too good to let go to waste. The next thing I knew, he was pulling himself

THE ACTOR

out of my mouth, whipping on a condom and I was bent over clutching the sink as he entered my front door from behind. He was strong, much stronger than I would have imagined, and he was pumping me like he was drilling for oil, past the point of pleasure, into pain. I was so aroused by the smell of his sweat, the feel of his touch, and the friction of him moving inside me; pain became part of the pleasure.

There was a mirror above the sink. I could feel him looking at me to see, asking without words, if I wanted him to stop. I shook my head and we kept on going. He buried his face in my back and hissed like a snake, and then he moaned so deep and so long I couldn't stop coming. He threw his head back like a wolf about to howl. As I convulsed, he pulled me tight, so tight to him, I could hardly breathe. Finally, the only choice left to both of us was to surrender to exhaustion.

I took a shower, dressed and left The Actor sleeping soundly in my bed, Philippe's bed. It was probably the first decent sleep he'd had for a good while. He looked content, sedated and a little dim-witted; just the way you want a man to look after a good fucking. Pickles and Mario must have been hard at work, because The Actor's bed was neatly made and his bedroom tidied.

The house was quiet — too quiet, in fact. I thought about knocking on Pickles' door, decided against it and continued down the stairs to the dual aspect living room: empty. The dining room was also empty, and the kitchen.

The boys had left a super-large mushroom and spinach pizza on the table with a note on top in big block letters that read: "BEER IN FRIDGE." Wherever they'd gone, they had to have just left because the pizza was still warm. In the fridge, next to the bottles of Mighty Oak Oscar Wilde beer was an envelope with my name scrawled on it. The note inside read:

Dear Babe,

Almost forgot about reading and book signing at Forbidden Planet. Roger is my handler for the night. If you need anything, Mario's business card is under the pizza box. Salivating for the scoopy-doop. I hope you took pictures.

Hugs, Pickles

CHAPTER 5

I adore simple pleasures. They're the last refuge of the complex.

— George Sanders as Lord Henry Wotton in
The Picture of Dorian Gray **(1945)**

Seduced and abandoned, left with all the beer I could drink, all the pizza I could eat and all the stromboli I could handle, snoring away upstairs. Nice touch, the Oscar Wilde beer, and not bad at all. I wasn't going to maintain my girlish figure if I kept on like this. I could do what I had been doing since I was fifteen: go on a mini-fast. Eat what I wanted for a few days and then not eat anything for a few days. It worked for me. I was so used to it by now, I rarely gave it much thought. Not something I'd recommend; just like I wouldn't recommend taking a stun gun to your lover on the first date, unless it was absolutely necessary. I wanted to feel bad about zapping The Actor, but I couldn't. I was amazed he had remembered it, because he hadn't remembered anything else. Well, on second thought, I suppose getting Tased is some pretty memorable shit.

The sun was setting, and the house was growing dark. I figured I should turn on the lights in the living room and the dining room to avoid any further accidents, but as I got up and walked towards the dining room I could see the rooms were already lit.

His back was to me. He didn't see me enter the living room. He was sitting at the piano, with a puzzled look on his face, as if he were trying to remember something. Then he turned around slowly and said, "I didn't think anyone was here." It sounded more like an apology than a statement. I felt as though I was intruding.

"I can go out, if you want to be alone."

"No, no don't do that," he said softly, "I never want to be alone. Come over here."

I sat beside him on the piano bench, not knowing what to expect. This was quite a different man from the one of the night before. He tilted his head to the side, searching my face.

"Why did you come here, Babe? To my house, I mean?" I started to answer. He cut me off.

"Was it the dreams? I saw you so clearly. It was so real.

I called on you to help me, and here you are. Am I still dreaming? Lately, I haven't been able to tell. I've just been so exhausted. I slept just now, really slept, for the first time in a long time."

I wanted to point out that I find a good fucking to be better than any sedative on the market, but he was being so sweet and so earnest I thought it better to keep that little tidbit to myself. I did want to explore the dream thing though, because it had been troubling me as well.

"See, I'm just not understanding this dream thing. I've never met you before, have I? I mean, I know who you are but why should we, all of a sudden, start having dreams about each other?" I said.

He still had that look on his face, like a dog when you've moved its bowl.

"I don't know. Maybe you're my guardian angel, maybe we were twins in another life, and maybe we were lovers who've crossed the seas of time to be with each other . . . damn, I'm sorry. I think that last line was from a movie I was in. Maybe . . ."

"As Professor Pickles would say, that's a lot of maybes, baby."

"I have all your recordings, you know, even the DJ remixes and the European vinyl dance releases. That's what I was trying to show you when I broke the lamp and cut my foot. I remember now. Whenever things got bad, your voice pulled me through. I mean it. When I found out you and Pickles were friends . . . but I was having the dreams before that."

"What do you remember about last night?"

"I remember we made love and it was really good. I wasn't dreaming was I? OK. And I remember you zapped me, with a stun gun. Was that before, after or during sex? And where the hell did you get a stun gun?"

"Never you mind where I got it. Suffice it to say, I did not bring it into this country illegally."

"It made me tingle all over. You'll do it again, won't you?" "Do you have any idea why I did that?"

"Love?"

"Because you were trying to force, emphasis on the word force, me to have anal sex with you."

"OK, now I remember. Sorry, I thought you were somebody else. I thought you were Philippe. It's his room, where he sleeps. I find it very hard to settle, toss and turn, talk in my sleep, so he kips there, in that room, where you were . . . are. Sorry."

It was time for Oscar Wilde. We retreated to the kitchen, where The Actor finished off what remained of the pizza, while putting a substantial dent in the cache of brew. He let out a belch that rattled the windows. We both laughed.

"That's better," he said, "Give us a kiss."

"You're not going to belch in my mouth, are you?" "Oh, you know that one."

"Honey, tell me about Philippe. What happened to him?"

Without warning his mood shifted, storm clouds gathered in his eyes, his shoulders rose and fell, as his breathing became heavier and for the first time I noticed how brutish he looked. He was clutching the edge of the kitchen table so tightly, his knuckles were transparent. He looked down and growled, with the ferocity of Richard Burton in *Look Back in Anger*.

"I told you I was sorry for getting into your bed uninvited. Can't we just leave it at that?" Then just as abruptly as it began, the storm was over; the dark clouds rolled back, and The Actor was all sweetness and light.

"I'm a bloody mess, aren't I?" he said, "Most of the time I can't stand my own company. I miss Philippe terribly, that's it. It's like a dull aching pain that won't go away. All I know is, we had a fight, one of many. It got physical, again nothing new," he continued matter-of- factly. Tears began to stream down his face, "I can't remember anything. I think we were here in this house. I think he'd left Italy before me. Anyway, when I got back he was here. I don't know. Did I dream that part? Oh, fuck. I just can't remember."

As he stumbled off to the downstairs lavatory, I thought about Lana Turner. Lana brought the whole blonde sexpot thing down to street level, especially in *The Postman Always Rings Twice* with John

THE ACTOR

Garfield. If you thought you were a tough guy, she'd show you just how tough you really were and you'd love every minute of it, just the way John Garfield's character did in the movie.

In 1958, Lana gave the performance of a lifetime when she had to take the stand and testify during her daughter's murder trial. There has been much speculation about the night Lana's daughter Cheryl stabbed to death her mother's boyfriend, reputed mobster Johnny Stomponato. Cheryl was about fifteen years old at the time, and Stomponato was a physically commanding guy, who some say worked as an enforcer for mob boss Mickey Cohen. People then and now have drawn their own conclusions about what actually happened that night.

The court verdict was justifiable homicide, because the court believed Cheryl did what she did to protect her mother, who — as both mother and daughter testified — was being attacked by Johnny Stomponato. The whole thing, whatever went down, must have been horrible for everyone involved, especially Mr. Stomponato. But to me, the most fascinating part of this whole story was Lana Turner's testimony at trial, which eerily resembled her witness stand testimony in a film she had completed not long before the real courtroom drama began. Was she in fact acting on both occasions? We'll never know.

Just like I will never know if the performance The Actor just gave was in fact a performance. What I do know is that in a pinch we all fall back on our available resources, even if those resources are courtesy of Metro-Goldwyn-Mayer or the Royal Academy of Dramatic Art.

The Actor was rejuvenated when he returned.

"Piss pills. Takes a while for the effects to wear off, have to use them when I'm working to keep my weight down. Drinking beer doesn't help."

"So, have you got anymore? Piss pills?" I asked. Diuretics, dammit! Why hadn't I thought of that?

"Sure, I'll give you as many as you want. Listen, I was thinking. I want to have a small dinner party, nothing fancy. You could meet some of my friends from the neighborhood. Would you like that?"

"Yeah, I'd like that, but who's going to organize it? I mean isn't this something that Philippe would handle?"

"Yes, yes you have a point. Didn't think about that."

He began to pace the width of the kitchen, nervously running his fingers through his hair.

"Look," he said, still pacing, "tomorrow you, me and Pickles will figure something out. It can't be that difficult. Then once that's sorted maybe the two of you can help me get organized. I know the house cleaning service is scheduled for tomorrow, early." He stopped short, focused his gaze on me intently and asked, "What do you think we should do about Philippe?"

Ah, the conspiratorial "we." I wasn't really sure what he was asking me to do. Help with the disposal of Philippe's body, the destruction of evidence, whether or not we should put Philippe on the guest list?

"I don't know, baby. Why don't we wait until tomorrow to figure that out? One more day can't hurt, can it? "I suppose not. Maybe he'll call."

"Maybe he will," I said. And maybe racism and poverty will end, and everyone will hold hands and sing, "We are the World."

The Actor moved towards me, "I'm hungry," he said. "Do you want to order out or maybe we can . . ."

He produced a Crown Zero-Zero Condom from his jeans pocket and ripped the package open with his teeth. "Not that kind of hungry."

In an instant, his tongue was plunged so deep in my mouth, I could taste the hops from the beer he'd been drinking. I stumbled backward. He caught me and steered me towards the kitchen table. Empty beer bottles fell and rolled across the kitchen floor, as The Actor slammed me down on the kitchen table, flattening the pizza box. He unzipped my pants and stripped them and my undies off in one forceful movement, like Harry Houdini. Then he spread my legs and buried his face in my kitty-kat. I could feel his tongue probing until it hit its mark. He worked it until I convulsed and screamed with pleasure.

He came up for air, tore off his clothes, whipped on the Magnum sized condom and was inside me. My arms encircled him, my fingers dug into his flesh. He gripped either side of the table. He was pumping hard now, with every thrust I rose to meet him. We were bathed in sweat, both of us grunting and moaning. The table began

THE ACTOR

to wobble, there was a cracking sound and just as we both were reaching for that critical moment, the table pitched to the side and collapsed, as we both arrived. We slid off the lopsided tabletop onto the floor. The Actor kissed me so slowly and sweetly it almost made me cry. He snuggled his head against my breast. I ran my fingers through his hair. He looked at what used to be the table. "Well, it was bound to happen sooner or later," he said.

That night we both slept peacefully in his bed for the better part of the night, until something woke me up at around 4AM. It sounded like someone was downstairs rummaging through things. I knew it couldn't be Pickles. No matter how late he came in he would knock on the bedroom door to see if I was all right. And, why would Pickles go through The Actor's things? I shook The Actor until he woke up.

"Are the cleaners here?" he mumbled, still half asleep.

"No," I whispered and pointed to the alarm clock on the nightstand.

"The driver's downstairs? Tell him I'll be right down. Get my script for me, luv."

"You're not working today. And keep your voice down. Someone's in the house and I don't think its Pickles."

The Actor swung both feet to the floor and said, "Blimey. Babe, lock the door." I did. He motioned towards the dresser.

I grabbed his mobile phone and handed it to him. He called the police.

"Yes, is this Sgt. Farrow? Yeah, that's right it's me. Fine and you? Listen, mate . . . can you send someone round? Yes. She's back. The door should be open. If not, I'll throw the keys down. Right. Cheers." He put the phone down and cradled his head in his hands. "Better throw some clothes on. I can't do this by myself."

We both dressed in silence. I had to pee. He followed me into the bathroom. He ran the tap and splashed water on his face. He said something, but it was muffled by the towel he was using and the sound of the toilet flushing. Someone was pounding on the bedroom door.

"Are you all right in there, sir? You can open the door now. It's the police."

The Actor grabbed my hand. As we emerged from the bedroom and made our way downstairs, I saw winks and knowing glances being exchanged. The police, it seemed, were everywhere. The Actor tightened his grip on my hand and bit down on his bottom lip.

The living room was a shambles. Books had been torn from the bookshelves and tossed on the floor. The cushions uprooted from the sofa, chairs flung about the room. The beautiful orchids were broken, their pots smashed on the floor. My vinyl recordings had been ripped from their jackets and the jackets torn in half.

There on the now cushion-less sofa, sitting between one male and one female police officer, was the whacky woman with the spiked hair, who had tormented me at Heathrow Airport.

The Actor let go of my hand and rushed over to the spot where my records lay. He knelt down, picked one up and examined it, then snapped his head around to the whacky woman on the sofa, "You bitch," he hissed. A policeman approached him holding a zip lock bag with a paring knife in it: "Had this on her. We're going to have to take her in again."

"You're not taking me anywhere," whacky woman screamed. "He's the one. Ask him about that assistant of his. Just ask him where Philippe is." She looked at me and said calmly, "You're next, you stupid cow."

She lunged at me but was quickly subdued by the two officers. After receiving a nod from the officer holding the evidence bag with the paring knife, the two officers wrested her away to one of the patrol cars outside. The remaining policemen and women began to file out.

The officer in charge, the one who had the knife in the baggie, took off his hat, slicked his hair back, put his cap back on, and said wearily, "This is getting as hard for us as it is for you. You'll have to do something. She needs care." The Actor, who had been kneeling over the vandalized albums, got up slowly, turned to the officer and extended his hand.

"I know. I know. I'm sorry for your trouble. Appreciate all you've done. Will she be all right . . . for tonight I mean?"

"We'll keep close watch on her. If it looks like she needs to be taken to hospital, someone will call you. Otherwise, we'll release her tomorrow. I hate to ask at a time like this, but my girlfriend will kill me if I don't . . ."

The Actor left the room and came back with an 8x11 glossy and a black Sharpie.

"What's your girlfriend's name?" After autographing his photo for the officer, The Actor slumped down on the piano bench. I escorted the officer to the door.

"Who was that woman?" I asked.

"His mum," the officer said as he closed the door behind him.

Over at the piano I could hear The Actor mumbling, "His girlfriend, my ass. Every time he comes here he's got a different girlfriend, probably selling the fucking things on eBay." I approached The Actor with caution.

"That woman is your mother?"

"Explains a lot, doesn't it? Well, I suppose I should get on to my lawyer, so he can be there when she's released. I can't have one shred of happiness . . . It's like she has radar or something. Oh my son is happy, let me go over there and fuck it all up. And I was sleeping, sleeping like a normal person, for once. Don't ask me about sleeping pills, bad experience."

"I wasn't. What's wrong with her?"

I sat down next to him and stroked his hair. It seemed to calm him. He put his head on my shoulder and sighed, "How much time have you got?"

As The Actor explained it, he had only recently been made aware of what was actually the matter with his mum. When he was a child her behavior had terrified and embarrassed him. It had, by his account, driven his father away. This last episode, apart from the paring knife, was pretty mild. The previous time The Actor's mum had broken into his house, it had taken four uniformed officers to drag her out, thus the heavy police presence tonight.

"She's bipolar. Tonight was the mania. When it's not mania it's depression. She won't take her tablets . . . and I forgot to turn on the alarm system like an idiot . . . as if that would stop her."

The Actor was worried about the Press, worried his mum would start babbling on about Philippe. Of course, no one would take her seriously, but they might. Just like the time she marched in the Gay Pride parade and it was in all the papers. What a mess that had been . . . the money and finagling it had taken The Actor to convince the public that just because she supported the LGBTQs her son wasn't one of them. He looked up at me with those big blue eyes and said, "I'm not gay, you know. I'm not. I'm not going to be put in some box. My needs cannot and will not be categorized."

I stroked his hair and kissed him on the forehead, "You tell 'em, honey."

The sun would be up pretty soon. The Actor decided we both needed a cup of tea, so he retreated to the kitchen to put the kettle on. I started tidying up the living room when he called out, "Leave it. It'll give the cleaners something to do."

At which point, the front door slowly opened. Oh! God, had she escaped, and me without my stun-gun. Then I heard Pickles' voice: "Damn, must have been a hell of a party."

Pickles could not hide his delight as The Actor detailed the recent events of the evening. Pickles had seen the kitchen table and just like the police had chalked it up to The Actor's mum. The Actor and I saw no reason to elucidate.

"Well, don't punish yourself about the alarm. That was my doing. I should have armed it when I left, remember you did show me how, but I was in such a rush . . . Did she break in the back door like she did the last time?"

The Actor got up and walked from the dining through the kitchen to the back door, which stood perfectly intact, not one pane of glass broken. Pickles and I brought up the rear.

We were just as surprised as The Actor. Pickles gently wrapped his fingers around The Actor's forearm, "I know you've been through some unsavory shit this evening, and I know that remembering things in the order they happen is hard for you at times, but did the police say anything about how your mother got in here?"

The Actor looked totally bewildered but I, "I thought I heard one of them say to the head guy, something about no forced entry." "She gets in, and always the first thing she does is fling open the front door. I don't know why . . . " The Actor said.

Pickles released The Actor's arm and let out a sound like air being expelled from a balloon: "She has a key."

"How the hell does she have a key?" The Actor raged. We were back to Burton in *Look Back in Anger*.

"There are four keys to the front door. Only I have a key to the back door. Each key is numbered. That's how I keep track of them. Pickles, look at your key."

Pickles reached into his pocket, "Key #3."

"And I have number one on my key ring," The Actor said. "Number four is on top of the dresser in my bedroom — it's for Babe."

"We'd better check to make sure . . . I mean you did say she had a knife," Pickles said.

So, off we all traipsed to The Actor's bedroom, where he produced keys #1 and #4. Pickles asked, "Where's the #2 key?"

The Actor looked at me, then at Pickles: "Philippe has it."

The three of us flopped down on the bed. Philippe again, for a guy I hadn't even met, he was sure getting on my nerves. We discussed the whole key thing for about a half an hour. The consensus was The Actor would get his lawyer to find out whether The Actor's mum had the #2 key among her personal belongings, which the police had probably confiscated when they locked her up for the night. But, my feeling was the police would be just as interested in that key as we were.

It was a little past six in the morning and a lot of yawning, and stretching was going on. We decided the best thing to do was to get some sleep. Pickles drifted off to his room. The Actor and I slept peacefully for about an hour, when the doorbell rang. The cleaners had arrived.

CHAPTER 6

Money is a sixth sense that makes it possible for you to enjoy the other five.

— Zsa Zsa Gabor

Zsa Zsa Gabor, the former Miss Hungary, Hollywood on-screen eye candy, and once described as the Hungarian H-Bomb was married nine times, once to the incomparable George Sanders. My fondest memory of the formidable Zsa Zsa is when she was performing in a dinner theater venue and reportedly asked the management to move the people in wheelchairs to the back, because they were depressing her. Sadly, many years later, dear Zsa Zsa had to have a leg amputated and ended up — in a wheelchair. Ain't life a bitch?

We were asleep-deprived and cranky lot when we convened in The Actor's study that evening. Pickles whipped up a pitcher of Bloody Marys to revive us, as we attempted to get The Actor sorted. Earlier, after the cleaners had been shooed away and we had ordered in some Thai food, The Actor dealt with the release of his mother from jail or "the local Nick" in Brit-speak. The telephone conversation between The Actor and his lawyer had been a long and heated one. The subsequent conversation with The Actor's publicist was equally protracted and intense. The lawyer thought it was the perfect time for The Actor to commit his mother to a mental institution. The fact that she was carrying a knife clearly demonstrated she was a danger to herself and others. What could be more sympathetic than a son dedicated to his troubled mother's care and well-being?

The Actor, on the other hand, felt committing his mother

THE ACTOR

would only open a can of worms out of which would wriggle the darkest secrets of his private life, including, but not limited to the disappearance of Philippe. The Actor's publicist felt that The Actor's mother, Philippe or anything to do with The Actor's off-screen life should be held at bay until after the release of his current film, in about six weeks. The Actor agreed to the latter.

This was the topic of conversation as Pickles, The Actor and I, tackled The Actor's email, snail mail, scheduled appointments and the household to-do list. Pickles took the emails, The Actor took the snail mail and I took The Actor's schedule. He'd already missed two appointments that week. The to-do list was divided among us. I got the dry cleaning — lucky me. Pickles discovered The Actor had a couple dozen emails from the same two individuals who were asking The Actor to please answer his phone. Apparently, a new script had been dropped off by courier and the writer/director wanted to speak with The Actor. In addition, The Actor was scheduled to do some dialogue looping at Pinewood Studios tomorrow afternoon, and would he please confirm he'd be there.

"Yeah," Pickles said as he swiveled the task chair around from the desk, "I tried to call your mobile and the land phone a couple of times last night, straight to voicemail."

The Actor, reading glasses perched on his nose, was on the floor sifting through a pile of mail.

"Not one," he said absently, "not one letter from Philippe."

Pickles looked at me, one eyebrow raised.

"What about your phones, Thespian? Maybe you should turn them on after we're done here."

"As far as I'm concerned we *are* done here," The Actor said, as he got up from the floor and stretched, "I have to go out for a bit. You two don't have to do anymore with this, not if you don't want to."

He grabbed me around the waist and gave me a kiss that was a little too passionate, what with Pickles in the room and all.

"I won't be long," he whispered."

A few minutes later we heard the front door slam. Pickles jumped up and clapped his hands.

"I couldn't wait one more minute. I want all the gory details."
"Can we go out to some place nice and get something to eat first?"

Thirty minutes later we were seated in Trojka, a sleek Eastern

European restaurant with al fresco seating. I preferred to sit inside, and of course Pickles wanted to sit outside. So, we compromised — we sat inside.

The place looked as though it had been populated by Central Casting for a James Bond movie, everyone with a very low body mass index, dressed in gradations of black, wearing designer shades. The waitresses were no different, except they weren't wearing sunglasses.

I took a deep breath; it smelled like Warsaw. Pickles ordered two double vodkas, which I thought was very gentlemanly of him until he asked me what I was drinking. I ordered one of the same. Pickles had the bigosz cabbage stew, and I ordered borscht and potato pancakes.

"Isn't this nice?" Pickles asked, "OK, I know when you said someplace nice you meant someplace really expensive . . ."

"Well, yeah. I don't like that waitress. Did you see the look she gave me? Like she couldn't be bothered, but she was fawning all over you."

"No, she wasn't. I didn't see a 'look.' Half of these perceived slights exist only in your own mind. Now, before we get down to the nitty-gritty, where do you think lover boy went off to in such a hurry?"

"If he didn't see fit to tell us, then we don't really need to know. And if you think I am going to sit here and give you a blow by blow . . . poor choice of words."

Our drinks were delivered and Pickles downed one double in a single gulp. He was salivating and it wasn't for the food. I didn't feel comfortable telling him everything, but I knew we could not move on to new business if I didn't throw him a bone.

"Crown Skinless Skin Magnums, by the case," I said sipping my drink slowly.

Pickles was working on his second double. My last remark made him stop in mid-gulp.

"Magnums? How many in a case?"

"One thousand, and we used twenty-four."

". . . In a thirty-six hour period. 'Jealousy, night and day you torture me.'"

"Pickles, how much do you know about Philippe?

THE ACTOR

Our food arrived in mid-sentence. Pickles got his Polish cabbage/meat stew, but I got herrings in dill sauce. An argument ensued with the bitch waitress until someone at another table shouted out he had the wrong order, and she realized what she had done, the cow. As the correct dish was finally placed in front of me, Pickles began.

"Well, you know, Babe, I only met him twice. Very sophisticated, very cultured, I mean you could come in your pants just from looking at him. Clean as the Board of Health . . . always. Mostly, because he wore Thespian's Tom Ford suits. Remember the way Tony Curtis looked in *The Sweet Smell of Success*, with those dark curls falling down over his forehead? That's Philippe, but creepy."

"Do you think he's still alive?"

Pickles dropped his fork, the color draining from his face, as he reached over and finished off my drink, simultaneously gesturing to the waitress to bring us both another round.

"My God, woman. You know how to ruin a good meal, but point taken. It is the sixty-four dollar question, isn't it? How could somebody, as fine as that boy, just disappear?"

"Here's the thing we don't really know if he's disappeared, do we? When we get back we're going to go CSI on this. We're going to call every fucking hospital in London and that place in Italy where The Actor was filming. We are going to search The Actor's house from top to bottom. I mean Philippe could have fallen down the steps or something."

"I don't like the 'or something' part," Pickles said as he slurped his fresh round, "And if we come up empty?"

"We'll have to start calling the morgues."

"Oh, God! Babe. Please, I'm eating. And may I ask Holmes, why are we doing all this?"

"Because of something The Actor said. Because I'm sick and tired of this Philippe, already."

Pickles leaned back in his chair, folded his hands across his chest and grinned: "Looks like the green-eyed monster's got a hold of your big toe."

The waitress bitch handed Pickles the bill and looked at me with contempt. I whipped out my credit card. She scurried off, returning sometime later with the receipt, which I signed then carefully placed

10p on the table, pushed it towards her and said, "Buy yourself a new personality."

Pickles looked at her with pity as we were leaving. "Don't mess with the Babe," his parting words.

Out on Regent's Park Road the still night air was conjuring up dreams. People quietly determined not to be touched by life strolled on as if in a trance. I just felt weary, tired of having to put one foot in front of the other. Pickles had been waylaid by another Friend of Cyberpunk. I remembered I hadn't asked him about the Forbidden Planet event, but so much had happened in the last twenty-four that I felt fortunate that I was able to remember my own name. I sighed loud enough for Pickles to take my hint, when out of the corner of my eye, I caught sight of a very tall, regal and fiercely handsome older man crossing the road. He was heading, straight for me. It was JD DeLongo, best friend of my late husband Gordon Burdett, and over the years, one of my best friends, as well. "I was just telling someone how much I missed you, and here you are. Fancy that?" JD said, as he held me in his embrace. How delicious to be held by a towering man, so reassuring after all I'd been through lately.

"Well, what am I? Chopped liver?" I heard Pickles remark.

"Raymond," JD said, "your escapades of late, have been thoroughly documented for the amusement and bewilderment of the local punters."

"Praise, Jesus. I had an SRO crowd at the Forbidden Planet and I made a small bundle, I don't mind saying."

"Are you taking care of our Felicia? She looks a bit knackered."

"I'm standing right here guys," I chimed in, as I whipped out my Salvatore Ferragamo aviator sunglasses, "It's been a rough day."

"And, the night before from the looks of it . . . I wish I could stop, but I'm meeting someone."

"You'd better watch it, JD. If they get any younger they'll be calling you a pedophile," Pickles sniggered.

"I'm going to ignore that remark, for your sake, old boy. I hear you two are house guests of The Actor. So, I take it I'll be seeing you on Sunday."

"What's happening on Sunday?" Pickles and I asked in unison. "He's throwing a dinner party. He hasn't told you? Have to dash. See you soon," and he was gone.

THE ACTOR

Pickles' mouth was wide open and his eyes were giant question marks. I put my foot down: "Don't start. I'm way too tired. Just get Mario to send us a car."

The Actor didn't show up until eight the following morning. Wherever he had been, he had changed his clothes. He stripped and crawled into bed beside me. I couldn't detect any fresh bruises, so I assumed he hadn't been satisfying his needs. I inhaled his scent- that mixture of whiskey, lemons and sweat now topped off with the strong aroma of marijuana. I stroked his hair. He snuggled up to me kissed me softly and then fell sound asleep.

When I woke again at 1 p.m. he was gone. I had just thrown a robe on when there was a knock at the bedroom door. It was Pickles with two big mugs of coffee, God bless him. He sat on the edge of the bed, barely able to contain himself.

"He's gone to the studio to do the looping. He looked happy. You're good for him, and he knows it. But, what about JD? How weird was that running into him? I thought he was still in LA. What do you think he's doing here? And what was that stuff about a dinner party?"

"Slow down, boy. It is way too early for this much curiosity. Anyway, JD is a Brit. England is his country, so why shouldn't he be here?"

"He's losing his hair, but I'd still do him." "You dog."

"Well, it had to be said. What's with Sunday? You know about this dinner party?"

"I vaguely remember The Actor saying something . . . no details, no date, just that he was thinking about it."

"How does he know JD? And when did he organize, no better yet how did he organize it? I mean Thespian is great if you tell him when and where to show up, but pulling things together, social things — not his strong suit."

"I hear what you're saying. When he first mentioned the dinner party I asked him wasn't it something that Philippe would normally take care of. He said yes, but that the three of us could sort it out, as he put it. But we didn't. So, who did?"

"Beats the hell out of me, but what about JD?"

"I don't know. JD's a producer now. Him and The Actor, they travel in the same circles."

"I hate to ask, because I know it's like asking about Lord Voldemort, but..."

"What about Philippe?"

There is an old vaudeville comedy sketch my father used to recreate to amuse his children. Either my brother or I became part of the sketch, taking on the role of the "straight man." The routine is known by several names, but I grew up knowing it as "Slowly I Turned," or "Niagara Falls."

In the routine, my father played the "wronged man." He and the "straight man" meet as strangers. The wronged man tells an impassioned story of how he was ruthlessly betrayed by his best friend and business partner, at Niagara Falls.

Sometimes it's over a woman, sometimes it's over a business deal...it really doesn't matter. What matters is the wronged man got his revenge, and in recounting this part of the story he begins with the words, "Slowly I turned..." This phrase causes the wronged man to get so emotionally wrapped up in the telling of the tale he re-lives it, and ends up attacking the "straight man." The straight man screams at the wronged man to stop as he fends him off; the wronged man comes to his senses and apologizes.

The two get to talking about something else. The straight man says something about Niagara Falls (maybe he went there for his honeymoon, I can't remember), which unbeknownst to him, are the trigger words for the wronged man, enraging him so much that he begins to re-live the actual events of Niagara Falls again, sending him into: "Slowly I turned..." and beginning his attack on the "straight man" again.

This cycle keeps going because the straight man can't help himself; the trigger words, Niagara Falls, keep slipping into the conversation. That's why this routine is also known as "Niagara Falls" or "Slowly, I turned..."

Now, when I was eight or nine, I thought this was the funniest thing on Earth. Even funnier was, I could say "Niagara Falls" when my father was snoozing on the sofa, and he would jump up and say, "Slowly I turned..."

I imparted this tidbit to Pickles who immediately agreed that from now on if anybody mentioned Philippe's name: "Slowly, I turned..."

THE ACTOR

We had a few hours before The Actor returned so we split up the London hospitals between us. After we eliminated the children's, eye/ear/nose/throat hospitals, and the walk-in centers, we had about fifteen or so a piece. The most difficult part was getting Pickles to give me some description of the missing man that we could use.

"I'm sorry, Pickles, but highly fuck-able is not a useful description. How tall is he, how much do you think he weighs, what color are his eyes? Stuff like that."

"Babe, I think of the whole package, not its component parts. Now, Mario's good at height and weight, and he's had more contact with . . . we're calling him 'the missing man' now, right?"

After Pickles called Mario we had more to go on: the missing man was around 42 years old, about 183 centimeters tall and 76 kilograms. His eyes were green. But, I was still not satisfied.

"For God's sake Pickles, what does all this mean in English?" "I hate to break this to you, honey — but it is in English, because we're in England. It's we, the barbaric Americanos, who are too dumb to convert to the metric system. Since I used to reside here, I will break it down for you: he's about 6 feet tall and he weighs about 168 pounds. I take it you understand the part about green eyes?"

"Highly fuck-able."

"Yes, Babe. I believe I've already covered that. Mario's on his way over says he's got something to show us. It must be funny, because he was still laughing when I hung up."

After Pickles and I finished calling the local hospitals, the missing man was still missing. There were only two hospitals in the municipality of Arezzo, Italy, where the missing man had initially gone missing; both had morgues.

Even though there were two men in one hospital, and one in the morgue of the other hospital, who matched the missing man's description, more or less, they all were Italian and their families had visited them or claimed the body. Finally, Pickles called the Office of Her Majesty's Coroner, and that turned out to be a dead end as well.

Mario arrived and offered to make some pasta if we'd help. He brought with him two bottles of a nice summer red wine, Domaine Ferrer Ribiere, Cotes du Roussillon; not pricey but good.

Mario suggested we all have a drink straight away, as he had news, urgent news, but first he wanted to know what had happened to the kitchen table. My response, "You don't want to know."

Mario produced his laptop and there on YouTube was a shaky, out of focus cell phone video of The Actor's mother being escorted out of The Actor's house by the cops. It already had 87,572 hits and had only been posted ten hours ago. The Actor had forgotten to turn the house phone back on, which may have been one of his smarter moves.

We watched the news. A statement issued by The Actor's agent said The Actor was saddened by his mother's deteriorating health, and felt sure that those who were struggling with issues surrounding their parents' onset of dementia would understand that deciding on the best course of care was not an easy task, etc., etc. There was also BBC footage of The Actor's mother emerging from the police station, under the protective wing of The Actor's lawyer, who was very adept at wading through the media swarm and deflecting camera lenses. The Actor could not be reached for comment.

"I thought there would be loads of Press camped outside,"

Mario said, "but there's just that black car sitting out front, the one that was following us that first day."

"Is there anyone in that black car?" I asked. "Yeah, two blokes."

Pickles was oblivious, due to the plate of food in front of him. Amidst his slurping and gobbling, he managed to chime in without lifting his head.

"I don't want to be here when he gets back. It's going to be like Heathcliff in Wuthering *Heights*."

"No, I have to disagree, more like Richard Burton in *Look Back in Anger*."

Mario dropped his fork, "What's the matter with you lot? Aren't you the least bit curious about that black car with the two blokes in it out front?"

"Maybe they're fans, or the press," I said, and Pickles agreed.

"Well, they look like Special Branch or the CIA to me," Mario said softly.

I said, "One of us should go out there and find out who they are, I vote for Pickles."

Pickles was choking a little as he frantically waved his hands and shook his head "No." He gulped down the remains of my glass of wine and said, "Negativo. We should do nothing until his nibs returns. I mean it. This is his house, his rules. Let him decide . . ."

"Let him decide what?" The Actor asked. He was standing in the doorway between the dining room and the kitchen. He must have come in the back way. How long had he been in the house?

"Not Heathcliff. Not Richard Burton. Not tonight. Too tired," The Actor said, as he threw a pile of newspapers on the table.

As I poured him a glass of what was left of the wine, he grabbed my free hand and kissed my palm tenderly. Pickles put a plate of food in front of him. We all sat in silence, for a moment, while The Actor ate and drank.

"Oh, by the way, Pickles," The Actor said between bites, "there are two gents from your State Department out front who'd like a quiet word. Shall I invite them in?"

Agents John Dowell and Stephen Small were ushered into the living room by The Actor, who, as the owner of the house, was asked to remain present, while they spoke with Pickles. Mario and I remained in the dining room within earshot.

Dowell and Small were from the DS, the Bureau of Diplomatic Security, the law enforcement arm of the U.S. State Department. The DS had been contacted by UK Immigration, who was being pressured to determine if Pickles should be deported, removed or forced to involuntarily depart the British Isles. Apparently, Pickles' ravings at the Oxford Arms had not gone unnoticed. The article in the *Camden New Journal* had been cited by the *Huffington Post* and gone viral in the blogosphere. Dowell and Small had attended the event at Forbidden Planet. Now they were seated in The Actor's living room in their Men's Warehouse suits, as part of their threat analysis of Professor Pickles. The Actor couldn't have been more calm or gracious. I was impressed; then I realized he was acting.

Dowell did most of the talking: the State Department was aware that Professor Pickles was a guest in The Actor's home and it would be less stressful for all parties concerned if they would interview Pickles here rather than dragging everyone down to the DS office. Agent Small leaned forward and asked:

"You are travelling with Felicia Lake Brown Burdett Ravelli, aren't you, Professor?"

All of my former husbands' names strung together with my own sounded like I was Elizabeth Taylor or something. I didn't like this guy Small, not one little bit.

"I understand," Small continued, "that she's a guest here, as well?"

"We'd like to speak with her," Dowell interjected.

"Oh, Babe will you join us please?" The Actor called out.

I looked at Mario, who was almost in tears and said, just like Susan Hayward in any movie she was ever in: "I will not let our Pickles go down."

Pickles crossed his legs yet again; his left foot tapping the air spasmodically. His hair was pulled back with a rubber band, which he kept undoing, shaking his hair out and pulling his hair back into the rubber band again. The Actor, to his credit, circled around behind Pickles and clamped his hands on Pickles' shoulders, all the while applying gentle force.

It had the effect of the swaddling sweaters that apply pressure to comfort nervous cats. Pickles' body relaxed and his nervous tics stopped.

I, on the other hand, was so fucking irritated listening to these two cyborgs drone on and on about being charged with the responsibility of maintaining a secure and safe environment in which our beloved country could administer its foreign policy agenda, that I just blurted out: "God bless America, goddammit!" There was a moment of uncomfortable silence after which the interrogation continued.

"Professor Pickles, we have gone over your background information — yours too, Ms. Lake . . . " Agent Dowell went on, "we can't find anything that would concern the State Department, but I hope you will take this to heart Professor, when I say: do your excessive drinking in private and keep your mouth shut about your President and the White House. We as a nation, along with our British allies, are engaged in an ongoing war against terrorism, and I for one don't want to waste my time running down God-less alcoholic faggots. Ms. Lake, the next time the State Department gets a call from UK Immigration about your friend here, we will assist the British government in deporting you both."

"But I didn't say a goddamned thing. Why should I be . . . ?" Agent Small said, "Look at it as an incentive to keep your friend in line. Ms. Lake, I was wondering . . ."

THE ACTOR

For a moment I thought Agent Small was going to ask me out, but he was holding one of my CDs, *Alone in the Night*, asking me if I'd sign it for him.

"Well, gentlemen, if that's all," The Actor said, "I'm rather tired, and I'm sure my guests must be as well."

"I know you hear this all the time," Agent Dowell began, "but my wife would kill me . . ."

The Actor left the room and returned with two 8x11s and a black Sharpie. "What is your wife's name?"

When he was done he stepped between Agent Small and myself and asked: "Wife, girlfriend?" Small said, "No, just make it out to me."

As The Actor showed the officers to the door, Pickles looked at me with tears in his eyes and sobbed, "They didn't want my autograph."

Mario moved quickly to embrace Pickles, now in the full throes of channeling Blanche Dubois.

"Look at it this way, Pickles," I said, "you'll have a great story for Celebrity Rehab."

"Those assholes," The Actor roared, as he returned to the living room, "all they wanted was to get in this house so they could go back to their bloody office and brag to their equally moronic mates . . . You OK, Pickles? That Dowell git was bang out of order talking to you that way, like the sodding Gestapo. I'll put the kettle on. We could all do with a nice cuppa. Help me, will you, Babe?"

As I trailed behind The Actor, I thought, how comforting it truly was to make a pot of tea for your friends, your family, your mates in times of trouble, and how comforting it must be to know that someone was making that cup of tea for you. My savage American heart was deeply touched by this British ritual. Somehow, there was more soul to it than making a pot of coffee. Making tea conjured up a loving mother, a soft blanket and a nice warm fire. I felt The Actor's arms around me pulling me close to him. He kissed me, a soft chaste kiss.

"Why, Babe, you're crying," he whispered.

"You're making me fall in love with the British people, I said."

The Actor laughed, "And all this time I was trying to make you fall in love with me."

We returned to the living room with tea and chocolate biscuits. Pickles, thanks to Mario, had regained his composure. I apologized to Pickles for my Celebrity Rehab remark. Although he did say it was cruel even for me, he forgave me. We all agreed that we were feeling pretty fragile — that maybe we should get some sleep. Pickles wondered aloud if he should cancel his reading and book signing at the Congress Centre the following day, but The Actor said no way. He told Pickles all the publicity was bound to bring the punters out in force. Hadn't Pickles had a standing room only crowd at Forbidden Planet? The Actor also told Pickles he should make a formal apology to both the British and the American governments, before he gave his reading, and he should also condemn public drunkenness. Pickles loved this idea and so did Mario.

Then that Classic Steve McQueen grin stole across The Actor's face. How about if the visit from the DS was leaked to the media by an anonymous source, and what if this source alluded to a homophobic remark made by one of the DS Agents? The Actor said he would take care of everything and the leak would take care of the two assholes. Pickles was a victim now, and the public just loves a victim. Pickles went into Blanche Dubois mode, and the waterworks started. He hugged and kissed The Actor, until his tears made a big wet spot on The Actor's shirt.

"You are diabolical," Pickles hollered.

Mario was pretty emotional as well. He hugged The Actor fiercely, "I just can't find the words, mate." We all kissed and hugged as if we were leaving another Thanksgiving dinner where Uncle Al had gotten drunk and pulled down his pants. Pickles and Mario departed. I was left alone with a man I now knew I could never leave. I began to tidy up, but The Actor said, "Leave it." I curled up on the sofa. The Actor removed his black Comme des Garçons PLAY Heart Zip Front Hoodie and gently placed it over me. "You must be tired, baby," he said, as he sat down next to me and cradled my head in his lap. When I looked up at him, it was as if I were seeing him for the very first time. He looked so extraordinarily ordinary in his white T-shirt and jeans, just another guy, who millions of women he would never know envisioned as they masturbated themselves to sleep.

"That was wonderful, the way you helped Pickles maintain his dignity."

THE ACTOR

"I'll make some calls tomorrow . . . have a statement issued on my behalf in support of Professor Pickles, whilst denouncing gay-ashing. I could use some good publicity about now, so you see I was not being totally wonderful."

"If you say so. How's your foot?" He wiggled his flip-flop off and held up his foot; it had been properly bandaged by a medical professional.

"Took your advice," he said proudly, "went to see a doctor. You were right, it needed stitches."

"Does it hurt?"

"Deliciously so, but reach inside my hoodie pocket." I did and found some prescription painkillers.

"Yeah, might come in handy." I said, thinking back to our first romantic night together, when he attempted anal penetration against my will. I wanted to ask him about his mother, but thought better of it. He was so docile, I didn't want to disturb the moment. Then I felt a wave of Catholic guilt wash over me, and the need to confess quickly followed.

"We called all the hospitals and the morgues here and in Italy while you were gone and we didn't find Philippe. I guess that's good news."

The Actor pulled away and my head plopped down on the sofa. He got up, seemed disoriented. He staggered towards the piano, sat down and began to play something, slowly at first, just picking the notes out with his right hand. It was a light melody that tripped easily across the keys, like a leaf caught in the wind. Then, he added the chords with his left hand and the rhythm became apparent: jazz swing, heartbreaking and joyous all at once.

The Actor began to improvise deftly; without effort the notes swirled and soared. His eyes were closed as his body rocked to the music. Then it was over. He went limp and sat staring at the keyboard.

"Why did you do that, call round about Philippe? Never mind. Doesn't matter. It was a thoughtful thing to do," he said with a distinct strain of irritation in his voice.

"What was that you were playing?" He seemed distracted by some movie that was playing in his mind.

"Oh, that was a Bill Evans tune, *Re: Person I Knew*. You have to hold onto me tonight. Promise me, Babe . . . you'll hold onto me as tight as you can," he said as tears filled his eyes.

"I will. I will," I said as I choked back my own tears.

We executed all the hygienic crap that people in the First World obsessively need to do before they go to sleep. When we finally got to bed we were too physically and emotionally drained to make love. I did as I'd promised and held him like a baby as we slept, or should I say as he slept.

My body was tired but my mind was racing. I knew he had gone to loop dialogue Friday, which was now yesterday, but where had he disappeared to the day before, when his mum was released from jail? And what about his mum, what was her fate? Had he committed her as his lawyer had suggested — and if not, where the hell was she? I couldn't imagine the cops letting her go out into the world with her paring knife. They'd have to have some assurances. And, what was this dinner party on Sunday all about? How did he manage to get it all sorted, as he said? These were the surface questions. There were much deeper questions that I just could not entertain, chief among them: where was Philippe?

I could see The Actor and Philippe getting into their king of pain competition, The Actor going into one of his crazed mood swings, things getting out of hand and someone ending up dead, someone like Philippe. Surely, an accident between consenting adults wouldn't be something my baby would have to do jail time for, but I was no lawyer and even if he walked away a free man he would be tainted for the rest of his life. His career would probably suffer. All of his peculiarities would no doubt be scrutinized by the prosecution. Yes, I'm no lawyer, but I've watched enough episodes of Kavanagh QC and Law and Order to know it would be all over for my precious baby-man. I just couldn't let that happen. Slow down girl, you don't have anything concrete and demonstrable to lead you to any conclusion that would hold water. I was jumping the gun. I needed The Actor to tell me the truth, or did I?

I was just at the tender threshold of sleep, when The Actor became restless and snatched me back into wakefulness. He was talking in his sleep, protesting in a deep angry growl: "No, you can't come in. Leave me alone. Stay away from me," all the while clutching at me, burying his face in my breasts. He awoke suddenly, sat up in bed and sunk his face in his hands as short shallow breaths shook his body. I have never felt sorrier for anyone in my life.

The Actor got up slowly and made his way to the bathroom.

He braced himself on the sink with one hand as he turned on the tap and splashed water on his face with the other. When he was done he slumped over the sink, almost paralyzed. I went into the bathroom and sat him down on the toilet lid as he dried his face.

"I have this dream, not every night but almost," he began, "I'm in bed sleeping and this bloke is pounding on the front door calling my name. I wake up. I go downstairs, I open the door and he has this whole crew with him. He shoves this official looking paper in my face and says, 'We've come to take it all back, because you don't deserve any of it.' That's when I wake up. I am awake, right?"

"Yes, sweetie, you're awake. Don't worry about that old dream. Everybody in Hollywood has it."

CHAPTER 7

I don't want reality, I want magic.

— **Blanche Dubois in** *A Streetcar Named Desire*

After I divorced the absolutely divine, but totally boring, Dr. Andy Brown, before I met the love of my life, Gordon Burdett, I went out with this lawyer named Norman Cohen. Norman and I weren't in love or anything, but we did have an awful lot of fun. He wrote a book of poems for me called *The Magic Bunny Poems*, not published, just written in longhand and stapled together, with hand-drawn illustrations, so very sweet. Norman would call me up and say, "Let's go down to that restaurant you like and pretend we're in Paris."

Then one day, I went by to see him and the concierge, who knew me, said: "Mr. Cohen isn't seeing anyone." I called his condo, no answer; went by his office, he wasn't there. About a week later I got a call from a mutual friend, who had gone to law school with Norman. He asked me to lunch, and it was there he told me that Norman had killed himself. To this day, people who knew Norman and know me think I was responsible for what he did, but whenever I think about what people had to say about me and what happened to Norman I always remember what his law school buddy said to me that afternoon at lunch, when he broke the news: "Norman was always a weirdo."

My stock and trade: the weirdos of this world. They are my people, and we are our own nation. I was now living in the capital of this mighty nation, with its supreme ruler: The Actor. The Actor was a magic bunny star. He could appear on screen and make doing

THE ACTOR

nothing riveting — electrifying, even. He was not only The Actor: he was An Actor, an artist, a master craftsman. Above and beyond all else, on screen he was Truth. Hell, even *I* wanted his autograph.

I woke up to an empty bed and the smell of hot coffee. The bathroom was still steamy, so The Actor hadn't been up long. I needed coffee badly, so I skipped the shower, splashed some water on my face, brushed my teeth, threw on a robe and went downstairs. He was lying on the sofa in his underwear, reading glasses on his nose, totally engrossed in something.

"Look," he said waving a big wad of white paper held together with two brass brads, "I found the script. It's damned good too. There are a few things . . . Come over here and give us a kiss." We kissed a good, deep, warm, energizing kiss that led us both to thoughts of other things.

"No, no, no," he said, "Wait 'til I'm done. I made some coffee. There's breakfast stuff in there."

As I walked through towards the kitchen, I noticed something was different about the kitchen. It just wasn't the same as it was the other night. Ah, the broken table was gone.

I sat at the kitchen counter, had my coffee, and ate a bowl of cereal. I didn't want to disturb him, but I really wanted to know what he'd done with that table.

He was all smiles, when he strolled into the kitchen, and threw the script on the countertop. He stretched and sat down next to me on one of the high bistro stools.

"I was a good boy last night, wasn't I?" he said, still smiling.

"My, my. You are quite a happy fella today."

"I love working on good projects, with good people, and this looks very promising. It would be a move in the right direction for me. Work makes me happy. You make me happy. I can sleep when you're in my bed. Ah, I feel safe."

When he said that last part, I wanted to cry, but I didn't because I wasn't going to spoil the moment for him.

"Baby, where's the table?" "Oh, I put it in the cellar." "You have a cellar? Wow!"

"They don't have cellars in the States?"

"Yeah, I just didn't think you had one for some reason." His mood changed. He eyed me suspiciously.

"Huh. Well, I wouldn't go down there if I were you."

Once he said it, there was no question in my mind. I had to go down there, no matter what, and soon. The Actor tilted his head to the side, smiling a knowing smile with a little menace around the edges, as if he were reading my thoughts.

"I know we are going to have to have that conversation, you know the one I mean, but I don't want to have it now." Slowly I turned . . .

I wanted to respond, but I couldn't speak. Something was happening in that moment, some kind of switch had been turned on in both of us. We turned to face one another, transfixed for what seemed like hours, wading deeper into each other's eyes, compelled by that beautiful, horrible, lovely, frightening energy, which had brought us together in the first place. Every molecule in my body was alive with the knowledge of what he wanted. What he wanted was no different from what the rest of us want: to be loved for the assholes we really are, without reservation. This is all he wanted, and all he wanted to give.

New information passed between us without words: love without a name, the redeeming power of sex, the purgative power of pain. We held hands, held on tight. We were communing in a séance of the senses. There was a rumbling in the blood. I felt feverish and moist. The Actor was flushed and covered with sweat. The labor of each breath soon fell into a shared rhythm, fueling the intensity of the sexual energy surging between us.

He was moaning, growling and crying for me. I was sobbing, pleading with him not to stop whatever it was he was doing. The Actor lowered his head struggling to hold back the eruption until he couldn't hold it any longer. I felt the tiny vibrations of a million butterflies between my legs that shook my whole body. We cried out to each other as we convulsed in waves. I thought we'd never stop coming and then it was over, just like that. He let go of my hands gingerly as if they were electrified. We sat with our palms pressed against the countertop, breathing slowly, watching each other, waiting in silence for the aftershocks. I could see he was as exhausted as I was. "What was that?" he whispered. "I don't know, but the counter's still standing."

We retreated to the relative safety of The Actor's bedroom,

stripped and huddled together in a placid sleep, for about two hours, when we were awakened by a knock on the door. It was Pickles.

"You know I wouldn't bother you two unless it was absolutely necessary but FYI: you have an army of reporters camped outside. I mean like a freaking circus, honey."

Pickles closed the door quickly and scurried down the hall to his room. I didn't move, I didn't breathe. I waited. The Actor sat up, pulled his knees to his chest, wrapped his arms around them and started humming, "It had to be you, it had to be you, I wondered around finally found somebody who . . . " He was humming, but he was really thinking.

"It's supposed to rain later," he said absently, "that'll drive them off. They're like rats really. On the other hand, if I show my face, they get what they want, they leave — we hope and pray — and that's that, except . . . I don't know what they're on about. Could be a shit storm waiting."

"I'll see if Pickles knows anything."

While I was in my room changing into my gold and pink cotton Ribbon Band sundress, and digging around trying to find my big lavender shawl, I could feel The Actor's eyes on me.

"Maybe we can be decoys, me and Pickles," I called over my shoulder. "He's got that thing at the Congress Centre, and I could go with him . . ."

But The Actor wasn't thinking about the press, or the Congress Centre, or anything else other than what had happened between us earlier.

When I walked back into his bedroom his face glowed with such contentment, it startled me. I sat down on the bed and listened to him recount what he had experienced at the dining room table. Aside from coming so hard he almost forgot who and where he was, The Actor had realized, beyond doubt, that we were meant to be together; in this life and the next. And, if this life no longer suited us, we could go hand and hand to what lay beyond, like Jean Simmons and Richard Burton at the end of the 1953 Biblical epic film, *The Robe*. Not exactly what I was prepared to hear, even though by now I knew that there was no bottom to his strangeness. More importantly, I felt compelled past reason to find out for a certainty, just how strange we both could get. That's how deeply this man had tapped into my inner freak.

Was this what happened to Philippe? Had The Actor reached down into Philippe's soul, with that killer charm harpoon of his, and skewered every twisted desire that was buried there, until pain wasn't enough, love wasn't enough? What had really happened to Philippe? I needed to know, because I was walking in his footsteps now, and I was beginning to feel sorry for the guy.

"I'm going to talk to Pickles," I called out as I headed for the door. Pickles was lying across a lavender and pink striped comforter clad only in his boxers, which, unlike The Actor's package-hugging Sloggis, looked like something Teddy Roosevelt was probably wearing under his uniform when he charged up San Juan Hill. He had a damp pink washcloth covering his face. I wasn't sure if he was asleep, so I hung back for a bit trying to decide if I should disturb him, when he said, "Child, just get in here, and close the door behind you."

I sat on the edge of the bed, waiting for a hug from Pickles, a hug that would leave me damp from his sweat and smelling like gin and mold, but he surprised me. He was not all sticky and clammy as per usual. He smelled like L'eau d'Issey Pour Homme, a very familiar smell because it was what The Actor used.

"Why Pickles, you look positively radiant."

"Oh, cut it honey. I'm a little miffed with you. I just have to put it out there: I've been feeling shoved, snubbed and unloved."

Apparently, when I refused to go all solidarity, and face possible deportation with him when the goons from the DS showed up, Pickles took my behavior as an act of betrayal and had been gnawing on that bone ever since.

"Pickles, I can only stand by one man at a time, OK? Jesus! Look, I got all dressed up just for you and the Congress Centre."

"You're coming with me? Oh, thank you, Babe. You're an angel. I was just lying here, because my head is pounding like it's going to explode. Is he going with us?"

"No, I don't think so. He's trying to figure out what to do about the reporters."

Pickles tip-toed to the door, pressed his ear against it and whispered, "They're asking about Philippe and Thespian's mother; apparently, she's missing too. My interrogation by the State Department is yesterday's leftovers, honey. Nobody's interested, except The Friends of Cyberpunk and the gays, who, according to Roger, will be packing the joint out tonight. Course, it's all peanuts to you, but you know some of us don't have rock-star divorce settlement money in the bank . . ."

"Are you on speed? What the hell! Sit down and slow down. No better yet, get some clothes on. What do you mean his mother is missing? We saw her on television, leaving jail with the lawyer, for Christ's sake."

"Yeah," Pickles said, over his shoulder as he rummaged through his bags (still packed), looking for the perfect ensemble, "that's the last time she was seen by anybody, including the lawyer. Just like you know who. I'm wearing beige and black, what do you think?"

"Do you know what The Actor's mother said to me, before the cops hauled her crazy ass out of here? She said, 'You're next, you stupid cow.'"

There was a knock at the door, and Pickles and I nearly jumped out of our skins. The Actor strolled in looking every bit the star, showered and groomed within an inch of his life. Dressed in grey Attachment jeans, a white vintage Triumph motorcycle T-shirt, a pair of black leather Cesare Paciotti slip-ons, the ones with a dagger strap across the instep and on his wrist a Maison Martin Margiela silver-embossed brass chain-link bracelet with a leather i.d. plaque. If I were a man this is exactly how I would dress.

He sat down beside me on the bed. "God, you look good," he said as he grabbed my hand. "I wish I could go with you two, but I have to be somewhere. Pickles! What are you doing over there, mate?"

"I just can't coordinate. Nerves, I guess. Promised Mario I would cut down on the drinking. What the hell am I going to wear? I mean look at you two, you're so perfect it's disgusting. I wish we could make a human sandwich right now, and that I could be the filling."

"Now who's being disgusting? I think we should just burn one before we do anything," I said, "Are you holding, baby?"

"I'll go into my stash," The Actor said as he stood up and headed for the door, "and whilst I'm at it, I'll get you sorted, Raymond. By the way, I want my cologne back."

Pickles ran over to me and stage whispered, "What do you think his mother was talking about? I mean where is she? You don't think . . ."

"My mother is a deeply disturbed woman," The Actor said as he returned, with some joints and a bundle under his arm. "She thinks I've done something to Philippe," he continued, brandishing three joints, one for each of us. "I don't care to talk about it now, if it's all the same to you lot."

He threw the bundle at Pickles, "See if you can wear these."

"I thought the paparazzi didn't know about Philippe," I said.

The Actor lit up. "Yeah, that's a little troubling," he exhaled, "I'm going to have to go out there and deal with it or they'll just doorstep us, no end. Don't look at me like that, Babe. As far as I know, Philippe's on vacation, and my mother is safe, getting the care she needs. That's what those little rodents will be told. I haven't killed her, if that's what you're thinking, although if there was ever a human who needed killing . . ."

"This is awesome," Pickles cried out, "I look good enough to eat." He was modeling off his new threads: a Hang Ten grey and red T-shirt, red drawstring surfer pants and the obligatory flip-flops, brown leather no less.

The Actor was slowly rubbing my left thigh, "Look up in the top of that closet over there, mate. There's a hat I think you'll like. My daughter nicked it from me. I think it's still there. I upgraded your flip-flops. You should bury yours. I'm pretty sure they're toxic waste."

While Pickles was looking for the hat, I took the joint from The Actor's lips. He gave me a look, "Didn't I give you one?" he asked slightly annoyed.

"You're getting just a little too wasted for someone who has to talk to the paparazzi."

The Actor leaned over and kissed me, a deep penetrating kiss, with that delicious rough tongue of his. When he pulled back, he looked so sad I thought he was going cry.

"Babe, you know I love you. I mean if another man hurt your feelings, I'd have to kill him with my bare hands."

I sat back and took a long toke on the joint and passed it back to him. Clearly, I was wrong: he needed more weed, not less.

"Oh, snap," Pickles shouted, "this is a Peter Grimm Black Chaos fedora. This is totally me. My God, I look good. Thanks a million, honey."

The Actor whispered in my ear: "You do know I'm afraid of you. I'm going to my club later. Pickles will explain it to you, won't you Pickles?"

"Sure," Pickles said, but please leave me out of this stuff in the future. Please."

Leave him out? He was so far in it wasn't even funny. Pickles and The Actor were huddled in the corner, involved in some sort of testosterone-driven conspiracy. My stomach started to growl. I realized all I had to eat that day was a bowl of cereal and a cup of coffee. The Pickles event was scheduled to go down at 19:00. It was now almost 17:00, still time to order in.

"I say we should give some Thai food delivery guy his fifteen minutes of fame and get some food up in here. Let him perp walk the gauntlet."

"Why, Babe. You're wasted, sugar," Pickles chuckled as he toked away on his perfectly rolled joint.

The room was now filled with a thick fog of herb. We needed to get out of there before our clothes were saturated with the smell. An hour and twenty minutes later filled with weed, Thai food and smelling like L'eau d'Issey Pour Homme and mouthwash, the three of us emerged from the warm cocoon of The Actor's lair to face the excrement of fame: the media.

There was a black BMW sedan waiting at the curb. Better to let the car wait on the street, because if the gate to the driveway was opened, the paparazzi would be swarming all over The Actor's property like cockroaches.

As we approached the small archway, where a sturdy-looking black door stood between us and the cackling throng, The Actor called Sergei, the driver, to let him know we were on our way out.

We could barely get through the door, because once it opened, a human wave surged forward and almost pushed us back in. The Actor hung back and let Pickles and me make a dash for the car. Holding the back door open for us was Sergei, a giant sequoia of a man, dressed in a perfectly tailored black suit, black silk T-shirt, a thick gold chain around his neck, black cowboy boots and aviator shades.

"Professor Pickles, are you still at war with the U.S. State Department?" a reporter yelled.

"No, we've kissed and made up, and I am inviting all y'all to come on down to the Congress Centre tonight and buy some of my books."

"Isn't that Felicia Lake?" a newscaster asked her cameraman, as she squeezed to the front.

Then a sort of frenzied clicking started, that I can only compare to the sound I heard once when I accidentally walked into a field of sleeping cicadas.

The swarm of paparazzi pushed forward in a single mass movement. The Actor was surrounded. Just before Sergei shoved Pickles and me into the back seat of the BMW, a reporter shouted out: "You're not going give us the finger this time, are you?"

"What's a finger between friends," The Actor responded as he pressed forward through the throng.

"Where's your mum?" "Where's your assistant?" "Where's Mr. Noiret? Where's Philippe?"

Still pressing towards the car, The Actor smiled and said, "My mum's off getting the care she needs, and Mr. Noiret is on holiday."

Someone shouted, "Why did your mum report Mr. Noiret as missing?"

I couldn't see what was going, Pickles was giving me the play by play. Sergei waded into the crowd, like a bulldozer, reporters tumbling over one another in his wake. He escorted The Actor to the car, using his massive body as a shield. It all happened in a matter of seconds. Sergei's skills were very impressive.

The Actor fell into the back seat looking dazed, and as the British would say, disorientated. His mouth was moving like a goldfish's mouth, but no sounds were coming out. We sped away and not a moment too soon. I asked Pickles for his whiskey bottle, which I knew was tucked in those surfer pants. I snatched it from him and made The Actor take a good, long slug. It helped.

The Actor took a deep breath, then the expletives came fast and furious. I never knew the British had such a command of profanity. When he finally stopped, he looked at me so sweetly and said, "I might not be back tonight, but I'll be back in time for the dinner party. Everything's all arranged. Pickles will fill you in. Won't you Pickles?"

"Oh yeah sure, just call me mister fill-in. I believe things took a turn for the worse back there, Thespian. How are you holding up?"

"I've been better. Look, I don't want to talk about this now, if it's all the same to you."

Then he slumped down and put his head on my shoulder, and we drove in silence to the Congress Centre. The Actor dropped Pickles and me off, then sped off into the night with Sergei. That Sergei intrigued me. Was he batting for the home team or was he on the other side? I made a mental note to ask Pickles.

Just as Roger predicted, the Congress Centre was packed out, standing room only, with a queue of the bitterly disappointed waiting outside. The Press was also out in force, no doubt feeding on the remains of Pickles' run-in with the DS, the homophobic fall-out, and The Actor's subsequent defense of his dear friend and house guest.

The LGBTQ front was making itself known with banners. The drag queens were carrying placards praising The Actor as a hero of the cause. It was a very carnival-like atmosphere, which I was thoroughly enjoying, until Pickles pointed out a drag queen dressed just like me on the cover of my biggest-selling CD of the 80s, *Alone In The Night*. I just wish it had been a better looking queen, but homage is homage.

Pickles had added one of his food stained scarves to his ensemble. It was casually slung over his shoulder. He was sporting a pair of tinted eyeglasses with shiny black plastic cat eye frames, so that any fashion sense The Actor's clothes might have given him was completely obliterated.

As Pickles approached, the crowd roared his name and the queens started chanting, "Babe! Babe! Babe!" It was thrilling and terrifying. Pickles turned to me, and said with tears in his eyes, "My people."

About half a dozen blood-sucking leeches from the tabloids started to close in on us just as we were about to enter the door, when out of nowhere these leather boys and a couple of really beefy queens intercepted and body-slammed them, to the delighted cheers of the geeky cyberpunk kids.

This was truly a festival of weirdness. I was so happy for Pickles, because he deserved a celebration, as well as the love and respect that all these people, all these sweet misunderstood people, had for him. The Actor would have been proud. Although it wasn't a nice thought, I was kind of glad The Actor wasn't there — it would have been all about him then.

The evening went well. Professor Pickles made his apology to the British and U.S. governments, gave the Press a good hiding and spoke up for his friend The Actor, whom the Press had savaged with wild, unsubstantiated accusations.

Pickles read from the galleys of his soon-to-be-published fourth novel with the fluid ease and grace that only a Southern upbringing and lots of marijuana and whiskey can produce.

He held the crowd spellbound, in the palm of his hand, when he spoke about his beginnings in Hot Coffee, Mississippi, and his beloved sister, Della, who died from an accidental overdose in her Hollywood Hills apartment. Della had introduced Pickles to my late husband Gordon Burdett and me.

Then Pickles asked me to say a few words. I told everyone that he was my best friend. That I loved him, and I was proud of him. I didn't cry, though, despite the fact that Pickles' publisher Roger, who was seated on the first row, was weeping like my Aunt Gladys at her dog Peppy's funeral.

That evening was a unique moment in time when the power of the human heart and magic prevailed.

CHAPTER 8

The best time I ever had with Joan Crawford is when I pushed her down the stairs in 'Whatever Happened to Baby Jane?'

— **Bette Davis**

Bette Davis was a mother in every sense of the word: a force to be reckoned with. No doubt it could not have been easy being her daughter. It must be difficult to be the child of anyone whose life is under constant public scrutiny and speculation, and who possesses an enormous talent, embraced and often misunderstood by the world.

Bette Davis' daughter B.D. Hyman (aka Barbara Davis Sherry) seized the occasion of her mother's ill health and subsequent stroke to tell all in the best-seller *My Mother's Keeper*. According to B.D., being Bette Davis's daughter was not just difficult, it was downright horrifying.

Now, B.D. Hyman's book was published just seven years after Cristina Crawford's tome *Mommie Dearest*, which agonizingly detailed the abuse allegedly suffered by Crawford's adopted children. Joan Crawford's friends divided into two camps, one side claiming Cristina exaggerated and even fabricated her accounts, while the other half supported the bulk of Cristina's depictions as accurate.

Not so with B.D. Most of Bette Davis' friends and even an exhusband, who had helped raise B.D., said the book was motivated by greed, and the characterizations of Bette Davis were far from the truth. Who knows?

B.D. Hyman wrote a follow-up book about her relationship with her mother called *Narrow Is the Way*, which maybe should have been called "Narrow Is the Mind." It didn't do well; beating a dead horse never does.

As for Joan Crawford, there once was a beautiful little boutique I used to frequent. Posted on the door was an 8x12 glossy of Joan Crawford. The caption read: "No Children Allowed."

He was at his "club" where women were not allowed, where three hundred years of tradition provided a safe and secret retreat for consenting, highly successful adult males, who enjoyed receiving and inflicting pain (not to hurt but to arouse — allegedly), could go to get their rocks off.

You could not gain membership into this club by filling out an application and sending in a few bucks; you had to be sponsored in by a member of good standing and undergo a rigorous screening process.

How was The Actor, who is about as stable as the San Andreas Fault, sponsored in, I wondered? According to Pickles, he was sponsored in by Philippe. And who sponsored Philippe? Well, that would be telling, wouldn't it?

All I know from Pickles is that the person who sponsored Philippe is somebody, "very high up," whatever that means. I let my curiosity rest, because there are some things better left unexplored, especially when you're hung over.

The mystery of who had sorted that evening's dinner party was solved. Maida Thorne, The Actor's agent and neighbor, had put together a menu and booked the caterer who would be arriving at around two that afternoon. She had also provided The Actor with a dining room table, on loan.

Maida had also been a friend of Lady Sylvia, JD DeLongo's late wife, thus the JD connection. There was another guest invited, but Pickles couldn't remember who that was.

I was missing The Actor something awful, when I heard a car pull onto the gravel drive outside. The front door opened and shut, but no footfalls on the stairs.

I padded barefoot down the hall to the stairway in the T-shirt and shorts I'd slept in, to find the downstairs dark, with all the curtains drawn.

I could hear the sound of ice cubes in a glass, liquid being poured, a chair being scraped slowly across the floor, the chair creaking with weight and the weight of a heavy sigh and then my name whispered tenderly: "Babe."

I cautiously entered the dining room where The Actor was sitting at the table with a bottle of Balvenie twelve-year-old single malt Scotch whiskey and a glass in front of him. I sat down beside him, grabbed his forearm with both hands and gently squeezed.

"I'm right here my darling. Why are you sitting here in the dark?" He didn't say anything, just grinned that crazy grin of his, the one that could make you forgive him anything, even murder.

He had returned wearing the same thing he'd worn when he left with the exception of a navy blue Baracuta jacket, very Classic Steve McQueen. Of course, I was curious, but I didn't say anything. He'd started drinking pretty early in the day. I took it as a sign that all was not well.

"They're still out there you know, some of them. Like vultures. Tried to follow me last night, one of them did, but Sergei lost them. How'd it go at the Congress Centre, any joy?"

"Baby, you would have been so proud of Pickles. It was like a Love-In. The place was packed, and they treated him like a king. He said some very sweet things about you."

"Did he indeed, the old cream of Hot Coffee."

The Actor topped up his drink. He looked down as he poured, so he wouldn't have to look me in the eye. I placed my hand on the top of his head very gently.

"What's the matter, baby? I mean it's ten o' clock in the morning, and you're already on your third drink."

"Pickles told you where I went last night? I wasn't cheating on you, but it felt like it, made me feel bad. I don't always want to be with a man, but sometimes I have to. You understand?"

The Actor pulled a cigar case out of his jacket pocket and a key ring with a stainless steel bullet punch on it. I got up and found an ashtray in the kitchen, by the time I got back he was rolling the Rafael Gonzalez Petit Cuban Corona between his fingers and puffing away. I had to admit that I didn't really understand, but I was willing to accept what I didn't understand and told him as much.

"Babe, you're the only woman who's ever said that to me." I was probably the only woman he had ever met who was as crazy as he was.

The Actor said he didn't want to hurt me, but that he might need to hurt me, from time to time. This thought had been troubling him, and he didn't know the right way to broach it, then he realized there was no right way. He simply had to know if I'd be cool with it. I asked him to define hurt and he said:

"What if I wanted to touch your ass with the tip of this cigar?"

I had to re-calibrate, because the concept did intrigue me and repulse me simultaneously. It would hurt, but I could probably endure hurt; however, real excruciating pain would be another matter altogether, and context would be important.

I realized this would require further discussion. I wanted to think about this a little more. I had been doing some pondering along these lines, after Pickles told me about The Actor's little all-male retreat.

"The cigar thing sounds intriguing. I was also thinking, maybe you might need a good spanking, and that I was just the chick to give it to you."

At this The Actor swiveled around in his chair, so that he was facing me. He put his cigar down and looked at me, as if he were seeing me for the first time.

"You do love me. You do. I know it now," he said with tears in his eyes, "I have a riding croup upstairs."

"Maybe later, baby," I said, "after the dinner party."

The dinner party, the goddamned dinner party, with the goddamned reporters outside; well, maybe it wouldn't be so bad. The guest list wasn't controversial. A little socialization, with relatively sane people, might be just the ticket.

"Blimey, the dinner party — thanks for reminding me. Pickles promised me he and Mario would deal with the caterer. I'm no good with that sort of thing. Where is Pickles?"

"Still sleeping, I guess. He'll be up by noon."

"Good, because there's something else I have to talk to you about, and it'd be better for him if he didn't hear this. I mean, I don't want him interrupting. I don't know what I mean."

I reached over grabbed his glass and finished off what was left of the whiskey. I motioned for The Actor to give me the bottle, which I put back into the liquor cabinet.

Then, amidst hand wringing, heavy sighs and cigar smoke, The

Actor haltingly recounted what had happened to his mother, why no one had seen her in days. She had been taken to a house The Actor had rented in Cornwall. Sergei was the driver of the car that had been waiting for The Actor's lawyer and The Actor's mum when she was released from jail.

Sergei had dropped the lawyer off, then jabbed the mother with a syringe full of sedative. He then drove her to Cornwall, where The Actor, a doctor and a psychiatric nurse were waiting. Once his mum was settled in with the nurse and a housekeeper, The Actor and the doctor, who happened to be a friend, returned to London.

This explained where The Actor had been the night he hadn't come home, and how he got his foot sutured. It also explained last night, because he had gone to visit his mother, after a brief stop at his club. Sergei had driven him back in the early hours of the morning.

"So, let's see if I've got this straight, you kidnapped and drugged your mother, and now she's being kept under chemical restraint, against her will."

"Pretty much," he replied as he stubbed out his cigar. "Don't look at me like that, please. What else was I to do? She left me no choice. We both could have been butchered in our sleep."

"With a dull paring knife?"

"OK, horribly disfigured, which is worse, much worse and she had this," The Actor slid a key across the table with the number two engraved on it — Philippe's key to the house.

"What do you make of it?" I asked, as I held up the key.

"I don't know what to make of it. I don't even want to think about it."

"Let's just say, for laughs, that your mother did something bad to Philippe. Why would she file a missing person report with the police?"

"One thing doesn't exclude the other. I'm fucked either way. I was Philippe's employer. The Old Bill's going to investigate his disappearance, and come straight to me. If you think the reporters door-stepping us last night was bad . . . The whole thing is totally shambolic, all because of that daft cow who gave me birth. I just want to make it to the premiere of the new film, that's all, without losing the bloody plot."

I wanted to tell The Actor to speak English, but he was speaking

English, the problem being that I had no idea what the hell he was talking about. This had happened several times before. I knew I just had to exercise patience, something I had very little of, and before long he would see the perplexed look on my face and translate — which he did so that I understood "the old Bill" meant the cops, "daft" meant crazy, "shambolic" was a disaster and "lose the plot" meant to go crazy. I knew what "bloody" meant.

I was putting in an effort to use bloody instead of fuck or fucking as an adjective like "bloody asshole" instead of "fucking asshole," because I thought it sounded nicer. But somehow "bloody asshole" conjures up a very graphic image, and saying "bloody face" instead of "fuck face" didn't work either; in fact I think it had a different meaning entirely. I had become fascinated by the word "gobsmacked" and was waiting for a chance to work it into conversation.

I loved when our worlds collided linguistically; it kept us in touch with our separate personal identities, vitally important, because at any given moment either one of us could have absorbed the other like the Borg. But, I couldn't indulge in these thoughts, not while the dinner party loomed large on the horizon.

"Maybe you should get some sleep. What time are the guests supposed to be here?"

The Actor sat with his head down, his chest rising and falling heavily. He had fallen asleep in the chair. I managed to wake him and help him to the sofa, where he collapsed and fell into a deep sleep, but not before I told him how much I had missed him, how lonely it had been.

He slept with a smile on his face. I watched him and tried to imagine what was going on in his head. I saw a ghost town from the old West with a single tumbleweed blowing down its deserted main street, as the sound of a coyote's cry floated on the wind.

Sitting in the dining room having a bowl of cereal with Mr. Pickles, it became clear to me why The Actor had engineered the impending dinner party, and why he insisted on going through with it despite all that had happened and was continuing to happen.

I put the pieces together when Pickles finally remembered who the other guest was: Mark Fragile (pronounced Frah-GEE-lay), the director. So, we had a producer, JD DeLongo; an agent, Maida Thorne; a director, Mark Fragile; and a star, The Actor — all of whom would indicate a deal was being brokered, a package was being put together.

Then, I remembered the new script The Actor was so psyched about. There had obviously been more than a tumbleweed rolling around in The Actor's head after all.

"Just when I think I've got him all figured out, there's more."

"Face it, sugar," Pickles said as he up-ended the cereal bowl and drank down the last drop of milk, "Thespian is like a lasagna. There's layers."

I could hear lasagna-boy stirring in the living room.

He called out, "I have to hit the gents, any chance of a coffee?"

"Sure," Pickles hollered, "I'll stick my big toe in it to make it sweet," he turned to me and giggled. "That's what my Mama used to say to me."

"What to wear, what to wear," I sighed.

"Wouldn't it just be a little slice of heaven if you sang tonight, Babe?" Pickles asked from the kitchen, as he made the coffee.

"Wouldn't it just," The Actor said sitting down beside me. He had discarded most of his clothes except for his jeans. His bare chest had several black and blue marks. His upper arms had red cuff marks encircling them. He leaned over and kissed me. That's when I saw them more clearly.

"What are those scratches all over your chest?"

"Oh," he said scratching his chest, "the hair's starting to grow back, itches like hell. You have no idea how uncomfortable this is, but apparently chest hair has gone the way of Sean Connery and the woolly mammoth. Fuck it, I'm letting it grow back."

Pickles entered with the coffee, cream and sugar and three cups on a tray.

"The bitch-goddess, Thespian . . . wants your balls and your chest hair," Pickles said as he put the tray down and started to pour.

"Well, I hope you're not referring to me, Raymond," I said.

"No, sugar. It's the DH Lawrence thing. Lady Chatterley's Lover. I believe the quote is, 'The bitch-goddess, Success, was trailed by thousands of gasping dogs with lolling tongues.'"

"You reckon I'm one of the gasping dogs?" The Actor laughed, "Well, you're too bloody right, mate, and I'm shagging the bitch raw."

No translation needed there. Pickles and The Actor clinked their coffee cups together and laughed until they cried. The Actor put his arm around me and said, "Pickles is right, it would be a slice of heaven if you sang tonight." Tears came to my eyes. I lowered my head and whispered, "I can't."

Pickles said quietly, "Babe's just like Pearl Bailey in the movie *All the Fine Young Cannibals*. If she sings again her heart might just break beyond all repair."

The Actor stroked my cheek, "I'm sorry, darling. I didn't mean to . . . You know what, I'll sing. I'll sing for you, Babe."

I couldn't hold back the tears. He was my bruised, scratched, semi-hairless knight in shining armor. I loved the big weirdo, in that moment, more than I'd ever loved anyone.

"Thank you, baby. I'll be looking forward to it. Now, boys, it is 13:00, and the caterers will be here in an hour. "We'd better get ourselves sorted," I winked at The Actor. He winked back, with a proud Papa grin on his face.

Upstairs we showered together and made love in the process. His bruises were tender to the touch. I instinctively knew not to ask how he got them. I did ask if he was in pain, but he just smiled and said he was a big boy, and I should stop trying to mother him.

Then, out of nowhere, he said he'd do anything I asked, even stop going to his club, if I promised not to leave him. I promised, he promised . . . I knew we would both keep those promises as long as we could. I was just hoping, in my case, it would be a little longer than usual.

I had some Taylor of Old Bond Street Chamomile talc that I persuaded The Actor to use on his chest to keep the itching down. It worked and he was grateful, grateful enough to give me a good, old-fashioned vanilla fuck, and that's when I realized how truly painful the stubble of his chest hair really was.

I wondered out loud if the tabloid Press were still outside. That elicited a string of expletives from The Actor, and a large ashtray being tossed across the room.

There was a faint knock on the door, and I heard Pickles ask in a trembling voice, "Is everything all right in there?"

The Actor reassured Pickles and asked him to peep through the curtain in the living room, to see if the Press was still camped outside. They were.

THE ACTOR

I was worried about the guests and poor Mario. The Actor's mood had changed. He said that he was the one I should be worrying about. The others could fend for themselves, wasn't as if the paparazzi were going to attack them or anything. The worst they could do was hurl speculation and innuendo, the bastards, the bloody bastards.

"We're not having any talk about Philippe or my mum this evening. Do you hear me? I have a very small window of time to explore the possibility of getting that script I showed you into production, because of the timing on this last film. I'm just weeks away from the premiere; right after, the Press tour and I can't think about anything else at the moment. You are going on the tour with me, right?"

"I think you should take a deep breath, and definitely burn one before the caterers get here."

He was wrapped in his bathrobe, pacing back and forth with pent-up hostility rising off him like steam. When I spoke, he stopped and tilted his head, but not in his usual charming way — more in a Travis Bickel, "You talking to me?" way.

I was scared, but I was damned if I was going to show it. I stood my ground, and yes, you crazy bastard, I am talking to you. He caught himself and shook off whatever demon was riding him.

"I'm all sixes and sevens," he said, as he got back into bed. "This whole Philippe thing, my mum, the fucking media, it's doing my head in."

"I think you should take a deep breath, and definitely burn one before the caterers get here. I mean it. Can't you hear the stress talking? We need a buffer between us and reality, right now. So, find your stash baby, and let's burn one for the gipper."

We could hear the caterers and Pickles and Mario rustling around downstairs. The caterer was a friend of Maida Thorne, The Actor's agent; therefore, discretion was guaranteed, but with the Press lurking about, we thought it best to be a little circumspect with the weed. We had about two and a half hours until the guests started arriving, but we had gotten way too mellow for any hanky-panky to ensue.

I guess we had smoked too much because The Actor went into his top ten regrets in life. He had regrets about a great many things, among them the attempted buggery on yours truly, but mostly about his daughter. Did I know the real reason his ex-wife wouldn't allow their daughter to stay over? No, it wasn't because of Philippe. Philippe would book into a hotel when The Actor's daughter stayed over. It was because of The Actor's mum.

Evidently, on one particular weekend when his daughter was safely sleeping in the room now occupied by Pickles, The Actor was awoken by a noise, and upon investigating, found his mother standing menacingly over her grandchild with a pillow in her hands. A fight between mother and son ensued, during which the daughter woke up screaming. Son panicked and socked his mum on the jaw, laying her out cold. The event had occurred almost a year ago. That was the last time The Actor's daughter was allowed to stay overnight in her dad's home.

Why did his mother attempt to smother her own grandchild? Because in his mum's warped and twisted universe, her grandchild would be better off dead than to have The Actor as her father. I was glad we were smoking the big G-weed because the psychic pain of this story would have been almost too much to bear otherwise. He saw it in my face and subtly changed gears.

He loved his daughter to no end, that was clear. His hatred towards his mother was not so much about her, as it was about how her illness always "threw a spanner in the works," as he put it, always disrupting his attempts to lead a normal life — at least this is what he told himself.

How could a man, an artist of his caliber, bring such joy to the public, and have such an agonizing private life? A rhetorical question after having lived in Hollywood.

I couldn't help thinking, maybe The Actor thought he deserved to be hurt, like a form of self-harm. And let's face it, with his mum, I could see love being tangled up with pain in his world view. I had totally forgotten to mention my encounter with his mum at Heathrow. When I did, I was sorry. "What the fuck was she doing in the airport?" he asked me totally perplexed. Of course, I had no idea, but I did tell The Actor she was looking for her luggage in the same carousel as mine, and I had flown in from Nashville via Toronto.

"That doesn't mean anything . . . She always claimed she was psychic, maybe she felt something, saw something about you?" The Actor sighed.

"Do you think she's psychic?"

"I tell you, luv, I wouldn't be surprised."

Surprised or not, the last thing The Actor's mum had said to me was, "You're next, you stupid cow," so naturally I felt compelled to see her, to talk to her, to ask her what the hell she meant by that remark.

I also wanted to find out if she had any insight into the whereabouts of Philippe; after all, she did have his house key. I had a feeling she wouldn't have to employ any psychic powers to elaborate on how it came to be in her possession. To top it all off, she did remind me of my dear, deranged, dead mother.

"Do you think I could go with you next time you visit her?"

Suspicion, surprise and curiosity all played across his face in rapid-fire succession. I was preparing myself for Burton in *Look Back in Anger*, when The Actor simply smiled and said, "OK."

We were silently drifting in a haze of marijuana smoke when there was a frantic knock at the door. It was Pickles:

"Y'all better get down here with a quickness."

We dressed in the uniform of the hurriedly dressed: T-shirts, jeans and flip-flops. There was an eerie, tense silence that pervaded the house. From the living room, I could see Sergei standing in the dining room, with his massive back to us.

We entered to find a skinny South Asian kid, head bowed, sitting at the dining room table. Sergei was standing behind him with his hands spread across the boy's shoulder.

The kid was about eighteen or nineteen. He was sporting a short skater boy haircut that made him look like someone had started building a bonfire on his head. He had carefully manicured sideburns and trimmed stubble on his upper lip.

His hands were folded on the table displaying his nails, which were bitten to the quick. He didn't look happy. The Actor strode into the room and immediately took charge.

"So, what's all this, then?" he asked.

Pickles and Mario were huddled together, standing off to the side. They both started speaking at once so it all just sounded like gibberish. The Actor shot them a look that silenced them.

"And what are you lot gawking at?" he questioned, as he turned on the catering staff, who were crowded near the open kitchen door. "What am I paying you for? Go on, then, back to work."

They all quickly scurried off into the recesses of the kitchen, closing the door behind them.

"Sergei, what the hell is going on, mate? Who is this?"

"Dunno guv, he slipped in with the catering staff. I escorted them in, didn't really notice him, since he was wearing a white jacket like the rest of 'em. Then Professor Pickles over there told me to restrain the lad 'cause he caught him taking pictures inside the house."

The Actor moved to the opposite side of the table so that he stood directly across from the kid.

"OK, mate," The Actor began with a sigh, "who do you work for?"

"Is that your girlfriend?" the kid asked without lifting his head. "No, I don't mean her," as he gestured towards me, "I mean the gorilla standing behind me."

At which point, said gorilla smacked the kid upside the head and growled, "Just answer the man."

The Actor sat down and leaned towards the kid.

"Look, just tell me your name, and who you work for, and maybe we can work something out; otherwise, I'm calling the filth and have you charged."

"Me charged? I'll have the hairy ape done for GBH and all. He assaulted me, and you're holding me against my will. There's witnesses."

I turned to Pickles and Mario. "You see anything? Because I sure as hell didn't see anything."

Mario shrugged and shook his head from side to side. Pickles said the kid must be tripping. I kind of liked this kid. He was feisty, holding his shit together against the odds. He had guts.

"OK, OK, seeing that I'm out numbered. My name is Paul and I'm a freelance journalist. Most of my stuff goes to PopBitch."

The Actor's shoulders rose and fell with yet another heavy sigh. I was thankful for the foresight I'd had in suggesting we fire up the big ganja weed, because it was this, and only this that was keeping The Actor from doing some real damage.

"Sergei, call your mates in to do some crowd control and to

THE ACTOR

escort my guests in when they arrive. You can leave us now. Job well done, Sergei. Cheers, mate."

Sergei disappeared into the living room. I went over to Pickles and Mario.

"Pickles please go out and tell the Press that The Actor's coming out in ten minutes to talk to them," I whispered. "Mario, if you could supervise the caterers and arrange transportation for Mr. Tabloid Journalist, that would be great."

"But Babe," Pickles pleaded. I gave them both a look, and they were gone. Back at the table I was surprised to hear The Actor and Paul laughing.

"So, it's a deal?" The Actor extended his hand across the table, Paul grabbed it and shook.

"It's a deal." he said.

"Baby," I said to The Actor, as tenderly as I could, "Mario's having a car sent around to take Paul home, and Pickles is out there letting the Press know you'll be making a statement in about ten minutes or so. I hope that's all right?"

The Actor turned and looked at me with curiosity and yes, admiration. He folded his arms across his chest and said, "That's more than all right, luv." Then he turned to Paul. "Fancy a coffee?"

While The Actor was in the kitchen organizing some coffee for us, I learned from Paul that The Actor had agreed to give him an exclusive interview with photos, which would probably bump Paul out of the tabloid slime pits onto the top of the tabloid garbage heap. The Actor had already given Paul a bombshell, the nature of which Paul would not disclose, but he did assure me that it would eclipse anything the media was honing in on concerning The Actor at the moment. I unleashed the full magnitude of my charm, which is considerable, but the little punk wouldn't spill.

"You know, he's not as bad as people say he is," Paul confided, "Oh, and congratulations," he added.

I wasn't sure what the kid was congratulating me for, so I just thanked him and let The Actor take over. After we had our coffee, Sergei escorted Paul out the backdoor to a car from Mario's service, that was waiting. I asked The Actor about Sergei and his mates. Sergei was an ex-squaddie or grunt, who owned a personal security company called Tight Security. His mates were other mostly ex- squaddies, who were also employed by Tight Security. They were all as big as, or bigger, if that's humanly possible, than Sergei. The Actor had been using Sergei for years, and Sergei was not gay.

"Should I change my clothes" The Actor asked, "or should I just go out there like this?"

"Don't change. Let them see that you're human."

"Yeah, but I need a shave," he said as he ran is hand along his jaw.

"Just go out there and be charming. Talk about the film you just wrapped. Answer a couple of questions. Tell them you've invited a few friends for dinner, and that you'd appreciate if they weren't hassled."

"Sounds good, I like it. Then I can wrap up by telling them to call my publicist who'll send a full statement to their editors, and Bob's your uncle."

"I think that should satisfy the legitimate press. As for the super sleaze bags, nothing satisfies them anyway, but at least they'll have some crumbs to gnaw on."

"We make a team don't we, Babe?"

"Yeah, honey just like Roy Rogers and Dale Evans."

CHAPTER 9

I'm not sure acting is something for a grown man to be doing.

— Steve McQueen

As I found out from Pickles and The Actor, at the Tate Modern Museum, to my chagrin, there are two Steve McQueens. The one I'm more familiar with, the one with the burning blue eyes and the honey-blond hair, who defined American cool and on-screen masculinity in the 1970s, Mr. H-F (Highly Fuckable) himself, I'm going to call Classic Steve McQueen.

The other Steve McQueen, the consummate visual artist and unparalleled filmmaker, the Brit, the majestic Black man, I am going to call 21st-Century Steve McQueen.

Now, that I'd become more familiar with The Actor, which is putting it mildly, I understood why he wanted to see the experimental silent short film called *Bear*, by 21st-Century Steve McQueen: sex and the threat of violence, two of The Actor's major hobbies.

It was only about ten minutes long, but the film *Bear* seemed to encase its audience inside a silent box with the two protagonists on-screen. It was cramped, almost claustrophobic, so you could feel the heat and the sweat, as these two naked Black men, one of whom *is* 21st-Century Steve McQueen himself, square off in a dance at once sexually provocative and menacing.

While watching PBS, the source of most of my real knowledge, I learned scientists have discovered through experiments with mice, those poor little sacrificial darlings, that the parts of our brain where violence and sex lurk can become tangled.

And here is where I now see a thread through the film *Bear* that links Classic Steve McQueen and 21st-Century Steve McQueen. I can think of no one in cinematic history who has intertwined the two elements of homo-eroticism and violence more than Classic Steve McQueen. He was a man known to take things to the edge to see how far he could push the envelope. A man who had a clear understanding of the profound complexities inherent in the visual nature of film, and how to use that understanding to his best advantage, kind of like 21st-Century Steve McQueen.

I'm pretty sure Classic McQueen was totally hetero and I'm sure sorry I missed out on that, real sorry. Hey, if I were a man, stylistically I'd be rocking it like Classic McQueen. As for 21st-Century McQueen, he is the most intellectually sexy man of the 21st century. I wish I had his brain; I'd be so super hot. I was sorry The Actor hadn't invited 21st-Century McQueen to his dinner party.

I also am sorry for all laboratory mice everywhere. There should be a statue, somewhere, to commemorate all the mice who have given their lives for the betterment of humankind. Amen.

Our little damage-control strategy had worked — at least it sounded as if it worked. I heard the paparazzi cheering outside. For a moment I thought I heard them chanting my name, but I was still a little wasted.

I swooped my crazy mass of corkscrew curls on top of my head and subdued it with a white scrunchie, which matched my white jeans. My approach to the evening: stylish yet comfy, because who knew? I decided to top the jeans off with a classic collar Eileen Fisher black sleeveless crepe de chine tunic and for my tootsies my white Jennifer sandals by Naot.

This wardrobe decision had preoccupied my thoughts for the better part of the day; therefore, I wasn't totally present for all the events that had transpired so far. The Actor and I had been fucking and smoking and drinking. I can't even remember if we'd eaten anything all day, so my ability to concentrate was not at its peak — although I had stepped up to the plate, and exercised some pretty deft organizational skills, if I do say so myself.

I could hear The Actor trudging wearily up the steps. I expected him to look as wrung out as a dish rag, but he was all smiles and manic energy.

"You look good enough to eat," he said as he grabbed me.

"I do, don't I? There's no time for all that now. You have to get dressed. Your guests will be here soon."

"Did you hear them out there? Give the people what they want. This may open up a whole new era with me and those vultures. I think they're actually starting to like me now."

"Whoa, big fella, the tabloids have always liked you. You sell. You haven't always liked them, though. Didn't you punch a photographer once?"

"That was a long time ago. I paid to have his nose fixed and settled with him out of court. He's out there now, all sweetness and light, worshipping the ground I walk on. Ha, ha, ha! Should I shower again? I'm wearing this. What do you think?"

My theory is, if you don't stink, why shower? Conserve the water and just change your clothes. Use baby wipes, if necessary. If I hadn't had sex or been to the gym, I'd just skip a day of showering and move on, my contribution to environmental sustainability.

I conducted a sniff test on The Actor, which ended with his tongue in my mouth. I declared him body-odor free, with some mouthwash not being a bad idea.

His bespoke white cotton dress shirt, with the vintage-look low-waist Armani stretch denim jeans were right-on for the dinner party. The black, calf-skin, Ferragamo classic penny moccasins he was putting on his bare feet made me hot and tingly all over.

Downstairs had been transformed. There were wildflower arrangements in every room, including the john, thanks to Mario and Pickles. The caterers had turned the dining room into an inviting culinary wonderland of chartreuse and white. The Actor was in the kitchen talking with the catering captain.

I was totally impressed by the Royal Stafford green and gold china, very much from a bygone era, so delicate and stately, something I'd hardly expect The Actor to own. And the beautiful blue and gold medallion patterned chartreuse linen tablecloth with matching napkins was also quite elegant.

There was a well-stocked bar set up on the sideboard, that I just could not resist: Laphroaig ten-year-old, single malt whiskey, Williams Great British Extra Dry Gin and Luksusowa Polish potato vodka, my request. Just as I was about to pour myself a nice tall glass, The Actor entered carrying a tray.

"Try this," he said as he plucked something from the tray and stuck it in my mouth.

"This is so good," I said, reaching for another one.

"Duck satay, there's peanut sauce, but I didn't know if you had allergies. What?"

"You must have been really cute back when you used to wait tables."

He put the tray down on the side board, grabbed a satay and gave me that grin.

"Unfortunately, it's a skill you never lose. Where are the boys? I hope they're not being naughty. We're going to need them, I mean for moral support. Maybe this wasn't such a good idea after all."

He was at the sideboard pouring us both a drink. I was eating the duck satay, so was he, in the hopes we wouldn't get totally plastered before the guests arrived.

"They'll serve everything from the canapés to the dessert," The Actor said gesturing towards the kitchen, and then we're on our own. They'll put the coffee on before they leave. Tomorrow they'll come back and clean up . . . Let's go sit in the living room."

I told him how much I admired the table setting, as he plucked at the explosion of hair on top of my head.

"Oh, all that stuff's Maida's. Nice isn't it?"

"Maida takes good care of you, doesn't she?"

"Uh oh, do I hear a twinge of jealousy? Why Babe, I'm flattered. Maida takes care of me, because I take care of Maida. Don't get me wrong: she's done incredible things for me, this last picture for instance, but we are friends to the extent that she can exploit me in the best sense of the word, and I remain exploitable. Pays to be realistic about these things."

"Look, I lived in Hollywood where the mantra is you can use me as long as you don't abuse me. So, this dinner is really business, right?"

"When does it ever stop being business? I'm not going to complain. This is what I do. It's the only thing I can do."

"And you do it so well," I said, just as he leaned in to kiss me. Before our lips met, we heard Pickles coming down the stairs with Mario not far behind. They were in the middle of an argument.

"No, I will not, sugar," Pickles said as he plopped down on the piano bench, folded his arms, crossed his legs and flexed his flip-flop back and forth. Mario looking as scrumptious as ever, in a blue Oliver Spencer floral patterned cotton shirt and Black Alpha Khaki Dockers, sat down next to The Actor on the sofa.

"Will you tell him, please," Mario pleaded.

"Tell him what, mate?"

"That he should wear something a little more appropriate."

"Well . . . what exactly are you wearing, Raymond?" The Actor chuckled, "I can't tell if you're going to service one of Mario's cars, or fix the plumbing."

"I'm rubber and you're glue, what you say bounces off me and, sticks to you," Pickles pouted. "I need a drink. All this humiliation's made me thirsty."

He marched into the dining room followed by a hail of laughter. I ran after him.

"Poor baby," I said as I rubbed his back, "you know not to pay attention to stuff like that. Everyone here loves and respects you, even if you are dressed like a maintenance man."

Pickles was pouring himself a very large glass of gin.

"My nerves are all aflutter, Babe. I mean, JD is coming. JD! And he really does take perverse pleasure in making fun of me. I'm sweating like a hog. This has wickability with vented cuffs so I can stay cool. I'm going to need to stay cool this evening, Babe. Can you explain that to Mr. GQ Mario in there," Pickles shouted.

Just then, the doorbell rang and if Pickles had even entertained the thought of changing his black cotton/polyester short-sleeved jumpsuit, it was too late now.

Maida Thorne swooped in like a gale-force wind, drenched in L'Eau Ambree by Prada, enveloped in a peach cotton batik shawl with little green and white embroidered flowers draped over a pale green sleeveless eyelet dress, which I suspected was Isaac Mizrahi. She was older and shorter than I had imagined, and a little over the top, with her tousled silver, jaw-length bob, her green toenails wiggling in her silver sling-back wedge sandals she was like a volcano spewing ice cream instead of lava. I liked her immediately. She hugged The Actor who in turn re-acquainted her with Mario. Pickles shot across the room, grabbed both her hands and kissed them. Maida threw her head back and roared with laughter.

Then she trained a practiced blue eye on me, as The Actor grabbed my hand and brought me over to her.

"So, this is the fabulous Babe," she said, leaning back on one leg.

"I feel like I know you already. It's a pleasure to finally meet you. Where's the gin?"

She grabbed me by the waist with one arm and ushered me into the dining room.

"My, you're a tall one," she said, pouring herself a glass of Williams Great. "Just don't wear heels in public with him, exaggerates the height difference. Drink?"

"That's my drink over there." She handed me my drink.

"The table setting is gorgeous," I said.

"Isn't it? Belonged to Freddie's aunt. Freddie's my husband. I thought the colors would be perfect, and I was right. I'm going to see how they're coming along in the kitchen. I'm here, we're drinking, they should be serving the canapés don't you think?"

With that she handed me her shawl and disappeared into the kitchen. The Actor walked into the dining room to find me standing there staring at Maida's shawl.

"Babe, where's Maida? What's that?"

"She's in the kitchen," I said as I held up the peach-colored cloth, "this is her shawl."

"What's the matter? You look strange."

"I believe I'm gobsmacked, baby."

Mark Fragile arrived. At first, I thought he was a friend of our wanna-be journalist Paul, but this was *the* Mark Fragile, the cinematic wunderkind, who everybody wanted to work with, but who, at this point in time, only wanted to work with The Actor.

His physical appearance was what you would expect from his name: thin, pale, slightly built, geek glasses and a little shorter than he should be, but he was cute, very cute. I looked into those smoldering brown eyes and I was in danger: a heterosexual man was in the house. OK, he was the one in danger.

As usual, I was checking out the wardrobe as we shook hands: vintage SuperDry logo T-shirt, slim mustard-colored chinos, a Levi's denim jacket circa 1967, and the coup de grace: classic black and white Adidas Gazelles. It was the Gazelles that really got to me. Pickles' nemesis and my old friend JD DeLongo arrived shortly after

Mark Fragile, bearing gifts in the form of a box of Cohiba Maduro 5 Cuban cigars and a bottle of Camus Extra Elegance Cognac, as if he were anticipating cause for celebration.

JD's ensemble for the evening was a study in uninspired quality: Black Armani lightweight sports jacket, Black Armani button-front sport shirt and True Religion Boot-Cut vintage-look jeans with the ever-present black Gucci Loafers.

JD handed his treasures to The Actor who raised an eyebrow, expressed his appreciation, and disappeared into the dining room, leaving me face-to-face with JD, who wasted no time in pressing himself against me, letting his hand wander across my ass.

As if on cue, a lively jazz tune played out from the sound system, softly underscoring the proceedings. Although my back was to the dining room, I could tell The Actor had returned, because JD's hand jumped off my butt, as if it were on fire.

The Actor walked past JD and me, without saying a word. He asked Mario if that was Grant Green playing and Mario said it was Grant Green's LP, *Idle Moments.*

We now had a soundtrack for the beginning of our evening, and how apropos. Pickles with his Oscar Wilde beer, Mario with *Idle Moments*, I just loved those guys. JD excused himself, saying he had developed a powerful thirst that only single malt Scotch could quench. Some little dark-haired girl was circulating around the room with a tray of canapés that included the duck satay and pear and Gorgonzola crostini. Maida was standing in front of the fireplace talking to Pickles. She could have sworn there was a flat screen TV over the fireplace.

Pickles said he was pretty sure there had been. Well, what happened to it, Maida wanted to know. The Actor said it had been damaged, and he had to chuck it out. Maida and Pickles exchanged knowing glances. Everyone seemed to settle in after JD returned with his drink and started bellowing about the Press being camped out front and how he was more in fear of the security The Actor had hired than he was of some little git with a camera. If it weren't for the young woman shoving the tray of canapés at him, he would have delivered a soliloquy of Shakespearean proportions, but he was stopped dead in his tracks.

Cue music: *P.Y.T.* (Pretty Young Thing) by Michael Jackson.

With JD they didn't even have to be pretty as long as they were young, real young, and this little server was a definite tender-roni, something JD preferred to nibble on much more than any old canapé. If any man was in danger of dying from terminal suave, it was JD. He took a canapé from the tray and shoved it so far down into the poor thing's mouth that she was sucking on his fingers, which is what he wanted. I moved to intervene, but The Actor beat me to it. He took the tray from the server and told her that we were fine, she could return to the kitchen. They could serve dinner in about twenty minutes. He then shoved a canapé into JD's mouth, and told him to keep his hands off the help. JD tried to respond, but his mouth was full of pear and Gorgonzola.

Mark Fragile asked me if I was Felicia Lake. Nobody who knows me (except my immediate family) calls me Felicia; everybody calls me Babe. I encouraged Mark to do the same. The first full-length feature he had ever directed was etched in my consciousness as one of the best films I'd ever seen, and I'd seen a few. I was starting to tell him so when Sergei entered the room to ask The Actor if he and his mates should pack it in. His entrance startled everyone, mostly due to his imposing physical presence. Maida and Mark seemed to take an unusual interest in him, for very different reasons.

Maida was definitely checking him out with her chin inclined slightly, so that she was looking up at him with this coquettish glance, as she sort of gnawed on her right index finger. Mark, on the other hand, was sizing him up not in a sexual way, but as if he were appraising some goods he wanted to purchase.

Mark excused himself from our tired little conversation and approached Sergei. We were all watching at this point, not really sure of what was going on. The Actor thanked Sergei, told him he and his mates could call it a night. Mark then asked Sergei if he'd ever acted before. Sergei said no, but of course he had thought about it. Mark told him he might have a part for him as a villain in his next film.

Mark gave Sergei a card and told him to call the following day. Sergei was all smiles, as he shook hands with Mark and The Actor, then made his exit. Maida scurried after Sergei, drink in hand, no doubt, to offer her services as an agent or agent provocateur, it was difficult to tell.

THE ACTOR

JD had sufficiently recovered from the Gorgonzola penetration to confront The Actor by throwing down the gauntlet with the words, "Now look here, matey . . . " to which The Actor, now all red about the ears and trembling, said in a menacing voice, just above a whisper, "Don't call me, matey!"

JD clearly in his cups shot back, "Call you whatever I like." The Actor, also slightly inebriated, countered with, "Don't push your luck, granddad."

"OK, boys, I think that's enough of 'quien es mas macho' for now. Let's eat," I said, grabbing them both by the hand and leading them into the dining room. Mark and Mario followed. Maida, slamming the front door behind her, swept into the dining room on her own breeze.

"What did I miss?" she asked breathlessly, as she clutched Pickles' arm.

"Round one," Pickles laughed.

"Nothing like two Alpha male actors going after each other. Next they'll be beating each other with their head shots," Maida quipped. The Actor sat at the head of the table, I sat to his right and JD sat across from me, Mark Fragile was to my right and next to him was Pickles. Maida sat next to JD and opposite Mark. Mario, who sat opposite Pickles, was on the other side of Maida.

Maida turned to Mario as we all dug into our cucumber salad and asked, "What must you think of us? You're the only one here who actually makes an honest living, you know."

Mario smiled and said, "I think you're all quite mental — lovely, but mental."

I could see Mark Fragile's left leg twitching nervously beneath the table. He was clutching his fork so tightly that his hand looked like a raw cod fillet. Despite all that, he looked The Actor straight in the eye addressing him matter-of-factly.

"Maida said you liked the script."

"I did. I do. I'd like to suggest a few things, but overall it's brilliant, mate. I'm just sorry I wasn't in your last film. I was otherwise engaged, as you know. Keep it up and you'll save the entire British film industry single-handed."

"You mean JD will," Mark said.

"Oh, I'm just the bag man. Mark's the creative genius writer slash director in one package. Saves us a few quid and all. We're doing this deal the same way we did the last, partnership film financing using a major bank as the broker. This way, we avoid the controlling stranglehold of Hollywood, and we actually can make some real money."

"Save the British film industry . . . " Maida chimed in, "We'll survive just as we always have. Remember 1981, JD? Remember?"

JD nodded as we were served the main course of pan fried Halibut, potato dumplings and sautéed spinach. For those of us who didn't remember 1981 in British film history, Mark filled us in: only about two dozen films were distributed.

"1981, you must have been an infant," I said to Mark.

"I'm a lot older than I look."

"Aren't we all, honey?"

Mark locked The Actor in an unwavering stare.

"The film you just finished was a leg up, this one will be a leg over, I promise you."

"My God," Pickles swooned "this is better than Inside the Actor's Studio."

"So," Maida said, clapping her hands, looking around the table eagerly, "I take it we're all in, and contracts can be discussed and drawn up?"

"Why don't we meet again at my office?" JD said, with his mouth full.

All concerned parties agreed. I could see what The Actor wanted: he wanted to see how the chemistry was between the major players, and just how badly Mark Fragile wanted him for his film. The Actor wanted a producer credit, as well. I figured that out from what he had said the other day.

All through dinner, The Actor's left hand was roaming over my lap. At one point I sort of let out a little squeal and jumped slightly out of my seat. Everyone pretended not to notice. The Actor could hardly contain his laughter, as I lamely swatted at him with my napkin.

"Babe seems to really be enjoying the fish," JD sneered.

Maida, ever the cheer-leader, said, "This is good isn't it? My goddaughter's catering company. She's such a dear. When she brings the dessert round I'll introduce her." "How's Freddie these days? Pity he couldn't be here," JD said, stifling a belch.

Maida grabbed Mario's arm and whispered to him, "Freddie's

my husband. Well, you know, JD," she went on, "the MS . . . he has his good days and his bad days. Today, was one of his bad days, I'm sorry to say. You must come round. He'd love to see you."

"Will I have to call him Sir Freddie?"

"JD one day soon you'll be up for Birthday Honors, I feel it," Maida gushed.

"I wouldn't hold my breath," The Actor snickered.

Just then the little dark-haired girl who had passed around the canapés entered, and began to clear away the dishes to make way for dessert. JD gave her a withering look that unnerved the poor thing, but only momentarily.

Maida extended her hand in a sort of Vanna White, Wheel of Fortune gesture and said, "This is my goddaughter, Charlotte. Twenty-eight years old. Cambridge."

I thought someone was going to have to give JD the Heimlich maneuver, but The Actor's forceful pats on the back seemed to quell the situation.

"Oh, leave off. I'm not one of your S&M rent boys." JD shouted, at which point little Charlotte scurried back into the kitchen.

Maida's face melted into an agonized question mark. I grabbed The Actor's hand, and squeezed as Pickles mumbled, "Why can't we all just get along?" Well, somebody had to say it.

There was the most uncomfortable moment of tense silence, so tense I thought I heard a drop of sweat fall from Pickles' forehead onto his dessert plate. It was then that I saw the true measure of Pickles, the man.

"You know, JD, they don't give OBEs to pedophiles," Pickles said, as he reared back in his chair, gripped the table with both hands, and attempted a jaunty head toss.

"The gay janitor has spoken," JD roared. "You think I don't know what gay stands for? Good-As-You, that's what it stands for, but you're not good as me . . ."

"Steady on," Mark shouted.

"You never were, and you never will be," JD went on.

Mario jumped up. "You're bang out of order, mate."

"Shut the fuck up JD, you're drunk," I said smacking my hand on the table, "Get a fucking grip. I can't stand a man who can't hold his liquor."

"Well stated," said The Actor, as he grabbed my thigh and grinned.

Of course, I was a little drunk myself, but I'd had enough of this men being men stuff.

"I say we retire to the drawing room, and have our dessert and coffee, lots of coffee, and I want you boys to kiss and make up, or I'll have to take a strap to you."

That snapped them to attention *and* gave them something to fantasize about, besides beating the shit out of each other.

"Oh my God," Pickles effused, "just like Margo Channing, in *All About Eve*."

Well, I was just drunk enough to feel as though I was channeling Bette Davis — good thing too, because, as we know, boys and girls, when men are confrontational there is always the threat of either sex or violence or both.

As everyone filed into the living room, I pulled Pickles aside.

"Raymond, that was pretty kick-ass of you, deflecting JD like that. I've never been more proud of you."

"I figured it like this, Babe, he was bound to get around to humiliating me sooner or later. I decided, why not make it sooner? Turned the tables on him, though; he wasn't expecting a frontal assault."

"Well, you're a popular little hussy. I saw two champions rise to your defense."

"Your Uncle Pickles still has a little vinegar left in him and a lot of piss," he kissed me on the cheek. "No kidding, I've got to hit the head, loo, whatever . . . you know what I mean." And he was gone.

The Actor and Mark Fragile had disappeared into The Actor's study. I overheard Maida and Mario discussing the volcano that erupted on Montserrat in the West Indies during 1995. Mario was from Montserrat, and so as it turned out, was Maida's mother, who was Irish.

Slumped in a chair, in the far corner of the room, was JD, now persona non grata, because of his alcohol-fueled homophobic outburst. He was sipping his coffee, in a half-assed attempt to sober up. I sat on the arm of his chair and wondered how it had come to this. JD was so dashing when I met him, every bit the leading man. Yes, he drank, but you never saw him wasted in public, and he was always the soul of discretion, courtesy. That was when his wife was alive.

JD was in his early sixties and still HF (Highly Fuckable) in every respect, proving the old adage that when you're hot you're hot. He was now richer than any man had a right to be, but there was no joy, not like there used to be when he was the life of those crazy parties my late husband Gordon liked to throw; the last of the old Hollywood guard.

"Coffee's cold," JD said without looking at me. "Give it here. I'll get you another cup."

"No, don't bother," he said, as he reached down to place the cup and saucer on the floor.

"Put my foot in it, didn't I?"

"Yes, you did. Very unattractive way to behave. We're all misfits here, JD. The least we can do is be kind to each other or at least try to be, make an attempt."

"I should apologize to Pickles. He's such an easy target, though."

"What about The Actor? Are you going to apologize to him?"

"Look, I can only take this mea culpa thing so far. I'm offering his lordship a deal, that no matter what, will net him twice the money he made from his last picture, for which he was paid quite handsomely, I might add."

"First of all, you're making a big money offer because you smell big money. I know you. Which leads me to believe, that you believe this film The Actor just finished is going to go through the roof, and you can ride the crest of that wave on through Mark's picture."

". . . and what does The Actor do? Whacks me on the back like he's trying to knock my teeth out. And don't tell me he didn't do it on purpose."

"What are you, twelve? You know he could probably write his own ticket now, especially with Hollywood."

"Babe, I'm glad I don't have you as an enemy. Look you're a pragmatist, I'm a pragmatist and your boyfriend's one as well. What's Hollywood going to offer him, some scripted version of a Marvel comic book? Why do you think he's in there with Mark now? Creative debate about the script, the tone of the film, points on the back end as a producer . . . The Actor knows this is the right move for him to make right now."

JD looked up at me and smiled like he used to when Gordon was still alive.

"I miss Gordon," I whispered. JD closed his eyes gripped the arms of the chair and whispered, "So do I."

Without warning JD unfolded himself to his full 6 foot 3 inches. He stood wavering like a flagpole in a strong wind, but managed to place his hands over his heart and say:

"I was a right bastard. I admit it. Raymond, I hope you can find it in your heart to forgive me. I apologize to everyone for being an ass," he turned to me, "Will that do?"

We all applauded and cheered. Pickles leapt from his seat and started dancing with JD. The mystery Deejay had continued the mellow mood of Grant Green's *Idle Moments* with Paul Desmond's album, *Summertime*. Just then The Actor and Mark entered, having missed the big apology scene.

"Not her, not her. No, mate. I don't care how hot she is right now." The Actor shouted.

"Do you have to talk shop now?" Pickles moaned as JD wriggled out of his grip.

"Raymond, you know who I'm talking about? Meena Grante, that's who."

"She's a nutter," Mario said.

"She stole your shirt, your favorite shirt. I remember that," Pickles laughed.

The Actor sat down at the piano. Mark Fragile drifted over to the sofa and whispered to Maida, "Do you know about this?"

"Everyone knows about this," Maida said, wearily. The Actor went on.

"I invited the cow over for a drink and a few laughs. Nothing serious. Then she gets it into her head that we're a couple or something. She's calling, texting, emailing . . . I call her. I say listen, luv, I don't know where you're getting this stuff from, but there is no you and me, full stop."

"She was seriously stalking you, man," Mario said. "The next week I'm with Philippe . . ."

"Philippe, isn't he the one the *Daily Mail* is on about? He's missing or something?" Mark asked.

"The *Mail, The Star, The Sun, News of the World*. Probably checked himself into rehab," Maida smirked.

". . . and we're driving through Islington," The Actor plowed on, "and there she is, bold as day, walking down the street wearing my favorite shirt, a limited edition Robert Graham sports shirt . . ."

Pickles smacked his lips.

"Well, honey . . . I would have jumped out of the car and snatched it off her bony behind."

". . . cost me five hundred US dollars."

"All the more reason," Pickles stated flatly.

"No, Mark." The Actor said, "I will not be in any film with that crazy, thieving, little bitch."

Mark shrugged his shoulders and said, "OK."

"So, I don't get it. What happened to Philippe?" JD said.

"He's gone missing," I stage whispered.

"Is that what all the paparazzi were about?" Mark asked. "I think we should change the subject," Maida said.

"Why? This is fascinating," JD went on, "Any foul play suggested? What do you think happened to him?" he asked The Actor.

"Maybe the same thing that'll happen to you if you don't shut it," The Actor growled.

"He'll turn up, you'll see. Probably just out on the piss," Mario said.

"Please change the subject," Maida pleaded.

Nothing Can Come Between Us by Sade was playing. Pickles and Mario were singing along. JD mumbled something about letting good cognac go to waste, as he retreated into the dining room. The Actor swept me onto the floor and started dancing the lindy, what they used to call the bop, where I came from, like we were on *American Bandstand*. "You've got some moves," I said. The Actor just winked and we kept on dancing. The Actor could dance, which kind of re-confirmed my theory that if a man can give you thrills on the dance floor vertically, he can also do the same horizontally.

From the corner of my eye, I saw Maida lean into Mark. He placed his hand on her thigh. She whispered something in his ear. Their cozy behavior led me to think that maybe more was going on there than met the eye. Maida was more than twenty years older than Mark. Go Maida.

The next thing I knew, Mark produced a little Ziploc sandwich baggie, about a quarter full of white powder. He dipped into the bag pinched off some powder, and sprinkled it into that little fleshy well between the base of his index finger and his thumb, then he held his hand up to Maida's waiting mouth and with a sharp, hard puff of air, blew the coke in.

"Do me!" Pickles squealed and Mark did. The it was round robin, The Actor blew into my mouth, I blew into The Actor's mouth and Pickles into Mario's and Maida into JD's.

We were all savoring the freeze, tripping on the verge of a serious tingle, when the secret DJ changed the mood. George Michael was belting out *An Easier Affair*. The pounding, hypnotic rhythm was infectious. Something primal overtook our little group. It became a free-styling free for all, even JD was rocking out. One partner was replaced by another in a whirling swirl of bodies. For an instant, I thought we had all levitated and were dancing closer to the ceiling than the floor. As George Michael called upon us to "celebrate the love of the one you're with," the mood of the music changed yet again back to Sade. Michael Fragile turned to me and said,

"Felicia, I mean Babe, would you sing for us, please?"

The music died down or someone had turned it off. "Please sing something, Babe?" JD implored.

I looked around, frightened. I felt like I was in a dark tunnel. Everyone sat down in anticipation. I looked furtively at Pickles who tried to intervene.

"Come on, people. If Babe were a surgeon, you wouldn't ask her to perform surgery for you right now, would you? She's here to enjoy herself, like everyone else," Pickles implored.

But Mark Fragile, coked up and siding with JD, egged him on. Maida tugged at JD's arm.

"If she doesn't want to sing, she doesn't want to sing," she said. I froze. I didn't know what to say. Anything I could think of was only going to sound lame. I must have stood there for longer than I realized, paralyzed by memories of things best forgotten, when The Actor started playing the piano. I recognized the tune. It was composed by Hoagy Carmichael and the lyrics were written by Ned Washington, *The Nearness of You*.

Everyone sat up in their seats, slightly amazed. Apparently, this was a side of The Actor they hadn't seen before. When he began to sing their jaws dropped, because he could really sing and sing he did, with such feeling.

His eyes never left mine, something welled up inside me. It spilled out and filled the room, took me a second to recognize the sound of my own voice singing along with The Actor's:

I need no soft lights to enchant me If you'll only grant me the right
To hold you ever so tight
And to feel in the night the nearness of you

"My God," Pickles sobbed, "just like Don Johnson and Barbra Streisand."

Everyone was sniffling and dabbing at their eyes, including me.

The Actor wrapped me in his arms, and whispered, "That wasn't so bad was it?"

"This calls for a toast," JD said. "Pickles, help me with the glasses."

JD and Pickles returned with glasses, and the insanely expensive cognac JD had brought with him.

"To Babe and The Actor's engagement," JD said lifting his glass, "Oh, you all haven't heard the good news? They're getting married."

Maida's mouth was opening and closing like a goldfish. I looked at The Actor, he looked down at the keyboard and bit on his bottom lip. I don't know if, in that moment, I was numb from all the booze, singing in public again, or the coke. I was definitely immobilized by this revelation. It was the first I was hearing about any engagement. What I really could not stand was JD was taking a little bit too much delight in delivering the news. He was passing out his Cuban cigars, damn him!.

"I heard it firsthand from Eagle-Eye Kenny as I was coming in tonight. Apparently you made some sort of announcement," JD said to The Actor, "You remember Ken, the photographer. You broke his nose."

The Actor started playing that pretty tune by Styne, Comden, and Green, from the Broadway musical, *Bells Are Ringing*: The Party's Over.

CHAPTER 10

Acting is like roller skating. Once you know how to do it, it is neither stimulating nor exciting.

— George Sanders

The suave, erudite British actor Brian Aherne was a Hollywood favorite in the 1930s and 40s. He was once married to Joan Fontaine, and he had an uneasy friendship with fellow actor George Sanders, who coincidentally co-starred with Fontaine in *Rebecca* (1940) and *Ivanhoe* (1942).

Aherne penned a biography about Sanders, published in 1955, entitled *The Dreadful Man: The Story of Hollywood's Most Original Cad.* According to the biography, George Sanders was a legitimate member of the Russian royalty, a distinction that was snatched from him by the Bolshevik overthrow of the Tsar — something with which Sanders never really reconciled.

Sanders deported himself regally on screen, until the day he died, lending class and sophistication to anything he touched, and yet, he really was an unscrupulous stinker, involved in various dodgy business deals throughout his life. *The Dreadful Man* also delves into George Sanders' second marriage to Benita Hume Coleman, the widow of English actor Ronald Coleman. In fact, her letters are really what make the book — quite literally.

The effect Benita had on Sanders was a stabilizing one. He still continued to be an eccentric curmudgeon, but without the excesses and self-destructive behavior, that marked his years after Benita's death.

Those eighteen years with Benita must have seemed short,

compared with the eternity of the five booze- and drug-soaked years without her until Sanders' own death, a death I continue to mourn.

The Actor's strategy for wriggling out of the nightmare of public scrutiny, brought on by his mother's madness and the missing Philippe, was to give the Press an even bigger story: our impending marriage. The fact that he hadn't bothered to tell me about it was apparently of little importance.

After everyone had gone, with the exception of Pickles and Mario, The Actor had silently retreated to his room. I suppose I was in a state of shock . . . it could have been the cognac. I don't know. I sat with Pickles and Mario on the sofa, as *Zen and The Art of Chilling, Volume Two* played in the background.

"Can I be the maid of honor?" Pickles asked. "This is not funny, Pickles," I said.

"I wasn't being funny. I mean it. I always wanted to toss rose petals in the bride's path, wear a crown of flowers . . . " Pickles said, dreamily.

"That's the flower girl, you moron," I said.

"Besides," Mario interjected, "you'd have to be the matron of honor, because Babe's been married before."

"I don't want to be a matron. God, it sounds so Eve Arden."

"Yeah," I agree, I said, "Eve Arden is way too butch for you."

"If you're the matron . . . OK maid of honor, I guess maybe that means I can be the best man," Mario beamed.

"What the fuck are you two talking about? Who said there was going to be a wedding?

"But you're engaged," Pickles and Mario blurted out in unison.

"I was never asked," I shouted, "I was never asked if I wanted to get married. Suppose I don't want to get married again, huh?"

"Babe, he wouldn't announce something like that, to the world . . . " Pickles said.

"You want to know what I think? I think, your boy has used this marriage thing as a way to squirm out of the negative publicity he's been getting."

"Oh, no, he wouldn't do that," Mario pleaded.

"You're just being negative," Pickles admonished, "You should march yourself upstairs. Talk to him. I know he feels bad about all this."

I was not concerned with The Actor's feelings at this point. I had some feelings of my own to be concerned about. I'd been divorced twice and widowed once. Any way you want to look at it, marriage had not been a successful enterprise for me.

Even though I didn't want to be alone and lonely, I had enough sense to figure out that starting a marriage this way, was not promising. Reluctantly I took Pickles' advice and climbed the stairs to The Actor's bedroom, but he wasn't there, nor was he in the bathroom or his daughter's room. I found him sitting on the bed in what was once Philippe's room, clutching a pillow as he stared out the window at the sun rising on the park across the street.

"You fucked up," I said.

"Yeah, I fucked up."

"Do you know how you fucked up? By not discussing your little Machiavellian tactic with me? Don't you trust me?"

"I trust you. I know my motives weren't entirely honorable."

"Let's not bring honor into this. I lived in Hollywood, the capital of situational ethics. It's just that you put me in a bad position." "You don't want to marry me?"

"Are you asking me to marry you?"

The Actor got down on one knee and grabbed both of my hands. "Felicia Lake, will you marry me?"

I was mortified. This was all wrong, but I loved him so much.

"Just get up, please."

He sat down on the bed with tears in his eyes.

"What's wrong? You don't want me?"

"I do want you. You have no idea how much I want you."

"Then just say yes. Marry me, Babe."

"I can't marry you, honey."

"Why, Babe? Why can't you marry me?" The Actor cried.

"Because, I'm already married!"

I had become a victim of my own subterfuge. I had never divorced Nick Ravelli, but we both had been telling the world we were divorced for so long, we began to believe it ourselves.

We had lived as man and wife for almost eighteen months, and believe me that was pushing it. I just couldn't take it anymore: the drugs, the guns, the shady characters. It was all a far cry from the genteel, sophisticated, benignly eccentric world I left as Mrs. Gordon Burdett.

THE ACTOR

Nick was burning a hole through his assets. You would have thought they had a revolving door at the Betty Ford Clinic; to make matters worse, he went on Celebrity Rehab, which did nothing for his career. Finally, he ran into trouble with the IRS. The upshot of the whole thing that based on my income during the time of our marriage and his present financial status I'd end up paying him a wad of cash, and he'd get a fresh start courtesy of bankruptcy court — if and when we divorced. I explained all this to The Actor.

"There must be a way round all this," he said.

"Yes, there is, but it involves me giving Nick money, and I just don't want to do that."

"How much money are you talking about?"

"A whole lot, seven figures."

"You have that kind of money?"

"Yeah, I do from my royalties, and more from Gordon's investments, and the business we built, the one my daughter and her husband run."

"It's practically extortion," The Actor said.

"No practically about it. Now that I'm hearing myself saying these things out loud . . . I mean Pickles doesn't even know this shit. It's only money isn't it? Look, I came to merry old England with some half-baked schoolgirl's dream of marrying an Earl. I figured Nick would let me go, if I was really serious about someone. I never thought that would actually happen. It was just something to keep me occupied, give me a purpose. You know? Because, I was getting so tired of being alive."

"I could top us both, if need be. I know people think I've done away with Philippe. I know. I could put up with that, I could put up with anything, even my mother, if I thought you'd be with me. I can't be alone, Babe. I can't. I won't."

"Honey, are you acting right now?"

"I'm sorry. I'm really knackered. The tendency is to fall back on technique in emotional situations, you know. Sorry, luv."

"Let's discuss this tomorrow. Are you too tired to give us a good fucking?" I asked.

"Let's have at it," he said.

It was around 2 p.m. or 14:00, take your pick, when I finally reached a semi-conscious state. I was all for just staying in bed until the next Presidential election, but The Actor had other plans. He was so strong and resilient, it was almost super-human. He and Pickles had this in common, this incredible physical constitution, equal only to that of Batman. Come to think of it, Batman had a lot in common with The Actor: both were sort of human and had that whole dark, brooding, obsessive, trippy dual-identity thing going on — all of which, masked something mystical and deeply disturbing.

I could hear The Actor in the shower singing, *What's So Funny about Peace Love and Understanding*. He emerged naked brandishing a long whip made from horsehair.

"Oh no, it's way too early for that stuff." I said, as I tunneled under the covers.

"I beg to differ," he laughed, "half the day is gone." With that he ripped the covers off me like he was performing a magic trick. Then he sort of brushed the horsehair softly back and forth across my body. It felt nice, a little coarse, a little prickly, but nice. Then he swatted, as if I had a fly on me. It did sting.

"You like?" he asked with a grin.

"I like, but what's all this about? You're pretty happy for a man who's created a public relations nightmare."

"I have been thinking, and I believe I have a solution."

"A solution to what? I mean there's no shortage of problems is there? Let's see: your mum, Philippe, marriage, the Press." "Party-pooper," he said, as he swatted me hard enough to give him a stiffy. "I'm talking about us now. If we solve us, everything else will fall into place. Now, I was thinking, suppose I give Nick the money he needs. We'd have to get something in writing . . . lawyers would have to be involved . . ."

"Oh, you are so sweet," I said, as I pulled him onto the bed, "you're my big sweet whacky guy. Don't you see, if I give Nick the money it's like I'm buying myself from him, and you need only look at me, to see why that idea is repulsive. By the same token if you give him money, that's like you buying me from him, again taking us back to repulsive."

"I see what you mean," he sighed, "We *could* kill him . . . have him killed . . ."

The Actor was not smiling when he said this. He was staring into space pondering. Then he snapped out of it.

THE ACTOR

"Well," he said, "what if we both give him the money, you know fifty-fifty? First we negotiate the price down, with the promise of immediate payment, if he signs the divorce papers within ten days."

"I could rock with that."

And so, the deal was struck. We decided that The Actor would contact Nick, man-to-man, have The Actor's lawyer draw up a document, then we could be married sometime between the premiere of the new film and its Press tour; otherwise, we might hold up the start of the Mark Fragile film.

The day seemed to be going well so far, that is until Pickles knocked on the door to tell us the police were downstairs and The Actor's publicist was on the phone. Of course, The Actor had to take the call from the publicist. Pickles and I served tea to the two police officers.

We were having a great conversation about the London Metropolitan Police uniform versus the LAPD uniform. We all agreed that the Met had a great uniform, geared up, practical and yet stylish. We all found LAPD to be too reminiscent of the Gestapo, while lacking the Gestapo style.

The Actor entered, a little the worse for wear. The phone call from his publicist had not been a happy one. I could see he was taking great pains to conceal his anger. I wondered whether the cops noticed this as well.

He forced a smile and exchanged pleasantries. He knew these two officers from their previous encounters with his mum. They were following up on Philippe's missing person report, doing what they called a "risk assessment."

Their questions were perfunctory, yet thorough: when was the last time The Actor saw Philippe, what were the circumstances, how did Philippe seem, was he unhappy, was he having financial problems, did he abuse drugs, had he been depressed, how long had The Actor known Philippe, did Philippe have any enemies, did he know if Philippe had family in the area.

Finally, the officers said that was all for now. If they needed any additional information, would The Actor mind coming into the Kentish Town Police Station — they'd call if it was necessary. The officers thanked Pickles and me for the tea. Neither of them asked for an autograph.

After the cops drove off, we convened in the kitchen over coffee and chocolate mousse with poached cherries, leftover from the night before: a night that now seemed like an old movie we had watched, a long time ago.

"My publicist read the headlines to me over the phone," The Actor began, "'His mum's gone mental, his assistant's gone missing and now he's getting married.' The photo of you was really good, apparently."

"Babe's so photogenic," Pickles gushed, "and you, Thespian, have never taken a bad picture in your life."

"I'm sharing tabloid space with Britney losing her kids, the State's X-ray spies wanting to see people nude . . ."

"Nobody with any sense is going to believe that crap about you. Lest we forget, these are the same people responsible for the headline 'Diana was still alive hours before she died.'" Pickles retorted.

"Unfortunately, a lot of people without any sense go to see my films," The Actor replied.

"Am I the only one concerned about the police? I wouldn't tell them that story you told me about the last time you saw Philippe. Better to be economical with the truth," I said.

"What story about the last time you saw Philippe? Am I going to need a drink to continue?" Pickles asked.

"Listen, mate. This is one of those times when the less you know the better," The Actor said.

Pickles got up and grabbed the exquisite Camus Cognac bottle from the counter, took a swig from the bottle and handed it to The Actor.

"Do you mind getting us some glasses, Pickles," The Actor said.

"Well, I think we should scour the house for any incriminating evidence and take care of it before they ask to search the house," I said, as Pickles put a glass of cognac in front of me.

The Actor narrowed his eyes and took a sip from his glass. "You think they'll do that?"

"It's possible. You should be prepared," I said.

"All right, can you and Raymond take care of that? I'll give the place another once over when you're done, and could you order some groceries in. I'll give you the number. Maybe we should get some takeaway for now, I'm starving."

We got the food situation sorted, ate and burned one. Thank goodness Pickles was on the case, getting up early to see Mario off. He was able to let the caterers in to clean up. We could relax without further disturbance. The Actor informed us that he had some business to take care of — he'd be back very late that night. I knew, at this point, not to ask. I had to grab Pickles' arm in a vise grip to prevent him from asking.

We had been fortunate. The Actor's mood had been pretty stable for almost twenty-four hours. I was too worn out to go through another last-angry-man episode.

We managed to get in a little sexual healing before The Actor left. He showered again and shaved. I knew by the way he was dressed, he was stopping off at his club during the evening. He warned Pickles and me not to get into any mischief, knowing full well we were planning to get into as much mischief as God and man would allow.

CHAPTER 11

I've always wanted to get an education and tonight's as good a time as any.

— **Burt Lancaster**

Burt Lancaster was once described as a brute with the eyes of an angel. He was also said to be a multitude of contradictions: self-indulgent and selfless, demanding and easy-going, detached and passionate.

Above all he was a man who always wanted more control of just about everything, and this drive led him to become one of the most successful movie stars-turned-movie-producers in his or any other era to date.

When asked about his success, Burt Lancaster said, "I had the luck of an obedient body." The meaning of that statement is wide open to interpretation, but the beauty and power of that body cannot be denied. And, if the stories are to be believed, Burt tried very hard not to deny himself or anyone else.

Rumors have been persistent, over the years, of Lancaster's bi-sexuality, primarily based on the assertion that he had a penchant for being on the receiving end of oral sex without really being all that concerned what gender was on the giving end.

The fact that he was also a champion of gay rights, before the phrase was coined, and that he was a close personal friend of Rock Hudson's, only keep the embers of the rumor smoldering.

That body, that face, that smile . . . When he walks across the screen in *From Here to Eternity* dressed only in a towel, flip-flops and that grin, well . . . I hope he was bi-sexual, because everybody deserved a shot at that.

THE ACTOR

Pickles produced a small stack of newspapers and showed me the tabloid headlines: "Did he shag his assistant to death?" "First his mum, then his assistant, is future wife, Felicia Lake, next?" "Met called in to investigate disappearance of star's personal assistant."

"We should have gloves," Pickles said as he rummaged through kitchen cabinets and drawers.

"And tiaras," I said absently, "if we're wearing gloves, we should have tiaras."

"Earth to Babe," Pickles shouted, "we're not going to a Ball at the Palace, sugar. Rubber gloves. We need rubber gloves if we're going to go over this place before the cops start snooping around — this is just so Alfred Hitchcock. Found them."

Pickles entered the dining room, ripped open the bag of latex gloves and snapped a pair on, as if he were about to remove someone's gall bladder.

"Where do you suggest we begin?"

"Well, doctor, after reading those headlines, the first place we should start is denial. The more we distance ourselves from the truth in our own minds, the better."

Pickles sat down and put his arm around me.

"Babe, I say we build that barge, and we float down that river of denial, but let's not get depressed about it, sugar. OK?"

"Raymond, there are so many things I want to tell you, but I just can't."

"I know, but eventually you will get drunk, and it will all come tumbling out. I can wait."

"Why must you always be right?"

"Because, I know you all too well and love you, you know that. So, are you two getting married or what?

"Let's look in the basement and see if we need to tidy up."

"You mean cover up. Over here, if it's the unfinished underground floor of a house it's called a cellar; if it's finished it's called a basement, just saying. Anyway, I don't have a key. Besides, I thought Thespian was very specific about you not venturing down there."

"A key? We don't need no stinking key. I looked at that lock: it's crap. I can get in there, no scratches, nothing. If there's no incriminating stuff down there, he'll never know the difference."

"And if there is? What then? I mean, I'm willing to do what I can, but I'm not as macho as you, Babe. I can't bury bodies or anything like that. They say, moving dead weight is really bad for your back, and you know I've always had problems with my back . . ."

"Is that what you think, that The Actor, your mate, my future husband, killed Philippe, stashed him in the basement or cellar, invited house guests over, then decided to have a dinner party, while boyfriend is rotting away below our feet?"

"Now that you put it like that . . . but he does go into these states where he blacks out and forgets things, you've seen him, and then if he's been drinking . . ."

"It's summer. If there was a body down there we'd smell it by now. I'd better get working on that lock. Look, I need you to call Mario. I'm going to have to stash my stun-gun with him for a minute. We may need him to help us with some other stuff, I don't know. Just put him on stand-by. Is he going to be cool with all this?" "You mean, as far as doing what needs to be done to protect Thespian? Mario's totally cool. It'll be just like old times."

That last remark gave me pause. Fuck it, in for a penny in for a pound. Talk about old times. This took me back to my youth when I was a wannabe biker chick.

I was dating this guy Skip, who was half Lithuanian and half Cherokee. He was twenty-three and I was fifteen. At fifteen, I was the same height I am now. I'm about 5'9". I've always been pretty zaftig, not the F word, never the F word, not Fat, just rounded. Consequently, I looked older than I was — then.

Skip and I would go into a bar and with shades, my hair all wild hiding my face, no one ever carded me. I saw some pretty crazy things, and did some pretty crazy things with Skip, like robbing a KFC drive thru.

When I saw him put his elbow through this guy's cheek in a bar fight, I decided my days as a biker chick were over at the ripe old age of sixteen. However, I did learn how to use a handgun and how to pick a lock, two things every girl should know. I will always be indebted to good old Skip.

As I was working on the basement or cellar lock, Pickles was calling Mario. Picking the lock gave me time to think. I supposed I'd have to get used to The Actor's disappearing act. I knew he wasn't rushing off to the arms of another woman, as they say in the soap operas. The Actor was merely a man of enormous talent, and men like him had enormous appetites for life and all life has to offer. Who could fault him for that? None of his excesses worried me. I had plenty of my own. Funny thing was, he didn't seem to care.

I thought about the pressure he must be under always having to please people and be pleasant, like in the restaurant when we first met, a meeting which precipitated me falling flat on my behind. Now, I knew what I only guessed then: he hated the whole adoring fan thing, the selfies, the Press, being a virtual prisoner in his own home.

The world he knew, during the almost two decades he spent working his way to the top, was now a foreign planet he could visit at his own risk. Don't get me wrong, my sympathy extended only so far, because the world he now inhabited showered him with millions of dollars, waves of adulation, recognition, accolades and respect. As he said himself, he was shagging the bitch-goddess Success raw and loving every minute, even though he, simultaneously, was somewhat contemptuous of it all.

No, it was my own fear of leaving the cocoon of relative anonymity, and stepping boldly into the incarcerating spotlight of mega-fame with my man, that was giving me the collywobbles, a term I had learned from Mario.

Let's face it, when I married Nick Ravelli, we were both Trivial Pursuit questions. There were at least a dozen tribute bands performing his glory days, Billboard chart-toppers, and I had female impersonators belting out my hits from the 80s like their lives depended on it. We were show business footnotes, not headlines like The Actor, and I was perfectly happy with that. I know this is tantamount to treason and very un-American, but I felt no obligation to be famous. I didn't mind the money, though.

Pickles and I stood at the top of the stairs leading to the unknown, both of us having lost our nerve, but afraid to say so out loud.

"What if there's something down there?" Pickles whispered as he grabbed my arm. I switched on the cellar light.

"We'll have to deal with it. Come on."

I took the first step, with Pickles practically piggy-back behind me. We got down to the bottom of what clearly was a cellar, with all the expected accouterments including a boiler, water heater, breaker panel and a ventilation system. In the far corner was a full wine rack, a play pen full of children's toys, a tricycle, two adult bicycles, shelving for tools and gardening equipment. Propped against the far wall was the broken kitchen table.

There were no apparent signs or smell to indicate that a dead body was rotting away inside a tarpaulin, but there was something almost equally as disturbing. I had to put my hand over Pickles mouth to muffle his scream.

Piled high in the middle of the cellar floor was a mound of men's clothing, expensive clothing: Tom Ford suits, Armani sportswear, jewelry, watches, ties, underwear, shoes, belts, bottles of cologne, aftershave — all just lying there in a big sloppy heap.

Thrown on top of the heap were photos of a tall man with an olive complexion, green eyes and black wavy hair. They looked like vacation photos with the black-haired man smiling, gesturing and making funny faces. There were also nude photos of him alone and him with The Actor.

"I think these must be Philippe's things," I whispered, "I'm not sure what we should do."

"We should march ourselves right back upstairs, finish off what's left of the vodka, smoke a joint and forget we ever saw this shit," Pickles said.

I knelt down at the foot of the steps, not sure if I was seeing what I thought I was seeing. A red amoeba shaped splotch about a foot in diameter dried into the concrete floor. I turned to Pickles, he looked at the splotch and all the color drained from his face.

"Let's get out of here," I said. After we burned one we went outside and sat in the narrow garden, that snaked around the house. We finished off the vodka, just as Pickles had so astutely suggested, and even that was not enough to dull the effect of what the cellar had revealed to us. It was painful, so painful we couldn't talk about it for at least ten minutes.

"I told you. Didn't I say we shouldn't go down there, didn't I?" Pickles was beside himself.

"It had to be done. Now, we know."

"Know what? What do we know exactly, Babe? If my best friend is a murderer, that's something I would be happy to live out the rest of my life not knowing."

"I thought I was your best friend. Really, I thought I was."

"Well, you're a couple now, aren't you? That means you're both my best friend, and how old are you, twelve? What the fuck does that matter, in the face of such calamity? This is messed up."

"If you're going to behave like this, we're going to need more alcohol."

We retreated to the womb-like comfort of the living room where we proceeded to tackle the gnarly problem of what to do next: whether we should finish off the single malt scotch or the beer. I proposed, that while we were at least sober enough to consciously direct our actions, we should make an attempt to get the S&M paraphernalia, and such things as the man-soap ring and the anal beads, lubricant, and the like out of sight. Pickles didn't think Mario would want to cart that stuff around, and what if the house was under surveillance or the Press was still lurking about, even a nosey neighbor? Taking bags out of the house now would look suspicious.

"I know," I said in the throes of a brainstorm, "why don't we put it into your luggage, then the cops can't link those things to The Actor?"

"My luggage . . . I'm the gay man, so of course I'm going to be carrying around whips, and anal beads and two dozen tubes of lubricant with me. What is the matter with you, woman?"

"I didn't mean to offend you, your highness. I'm thinking on my feet here. OK, so we split those things, half in your luggage half in mine."

"That's acceptable. When are the cleaners due back? My bathroom's starting to need some attention, and I could use some clean sheets."

"Tomorrow, I think. The cleaners are here tomorrow and they won't change the beds; they'll do the laundry, but they're not making the beds. We'll strip all the beds and change the sheets ourselves. You get the sheets from the linen closet, while I deal with the sex toys."

I followed Pickles as he climbed the stairs, all the while, mumbling under his breath something about me not being the boss of him, when suddenly he stopped short and turned around.

"Babe, we don't have to ever speak about the cellar again. Promise me." I promised.

I was counting out the tubes of Astroglide, there were a lot more than I thought, when I heard Pickles scream and the sound of something heavy hitting the floor. I ran out of the front bedroom, through The Actor's room and out into the hallway, where I found Pickles in front of the open linen closet crumpled in a heap, on top of a pile of fresh sheets that littered the floor. His breathing was labored, but at least he was still breathing. I gently tapped his cheek and called his name. He slowly came to.

"Am I dead?"

"No. You fainted. What happened?"

Pickles pointed a trembling finger to the linen closet. I helped him to his feet. He started backing down the hallway. I stepped over the sheets, on the floor and drew closer to the linen closet. There, lying on top of the remainder of neatly folded bed sheets, was a Webley Service Revolver.

At first glance I thought it might be a Smith and Wesson .38, but it was a Webley, all right. I opened it. It wasn't loaded. I showed it to Pickles.

"It's not loaded, Pickles," I said as I snapped it shut.

"That's a real gun. What's he doing with a real gun?"

"Let's sit down. Come on," I said as I guided Pickles into The Actor's bedroom, "you don't look so good."

Pickles sat down on the bed. I placed the gun on top of the dresser then went into the bathroom, to get him a glass of water from the tap.

Pickles held the glass with both hands to steady the trembling. When he finished, I took the glass from him, placed it on the dresser and held up the gun to get a better look at it. It was in mint condition.

"Do you have to hold that thing like that? I can't stand guns."

"Well, it's not loaded or anything, nothing to be afraid of."

"I grew up in a community where men were always going out and shooting something: squirrels, deer, turkey, Jews, Black people, each other. I just don't like guns, so can you please put that away?"

I stuffed the gun down the front of my jeans and pulled the bedazzled T-shirt I'd bought at Nashville's Wild Horse Saloon over it.

"Let's not jump to conclusions. We don't know if this belongs to The Actor. For all we know, it could be Philippe's or a prop or something. Pickles, are you all right? Want an aspirin or some painkillers?"

"I'll be OK. This is all a bit too much for my delicate sensibilities, sugar."

I sat down next to Pickles and hugged him tightly. He hugged back. I kissed him full on the mouth. He didn't resist. I grabbed his hand, and we just sat there for a long time, tears streaming down our faces. What were we going to do about our wayward boy, The Actor?

We'd finished changing the beds and replacing the dirty towels with clean ones. We were on our way downstairs, heading to the laundry room with the dirty linen, when the doorbell rang. I thought Pickles was going to jump out of his skin.

"Here," I said giving him the pile of dirty linen I was carrying, "I'll get the door."

Pickles whispered frantically.

"The gun, I can see the gun sticking out."

I removed the gun from my jeans and stuffed it under a sofa cushion, as Pickles scurried off to the laundry room. I took a moment to compose myself.

Even though I could feel my heart pounding and my knees shaking, I tried to look calm as I opened the door. It was Mario, thank God. I pulled him inside and gave him a big hug and a kiss.

"I have never been happier to see anyone in my whole life."

CHAPTER 12

I am forever being punished by the gods for stealing fire and trying to put it out. The fire, of course, is you.

— Richard Burton to Elizabeth Taylor

When asked about the movie *Cleopatra*, the movie that pretty much destroyed 20th Century Fox, financially and jump started the most famous, and infamous, love story of the last half of the 20th century, Elizabeth Taylor is reported to have replied that she didn't really remember too much about the movie, because there was a lot of other stuff going on at the time.

That "stuff" was Richard Burton. If I had been having an affair with Richard Burton, I probably wouldn't remember my name, let alone any old Hollywood-studio-destroying mega-million-dollar movie.

Richard Burton had so much raw sex appeal, it was barely containable by a movie screen. Everything about the man was super-high wattage: his voice (which I would gladly take as a sex-substitute), his talent as an actor (see *Becket*), his command of the English language (*Hamlet on Broadway*), those eyes, that body (see *The Robe*), his love for Elizabeth Taylor, his battle with the bottle. I'm just sorry I never got to see him on stage.

Two or three times a year I'll watch *Look Back in Anger* with salivating awe and lust. The *tirades* of the main character in that film, Jimmy, when invested with the volcanic power of Richard Burton, leap out of the screen and grab the audience by the throat.

More than any other actor, when it came to communicating the power of unbridled emotion on screen, *The* Actor came closest to

Richard Burton, when Richard Burton was at his best. However, dealing with such unbridled emotion in person could be a little scary.

Mario and Pickles helped me scour the house once more, including the third floor, which I hadn't realized was there, and divvy up the sex paraphernalia between my luggage and Pickles'. Mario agreed to hold onto my Taser for a while. I was sure there was something I was forgetting, but I just couldn't think of what it was. Pickles and I decided it best not to tell Mario about the cellar: plausible deniability. Pickles and Mario wanted to go out to eat. I wasn't in the mood. We burned one, they left. I made a sandwich and had a beer.

I called my daughter, Veronica, to see how she and her husband, Matt, were doing. I wanted to give The Actor a new kitchen table from our catalog. I described the kitchen and Ronnie said she knew just the thing. I also told her I was getting married — again. She asked me if I'd divorced Nick yet, at which point I said I'd email her with the details. Somehow, that girl always knew what I thought were my secrets.

I took a shower then slept for a couple of hours. I'd slept longer than I wanted. I must have needed the sleep, because I did feel better. I was hungry again. I could hear music. I wasn't sure if it was inside or outside my head. As I walked into the hallway, the music coming from the sound system downstairs filled the house. It was *Motorcycle Emptiness* by Manic Street Preachers.

He was back. The Actor was home. I had to stop for a moment, catch my breath, and compose myself. I didn't want him to see how much I'd missed him. He was standing at the kitchen sink, his back to me. I watched him from the doorway as he filled a glass full of tap water, and drank slowly. He bowed his head, the glass clutched so tightly in his hand, I was fearful he'd squeeze it until it broke. I opened my mouth to say something, but I saw the mood he was in and thought better of it.

Then he said quietly, without turning around. "I went to see my daughter, Zoe, to tell her about us. She said we should be very happy together, because we deserved each other. Whatever the hell that means."

He threw the glass in the sink, it didn't break. He stood there, palms flat, pressing down on the edge of the sink, silent. The muscles in his back, visibly tightening. Then, all at once his shoulders slumped, and he began to sob. "She called me a freak. What I do for living, the way live, what's being said about me online. 'Why can't you just be a normal dad?' That's what she said to me. I was gutted, Babe. I can't take it from her; anybody else, but not her."

I walked over to him, slowly gauging where I thought his mood would fall. I wrapped my arms around his waist and pressed my cheek against his back. The smell of him, the warmth of him, the goodness in him filled me with tenderness and compassion.

"Do you think we could be happy, Babe?"

"I think happiness is overrated," I said hugging him tight. "How about just being thankful, thankful that we have each other. How old is Zoe?" "She's thirteen."

"Well, she's at just the right age to be a fucking idiot." He laughed.

"Yeah. What did I know when I was her age? I thought my dad was a big stupid git, and all. It was only after he left I realized he was an OK bloke, did the best he could. He was up against it. He loved me, never missed an opportunity to say so. All these years dead, and sometimes I'll pick up the phone to call him . . ."

He was in a mood. The only thing I could do was let him cry it out, cry with him, hold him, let it pass. Manic Street Preachers was blasting out *You Love Us* over the sound system. It was time for alcohol.

"I'll turn the music off," he said. "Pour us a drink, will you?"

When he turned around, there were several small splotches of what looked like blood on the front of his shirt.

"Is that your blood?" I said, as I tried to unbutton his shirt. He pulled my hands away, kissed me on the cheek and smiled. "That would be telling, wouldn't it?"

I cracked the last bottle of the good single malt and poured out doubles. The Actor returned. I was concerned about the blood on his shirt. He could see the distress on my face. He told me not to worry about it. But, I was worried about it, very much worried.

"I see you had groceries delivered. Shall I make omelets?" he asked, giving me that killer grin.

"Please. I'm starving. Will I have to learn to cook? You know I'd do that if you wanted me to."

THE ACTOR

"You don't really mean that, Babe, do you? Besides, I like it that you don't cook; it means I can cook for you."

We ate most of our meal in silence. The tenseness had evaporated, his mood had shifted, but there was something dark stirring in him. It put me on edge, like waiting for a bomb to explode.

"I understand you and Maida are having lunch tomorrow," he said, without looking up from his plate.

"Yes, that's right. I thought it might be nice to hang out with someone from my own gender for a change."

"Your own gender?" he laughed, "Yeah, I see the point." He was pensive for a moment, then the anger started to rise in him, slowly transforming his features.

"Do you think I'm a ponce, poofter, a queer, a faggot?"

"What kind of question is that? Why is it a topic at all?"

"For me, this is always a topic . . . My bloody ex-wife, Tessa, always wants to know why I don't just come out of the closet. Every time I see her, it comes down to the same old bullshit. I am not gay, Babe. I have sex with men, because I need to, but I am not gay, I am not bisexual . . ."

"I know, baby. I know that."

"What do you know really?" he said as the veins in his neck began to bulge. "I'm just who I am. I see no reason to imprison myself with labels. Can you understand that?"

What I understood was that no matter what I said it was going to end badly. He had turned mean, like a dog who's been hit too many times, that's the look that was in his eye, as he lifted his head to give me a sideways glance, a glance that reeked of hatred. I was sure, even though he was looking at me, he was seeing someone else. "You've had too much to drink. You're thinking crazy thoughts, baby. I'm not the enemy."

"Everybody's the enemy. I love you and you could be the enemy. You ever think of that? Huh?"

"Why don't you let me hurt you, honey? In a sweet and tender way, you know, to make you feel better. Wouldn't that make you feel better?"

He put his knife and fork down folded his arms on the table, leaned forward and stared at me eagerly.

"How do you want to hurt me? I want you to tell me all the things you'd do to me — in detail," he said.

I leaned forward and smiled.

"First I'd strip you naked then I'd blindfold you."

"Go on."

"Then I'd make you lie on your stomach and I'd tie you, spread-eagle to the bed."

"Tie me to the bed . . . with your panties," he said closing his eyes.

"That's right, baby, with my panties. Then I would tell you that you've been very naughty, that you've left me no choice, but to give you a good spanking."

". . . a good hard spanking."

"Yes, a good hard spanking."

"And what will you use to spank me? What do you think this naughty boy deserves?"

"Hmm, I don't think a belt will do."

"No, not a belt . . . maybe a riding crop."

"No, not a riding crop, I'm thinking a warm stainless-steel spatula."

"Oh yes, Babe. That's it . . . a warm stainless-steel spatula. Until my bottom is red."

"Red as a beet, baby. And then I'd finish you off by diddling your bum with a pulsating dildo, until you came by the bucketful." At this point, he was moaning, "Yes, yes, oh yes. My wallet, oh yes." I found a condom in his wallet and the sex we had on the dining room floor was transcendental. Needless to say, he was in a much better mood after that. We lay naked, sweating and intertwined on the dining room floor like Deborah Kerr and Burt Lancaster on the beach in *From Here to Eternity*. For a moment, I actually thought I heard roaring ocean waves, breaking on the shore.

The Actor was humming a sweet melody in my ear. I didn't recognize it. He said it was *Lovesong* by The Cure. What a zealous romantic. He believed in the power of love and had been trying to convert me since the first moment we met. I realized that I trusted him more than I loved him. Maybe that should have been the other way round.

It's amazing how the throes of passion can make the floor seem as comfortable as a bed, however, once the love frenzy is over the floor is . . . the floor. We got up, and began to put our clothes on when I noticed there was no blood or cuts or anything on The Actor's chest, just the hair that had grown back. I was staring at his chest so intently, it was obvious what I was thinking. He didn't bother to button his shirt. He stood there trying to figure out whether he should tell me the truth, or divert my attention.

"OK, I got into a fight," he said, holding up his right hand so I could see the bruised knuckles, "Happy now?"

"Why would I be happy about that? Were you drunk?"

He looked down, took a deep breath, looked off into space for a moment. I braced myself, well aware of how his mood could change in a nanosecond.

"Fair question," he said, "that's a fair question and the answer is: no I wasn't drunk, because if I were drunk I would have killed the bastard."

"Context baby, context. Killed who?"

"That cunt my ex-wife is screwing, that's who. Gary or Larry something . . . throwing me out of a house I bought and paid for. I think I broke his nose."

"Jesus, honey. Don't you ever get tired of being in the tabloids? He could sue you, press charges."

The Actor poured us both a drink and led me into the living room. We sat down on the sofa.

"Damn, I wish we still had the flat screen, it'd be nice to cuddle up and watch a movie with you," he said.

"Pickles said the flat screen was trashed during a fight you had with Philippe."

"I think that's probably true, but I was drunk when that fight started, so I don't remember much."

"Oh God, what am I going to do with you?"

"Love me, never leave me, be my wife and let me worship you like a living goddess, for the rest of my days. I talked to Nick, by the way. He's willing to accept our offer, happy in fact. He's skint."

The Actor put his drink down got up abruptly, mumbling something about " . . . you'll like this just wait," and the next thing I knew Johnny Mathis was singing *Chances Are*. The Actor walked towards me with both arms outstretched.

"Dance with me? Come on."

"Take off the shirt first, please. I don't want Larry Gary's blood on me."

We danced like we were two love-drunk teenagers at a high school prom: eyes closed, hands wandering, our breaths heavy, our souls trembling. I could feel the texture of his bare back against my hands; the smell of sweat and whiskey on him was like a narcotic. I was completely consumed and subsumed. He was my drug of choice. I would have done anything he asked, anything.

The song was over, I opened my eyes and there was a man staring at us through the window. I screamed, "There's someone at the window." The Actor ran over, looked, then turned on the outdoor lights and went to the door.

"Don't open the door," I shouted, "he might still be out there."

"I didn't see anyone, Babe. Should I call the police?"

"No more publicity, please. He's probably long gone by now anyway."

"Are you sure you saw someone? He'd have to climb over the wall . . ."

"I saw someone."

The Actor wanted to know where Pickles was. I told him Pickles was probably with Mario and wouldn't be back anytime soon. We made sure all the windows and the back entrance were locked. We closed all the curtains. The Actor armed the alarm system and left the outdoor lights on. We retreated to his room, locked the door and proceeded to burn one. I remembered what I had forgotten earlier that day — the gun. Where had I put it? I was way too tired to even think about it. I was drifting towards sleep, when I heard The Actor say before he nodded off, "I don't give a toss if he does sue me, it was worth it."

Several hours later The Actor was shaking me awake. I was terrified, gasping for air. I had no idea what was happening.

"You're having a bad dream, Babe. Come on, wake up," The Actor said as he cradled me in his arms.

"I was so, so scared. I thought he was going to get me. It was dark, I couldn't see . . ."

"Why don't you tell me the dream," The Actor said softly, "that will take all its power away and it won't seem so scary."

I'm sure this is how he must have comforted his daughter on many a night. It made me feel like a big baby, but I was glad he was there to hold me and stroke my hair. This man never ceased to amaze me.

It took a moment until I was breathing normally, then I began: I was walking in the park across the street, the sky was overcast and then in a matter of seconds the sky had turned black. All I could see was the pathway in front of me, which was illuminated by some unseen light source. I kept walking as a fog started to roll in and the pathway turned to wet cobblestones. I could hear my every step reverberate against the stones. In the distance, a church bell started to chime.

I thought I heard something behind me. My heart was pounding with fear. I stopped, the echo of footfalls not my own stopped at almost the same time. I had to get out of there. I started to walk as fast as I could. The footsteps behind me picked up their pace as well. Then, totally terrified, I began to run. The footsteps were chasing me. Out of nowhere, I heard a witch's cackle and there besides me was The Actor's mum on a bicycle pedaling fiercely, "You stupid cow," she screamed and then like the witch in the *Wizard of Oz* pedaled off into the sky. I slipped and fell, sliding on the wet cobblestones. I was hurt and struggling to get up when I felt a hand clamp down on my shoulder. I was crying now, sure that this was the end of me, when I heard The Actor's voice say, "Let me help you up." I turned around shaking with fear, tears streaming down my face thankful to find that it was, indeed, The Actor helping me to my feet, telling me not to be afraid. I relaxed into his embrace, but I felt something lurking in the distance. I looked over his shoulder, and there down the path half in light, half in shadow was a tall man with eyes burning like a demon's staring at us, just staring. I started to scream. This is when

The Actor woke me up.

We slept an uneasy sleep wrapped in each other's arms. Even though he had put up a brave front I think my nightmare had scared The Actor as much as it had scared me.

CHAPTER 13

Fame gives you everything you never wanted.

— Ava Gardner

Men had a habit of trying to force their attentions on Ava Gardner. Is there any wonder? Just watch her in *The Killers* with Burt Lancaster. She doesn't have to do anything but breathe to be fabulous. She had a captivating sexual presence that was elemental, feral and unpredictable — just the kind of qualities that fascinate men, as well as fuel their desire to tame the woman who possesses those qualities. Ava would not be tamed.

According to Hollywood legend, Ava cold-cocked Howard Hughes with a candlestick holder and laid him out flat, because he wouldn't take "No" for an answer.

On another dicey occasion, with actor George C. Scott, Ava proved her mettle. The story goes old GCS, as Ava called him, could be a dangerous man when drunk. One night, when he was in his cups, he allegedly cornered her with a broken liquor bottle. Even though she was terrified, she sweet-talked the potential weapon out of his hand. Now, that's my kind of woman. Pity she didn't have a stun-gun.

Ava could dish it out as well as take it. When she threw a glass of champagne at an Australian reporter, by his own account, all he could think about while it was happening was Ava's beauty.

Ava could be difficult. Towards the end of her career, she reportedly became so problematic during the filming of one picture, that her character was prematurely killed off just so the director and producer wouldn't have to deal with Ava anymore.

Ava could be salty. Reportedly, her use of expletives was so extensive off-screen, listening to her would make a Marine drill sergeant cringe. I want to say that she was a free-spirit ahead of her time, but up to now there never has been a time for a woman who takes no shit, chooses to deal with the world on her own terms, is fucking unapologetic about it, and drop-dead gorgeous to boot.

It's a heartbreaking business trying to be your true self in this world. When you're a woman it not only breaks your heart, it can break your spirit beyond repair. Maybe, that's why Ava Gardner sought solace in the bottle. I'm not judging.

Ava was a better actress than she ever gave herself credit for. Weigh her nuanced performance against Susan Hayward's hand-wringing in *The Snows of Kilimanjaro*. Getting past her beauty was even hard for Ava Gardner to do.

Sometimes the gods give people gifts that they are not emotionally equipped to handle. The gods don't punish these people, they just allow them to punish themselves.

I had a lunch date with Maida that afternoon. I was looking forward to it. I could tell The Actor was a little apprehensive about his two favorite ladies harmonically converging. He was convinced the only reason we were getting together was to dish about him, the self-centered bastard. OK, so he was right, but I wasn't going to let him know that.

"Women all over the world talk about me . . . probably not a second goes by without my being the topic of some woman's conversation somewhere on Earth. Why should you and Maida be any different?" The Actor laughed.

He sat on the edge of the bed, fully dressed, wiggling his feet into some flip-flops. I was still in bed feeling like I wanted to stay there.

"Oh, why limit it to Earth women. What about Alpha Centauri?" He leaned over and began to tickle me.

"Are you jealous? You know, I've got quite a thing for those Alpha Centauri chicks."

He was in such a good mood I was sure there had to be illegal drugs involved, but his pupils weren't dilated and he didn't seem to be artificially hyped in anyway. It had to be me.

"Are you feeling like a loved man today? Is that why you're in such a good mood?"

"Yes, that and the fact that now I know you'll hurt me if I need hurting, in a way that can make me feel... You get me, Babe. I like it that you get me."

"Well, let's not delve too deeply or we'll only end up freaking each other out."

Though I knew his need to be hurt was a profound one, I couldn't help feeling that my bad dream had given him the opportunity to comfort me, and that he had enjoyed that more than any old whipping I could have given him with a riding crop or a warm spatula.

The Actor had gotten up early to let the cleaners in. By the time they'd finished, Pickles had returned. He was downstairs making coffee. The Actor said he and Pickles were going to walk around outside to see if they could find evidence from the intruder the night before.

I got up and headed for the bathroom, I could hear The Actor say as he left the room, "Time I sold this bloody house, anyway."

I must have slept through the damn cleaners, because the bathroom was spotless. When I returned to the bedroom, I noticed the rugs had been seen to, and all surfaces had been dusted. After I showered, I went into Philippe's old room because all of my belongings were in there. I still hadn't really unpacked; half of my clothes were in suitcases the other half strewn across the bed, but the clothes on the bed were now in neat piles. The curtains had been drawn back. There was no sun pouring in; the sky was overcast. Rain was just beginning to come down in a fairly steady stream. I watched the rain fall on the empty park across the street, when through the rain I saw something slowly rise from behind a slope to the left, a black billowy thing that turned out to be a huge umbrella. Holding the umbrella was a tall man wearing a black fedora and a long black raincoat. He stopped when he reached the crest of the rise. He stood there staring in my direction, just as the man with the demon eyes had stared in my nightmare.

I threw some clothes on and ran downstairs. The Actor and Pickles, wet from the rain, were playing around in the kitchen, trying to dry each other with dishtowels. They didn't notice me as I stood in the doorway. They finally caught sight of me.

"Sugar, you look like you just saw a ghost," Pickles said.

The Actor walked over to me slowly with a puzzled look on his face.

"What is it? What's happened?"

"He's out there in the rain, in the park, the evil man from my dream."

"What's she talking about?" Pickles asked.

"Babe had a nightmare last night, about a man chasing her at night in the park. You're trembling. Pickles get us some brandy, please."

The Actor led me into the living room and sat me down on the sofa. I felt dazed, as if I weren't really awake. Pickles came in with three glasses and a bottle of cognac.

"We did find footprints outside beneath the window. They started at the foot of the wall, near the gate," The Actor said as Pickles filled our glasses.

"They're probably all washed away by now," Pickles said as he slugged one down.

"I'm going upstairs to take a look," The Actor said, setting his glass down. Pickles poured another one and eyed me suspiciously.

"You're not cracking up on me are you, sugar?"

"No, I am not Raymond. Listen, we have to make some time to talk. I hardly see you anymore."

"Well, we've both been otherwise engaged. Mario wanted to go on a day trip to Paris this afternoon, but I don't know about this weather."

"Pickles, screw Paris. I need you here."

"I didn't see anyone," The Actor said as he descended the stairs, "but that doesn't mean he wasn't there."

"It's the vultures from the Press. I'll bet you a nickel," Pickles said.

"I guess you're right," I said, but I really didn't believe it.

Neither did The Actor, from the look on his face. What had he really seen from the front bedroom window, I wondered? The boys made a light meal of bacon, toast, sliced tomatoes, and fresh coffee which we consumed in silence. The rain stopped, and an eerie stillness pervaded, thrusting everything into a state of apprehension. When the phone rang, we practically jumped out of our skins.

"I don't want to answer that," The Actor said.

Pickles got up and strode over to the phone, with booze-inspired confidence.

"Yeah, I remember you. How'd you get this number? Really. You're shitting me. Uh-huh. All right, I'll tell him. I know it's important. OK. Well thanks, honey."

"What was that all about?" The Actor asked.

"You remember that kid who crashed the dinner party, posing as catering staff?"

"Paul," I said, "the wannabe journalist."

"What did he want?" The Actor asked.

"He wanted me to tell you not to use your phones, the house phone or your cell phone, and to delete all of your messages, because the tabloids are hacking people's phones, especially their texts and voicemail . . ."

"There must be some kind of law . . . " I said.

"Bunch a bollocks. They can't do that, can they?"

"Apparently, they can," Pickles went on, "the kid kept saying that it was important . . . that you and everybody you know could be hacked."

"Better get the word out then," The Actor sighed.

"The kid said there's a list, that it'll all be public knowledge soon."

"Why's this kid doing this?" I asked. "What do you think his angle is?"

"Maybe he's a decent bloke, who found out he doesn't want to roll around in the gutter just to make a living," The Actor said.

How we were going to operate phone-less was a challenge. Then there was email, Pickles reminded us. We couldn't take any chances. Mario, Mark Fragile, JD DeLongo, Sergei and The Actor's ex-wife, publicist, and business manager were called before the house phone was unplugged, and our mobile phones turned off, their SMS Cards removed. I would alert Maida since I was going over to her place later.

We devised a plan to use Mario's mini-cabdrivers to deliver hand-written messages to and from whomever we needed to contact. The Actor speculated that the phone hacking thing was how the Press knew his mum had spent the night in the nick. This also meant I was incommunicado, for the time being, with my family back in the States.

THE ACTOR

Our lives would be totally disrupted, indefinitely. Food delivery, pick-ups, ordering out and most crucially liquor deliveries would be affected. The three of us agreed. It was imperative we sort out the liquor delivery, posthaste, because supplies were running dangerously low.

It was exasperating and exhilarating, all at the same time. We were under siege; therefore, we had to hunker down together, fill the moats, lift the drawbridge and man the battlements, but first we had to burn one and listen to some Bob Marley to chill out. Afterwards, I prepared to go to Maida's.

The Actor, Pickles and Mario huddled together devising some new strategy to deal with the hacker situation, at least that's what I supposed they were doing, the day trip having been called on account of the weather. But the boys seemed vague when I asked them if it was raining in Paris.

Maida lived down one block and around the corner. It was only one o'clock in the afternoon, but it looked like dusk outside. The rain hadn't really stopped; it was merely misting, so that you didn't really notice it until you were out in it.

The street and the park were empty. I looked behind me. No one. As I walked farther on, I could have sworn I heard footsteps that were not my own.

I knocked on Maida's door and was greeted by a short, plump, youthful woman with a Russian accent. She guided me through the immaculate Victorian townhouse, from the subdued entrance with its whisper of yellow damask wallpaper, to the truly English library, with its deep red wallpaper and red and white vintage floral chintz upholstery.

Roses, of varying hues, exploded as centerpieces, from huge ceramic bowls placed strategically throughout the house. Care and attention to detail made themselves known everywhere I looked, giving the house a distinct museum-like quality. It reminded me of the controlled hysteria of my childhood home.

The library was connected to a glass enclosed conservatory, a study in gleaming white, where under a peaked roof, straight-backed chairs with plump chartreuse cushions surrounded a huge round table with a glass top, under which was a billowy chartreuse and brown, paisley print tablecloth, starched so hard it looked as though it had been chiseled from marble.

Maida was standing in the conservatory with her back to me, arms folded, staring out the window shaking her head in disapproval. She turned when the Russian maid announced me, looking a little rumpled, in her blue-grey smocked-bodice cotton shirt dress. Her white leather slides, with their little cork wedge heels, click-clacked as she walked towards me.

"I wish I could do something about this weather," she said as she hugged me, "I was hoping we could lunch out here, but it's so dreary . . . Let's eat in the library, shall we?"

Sir Freddie, Maida's husband, would have joined us, but he was having a bad day. It was decided that he should remain in bed where he was engaged in a game of gin with his nurse, Russell. After lunch, we would go up and see how Freddie was doing.

Maida had staff, which I loved. Eugenia, who answered the door, was the maid. She split the housekeeping duties with the cook, Keiko, while Russell was Sir Freddie's live-in nurse.

We sat down on the fat library sofa, with our double gin and tonics. I confided in Maida how much I'd missed having a household staff, but when Gordon died it just seemed pointless. Then, I got married to crazy Nick "Ravioli." His only staff before we married was a personal assistant whose main gig was scoring drugs.

I explained how I tried to use my former housekeeper and her gardener husband, but the rock star atmosphere was too scary for them, after the sedate environs of the home I had made with Gordon. Graciela, my faithful housekeeper of ten years, told me her family thought she had become a drug addict, because her clothes reeked of marijuana. After a conversation with her son, she was adamant. She did not want "contact with the pot." It took me a while to figure out she meant she didn't want to get a contact high from pot smoke. I admitted that I was somewhat guilty in the pot smoking department. Before Nick, I had only been in the minor leagues as an herb smoker. However, during and after life with the rock idol,

I had become an MVP in the majors.

Gordon and I, we'd been pretty conventional. We just got quietly drunk as the day wore on, and passed out. We didn't whip out the Stratocasters, plug in the Marshall amps and start cranking out heavy metal anthems. My anecdote amused Maida to no end. Over lunch, she suggested I write an autobiography. She said she had a publisher in mind.

"Are you wooing me, Maida? You must know that I don't have an agent right now."

"And just suppose I am wooing you? You could do a lot worse." "It wouldn't harm your boy, either, especially if the book ended with how we met and married."

"It would do him no harm at all."

"You little, vixen. Honey, I've got to hand it to you, I didn't even see the wheels turning."

"I'm not a woman who's given to spontaneity, as you may have guessed. I've discussed the possibility with your future husband, and he was all for it, providing you're all for it."

"What the hell else have I got to do, besides run the institute for the care, feeding and study of my future husband?"

"Oh, goodie. Well, there are contracts to be drawn up and so forth, all the boring details, which we can save for later. For right now, in all seriousness, I want to thank you for taking such good care of him."

There were tears in Maida's eyes. Despite her unrelenting quest for the next deal, Maida actually cared about The Actor. I was profoundly touched by this. Then, I thought of Pickles and Mario and Sergei, who also genuinely cared about The Actor. Then, I thought about Philippe. I told Maida it was easy to take care of someone you loved. After she had gotten up and closed the library door, she began to talk about Sir Freddie. Maida spoke in a very quiet voice, about Sir Freddie's prodigious gambling habit and his foolish extravagances, all of which had decimated his inheritance and the profit from the sale of his business several years ago. Unfortunately for Maida, good old Sir Freddie still thought he was in the chips, and behaved accordingly, albeit in a somewhat limited fashion, because of his multiple sclerosis.

It was Maida who had kept the ship afloat on choppy seas, as her husband's gambling debts mounted and his health declined.

I commiserated by referencing my experience with Gordon in his waning years. What we women go through . . .

"I think this calls for another round," I said.

Maida agreed with me.

"Any new developments in the Philippe saga?" Maida asked, as she poured gin into fresh glasses.

"I guess you know about the police visiting. They're probably going to ask The Actor to come in for questioning."

"Because, he was the last one to see Philippe before Philippe disappeared..."

"That's right. I can't seem to get a handle on this Philippe dude."

"Join the queue. At first, he seemed harmless. We were all grateful for his presence. You see, in the absence of someone to love and torment, The Actor is, well, let's say he can be a vicious sod, bordering on mental, quite scary in fact."

"I've noticed. Why hasn't anyone suggested medication, I mean based on his mother's history?"

"To his credit he did try medication to control his mood swings, but his acting suffered, or at least he felt it did, and that was that."

"Well, how much do you know about Philippe? Where are his people? What did he do before?"

"Babe, that's just the point. No one knows. Believe me, I had him checked out and there's nothing, nothing. It's as if he just emerged from the ether, and strolled into The Actor's life..."

"Out of nowhere..." I said.

"Exactly, but not exactly. Philippe had attached himself to The Actor's mum. I believe Philippe targeted her, using her as a way to get to The Actor. It was planned, and the plan worked."

Maida went on to describe how Philippe and The Actor had become inseparable; their rough sex the stuff of legend. As much as Philippe loved The Actor he resented him, relished his hold over him, and used it to advantage. The Actor, for his part, was no pushover, and gave as good as he got. The one thing Philippe had not factored in was The Actor's wild mood swings and drunken blackouts, which could lead to Philippe's public humiliation at the hands of The Actor, as well as dangerous moments where Philippe's life was thrust into real jeopardy.

"You know, being in love with an actor is always a love triangle where you are both in love with him, and I don't think Philippe was ever able to accept that," Maida said.

And I did, was the inference. Truth be told, it was our mutual narcissism, The Actor's and mine, that bound us to ourselves and each other. Being with him was like living in a house full of mirrors, where we could admire ourselves and each other unobstructed and uninterrupted, ad nauseam. Of course, we were both unselfconscious about this, because we were basically shallow people and proud of it.

Maida went on.

"I think Philippe also made the mistake of thinking The Actor is somehow confused about his sexuality. Well, my dear he's not confused, he's just ambivalent. He's ambivalent about most things in his life. Most people, including Philippe, put it down to The Actor simply not caring about anything or anyone. My theory is that the ambivalence comes from him caring too much. That, and the fact that he thinks he's sold his soul to the Devil."

"Define Devil. I like what W. C. Fields said, 'Show me a great actress, and you've seen the Devil.'"

We agreed that truer words were never spoken. The rain finally subsided. The sun was struggling valiantly through the clouds. Once we finished our lunch, Maida suggested we move into the conservatory for coffee, which we did. I had learned a lot from our conversation, but not nearly enough.

"Tell me straight up, Maida, do you think Philippe's become the victim of some sort of foul play?"

"Has he come to harm? I think it's quite possible, don't you? But, what you really want to know is whether I think The Actor has anything to do with it. My answer is yes and no. The Actor. . . Well, I just adore his Ashley Wilkes routine, where he's always the victim of other people's desires, when ultimately everyone ends up becoming the victim of his. We all love him, don't we? Despite everything there is something so lovable and loving about him . . . like a child . . . almost." We drank our coffee, topping off our cups with some Jack Daniel's Maida had produced. The sun streaming in through the conservatory caressed us and conspired with the booze to create a relaxed mood conducive to unburdening oneself of secrets.

"I met him when he was fresh out of RADA, slowly starting to make a name for himself in the theatre," Maida continued.

"He used to come over here almost every day, play cards with Freddie, watch telly with us, take the dogs for a walk. He even played with Charlie, our son, when he was little. This was before The Actor was married. Even when he had the flat with Mario and

Pickles, he'd still come over to spend the night. He never could sleep. I remember more than once he'd just appear in the doorway of our bedroom, like Charlie, and ask could he get into bed with Freddie and me, nothing kinky, but just as a child would ask when they're afraid. He's always been brilliant and he's always been odd, and yes there have been times when I've been afraid of him. Even though you are a tough cookie, Babe, don't be afraid to jump ship, if you have to."

Maida informed me that The Actor's ex-wife had called Maida about the punch up The Actor had had with Larry/Gary what's-his-name. I assured her that Larry/Gary had gotten the worst of it. Maida wanted me to assure The Actor that his ex-wife had dissuaded her boyfriend from taking legal action, for the daughter's sake, thereby obviating any onslaught by the media.

I was tired and I was curious about what the boys were up to. Maida said I couldn't leave without saying good-bye to Sir Freddie. As we trudged up the narrow staircase to the second floor, I could hear dogs barking. There, at the top of the stairs, were two identical Welsh Corgis, the most willful breed of dog that ever drew breath.

When I was a child, we had a Welsh Corgi we called Digby. He was strong as an ox. You never walked Digby; he walked you. These two little demented darlings, Honey and Rose, were so happy to see Maida they were beside themselves, jumping and falling on their backs, so Maida could tickle their tummies. Maida said, "They need a good run."

We turned to the left and there, resplendent in a red brocade smoking jacket, sat Sir Freddie Thorne propped up by a sea of pillows, in a comfy four-poster Queen Anne bed. By his side sat Russell, the live-in nurse, who reminded me of David Hasselhoff from his Mitch Buchannon days on Baywatch. Maida introduced us and I thought I heard a trace of an accent. I was not mistaken. Russell said he was from Holland.

Sir Freddie was considerably older than Maida, who was no spring chicken. Although his white hair was thinning and he was probably a shadow of who he once was physically, it was quite apparent that he had been, and still was, in a way, a hunk. He extended both hands to me and smiled broadly.

"Give us a kiss you sexy thing," he gushed, "Oh, I've been dying to meet you."

Russell got up and stepped back, as I leaned in to give Sir Freddie a hug. Apparently, his MS had no effect on his hands, which seemed to roam nimbly, at will, all over my body. I felt as though I'd had a Swedish massage, when I finally extricated myself from him.

Maida and Russell had positioned themselves at the foot of the bed where Russell was blatantly rubbing his hand up and down the back of Maida's thigh. Was this why she looked kind of rumpled when I first arrived?

Sir Freddie's eyes darted from his wife's thigh to her face, then to Russell's face, and back to Russell's hand on Maida's thigh. Then, Sir Freddie looked at me with eyes twinkling and said, "I like to watch."

On that note I said my farewell and promised to return at some unspecified time in the future.

Maida said she'd walk me back around to The Actor's house, because she wanted to take Honey and Rose for a run in the park. As we were leaving, I told her that someone had been watching The Actor and me; that I had distinctly felt as though someone were following me.

"Could be the Press," Maida said, "they're always lurking about." I then told Maida about the phone hacking tip we'd gotten. She stopped and looked at me very thoughtfully for a moment, as the dogs smelled the pavement eagerly.

"That would explain a lot of things," she said pursing her lips.

When we finally reached The Actor's gate, Maida kissed me on the cheek and said, "You know, JD has changed since his wife died. Now, there's a man I'd watch out for, if I were you."

CHAPTER 14

I'm still in the shell, and you haven't cracked it yet, honey.

— **Dirk Bogarde to Russell Harty, during a 1986 interview**

Dirk Bogarde saw himself not as a matinee idol or a sex symbol, but as a character actor who "got diverted." He described, with utter disgust, how mobs of teeny-boppers would attack him, and attempt to tear the fly off his pants.

He was a man who was very specific about keeping his private life totally separate from his public life, despite the fact that, especially in the 1950s and early 1960s, he was Britain's biggest star, as well as a big hit with American audiences, making him arguably Britain's first international movie star.

There is so much mythology surrounding Dirk Bogarde, some of his own making. Ava Gardner reportedly stated that once when he'd gotten drunk, and subsequently fallen down the stairs, he told the Press that he'd had a stroke.

During the same year that Bogarde made *I Could Go on Singing* (Judy Garland's last movie), he made what would become a cinema classic, with director Joseph Losey: *The Servant*, adapted for the screen from Robin Maugham's novella, by the great Harold Pinter. This is not an easy movie to watch, because it's so brittle, so raw.

Dirk Bogarde as Barrett, the titular character, is sardonic, insolent, bitchy, slovenly and devious. His manner towards his employer quickly devolves from servile to mocking and demeaning. In the end, Barrett subsumes his employer's life, rearranges it to his own design, so that the roles of servant and master become completely reversed.

THE ACTOR

My favorite scene, among many favorites, is when Tony (James Fox), the upper-class employer, barges into Barrett's room demanding to know about the "tea dregs on the carpet." This argument is rife with homo-eroticism, the possibility of sex and violence, as well as all the things that the upper and lower classes hate and envy about each other. This "tea dregs" scene is like *Who's Afraid of Virginia Woolf* with James Fox as George and Dirk Bogarde as Martha.

Dirk Bogarde's real-life relationship with his live-in lover, Tony Forwood, by all accounts, was not volatile or depraved as the relationship between Barrett and Tony in *The Servant*, but it was an employer/master, employee/servant relationship, because Tony Forwood was Dirk Bogarde's manager.

Tony Forwood has been described as likeable, funny, and always deferring to Bogarde in a subservient way; however, unlike Barrett, Tony Forwood apparently enjoyed his role.

He and Dirk Bogarde were also described as being mutually dependent upon one another. They were together for forty years, until Forwood's death in 1988.

Although Dirk Bogarde never came out of the closet in a way that might have satisfied some gay activists, if you look at his films he was coming out all the time: as the married, homosexual attorney Melville Farr in the groundbreaking 1961 film *The Victim*, which was released six years before homosexuality was decriminalized in the UK, and in the repressed Gustav von Aschenbach in Visconti's 1971 film adaptation of Thomas Mann's *Death in Venice*.

Dirk Bogarde was not a stupid man. He knew what he was doing when he refused to come out; he just lived his life. I'd like to think he felt he didn't have to give love a label or people the satisfaction.

As I opened the gate and locked it behind me, I realized I wasn't ready to go in just yet. Maybe I should have accompanied Maida on her walk with the mad Corgis, but I just wanted to be on my own and think about a few things. I walked around the side of the house to the little garden and sat down on a ledge near the rose bush.

I have to be honest, at first when I met Maida, even though I liked her, I thought she was Deborah Kerr on crack. My respect for her had grown immensely through the time we had just spent together. I can only imagine what it must have been to deal with Sir Freddie Thorne before he was impaired by a degenerative disease. Maida had got me thinking with her talk about The Actor's ambivalent nature. Maybe that, too, had something to do with what clicked between The Actor and me: a deep ambivalence about being alive, not because we cared too little, but maybe like Maida had said, because we cared too much.

I had to laugh out loud at the thought of our suicide pact, because it was totally befitting two drama queens who could take or leave this life, purely on their own histrionic terms.

Then I thought of George Sanders and my mother. Maybe it was all about just being too bloody bored, bored and wearied by all the bullshit. Maybe, when things got to that level, it was either, "To be or not to be . . . " or "Who holds the Devil let him hold him well . . . " Hadn't we all sold our souls, in some form or another?

Pickles' mother had embroidered a quote from Ralph Waldo Emerson which Pickles had framed and hung on his living room wall: *To be yourself in a world that is constantly trying to make you something else is the greatest accomplishment.*

I heard the back door open, well technically it was the side door, and turned to find Pickles poking his head out, like a turtle afraid he's going to be soup.

"I thought I saw you walk by the window, when you didn't come in . . . Is everything all right, sugar?"

"I don't know, Raymond. I don't know."

"Well, you look like you could use a nice hot cup of tea, with some cognac in it."

Inside, we sat down at the dining room table with our tea. The Actor was at Mark Fragile's. There was some aggro that had erupted at the minicab business. Mario had gone to sort it out.

"So, how was your visit with Maida?" Pickles asked.

"I think she's fucking Sir Freddie's nurse."

"Male or female? On a scale of one to ten . . ."

"Male. I'd give him a definite nine. He looks like Mitch Buchannon."

"Mmmm, Hasselhoff the Baywatch years, I'd do him. If it were actually Hasselhoff . . . I'd say a ten. Did you meet Sir Freddie? He's a grabber, you know."

"If it were actually Hasselhoff I'd say a six and a half, and yes, I met Sir Freddie, and yes, he is quite a grabber. He likes to watch, too. He told me."

"Get out of Dodge. Maida just has all the fun. What about her and that young director, the one The Actor went to see, are they at it, you think?"

"Oh, yeah. I tell you I don't know how she finds the time. God, I hope The Actor's not fucking him, as well. Anyway, I might be signing with her for a deal to write my life story."

"No, the director's totally straight. Your life? My God, it'll be more volumes than Churchill's *History of the English People*. Let me help you. Wouldn't that just be a hoot, you and me collaborating?"

"*English-Speaking Peoples* and yes, Pickles, it really would be a hoot. Thank you. I believe I *could* do it if you helped me. I'm not being disingenuous, or full of shit or anything. I really mean it."

"Why, Babe, I'm touched."

"OK, enough sentimentality. What the hell were you boys up to while I was gone?"

"Ask me no questions, and I'll tell you no lies. Babe, I'm sworn to secrecy. Seriously, I believe Thespian would kill me if I spilled the beans."

"What beans? Come on, Raymond. Give."

"Please, Babe. Don't pressure me. You know I can't stand pressure. I'll crack like a walnut."

"So crack, already."

"This may seem very hard for you to believe, but I am a coward, and I am actually more afraid of The Actor than I am of you. It's a toss-up though, very close, a hair's breadth . . . but, on the scare the fucking be-Jesus meter, he's totally in the red, for me. Look, I'm sure he'll tell you . . . when he's ready, anyway . . ."

"Are you two talking about me behind my back again?" The Actor asked as he strolled into the dining room and threw his keys on the table.

"How do you do it? You just appear unseen and unheard . . . It's spooky," I said.

"Just like a Ninja," Pickles said in awe.

"Babe," The Actor said as he bent down and kissed my forehead, "a bit testy, aren't we? No 'Hello, how's my man?' I knew the stimulation of all that estrogen being churned up between you and Maida would lead to no good."

"You're in a funny mood," I said.

"I could say the same about you," The Actor retorted.

"Isn't this the part where Bette Davis sashays in with, 'Fasten your seat belts?'" Pickles chimed in.

"Would you like a cup of tea, honey? You Pickles?"

The Actor sat down and started to laugh.

"You're going to make tea for me and Raymond? Well, I have to say, Babe, it's finally happened. I do believe there is a God."

With that remark, The Actor leaned over and kissed me properly with a great deal of passion, then sat back in his chair with a self-satisfied look. "I missed you," he said. "Think you're so smart." I said.

I demonstrated that I could boil water, with proficiency. The Earth did not reverse polarity, the stars did not fall from the heavens, nor did lightning strike the Queen. I even made sandwiches and threw a few chocolate biscuits on a plate. The Actor and Pickles enjoyed their tea, especially since the actual beverage itself was mostly cognac.

The Actor was regaling us with stories of Sir Freddie's pre-MS exploits when the doorbell rang followed, by a loud deliberate pounding that could only mean the police. Thank God, we hadn't burned one.

As a consequence of having the Press camped on the doorstep in the not so distant past, and the presence of the unknown Peeping Tom, the front gate and the sentry door, adjacent to the gate that led onto the property, were now both locked. The gate could be electronically opened from the house and The Actor made that happen, allowing the police to enter.

Detective Sergeant Gerald Crawford and WPC Greenway, one of the police officers who had responded the night The Actor's mum broke in, were very apologetic. DS Crawford actually wiped his feet on the outdoor mat, a sign of his age and proper home training.

The Actor showed them to the sofa, as he sat down at the piano, while Pickles and I took up positions in the two comfy chairs off to the side. There was a rug, a coffee table and a gulf of suspicion, between us and the cops. There was also a pretty important thought sneaking up from the back of my brain. Just as Detective Sergeant Crawford sat down, I remembered where I had hidden the Webley service revolver.

"Hate to bother you like this, Sir," Crawford began, "just following up on the disappearance of your. . . of Mr. Noiret. Philippe Noiret. What exactly is the nature of your relationship with him?"

"Would you two like some tea, or coffee or anything," Pickles blurted out.

They didn't want any. The Actor shot Pickles a look. I wondered just how thick that sofa cushion was.

"I've been Philippe's employer for three years. He's my personal assistant. He runs the house, schedules my appointments, handles my correspondence, that kind of thing."

Greenway was frantically scribbling away on a notepad. Crawford edged forward in his seat. I looked up and Crawford and Greenway were looking at me. I guess they thought I'd been staring at Crawford's crotch, but it was the sofa cushion, the one with the gun stuck under it, that had my attention. I grinned nervously and pretended something was in my eye.

"I understand Mr. Noiret lives here with you."

"Yes, he does, well . . . he did until he went missing. See here, I'm not sure what you're getting at," The Actor said.

"Not sure I'm getting at anything, Sir. I do apologize, but I may have to ask you some questions that may make us both uncomfortable, but I have to ask them nonetheless. Do you and Mr. Noiret have an intimate relationship?"

"What do you mean by intimate?"

"I think you know what I mean. OK. Let's just assume, for the sake of argument, that you and Mr. Noiret enjoy a relationship that goes beyond employer/employee. Would it be safe to say, that you and he might have arguments of a more personal nature . . . arguments that might set him off?"

"That's possible, yeah."

"And do you think, if Mr. Noiret was in an emotional state, he might run off, harm himself?"

"It's possible, especially if he's been drinking."

"Heavy drinker, is he? Does he have any mental or emotional problems you're aware of?"

"Look, I was asked these questions before, by the two officers who came here to do the risk assessment. I don't understand why we're going over this ground again. Don't you have any leads? I mean, he could be lying in a ditch somewhere for all we know!"

"Does Mr. Noiret use drugs? Is he on any type of medication that you know of?"

"We probably drink more than what's good for us. On occasion, and I'm telling you this in confidence, we'd smoke some marijuana just to unwind. Philippe doesn't have a drug problem. He's healthy as an ox . . . he's high-strung, but he's not . . . mental or anything."

I had to suppress a smile, because it was starting. I could just about tell, when he was doing it and he was starting to do it. He was acting. Pickles was getting fidgety and giving me telegraph eyes. I gave him my best please-pull-your-punk-ass-together look, at which point he leapt up like his butt was on fire and said, "Sorry. Have to spend a penny," and darted out of the room.

DS Crawford and Constable Greenway exchanged amused glances, were silent for a moment, then Crawford continued.

"Is there any reason Mr. Noiret . . ."

"Mr. Noiret... Can you just call him Philippe, please so I know who you're talking about?" The Actor pleaded.

"Is there any reason Philippe might want to disappear? Was he in debt?"

"I would have paid off his debts. I *have* paid off his debts. No, I don't know of any reason Philippe would just want to get lost. What do you really think has happened to him?"

"We don't know. That's why we're here. It's been over a month since Mister . . . since Philippe has gone missing. We're getting pressurized by the media about his disappearance, as you can well imagine. Since he's not made any contact with you, and no one has contacted you about ransom money. No one has contacted you about a ransom, have they?"

The Actor's face drained of all color, his eyes filled with tears. I wasn't sure what was going on, but dammit it was time for a drink. "You look like you could use a drink, sweetie" I said to The Actor as I rose. "I know you all are on duty, but just a little one?" Crawford and Greenway didn't reply. I returned with drinks for the civilians. Pickles had returned from the lavatory looking as if he had just puked up his guts. He was grateful for the alcohol.

Crawford looked like a man who appreciated a good single malt

Scotch, so I gave him mine. He didn't refuse. I asked Greenway if she wouldn't mind a cup of tea, and she said she was gasping, which translated meant she could really use a cup.

I was prepared to boil the water, but Pickles volunteered. I followed him and poured myself another drink. Pickles grabbed my drinking arm, splashing Scotch over both of us.

"Babe, I'm shaking like a leaf. This is nerve wracking. Don't you find this nerve wracking? I thought I was going to do number two right in my pants. Lord Jesus."

I topped up both our glasses. "Just go make the tea and keep drinking that Scotch."

When I returned to the living room the mood had changed. Detective Sergeant Crawford was sprawled comfortably on the sofa, devoid of all formality discussing one of The Actor's movies with him. For a moment, I could have sworn Crawford was flirting with Thespian. Officer Greenway, pen and pad on her lap, her hands folded on top, stared dreamily at The Actor as he duologued with Crawford.

"So, you did that stunt yourself then did you?"

"Yes, I did. Not one of my better decisions, could have broken my bloody neck, but don't you think, as the audience, it's so much better…"

"Oh yes, yes." gushed dewy-eyed Officer Greenway, completely breaking character as the efficient police constable.

"Thought about being a stunt-man once, way back when my tour of duty in The Corps was up," Crawford said.

"You were in the Royal Marines?" The Actor asked.

Pickles served Greenway her tea as the two men continued the testosterone fest.

"Aye, saw combat in the Falklands and Iraq," Crawford answered.

The Actor leaned forward eagerly, "Did you see 'Commando Brigade'? What did you think, I mean as far as the authenticity?"

"I thought your character was spot-on. The action sequences were bloody well done, quite believable, in fact."

"Cheers. I was well pleased, I don't mind saying. Now, with the last two films, and the new project, well . . . I've become an action hero, haven't I? It's frustrating, because that's all people will expect of me now."

"But that's more than enough, I think," gushed Officer Greenway.

Pickles and I just sat back and shook our heads as we emptied our glasses. I couldn't wait for these two boobs to leave. Crawford sensed that things had gotten off-track and he attempted to refocus. He put his glass down on the coffee table, the effect being like a period at the end of a sentence.

As he scooched forward on the sofa, my heart sank. I thought for sure the gun would tumble out this time, but it didn't. Crawford pulled his squat, muscular body up from the sofa, which caused WPC Greenway to snap to attention, note pad and pen at the ready. "Well, I think it'd be a good idea if we could see the missing man's room, then if it's all right with you, sir, the rest of the house." I looked at The Actor and then at Pickles and back at The Actor.

Why was I the only one who seemed panic stricken? My heart was pounding so hard I thought everyone in the room could hear it. Just when I was starting to feel OK about the hidden gun, the police were going to find all of my things in Philippe's room . . . and the basement. I mean cellar. Oh, God, the cellar.

CHAPTER 15

Did I behave like a pink powder puff or like a man?

— Rudolph Valentino's first words, after surviving surgery

Shortly before his death from peritonitis, resulting from emergency abdominal surgery, the great silent film hunk Rudolph Valentino, was the subject of ridicule by the *Chicago Tribune* newspaper, which featured an editorial on Valentino's so-called feminization of the American male entitled: *Pink Powder Puffs*.

Valentino was so enraged that he challenged the unknown author of the editorial to a boxing match. That match never took place, because Valentino collapsed not long after, throwing down the gauntlet, and was hospitalized.

I know I'm jumping past my areas of expertise into silent film, but Rudolph Valentino continues to be maligned and called out of his name well past his initial era of interest, and it bugs me. It bugs me that he gave so much to cinema, to his audiences, and all history has to give him is an erroneous reputation.

On screen, where he needed no words, he had the ability to project not just the promise of the best sex any human could imagine, but something mystical, something transcendental, even something supernatural. When he died in 1926, legend has it, women all over the world committed suicide; however, that is just one of the many legends, most of them unpleasant, that have dogged his memory.

He was born in 1895 in the southeastern tip of Italy and given the name Rodolfo Alfonso Raffaello Pierre Filibert Guglielmi di Valentina D'Antonguolla. I know.

Spoiled by his mother, he never learned how to manage his

money. His estate, when he died, was in debt to the tune of $300,000. By all legitimate accounts he was a kind, sweet, gentle man, although maybe not too bright. He never learned how to manage women either.

His first wife, actress Jean Acker (born Harriet Acker) was a lesbian, and about as out as you could be in Hollywood in those days. Valentino fell head over heels for her. She married him to get out of a sticky situation. They remained friends until Valentino's death. His love letters to her (many still extant) reveal that he was clueless. He thought she wouldn't have sex with him because of some personal flaw he possessed. His heart was broken. He thought Jean wasn't into him, and of course she wasn't, but not for the reasons he thought.

If the sexual habits of a lifetime are any proof, Rudolph Valentino was not gay. The fact that he married a lesbian, and had many gay friends is just a tribute to his expansive nature or his thickness — or probably both.

Enter set and costume designer, and all-around wild woman, Natacha Rambova (born Winifred Shaughnessy), the second wife of Valentino, whom he married while still married to Jean Acker.

Rambova was a bossy chick, probably what we'd call a feminist, but not a lesbian. She ran Valentino's life with an iron fist, and he apparently loved every moment of it. He loved her so much he never stopped pleading with her to return to him once they had split up. He was so distraught he tried to commit suicide. Their relationship had been extremely passionate and volatile. Rambova was quoted as saying that the sex was incredible, and that Valentino looked his best naked.

Rudolph Valentino did not give silent film star Ramon Navarro a black Art Deco dildo, as has been reported in books and magazine articles.

Ramon Navarro, born José Ramón Gil Samaniego, *was* gay, but he said in an interview that he had only met Rudolph Valentino once, briefly. Navarro swiftly rose to stardom after Valentino's death, because there was a huge void to fill left by an actor Hollywood had once pronounced too ethnic to be a leading man.

At a point when his brilliant silent film career was all but forgotten, Navarro was brutally murdered by two hustlers he had hired for sex. Legend has it that the murderers stuffed the Valentino dildo down his throat.

Crime scene reports from LAPD showed no such item found on the scene, but this non-existent dildo has linked Valentino and Navarro together in some perverted version of gay celebrity history, for all time. I wondered what rumors about The Actor and Philippe would transmogrify into legends, that would outlive them both.

I tried to move, I really did, but I was paralyzed with fear. The Actor was preoccupied as tour guide to the cops, merrily leading them into circumstances that could only serve to incriminate him in Philippe's disappearance.

I was rubbing the back of my neck like it was Aladdin's lamp, hoping for a miracle or a genie to pop out of my head. "Pull yourself together, they'll think we're up to something," Pickles whispered, as he grabbed me by the hand and dragged me up the stairs. "Well, aren't we?" I whispered back.

As The Actor led the cops through his room into Philippe's room, I noticed The Actor's bed had been made, a first since I'd been sleeping in it. I was about to cross the threshold into Philippe's room, my room, the room, when I decided I just couldn't go in there. Pickles was behind me and he shoved me into the room so hard, I bumped into WPC Greenway.

I was about to say I was sorry, when I noticed men's toiletries in the bathroom. My clothes were gone, so was my luggage, not even my toothbrush remained. The Actor opened the armoire and it was filled with men's clothing. I looked at Pickles and he gave me the "just be cool" look. I was sweating like a hog, but I was cool.

DS Crawford asked The Actor if he had anything with Philippe's DNA on it, like a hairbrush or toothbrush. The Actor went into the bathroom and emerged with both. Greenway snapped on a pair of gloves and produced two large Ziploc baggies from somewhere in her uniform and bagged the toothbrush and hairbrush, respectively. I gave The Actor a "what's going on" look. He just smiled and grabbed my hand, squeezing so hard I thought I heard bone cracking. I had to stifle a whimper of agony, as The Actor pulled me close. I may have looked as if I was smiling, but I was actually grimacing with pain.

"Nothing like being in love, eh," DS Crawford chuckled.

"Nothing like it," I hissed between clenched teeth. "One thing I don't understand, sir, if you'll forgive me," Greenway asked, "why doesn't this room have a door?"

"Oh, it does," The Actor said. He then walked over to the wall, pressed a spot in the molding, and a door opened onto the hallway. "It can only be opened from the inside — used to be a library."

As we all marveled at the quaintness of old Victorian houses, The Actor continued, with his walk-in closet, his daughter's room, now occupied by Pickles, ending the tour of the second floor.

"Is there another floor?" Crawford asked, "These houses usually have another floor."

"Well, this one doesn't," The Actor said curtly. It did. I think DS Crawford knew that it did, but he didn't press the issue, to my surprise.

The Actor had eased his grip on my hand, after I indicated I'd gotten the message. We continued showing the cops around the house, traipsing through the downstairs study, back through the living room, through the dining room and on into the kitchen.

WPC Greenway examined the shed adjacent to the kitchen which was the laundry room and led through the side door to the garden. She and Crawford strolled along the perimeter of the house and back to the garden, looking for God knew what. They both returned to the kitchen, Greenway scribbling away on her note pad.

"Is that the door to the cellar, sir?" Crawford asked.

"Yes, it is," The Actor said, a little too calmly.

"Mind if we have a look?"

"In for a penny, in for a pound," The Actor said, under his breath. "I don't see why not, go ahead the door's open."

I don't know what it feels like to have a stroke, but I was sure I was in the beginning stages of one. The Actor kissed me on the cheek, opting to lead the way down the cellar stairs.

Seeing the state I was in, Pickles suddenly appeared beside me and said, "Just stay where you are, and I'll explain everything later."

"I don't know about you, but I need a drink." Pickles poured us both a couple of stiff ones. I had to use both hands to bring the glass to my lips, my hands were shaking so.

WPC Greenway was the first to emerge from the cellar, with yet another plastic baggie in her hand. She held it up to the light and examined its contents, which I could barely see.

THE ACTOR

"It's been there for ages," The Actor said, "I guess I stopped noticing it."

"I could see how you would. You don't remember anyone falling down the stairs or injuring themselves?" Crawford asked.

"No, no I don't. Like I said, I do remember dropping a bottle of wine, but that was a while ago." The Actor said.

Crawford turned to Pickles and me, "Do either one of you have any ideas about that stain at the foot of the cellar stairs?"

I was totally flummoxed. No mention of the clothes or the porno-type photos, only the stain. I started to laugh. Pickles' eyes got wide as saucers then he started laughing too, and with his best Southern drawl he said, "Honey, why on earth would we be going into this man's cellar?" There was a short round of nervous laughter, and then the cops were on their way to the front door, when it occurred to me . . .

"Excuse me, Detective Sergeant Crawford, there was a man prowling around outside the other night . . ."

"Yes, I didn't see him, but Pickles and I found his footprints outside; the rain washed them away," The Actor said.

I told Crawford I hadn't got a good look at the man.

"It was just a split second between when I saw his face in the window and when he ran off."

Crawford said it was probably the Press, but The Actor said he had gotten an injunction.

"They can jump out from behind a bush down the road, but they can't be within fifteen meters of the house." The Actor added triumphantly.

"Well, since we're having Q&A," Pickles said, "what do you know about the daily rags' phone hacking of celebrities?"

"Isolated cases. Limited to the Royal family, and a handful of others. We've got it well in hand. Nothing for you to worry about, sir," Crawford said to The Actor.

Crawford was half-way out the door when he turned around, and pulled The Actor aside, "Don't suppose there's any chance we can talk with your mum? She did file the report, you know."

Up until that question The Actor had conducted himself with the composure of a Zen master. I could tell he was just about to lose his shit, so I dropped my glass of Scotch and it broke, thank God. I made the expected female noises about "oh clumsy me" and "what a mess I've made" and my "butter fingers." Crawford warned me to mind the glass shards. Pickles ran to get clean-up equipment.

The Actor had the faintest trace of a smile on his lips, as he assured Crawford that we'd manage, and that he would check with his mum's doctor to see if and when she'd be fit for questioning. Crawford seemed satisfied, and to his credit left without asking for an autograph. I was sure Greenway already had one.

As the police exited, the front door seemed to close behind them very slowly, of its own accord, the sound of it slamming shut reverberating with a loud echo that filled the entire house. The reverberation gradually de-crescendoed until there was only the sound of our collective exhalation.

"God! Am I glad that's over," The Actor said as he plopped down on the sofa, on the very same spot where Crawford had been sitting. I just stared at him waiting for him to ask me what that lump in the sofa was, but he didn't. He just tilted his head to the side, in that way he does and asked me what was going on. "That's one hell of a sofa," I said.

"Well, now I have to spend a penny," The Actor said as he jumped to his feet, "Don't look so distressed, Babe," he said on his way to the toilet, "Everything's under control."

Pickles was tidying up, putting the liquor glasses on the tea tray, when he looked up at me,

"Whatever you feel you have to tell him don't tell him and whatever you feel you need to ask him don't ask him."

Of course, I wanted to spill my guts about the gun and I wanted to know about the cellar. If I asked The Actor about the cellar then he would know I'd been down there. I'd have a lot of s'plaining to do, and what about Philippe's room? And what the hell happened to my things? Pickles was right. I needed to keep my mouth shut. The state I was in, whatever I said would be all wrong. I just had to have patience, confidence that everything would be revealed to me, in its own time.

"Look what I found in the loo, in a box in the cabinet under the sink," The Actor said waiving a handful of joints as he entered the room. "Just think of me as Father Christmas, boys and girls."

Pickles was fluffing the cushions on the sofa like an idiot, but then he didn't know about the gun.

"Oh, thank you, Jesus. My nerves . . . I was just about to jump out of my skin. What's this?" Pickles had found the gun.

"What have you got there?" The Actor asked.

"Oh, it's nothing. I'll just go rustle us up some eats, I don't know about you but . . ."

"Raymond, show me what you have in your hand." "Babe, help."

I walked over to Pickles, and gently pried the gun from his trembling hand."

"It's a gun, baby. I found it in your linen closet."

The joints tumbled from The Actor's hand to the floor in what seemed like slow motion. He took a step back and held up both hands as if he were trying to stop traffic.

"It's not loaded," I said.

"You found a gun in my house?" The Actor whispered rhetorically. "What the fuck is a gun doing in my house?" he screamed.

"Keep your voice down," I said. "We were hoping you could answer that one."

"Yeah," Pickles said as he picked up the joints and threw all but one on the coffee table.

"I have no fucking idea. Maybe it's a prop, something I used in a film. Let's have a look at it."

"Are you going to light that joint or what, Pickles?" I said, as I handed The Actor the gun. I explained how it came to be under the sofa cushion, and how I had forgotten it was there.

"Well, it's real all right," The Actor said as he examined it, "but it's not mine. I've never owned a gun in my life. It must be Philippe's. It must be."

At this point, I was really hoping Philippe was dead otherwise I'd have to kill him. He had been nothing but trouble, and he wasn't even there or anywhere as far as anyone knew.

Pickles passed the joint around, plugged the phone back in and ordered some food from the Thai place. The three of us collapsed on the sofa exhausted, yet again, by the aftermath of Philippe's vanishing act. It was like a stain you just couldn't get out of the carpet.

I passed the joint to The Actor and asked, "What if he staged the whole thing?"

The Actor, shrouded in a haze of marijuana smoke, thought

about my question for a moment, then turned to Pickles. "What do you think, mate? You're the science-fiction writer."

Pickles began to giggle. "Come on, Thespian. Babe's got a point."

"And what point might that be? Oh, don't tell me. Philippe isn't really missing. It's all an elaborate wind-up to teach me a lesson."

"It's possible," I said.

"As the science fiction writer in the house, I say it's possible he was abducted by aliens. Just think of those anal probes," Pickles laughed.

"Why is no one willing to entertain my theory?"

"Because, for Philippe to do something like that, to me . . . " The Actor said as tears streamed down his face, "he'd have to hate me."

I felt sick with self-contempt. I had upset my baby, made him cry no less. I knew how he felt about Philippe. I knew he missed him, but I wanted Philippe to be the biggest contemptible asshole in the universe and I wanted The Actor to see him that way. However, it wasn't that simple; nothing ever is. Now, I had to apologize, kiss and make it better. Dammit! Pickles was right, I should have kept my big mouth shut.

So, even though I wasn't in the mood, even though I knew I was jealous and thought I was right, I capitulated, broke one of the primary codes of womanhood, and apologized. I even whispered in The Actor's ear that we could try the warm spatula thing later. That made him very, very happy indeed. I basked in the warm knowledge that my job as humanitarian had been successfully completed.

The Thai food arrived. Pickles had ordered way too much, as usual, but Mario returned and solved that problem. Pickles gave Mario a very animated account of the coppers' visit. It was almost like charades in a way, because Pickles was eating as he was talking, so Mario had to guess words. We finished off two very nice bottles of 1975 Château Rieussec Sauterne with the Thai food. Pickles had produced the bottles from the disaster area that once was The Actor's daughter's room. Pickles wouldn't say how he happened to have the wine. We knew better than to ask. I could see The Actor growing more melancholy, as Pickles and Mario grew more restless.

"Let's all go down to The Black Cap," Pickles said as he ran his fingers through his hair and bundled it up in a scrunchie. Mario was all for it, but Thespian wasn't.

"I hate that place," The Actor said.

"What's The Black Cap?" I asked.

"You hate that place, because they kicked you out — twice," Mario said.

"What's The Black Cap?"

"Drunk and disorderly," Pickles said, smacking his lips.

"Come on guys, what's The Black Cap?"

They all looked at me as if I was one of the aliens that may have abducted Philippe. Then they looked at each other and nodded in fraternal agreement, as if to say, of course, how could she know.

"The Black Cap is a gay cabaret on the high street, used to be known as 'The Palladium of Drag.' It's not quite that now, but it's a hoot, a definite hoot," Pickles said.

"We'd better shake-a-leg, Raymond, if we're going. Can't entice you two?" Mario asked.

"I hate that place," The Actor repeated.

"Yeah, so you said. Come on, Babe," Pickles enthused, "it'll be fun."

"I want to watch a movie. What happened to the flat screen?" The Actor whined.

"You broke that flat screen, honey. Looks like I'm babysitting tonight, fellas," I sighed.

"Next time, then," Mario said as he bent down and gave me a kiss on the forehead.

"You don't deserve a kiss, abandoning us for the big baby man," Pickles said as he searched for his missing flip-flop. "Anyway, Thespian," he continued "if you want to watch a movie you can use the computer in your daughter's room. That's what I've been doing. She's got a stash of movies in the bookcase by the window. I'll blow you one and owe you one." Pickles blew me a kiss, and he and Mario were gone.

"Why doesn't your daughter have her own flat screen?"

"Her mother's orders . . ."

"OK, wrong question. Do you have any popcorn?"

No popcorn, but then there was plenty of the big ganja weed. This became a catch-22 because we were going to need snacks if we were movie watching and smoking dope. I had the feeling Pickles had a stash. I looked for the snack food stash while The Actor looked through his daughter's DVDs. We both struck pay dirt. I found about a dozen bags of Frazzles under the bed, sort of like bacon flavored Fritos. What The Actor found stunned and confused him.

"She has all my films," he said holding up a DVD. *The Reality of Desire*, for God's sake. She's too young to be watching this. I'm stark bollock naked in this one, you know. How'd you like to see your father's bare ass?"

"Don't make me nauseous. Look, I think this just shows that she was trying to get to know you better . . . I don't mean by seeing you naked . . . I'm sure she fast forwarded."

"There's everything here, even from the series I did for ITV before I had my teeth fixed. God, how embarrassing. I was kind of chubby then. Still had my baby fat."

"Looks like the baby fat may be making a return engagement. Here have some Frazzles."

"Really, do you think so? I've done sod all about working out. I just wanted to relax and not feel like I'm training for the fucking Olympics all the time..."

"I'm kidding, c'mon. What's that one?"

"This is Commando *Brigade*, the one the filth liked. Let's watch this one. Babe, do you think I should talk to Zoe about the DVDs? I don't approve of her watching some of this stuff."

"And what would you say? She'll only resent you for going through her things. Even if we do go through their things we have to let children believe that we are totally above that shit. Here, take a hit and let's watch you being wonderful."

The Frazzles were not the ideal snack for movie watching, too noisy when chewing, but they actually weren't bad. They had that dope-like addictive quality that any really good snack food strives to achieve.

We snuggled on Zoe's bed, which now smelled like gin, patchouli and hot sauce, courtesy of Professor Pickles, and watched *Commando Brigade* on Zoe's 17-inch laptop.

The story centered on a group of Royal Marines who were part of an amphibious assault on the Al-Faw peninsula in south east Iraq during the 2003 invasion, and what happens to them when they return to civilian life, after losing one of their mates, in what might have been friendly fire. The Actor was the main character who couldn't let go of the death of his friend.

THE ACTOR

"I thought I did a good job right there — some of it's rubbish, but right there . . . I'm proud of that."

"It's really good. I don't like war movies — but this, I like this. And that guy playing Sgt. Mark Davis is kind of cute. I'd do him."

"Would you do him right now?"

"I sure would."

"I got a BAFTA Best Actor Award for that role. I loved playing that bloke."

"Well, where is it? It's some kind of statue, like the Oscar, right? So where is it? Where are your awards?"

"My mum stole that particular BAFTA award. I have no idea what she did with it. I searched her house. I just gave up trying to find it. As for the rest of my awards, I had to hide them because she kept breaking in. They weren't safe on the shelves in the lounge or anywhere else, for that matter."

"I didn't mean to upset you. I always end up asking the wrong questions."

"No, it's not that. I have to see her. You heard Crawford. She filed the missing person report on Philippe. He wants to question her? Fat lot of good that'll do him. The daft cow. Well, you wanted to visit her, so you'll get your chance."

"Where is she?"

"Cornwall, I thought I told you. I'll have to ring the doctor and Sergei. It's a five-hour drive. We'll spend the night, maybe a couple of days. I like it down there, I can walk around, go to a pub. Nobody bothers me. You'll like it. It'll be a honeymoon before the wedding. We'll take that Webley revolver with us and toss it in the ocean."

Slow dissolve to indicate the passage of time. The beginning of a fantasy sequence: a video of The Actor tossing a gun into the Atlantic Ocean off the Southwest tip of Cornwall goes viral on YouTube. Quick cut back to the present and The Actor agreed with me that tossing the gun into the sea was a bad idea.

"Why don't you ask Sergei to take care of it, have it broken into parts, and the parts tossed in various locations?"

"You're diabolical. What can I do to make you happy right now?

"You can tell me what happened to my things."

"Upstairs in my walk-in closet, neatly arranged, hung up and put away, and before you ask me about Philippe's room . . . I know you were in the cellar."

"That fucking Pickles . . ."

"He couldn't help himself. He tells me everything."

"So, while I was at Maida's, Mario and Pickles helped you put Philippe's things back in his room and my things in your closet."

"Yeah, and I swore them to secrecy. I have to tell you, luv, when Pickles told me how you picked that lock . . . it gave me a stiffy, in fact I'm getting one now, just thinking about it. Where are you going?"

"I'm going to warm up the spatula."

The idea of taking a five-hour road trip to Cornwall was less than appealing to me. I was prepared to charter a plane, but The Actor was against it for many reasons, mostly having to do with his own personal weirdness and privacy issues. In the end, I just accepted it and let go of the need to understand, just as I had, for the moment, let go of the need to find The Actor's stash of awards. Surely, we could display them now that his mum was psycho-pharmacologically imprisoned in the wilds of far-off Cornwall.

That night as we lay in The Actor's bed, exhausted from extensive canoodling and spatula experimentation, I couldn't sleep. As I listened to the sound of The Actor sleeping, I had a feeling that we were being watched. My parents' craziness had made me hyper-vigilant. Let's face it: if you're a woman of color, paranoia is a survival tool.

Maybe it was the visit by the law that was making me jumpy. Maybe it was the thought that Philippe was in fact out there somewhere in the dark, none too happy about a woman taking his place in his boyfriend's bed. I curled up next to The Actor, pulled the covers over my head and tried to stop thinking.

Then, The Actor starting writhing around, moaning — and not in a good way.

"Will you stay within the speed limit? Will you?" he cried out. "Yes, yes I will," I said, not knowing what else to do. With that he just sighed, rolled over and said, "Good." That was the end of it, or so I thought. I lay on my back staring at the ceiling, now fully awake and unable to sleep.

Why had The Actor chucked all of Philippe's belongings in the basement in the first place? Where were the bullets for the Webley and whose gun was it? Who followed me to Maida's, who was the man peeping through the front window and who was the stranger in the park? My mind was spinning.

I decided to go downstairs to make myself a cup of warm milk and top it off with a couple shots of brandy. The Actor was snoring softly now, a slight vacuous grin on his face. Well, at least one of us was getting some kip, as he called it. I was knackered, too knackered to sleep.

While the milk was heating up, I closed the curtains and armed the alarm. Philippe must have done these things on a regular basis. This may have been why The Actor never paid the slightest bit of attention to home security, because someone else always had.

As I poured the milk into a mug I thought I heard a noise, but I couldn't tell if it was coming from inside or outside the house. I quickly retreated to the dining room, where I found the brandy. I had to gulp down some of the hot milk to make room for it and scalded my mouth in the process. I just drank the brandy straight out of the bottle, thinking it would sooth my burning mouth, but it just made it worse. Then I thought I heard a noise again, like a thump, just once. The Actor came running down the stairs in his undies, calling my name.

"I'm in here," I mumbled as loud as I could, my mouth still burning.

The Actor slid into the dining room like Tom Cruise in Risky Business: "Are you all right? I heard a noise, it woke me up and you weren't there . . . and I thought . . . What's the matter? You look like you're in pain."

"I burn my mawt."

The Actor took the mug of hot milk from my hand and put it on the dining room table. He went into the kitchen, returned and stuck an ice cube in my mouth. I felt so much better.

The Actor took a few swigs from the brandy bottle and released a pent-up breath. He wanted to know if Pickles had returned. I shook my head from side to side. Then, he asked me if I'd heard a noise. I shook my head up and down. I took the melting ice cube out of my mouth for a minute so I could tell him I heard a thump. He said not to worry, that was just him falling out of bed. No, there was a noise before that. I told him yes, I'd heard it, but I couldn't tell whether it was coming from inside or outside. He said he thought it was both. I disagreed.

We sat in silence for a while thinking what it could be, what we should do. I mentioned that I had armed the alarm and closed the curtains. The Actor reminded me about the outdoor lights. I reminded him that I wasn't the butler. He said he'd see to them on our way back to bed. We finished off the brandy and left a light on in the kitchen and the living room for Pickles, just in case. The Actor switched the outside lights on, and we trudged carefully up the stairs on unsteady legs. When we reached the landing something just wasn't quite right.

"I feel a draft," I said.

The Actor pulled me close and whispered in my ear, "I want you to stand right where you are, don't move. I'll be right back."

He ran into his bedroom and I could hear him rifling through some drawers, there was about a five second pause and I heard a distinct snap click of metal, another pause and then the light in Philippe's room came on, but how could I see it? Then I realized that the door to the room, the one that could only be opened from the inside, was ajar. I could see the shadow of someone approaching the door. I wanted to run, but I couldn't. I was way too wasted. My breathing was audible as my chest rose and fell with anxiety. I let out a little yelp when the door burst open. Thank God, it was The Actor. "The double doors to the terrace were wide open and there footprints on the rug, big ones. Whoever was here is gone now."

I looked down at The Actor's right hand; it held the Webley revolver. He saw me staring at the gun and before I could ask he said, "I found the bullets."

CHAPTER 16

You just happened to walk in on this and if you know what's good for you, you'll turn around and walk out.

— **Ray Milland as Don Birnam in** *The Lost Weekend* **(1945)**

Ray Milland was the other moody Welsh actor who at one time was Paramount's highest paid male star, and the first actor to win a Cannes Film Festival Award and an Oscar for the same performance. That performance was as alcoholic writer Don Birnam in the 1945 Billy Wilder film, *The Lost Weekend*.

Milland was at least a generation before Welsh actor Richard Burton. Unlike Burton, Ray Milland was a movie star who happened to be an actor. Richard Burton was an actor, who apparently was never really comfortable with the whole movie star thing. He liked the movie star money, though.

I remember my father, T. Laurence Lake, telling the story of the time he and a buddy of his, Larry Stanton, went to see *The Lost Weekend*. They each had managed to smuggle a bottle of booze into the movie theatre. Every time the Ray Milland character took a drink in the film, my father and Mr. Stanton took a drink. Halfway through the movie, they both passed out. My father said it was the best movie he never saw.

There were many times, some I can remember some I can't, when an abundance of liquor in my system was the perfect prophylactic barrier to unwanted information from reality. This was one of those times. I was beginning to think it had been a very bad idea to watch *Commando Brigade*.

"You know how to use that thing?"

"I've done four action films in a row, OK?"

"OK, Rambo what do we do now? This is a goddamned home invasion, buddy."

"Babe, you're drunk."

"Well, so are you, but I don't have a loaded gun in my hand, do I? Firearms and alcohol, I'm just saying."

"Well said, and duly noted. I can't have the filth over here again. We should just go out and track the bastard down. Shouldn't be hard to find with those big feet."

"*Commando Brigade*," I muttered.

"Listen, I heard that. I know I'm getting a little too gung-ho, but my blood is up. You think I'd let anyone harm you? I'd kill the bastard."

"Can we discuss this in bed? I need to be horizontal right now. You've got a gun. The alarm, the lights, and the phone are on. We have weed and Frazzles. I say we lock ourselves in and get some sleep."

"I can rock with that."

We agreed that the whole discussion about the gun and the bullets was way too much at the present moment, so it was tabled until sobriety prevailed. However, speculation about the intruder was wide open for a five-minute debate: that's how long either one of us had before we either fell asleep or passed out.

The Actor said he thought it was probably some mentally unstable fan. I told him that made me feel so much better, and then we got into a slight row about me being "so bloody sarcastic."

After we both simmered down, I asked about the actress, the crazy one who stalked him and stole his favorite shirt. He didn't think it was her, because you'd have to be in pretty good shape to climb up to the terrace from street level. Her arms, according to The Actor, were like twigs, but she did have big feet.

I told him not to discount the super-human abilities of a crazy person, take his mum for instance. Well, she was not a suspect, not unless she had taken to wearing men's size thirteens. Anyway, she was five hours away by car — three by train — and heavily medicated.

In the end, we decided that if the cops called The Actor into the nick for further questioning about Philippe, he'd tell them about the intruder and not about the gun, which, for the time being, was not going anywhere.

That night I dreamt about the 1948 film *So Evil My Love*, a chilling period thriller about love, depravity and murder set in Edwardian London. Instead of Ann Todd as the virtuous widowed ex-missionary, Olivia Harwood, in the female lead, it was me. The Actor had replaced Ray Milland as Mark Bellis, the totally evil, all-around criminal, with a talent for forging masterpiece paintings.

By the time Mark Bellis has finished working his voodoo on Olivia Harwood, she has devolved into a fornicator, consummate liar, blackmailer and cold calculating murderer. On the other hand, upon seeing what his woman will do for love, Mark Bellis begins to evolve into a kinder, gentler crook who wants to stop fooling around and settle down. Of course, it's too late for both of them by that point. This dream left me with the same question and the same sick feeling I had when I saw the movie: Does evil lie dormant in everyone, just waiting for the right person and circumstance to awaken it?

The next morning, I felt so exhausted. The bedroom door was open. I could see The Actor, still in his tighty whiteys, gun in hand by his side, pacing up and down the hallway past the open bedroom door like *Commando Brigade*. He was talking to himself, carpet F-bombing, something about "defiled," which I couldn't make out. The dark cloud was over his head, and a storm was brewing in those blue eyes. I would have to pull my shit together PDQ, despite the fact that I was way too hung over to play Cathy to his Heathcliff. I sat up in bed, pulled my knees up to my chin and watched him until he felt me watching him.

"He's been in the hallway, you know. I found footprints that led right up to the bedroom door," The Actor said, trembling with anger. "He's gone now, baby. Why don't you put the gun away before an accident happens?"

"I feel like murder."

I didn't know quite how to take that; in fact, I was getting pretty scared. I'd seen him like this before, when he did and said things he didn't remember. I didn't want my accidental death by gunshot to be one of them, so I just sat there without moving a muscle, waiting for whatever happened next to happen.

One of those hour-long minutes passed without either one of us moving or saying a word. Then he walked into the room, put the gun in the top drawer of the dresser and sat down on the bed.

"Why is this happening, Babe? I don't understand it, just when things were really looking up. It's like someone has it in for me. The premiere is in a few weeks, then the Press tour, chat shows, the new film goes into pre-production . . ."

"My father taught me that at times like these it's best to use the salami method: just take one slice at a time."

This brought a grin to The Actor's face as well as a sigh of relief. He snuggled up next to me.

"I liked the spatula," he said as he wrapped his arms around me.

"We can try it again, tonight," I whispered as I kissed his neck.

"Won't be around tonight, luv," he said as he caressed the inside of my thigh. "I'm going to my club tonight."

I pushed him away. "You can be such an asshole. I don't mind you going to your goddamn club, but just don't use these corny tactics. Don't go all husband on me. Please. Tell me whatever you have to tell me — man to Babe. OK?"

He looked genuinely hurt.

"Babe, at the end of the day, I am just a man and when a man is with his mates he's one way, and when a man is with his woman he's another. The company of men is less confusing to me. What I tend to forget is, I don't have to shift gears with you, I can act and talk pretty much like I'm with my mates. Do you have any idea how fantastically comforting and scary that is?"

"It's come up in conversation, before. Don't weasel."

He was on the bed, sitting back on his heels with his hands clasped under his chin looking at me like one of those dirty faced kids in a Save the Children commercial.

"You know those black paper clamp things? Do you think you could . . . on my nipples. Please. Now?"

And so another hour and a half passed, as I pleasured him with pain, and he tortured me with pleasure.

In the shower I made a mental note to tell my future husband that even though I preferred the company of men for the same reasons he did, I was not a man. I had made the mistake of not reminding him of that difference on one occasion and had the bruises to show for it. Not that he had deliberately intended to hurt me, he's just incredibly strong and very fit and in the throes of passion he forgot I was a woman, for a moment, and in that moment I thought I was reliving some past life when I was in the World Wrestling Federation.

He was listening to The Brand New Heavies with N'Dea Davenport, one of my favorite singers, not blasting — it more like background, soundtrack music.

He spied me from the kitchen, as I sat down at the dining room table. He smiled and appeared with a tray containing the giant French press filled with delicious-smelling coffee, two cups, cream, sugar and a plate of chocolate-filled croissants.

"This should help," he said as he kissed me ever so sweetly.

I bit into a croissant and it was heavenly. "Why, thank you, baby. You're in a much better mood."

"You have the power. That's a nice dress. Are you going somewhere?" he said as he poured me a cup.

I was wearing a white poplin sleeveless eyelet shirt dress from Lafayette 148 New York.

"I thought maybe we could do something today. Go out for lunch or something, maybe to that place Pickles is always talking about in Hampstead Heath."

"I have to meet with Mark Fragile today. I thought I told you. Then . . . well . . . you know. I have Sergei on call." He sipped his coffee sheepishly, eyeing me with caution.

He knew damned well he had said no such thing to me, but I let that slide. He was looking very James Dean today, in those black slim straight-legged Diesel jeans, white V-neck T-shirt just veed low enough to expose the return of his fluffy dark blond chest hair. The hair on his head was still wet, slicked back with that one errant piece that flopped over his forehead and almost covered his eye.

My first thought was that The Actor, Sergei and Mark were scheduled for a three-way, and he hadn't even had the decency to ask me if I wanted to watch. He was onto my thought processes, because he cocked his head to the side, in that way of his, pursed his lips and just stared at me for a moment, then said:

"Don't even go there. I know what's rolling around in that head of yours and no, this is strictly business and that's all. Besides, Mark only fucks women, and I'm not sure if Sergei's actually human, so I don't know what his story is."

"All right, all right, what about your meeting with JD, how'd that go?"

"Funny, you should ask. Apparently, he's in, but now, only marginally," he said in full dish mode. "Maida and Mark don't want to deal with him, his behavior, his politics, the teeny-boppers, the gambling. He hates the gays. I think you're the only Black person he knows, and you're half-White. Well, you heard him at the dinner party."

I was surprised. This was not the JD I knew and loved. What had happened to him?

"Maybe Lady Sylvia's dying like that . . . maybe he's depressed or something."

"That may be, luv, but we're making a movie, not starting a psychiatric clinic. I know, I should talk, but when I'm on the job, I'm on the job. My beliefs, personal life, my eccentricities are not in play while I'm engaged in a project . . . only, if those things serve the part I'm playing . . ."

"Ok, I get it. This isn't a chat show interview."

"Sorry, my love. I've got a lot on my plate at the moment. You know, I was thinking maybe we should try to cut down on the drinking and smoke more weed, probably healthier."

"Are you down with burning one right now?"

"I'm down."

The Actor was worried about the intruder and didn't want me in the house alone. When I suggested maybe I could visit with Maida, he told me Maida was going to be at the meeting with Mark. The Actor had spoken with Pickles, and he and Mario were in Brighton. Don't ask. It would be hours before they'd return.

"Go shopping. You haven't done that since you've been here. Retail therapy would do you good. I've kept you cooped up with me, but I'd keep you in my pocket if I could, I love you that much." We left the house together, arming the alarm system, after we made sure all the doors and windows were locked. On the pavement, as the main gate automatically closed and locked behind us, we embraced as if this would be the last time we saw each other. It was a sad and tearful parting for both of us drama queens, because we truly missed each other when we were apart.

As we disengaged, once again, I had the feeling we were being watched, and told The Actor so. He said it was probably some paparazzo hiding in the bushes. We waited until my cab arrived. I was going to St. Christopher's place to check out a shop I'd fallen in love with online. The cab pulled up to the curb and The Actor put me inside. Through the rear window, I watched him walk away in the opposite direction until I couldn't see him anymore.

"Wasn't that, you know. What's his name?" the cabbie asked in a flush of excitement.

"Commando Brigade?"

"Yeah, that's the one. Oh, I loved that film. That was him, then? Wait 'til I tell the missus."

The cabbie's summary and review of *Commando Brigade* was Roger Ebert worthy: knowledgeable, nuanced and comprehensive. It was like watching the special features on a DVD, and I told him so. He really liked that. We kept up the chit-chat. Wasn't I that one he was going to marry? And what about that assistant of his, did they ever find the bloke? Wouldn't keep my hopes up on that one if I were you, he cautioned.

The cabbie dropped me off on Bond Street and wished The Actor and me luck on our upcoming nuptials — couldn't wait to tell that missus of his. I gave him a twenty-pound tip and his teeth almost fell out.

The Actor had given me explicit directions, so I knew to find the purple clock landmark for the entrance to St. Christopher's place, so hidden I felt as though I was the first person to discover its charms. It was the perfect spot for me to hide for a while, not as crowded as Bond Street. I purchased the cutest sleeveless flower linen dress in all four available colors, a gold crystal beaded sleeveless top with a scooped neckline and a gold evening clutch. I would have bought more, but I started to feel a little lightheaded. I needed food. I forgot I was functioning on a chocolate croissant, two cups of coffee and a joint.

I needed a child-free environment, that was close by. When I finally stumbled onto Pontefract Castle, I thought I had died and gone to pub heaven. I could get some serious drinking done in this place, but I needed to eat something first.

I burst in with my bags, my hair flying in the breeze and a Hunger-induced bad attitude, and believe it or not people made it a point to get out of my way. I walked up to the bar, told the bartender I needed to sit down and eat immediately and I was quickly shown the spiral staircase, that led to the full table service dining area upstairs.

I didn't have time to have an internal debate about reducing my alcohol consumption. I was in desperate need of fortification. I had a Nicholson's Pale Ale, while I waited for my roast beef salad. I mean it was pale ale, I don't see how anyone could call that drinking. Anyway, I didn't have to tell The Actor.

The salad arrived, and not a moment too soon. It was delicious. I looked at the empty plate when I'd finished and tried to remember actually eating it, that's how hungry I'd been.

I didn't want to be one of those annoying chicks who talks on a cell phone in a restaurant, when other people are trying to eat in peace, but I decided what the hell? I'm an American, we don't have any manners — and I just had to call Pickles.

When he finally picked up the phone, I was happy to hear his voice. I told him about the home invasion, that The Actor was going to be out all night, and I didn't want to stay in the house by myself. He and Mario were back from Brighton and at the house, so I should just toddle on back, Pickles said.

"Pickles, you'll never guess who just walked in," I whispered into the phone.

"In where, where are you anyway?" Pickles asked in a panic.

"A pub in St. Christopher's Place. JD, what are you doing here? Pickles, JD just walked in. I'll have to call you back."

CHAPTER 17

When I'm off (not acting) I'm a different breed of cat entirely.

— Robert Mitchum

If someone ever gives you a sideways look, with their nose tilted in the air, and their eyes looking downward at you, with an expression on their face that says, "What the fuck did you just say?" and you, my friend, haven't said a word, I guarantee you that person is a full-on whacko crazy. Tread lightly.

This is something I think everyone who ever interviewed Robert Mitchum had figured out, and yet because of the oblique way in which Mitchum communicated, although treading lightly, the interviewer would come dangerously close to the precipice. As a consequence, many of the earlier recorded interviews with Robert Mitchum are as fraught with tension as the movies he made, because the possibility that Robert Mitchum would just haul off and pop the interviewer was always percolating below the surface.

Now, this may have gone through the filters of time and my imagination, but I could swear I saw a clip of Robert Mitchum on the classic *Tonight Show with Johnny Carson*, where Robert Mitchum is talking to Johnny and stops in mid-sentence to address someone off camera. He tilts his head in that crazy person way pulls his glasses down on his nose and in that deep baritone voice, dripping with menace says: "Are you eyeballing me?" It was chilling, as chilling as Max Cady.

In the fledgling days of his career, Robert Mitchum had hauled off and popped an uncooperative horse. During the peak of his forty-year career, he had hauled off and bitch-slapped Austrian director

Otto Preminger. This was in response to Preminger's insistence that Mitchum repeatedly slap actress Jean Simmons — for real — in a scene for the movie *Angel Face*.

When Preminger went to studio brass and told them he wanted another actor for the role, the answer was: around here when it comes to Robert Mitchum, you don't get another actor, we get another director. That's how revered Robert Mitchum was, not only by his fans, but by the studio.

In the wee hours of an August night in 1948, just before he was to give a speech on the steps of Los Angeles City Hall later that day, in honor of National Youth Week, Robert Mitchum got busted for smoking herb at the Laurel Canyon home of a Lana Turner look-alike, actress Lila Leeds.

It was a set-up, and Mitchum knew it, but he took it like a man and did his time at County, and when he walked out of jail he was a bigger star than when he walked in; a feat unprecedented in Hollywood at that time, or any other time, to my knowledge.

Yet, Robert Mitchum constantly referred to himself as an "actress." The highest praise he would cop to was to being "a good journeyman actor." Like Classic Steve McQueen, Mitchum thought there was something inherently sissy about being an actor. I'm not going to attempt to define the word sissy, because some men think it's sissy to have sex with women. All I know is that on or off screen, Mitchum at his peak was divine, dangerous and dead sexy. With Robert Mitchum, you never knew what would happen next, and that's what really makes a man exciting to me, as long as he's not like a serial killer.

This was the second time JD had just popped up out of nowhere. I didn't like it.

"What are you doing here, JD?"

"I could well ask you the same question, darling," he said as he bent over and kissed me on the mouth. The stubble from his permanent 5 o'clock shadow grazed my face.

"We must have just talked you up."

"Oh, is his royal highness here? From the looks of it I thought you might be on your own."

"I am. Oh, put those bags on the floor and have a seat." At this point a waitperson came over and asked JD if he was joining me.

THE ACTOR

JD ordered "whatever she's drinking." I'd stopped drinking at that point. I had to have the gin and tonic sorbet for dessert, so I could tell Pickles about it.

JD was majestic, standing well over six feet tall, with that distinguished animal-sexy look that some men who were sizzling hot in their youth mature into with ease.

Some heads were turning. People always recognized him, but few ever asked him for autographs. His most memorable performance, for which he earned an Academy Award, was as a brutal Nazi SS General.

He was in another uniform this evening: the impeccable Italian-made white cotton shirt, always crisp and gleaming, a black Armani suit jacket, tailored jeans and black loafers. He smelled like fresh laundry and really good single malt Scotch. He was giving some punters the cold blue stare, letting them know: approach at your own risk.

It was almost dark on Wigmore Street when we finally emerged from the Pontefract Castle Pub. That's when I noticed that JD was limping. Something told me not to ask. I was anxious to get back, so I could show Pickles my purchases and to find out what went on in Brighton.

JD helped me with my bags, hooked his arm through mine and led us out onto Bond Street, where he hailed a cab. I expected to say goodbye to him there, but he jumped in the cab with me.

"Where to?" the cabbie asked. JD said, "Abbey Lodge, Park Road."

I just assumed he was hitching a ride. However, when we got to Abbey Lodge, JD paid the cabbie and pulled me and my purchases, unceremoniously, out of the cab. I was yelling for the cab to wait a minute, but he was already gone.

"What? Are you kidnapping me now?"

"I just thought you might like to come up and have a drink with me?"

"Well, you could have just asked, like a normal person," and as soon as I said it a little voice in my head was whispering, "He's left normal. The eyes look at the eyes."

Abbey Lodge is an impressive block of stately residential flats that costs a bundle. Any other time, I would have loved to check it out, but not this night and not with JD, because he was being

Robert Mitchum scary. There was a frenzied quality about him, as if my having a drink with him right now, at this moment, was imperative to the survival of mankind. Also, the fact that his fingers were digging into my arm like a hawk's talons, as he practically dragged me to his door, was a little unsettling. I decided to keep my mouth shut, for as long as I could, and placate him, always the fallback position when someone is nutting out, until I could hatch an escape strategy.

Just as we entered JD's flat my cell phone started to ring. The next thing I know JD rips my handbag off my shoulder, starts rummaging through it until he finds my cell, turns it off and stuffs it in his pocket. Only a crazy person could have found the phone that fast in my handbag. I stepped back and just stared at him, trying to calculate just how fast he could move.

"We don't need interruptions, do we?" he said.

Sweat was trickling down his flushed face, as his chest rose and fell with each labored breath. I'd known JD for twenty years. I'd never seen him like this.

"Let's have some champagne. Sit, sit."

Sit, beg, rollover, play dead. What was next? JD returned to the cavernous reception room (read, living room) with a bottle of 1998 Philipponnat Clos des Goisses Brut, Champagne and two glasses. I noticed the limp again.

"Talk to me, Felicia, you have to talk to somebody. Talk to me."

"Nobody calls me Felicia, except you and my father." "Gordon called you Felicia."

I began to cry. It was too much. To bring up Gordon now was just too much.

"I've upset you. I'm sorry," JD said as he struggled with the champagne bottle. "Once you get a glass of this down you, you'll feel better."

We toasted to long life, happiness and Lady Sylvia. Lady Sylvia. She was a real Lady by birth, didn't have to work at it like the rest of us. The great stage actress and acerbic personality Tallulah Bankhead once said: "I can say shit if I want, darling. I'm a lady."

Lady Sylvia must have heard this and taken it to heart, because she cursed like Richard Nixon. Lady Sylvia was what Frank Sinatra would call a "real broad," meant totally as a compliment. Lady Sylvia died after passing out drunk on the sofa, at the home of a friend, when the house went up in flames due to an unattended cigarette. JD's hand was shaking like a leaf fluttering on a twig, as he brought the glass to his lips. His eyes still had that glazed-over look. He was sweating profusely. He had to use both hands to lower his glass to the coffee table, so that he could retrieve a handkerchief from his jacket pocket to mop his brow. When he finally removed

his jacket, his shirt was soaked.

"This is some place you've got here. I can't believe the size of this room. I could ride a bicycle in here."

"Largest flat in the building . . . Ride a bicycle with all these priceless antiquities? Lady Sylvia would have my head," JD said.

I looked over at the two ancestral portraits which hung over the ornate fireplace, relatives of Lady Sylvia's, no doubt. I was hoping, praying, begging they'd give me a sign, speak to me telepathically through the haze of history, and tell me what the fuck to do. But, they just stared at me with grim intensity, as if to say: you're on your own, kid.

I knew better than to correct JD, even though he had spoken of Lady Sylvia as if she were in the bedroom changing. So, I decided to try to keep the conversation light. Maybe he'd pass out from the drink or have a stroke or something. I could get my phone off him and then I could . . .

"A penny for your thoughts," JD said. From the looks of the place JD could afford more than a penny.

"So, how much did this set you back?"

"Look luv, I'm a tradesman's son from the Midlands. This is her Ladyship's flat with her Ladyship's things in it. I include myself among those things."

The champagne was disappearing at an alarming rate. JD had mellowed out considerably, thank God; still, my right foot was fluttering like a butterfly at the end of my crossed leg.

"If I sold this mausoleum today, I could probably get four and a half million quid for it; that's without the contents, mind you," JD continued.

"You're not planning on selling, are you?"

"Do you want me to sell? I'd sell it tonight if you wanted me to.

Why on God's earth are you with that ponce, that poofter? Do you have any idea where his dick is tonight?"

"OK, JD. Out of bounds and give me my phone back, I have to call Pickles. He'll be worried."

"And there's another one. If it were up to me, they'd be burned at the stake, the lot of them. Like a pestilence. They need to be contained, then destroyed by cleansing fire."

"Who are you? Professor Abraham van Helsing? I think you're getting real life confused with some movie you were in. You don't seem well to me, JD. I mean, to hear you talking this way . . ."

"I'm trying to save your life. I could have played van Helsing. Hell, maybe I did — I can't remember, now. I miss acting like a double hernia. Do you have any idea how painful it is sitting astride a horse in fake armour, or walking around in the blazing sun in a leather skirt, sandals and a helmet, dragging a sword behind you? And I was not exactly in the flower of my youth when I was doing some of those things. Couldn't fuck my way into a part set in this century or the last one for that matter."

"We're getting drunk, and way off the point; besides, it's past my bedtime, so please return my phone like a good boy."

"And you'll what, dance naked with me to Johnny Mathis, beat my bum with a hot spatula? Don't look at me like that. I promised Gordon I'd watch over you. I'm your avenging angel."

"Guardian angel, guardian angel, and Gordon was a good man, he would never want this, you spying on me."

"Gordon was my best friend. If it wasn't for Gordon I would have nothing. Believe me, I have only the profoundest respect for that man's memory, but he would want you to be with me, not that abomination."

I bolted for the door, but he intercepted me, sprained ankle and all. He was so big, so strong I couldn't break free. His massive hands were clamped around my upper arms and he was shaking me like a rag doll.

"With me, right here and right now, don't you see? We're alone we have no one, just you and me, Babe."

I stopped struggling. I was afraid he was going to break my arm. I stamped on his left instep with all my might. He let out a short, sharp yelp of pain, releasing his grip on me, just enough so that I

THE ACTOR

could wriggle free. I had to think fast. I grabbed the champagne bottle from the coffee table, as he rushed me, and laid him out flat. It took me a minute to catch my breath. I checked to see if my clothes had been torn; they hadn't. I checked to see if JD was still breathing and he was. There was a big gash on his head, and blood was gushing out all over Lady Sylvia's beautiful Persian rug.

I dug into JD's pocket found my phone and called Pickles. I told him there had been an accident, that JD was drunk and hobbling around on a gimpy ankle when he'd fallen, hit his head and knocked himself out. I didn't know the London emergency number to summon an ambulance. Pickles told me to dial 999 and to call him back.

I called for an ambulance. Then I looked for incriminating evidence. I wasn't going down for something that was clearly self-defense, and I wasn't going to have my picture smeared all over the tabloids and the internet for cold-cocking one of Britain's veteran movie stars, turned mega-movie producer and nut job.

This was bad business all the way round. I was determined to come up smelling like a rose, no matter what. God, I wished I had a publicist. If there was ever a time I needed one, this was it. Maybe The Actor would let me use his.

If JD wasn't dead, The Actor would surely kill him if he ever found out that it was JD who had "defiled" The Actor's home. I had to get my game brain working, because damage control was the most important thing at the moment. OK, so JD was bleeding all over the rug, but the paramedics were on the way to take care of him. Who was going to take care of me?

There was blood on the side of the empty champagne bottle so I walked across the hall to the kitchen and washed it off, got some dish towels, brought them back with me and wrapped them around JD's head then I put the champagne bottle back on the coffee table. JD's head was right near the table, so I took off my shoe and with the heel banged a dent into the wooden edge, then smeared the dented edge with JD's blood. I went back into the kitchen, one shoe off, washed my hands, returned to the reception room, put on my other shoe and called Pickles. By the time I hung up, the ambulance had arrived.

There were so many questions from the paramedics, in between comments about the flat, how the other half live, and so forth. Then, this trauma team arrived with another paramedic and a really good-looking doctor. I was in tears, because I had no idea what I would do if JD regained consciousness and ratted me out.

I tried to answer the questions as best I could, without jeopardizing myself. Yes, we had been drinking since that afternoon and JD had had a few before that. No, I didn't live here. I explained that I'd known JD for twenty years, that he was my deceased husband's best friend, and best man at our wedding.

Then, the really good-looking doctor, Dr. Kazuo, who was on his knees, pulling back JD's eyelids and shining a light in his eyes, looked up and asked: "Is this who I think this is?"

"It's JD DeLongo, yes," I replied.

"And are you who I think you are?"

"Yes, I am, and I'd appreciate it if you'd be discreet about this."

"Blimey," one of the paramedics said, "JD DeLongo, SS General Richter, wait 'til I tell my gran."

"This man is pissed," Dr. Kazuo pronounced.

JD was drunk, which was not helping matters. His blood pressure was elevated, and he needed stitches. His age, and the fact that he was still out cold, was cause for alarm. He could have sustained a concussion. I told them about his sprained ankle, and how that had contributed to the fall.

After getting him stabilized, the ambulance took us to St. Mary's Hospital A&E. I rode in the back with JD and was constantly referred to as "the poor thing." I was crying my eyes out, but not for the reason they thought.

JD might come to and put the finger on me *and* I had left all my pretty things from my shopping spree in JD's flat, dammit. And the day had started out so wonderfully. I was beginning to think I was cursed.

I waited for what seemed like days, for news on JD's condition. It seemed like days, because I'd fallen asleep and woken up sore and hungry. Thankfully, a nurse came out with a cup of tea, in a real cup, and asked how I was doing.

"You're the one's going to marry my favorite actor. Oh, I've got such a crush on him, you wouldn't believe. When I saw him in *The Reality of Desire* . . ."

"Was that the one where he was stark bollock naked?" "Oh, yes."

The nurse told me JD had been concussed and would require an overnight stay for observation and to dry out.

"You look done in Ms. Lake, you should just go home. Come back tomorrow."

"My battery's dead. I need to call someone. Can I use the phone at the nurses' station?"

I called the phone at the house and Pickles answered. He was frantic, wanted to know where I was calling from, the total lowdown on the whole deal.

"I'm at St. Mary's Hospital, Pickles. Please just get your ass down here, I need a ride."

"Sugar, we'll be there in fifteen minutes."

Forty-five minutes later I almost fainted when Pickles arrived. When he said "we" I'd thought he meant Mario was coming with him, but as I looked down the long fluorescent corridor, who should I see walking side by side with Pickles, in his black Baracuta jacket and New York Yankees cap, but The Actor, and he did not look well pleased.

CHAPTER 18

I lived a few weeks while you loved me.

— Gloria Grahame as Laurel Gray in the film *In A Lonely Place* (1950)

Gloria Grahame (born Gloria Hallward) was the perfect film noir bad girl. She had the kind of tough, blonde dame look and pouty mouth that made men want to slap her and then fuck her. Grahame was at her peak in the 1940s and 1950s in such noir classics as *Crossfire, The Bad and the Beautiful,* for which she received an Oscar for best supporting actress, and *The Big Heat,* in which her character received a hot pot of coffee in the face courtesy of Lee Marvin, that evil, sexy bastard.

Gloria Grahame had cosmetic surgery to correct what she felt was a flawed upper lip. The surgery was botched, leaving her with nerve damage and partial paralysis, that gave her a kind of lisp, which, in the end, made her more identifiable and loads sexier.

She was married to film director Nick Ray (*In A Lonely Place, Rebel Without A Cause*) who was a friend of my Gordon's, and always good for some delicious gossip. I remember him telling Gordon that he had loved Gloria Grahame, but he never liked her.

I suspect the fact that she had had an affair with Nick's son from another marriage, while she was married to Nick, might have something to do with the way Nick felt.

Grahame eventually married her stepson, Anthony Ray, making her ex-husband Nick her father-in-law. I don't know why, but there's something in that, that I kind of admire.

I gave Pickles the stink-eye, and he hung his head like a dog that had been caught peeing on the carpet.

"Don't look at Raymond that way. It's not his fault," The Actor said, as he grabbed my arm and pulled me into a corner.

"Pickles had no idea what state you were in, he was frightened so he called Sergei. Sergei came and got me. Are you all right?"

That's when I lost it. I was tired and hungry. I needed to pee. I was sobbing uncontrollably onto The Actor's chest. Pickles rushed over, beside himself with worry, "Babe, I'm sorry. I had to tell him."

"Raymond, give us a moment, mate."

The Actor grabbed my hand and walked over to the nurse who had given me the tea earlier. "Sister, where's the gents?" The Actor asked. When the nurse realized who it was, her eyes widened, she clasped her hand over her mouth, made a kind of stifled cry, and pointed down the corridor.

"I'll come with you, I have to pee something awful," Pickles said.

"Use the ladies'," The Actor said curtly, as he led me down the hallway.

The men's room was empty. The Actor unzipped and used a urinal. I ran into a stall. After we'd both finished, we met at the basins. I was grateful for the cool water, I splashed on my face. The Actor handed me some paper towels. Then he stationed himself against the entrance door, folded his arms and gave me that killer grin.

"Now, I want you to tell me what really happened."

Ten minutes later I'd detailed the unexpurgated version of that evening's events. Someone was pushing on the door to get in. The Actor pushed back: "Under repair, mate." "So, I guess that makes you an accomplice after the fact," I said softly.

"You mean because you told me the truth, and I'm not going to grass. Well, I guess you're right. I am damned proud of you, girl. Come over here and give us a kiss."

"Is he going to live?" The Actor whispered

"Yes, I think so. That's what the doctor said, anyway."

"Pity."

When we found Pickles, he was having tea with a male nurse in an unoccupied urgent care room. The Actor called out in his most imperious baritone, "Raymond!" as we whisked past on our way down the corridor to the side entrance, where the ambulances brought the injured. Someone shouted, "You can't go out that way!"

Pickles shouted back, "I don't see why not, it's the way we came in. Hey, y'all wait for me!"

It was like a heist movie: Sergei at the side entrance, in the dark sedan, with the motor running — dodging an incoming ambulance as we sped off into the night. It was actually almost three in the morning. Pickles pulled out a hip flask. We all had a much-needed taste, and then The Actor, always prepared like a damned Boy Scout, pulled out a joint and we burned it. All we needed was a bag of Frazzles and we were in business.

"Do you think we should have left him just like that?" Pickles asked.

"What's the matter? Didn't you get his phone number?" The Actor laughed.

"I meant JD, asshole."

"What the fuck? Why are you calling me an asshole, Raymond?"

"Boys, please. It's been a long night for all of us. We're all on edge," I said passing the joint to Pickles. "Anyway, the nurse told me to go home, because they're going to keep him for observation. He's been concussed."

"Yeah, that's what Nigel was telling me, plus the fact, that when JD was admitted he was stinking drunk. They've called his nephew and his brother."

"JD has a brother and a nephew?" The Actor asked as he took the joint from Pickles. "I don't know why, but I find that hard to believe."

"Well, believe it. I met them both years ago. They're from West Bromwich, wherever the hell that is. Nice people, nephew was a kid then. I think his brother is a mailman, probably retired by now. You know, salt of the earth, blah, blah." I said, wearily.

We drove on in silence, for a while. The joint was now a roach. We were all pretty chill, on the verge of just dozing, when Pickles asked, apropos of nothing:

"Were you two having sex in the loo, 'cause you were in there for a long time?"

"We weren't in there that long. Give me some credit," The Actor said.

"Sex in a hospital men's room, just strikes me as unhygienic," I said.

"You wouldn't . . . " The Actor teased.

"No, I would not."

"I would," Pickles laughed, "Especially, if it were you, Sergei."

"No offense, Mr. Pickles. But, you're not my type." Sergei said, keeping his eyes glued to the road.

We pulled up in front of the house, but not into the driveway. Pickles leaned over and kissed me on the cheek, then he winked, got out of the car and closed the door. Sergei slowly drove on as Pickles stood in the middle of the road, dramatically waving goodbye and throwing kisses.

"What's going on, where are we going?"

"We're going to Cornwall, by way of Bristol. Don't worry, we packed some things for you. Our bags are in the boot, along with some booze and food. Sergei has some bottled water up front, and I've got a cigarette case of fatty spliffs in my pocket . . ."

"What are we doing? Going on an expedition? And when you say, 'We packed some things,' who's we?"

"Well, me Sergei and Pickles."

"My undies and everything . . ."

"Yes, luv, and it was pretty damned labor intensive, matching things and colors and . . ."

"Jesus! Never mind. What's in Bristol, where is Bristol and why do we have to go this absolute minute?"

"We have to get out in front of the publicity shit-storm that's brewing, thanks to JD's accident. Pickles will manage things at the house whilst we lay low for a few days. My publicist is issuing a joint statement from you and me. Maida's sending flowers from both of us to JD, and contacting his family to let them know we're willing to be of whatever help we can, and so forth. Ow! The back of my thighs . . . " "That must have been some night at the club. Listen honey, what if JD regains consciousness?"

"Let's talk about that later. Are you warm enough? I've got a rug here if you aren't. Sergei, put some music on, will you, mate? Do you need anything, Babe?"

"I'm good. Do you need a painkiller?" I said as I snuggled up next to him. He threw what I call a blanket, and he called a rug, over me. "What's Bristol?"

"Bristol is a city about two hours from here. It's where I was born and raised," The Actor said as he put his arms around me. "Normally, I'd take you up on that painkiller. Let's just try to get some sleep, yeah."

It was almost four in the morning, as we hurdled through the night down the M25. I was lulled to sleep by the sound of The Actor breathing softly in my ear, the whoosh of passing traffic and Groove Armada's *Inside My Mind*, gently pulsing through the sound system.

I dreamed that The Actor and I were naked, lying on a lounge chair on a beautiful veranda full of lush pink and purple bougainvillea. The veranda overlooked a beach of sugar-fine white sand. The water lazily lapping the shore was as blue as The Actor's eyes. The sun was full in the sky, yet it didn't feel hot — just warm and caressing. Every once and a while a breeze would stir. I can't remember ever feeling so good. The Actor turned his head to look at me. He was smiling with such contentment. Then suddenly it was dark, even though the sun hadn't set. There was a tall, shadowy figure standing over us, blocking the sun and making it cold.

When I woke the sun was just beginning to rise to the strains of *Hands of Time*, another Groove Armada tune, as we crossed an elegant suspension bridge over a majestic gorge. I had no idea where we were, but I liked this place, as well as Sergei's taste in music.

I looked at The Actor, who was sleeping with his head tilted back and his mouth slightly open. He probably looked just like this when he was a boy, all innocence and sweetness. I was feeling like a wilted flower, in my once beautiful white dress, now stained with my own sweat, droplets of JD's blood, tea and The Actor's drool.

"Sergei, where are we?" I asked.

"Bristol, Clifton Wood. Better wake the guv."

I woke the guv, and he was none too pleased. He gave me a look that would curdle milk.

"What time is it?" he wanted to know, as he stretched his arms.

"About six," Sergei answered.

"Where are we going?" I asked

"To my mum's. We're almost there. See, just around that corner there. Sergei, bottle of water, mate."

The Actor handed me the bottle, I drank some then gave it back to him; he finished it off. I said, I thought his mother was in Cornwall and he said she was, but we were going to her house, the one he bought her years ago when he made his first million. It was in a swanky neighborhood of Bristol called Clifton Wood; in some ways it reminded me of Potrero Hill in San Francisco.

The house we were looking for was on a small, winding slope that dead ended. There was no parking on the narrow street, so Sergei dropped us off, helped us take the bags into the house, then backed the car down the street to find a place to park.

The smooth, pale yellow, stucco façade of the townhouse made it look as though it were made of butter. Once through the door, it was amazing how deceptively spacious it was. Although it looked bright and airy with its connecting reception rooms and fireplaces, there was a heaviness of spirit hanging like a stench in the air.

The Actor opened a cardboard box that had been brought in from the boot (read, trunk) of the car. He pulled out a bottle of single malt Scotch. He then proceeded towards the kitchen/breakfast room which had bi-fold framed glass doors that opened onto a small, secluded courtyard garden. I followed him and unlocked the garden doors so we could sit down on one of the comfy chairs in the courtyard. The Actor retrieved two glasses from a cabinet over the sink.

"Oh, God, I never want to go through another night like that again in my life," I said as I took off my once lovely shoes.

The Actor poured out the Scotch.

"You'll want to get rid of those, I expect," he said, as he nodded towards my shoes, and handed me a glass.

"I really like those shoes. But you're right, of course."

Just then, we heard the front door open. I jumped.

"It's only Sergei. He's staying here with us. There's enough room. We won't get in each other's way."

Sergei called from the outer reception room, "If it's all the same to you, guv, I could do with some kip."

"Sure mate, the day's yours," The Actor shouted back.

The Actor sat down opposite me in a plump love seat, that was a complement to my comfy chair. He kicked his shoes off and put his feet up on the small coffee table that was between us. As he lifted his glass to his lips, I could see how black and blue his wrists were. Involuntarily, I clamped my hand over my mouth and tried to swallow my tears, but they rolled down my cheeks despite my effort.

He was visibly upset by my reaction. He put down his glass, stepped over the coffee table and knelt down before me placing his hands on my knees. I was sobbing by now, unable to get a grip, thoroughly embarrassed by this display of weakness.

"Babe, look at me. It's not as bad as all that, really. I was only hurt as much as I wanted to be and in saying that I just want you to prepare yourself for the state of my legs. Anyway, I think seeing my wrists, was just a tipping point. You need to finish that drink, get straight into bed and just sleep."

He was right; I was practically hysterical. I tried really hard, but I just could not stop thinking about what would happen to us if JD died, and somehow it was traced back to me. Everyone knows the French make the greatest champagne, but let it be known, their champagne bottles are pretty fucking formidable.

Upstairs were three fairly large bedrooms, and a family bathroom. Our bedroom, the guest room, had a balcony. It also had a large walk-in shower with a skylight. Next to it was The Actor's mum's bedroom, on the other side of which was another bedroom, now occupied by a sleeping Sergei.

The Actor led me to the bed. I was so tired I couldn't remember climbing the stairs. He was talking to me as he undressed me. His voice sounded distant, as if it were coming from a cloud floating by — something about Clifton Wood, a suburb of Bristol, between Clifton village and the harbor side. How his mum dreamed of living here when he was a boy, took him for walks on Clifton Down when they lived across the bridge in a run-down Council house, and something about the Lion pub. By the time he'd taken off my dress and wrapped me in the covers, I was fast asleep.

CHAPTER 19

I got a part as a chorus girl in a show called Every Sailor and I had fun doing it. Mother didn't really approve of it, though.

— James Cagney

At least once or twice a year I have to go back and re-watch a James Cagney movie, like *Public Enemy*, to remind myself just how utterly fantastic he was. When Cagney comes on screen he's electric. The man generated so much energy, that sparks fly even when he's standing still.

Too bad the moviegoing public only got to see him in black and white, during the earlier part of his career, because with that wavy red hair and those blue eyes he was fit as fuck, and I'm not really into short guys.

That's another thing I like about Cagney, he was totally cool with being 5'5" tall; in fact, he reportedly asked that certain scenes be shot to emphasize his lack of stature, especially when he was kicking some guy's ass, which makes him a big man in my book.

One of his most enduring roles is as the completely unhinged criminal Arthur Cody Jarrett, in Raoul Walsh's film *White Heat*. To call the character Cody Jarrett a psycho is a failure to appreciate just how crazy he truly could be, as well as an insult to psychos everywhere.

In one scene, Cody hides a fellow criminal in the trunk/boot of his car. When the guy in the trunk tells Cody it's getting a little hot, Cody tells him he's going to give him some air and proceeds to ventilate the trunk with bullets.

By far, the most — and there are many — twisted element of

the film is Cody's relationship with his longtime partner in crime – his mother – played to the hilt by British-born Margaret De Wolfe Wycherly.

Cody suffers from what appear to be severe migraine headaches. In one scene, his mother sits him on her lap, and feeds him whiskey to help relieve her poor, murdering sonny boy's pain.

Cody's insanity reaches its apex when his mother is gunned down by Cody's wife (played by a Warner Brothers' favorite, Virginia Mayo, giving it her hard-boiled all) who, in an adept move to shift the blame, fingers her lover, Big Ed Somers, one of Cody's gang, portrayed by the always delectable Steve Cochran.

The things that go on, or don't go on, between a man and his mother are for me like the Forbidden Zone in *Planet of the Apes*. I'm not going there. Really, does the Oedipus complex exist as a viable psychological condition in Western culture anymore? I have no idea. For sure, it did in 1949, when *White Heat* hit the screen.

When I think of the way The Actor's wrists looked, I can't help thinking, even though I don't want to think about it at all, I can't help thinking: there's a mother at the core of that, too.

I awoke in a warm bath of sunlight streaming through the balcony doors, and the sound of birds chirping. I was waiting for the strains of Rossini's opening to the *William Tell Overture* to begin, when The Actor rolled over, grabbed me and whispered, "It's been two days. Two whole days."

Two whole days since he had sex with *me*, but not two whole days since he had sex, because I know when he went to that club of his he was having it off with some hot young guy, who was probably cuter that I was, goddammit. Anyway, to his credit, even though he started things off in a sort of sex-starved frenzy, he relaxed into love making with a great deal of attention to my pleasure. He slowed down and took his time about it, too, which was wonderful, but unusual. Normally, he was in there banging away like it was his last night before the electric chair.

We both came slowly this time, and so hard that I forgot what century it was. I'm not kidding. I really thought my mother was going to come upstairs and catch us, because she went to pick me up at Onteora High School and found out I hadn't been there all day.

"Hurry, hurry, get your clothes and go down the back stairs." I mumbled in an erotically induced semi-comatose state.

"Babe, what the hell are you on about?"

"I thought we were in high school, in my old bedroom . . . I thought my mother was coming up the stairs . . ."

"Blimey. Maybe you're still in shock. Should I call a doctor?"

"No, silly. I'm fine. It's you. You fucked me into another century."

"You mean, I made you come until you time travelled? God, I'm good. Next time, do that to me."

"I honestly don't know if I can."

The Actor got up and opened the bi-fold doors to the balcony. I felt a rush of warm air.

"You can see Ashton Court estate beyond the rooftops, from here. Come and have a look."

It was breath-taking. I learned from The Actor that Ashton Court estate had belonged to a single family at one point. Now, the old mansion, as well as the woodlands and grasslands surrounding it, were historically preserved for public use and wildlife conservation. He was staring off into the distance, with tears streaming down his face.

"Philippe loved it here," he said softly.

I know that it's horrible to even think it, but I was really hoping Philippe was no longer among the living. The painfully tender memory of Philippe passed like a drifting cloud, and we showered and dressed in silence. Sergei had dutifully deposited our luggage in our room the night before. I started digging through mine, looking for something to wear.

"That white dress you liked so much is done for," I said to The Actor as he pulled on his underwear.

"Find anything interesting in there?" he asked, with a twinkle in his eye.

"Like what?" I asked as my hand lighted on a beautiful red brocade box, about the size of a small book.

The Actor was standing behind me now, with his hands on my shoulders. I opened the box. Inside was a gorgeous gold, ruby and diamond necklace. There was a band of small rectangular diamonds at the throat, followed by a band of small, round rubies next to a band of smaller diamond hearts, all set in gold. From the diamond hearts, dangled various size and shapes of small teardrop rubies.

"It's from the Mughal Empire, late 1700s, I think. A gift from a Maharaja to his wife. That's 22carat gold. Do you like it?"

I gently removed the necklace from its case and held it to my throat. The Actor fastened the clasp and kissed my neck. I stood there naked, dressed in my beautiful necklace, and The Actor's arms. I was overcome with so many conflicting emotions I couldn't speak. Finally, I was able to utter, "I've never liked anything so much in my life." Then The Actor dropped to his knees and after a few moments, I placed my hand ever so lightly on the top of his head, and began to time travel again.

The necklace, I learned, was my engagement present. The Actor had spoken to Nick, my current husband. The signed papers, releasing us from our marriage, were on their way, along with the "buyout" agreement. As soon as we received the paperwork, Nick would get the other half of the agreed upon sum. Everyone was a winner, despite the fact that The Actor and I were, respectively, one million dollars poorer.

As we finished dressing, The Actor confided that he liked Nick, that he thought maybe Nick and I should go into the studio and drop some tracks together. As far as I was concerned, he may as well have said that Nick and I should make a baby together. I was disgusted and repulsed as well as intrigued.

"Have you boys been talking about me behind my back?" "Only about our admiration and love for you."

"Uh, huh."

"Now, Babe," The Actor said as he blocked my way to the door, "I want you to just think about how you're going to spend your time, when I'm preparing for a part, or I'm on location or doing the chat shows. I think you should sing again . . . if there was ever a time the world needed to hear your voice it's now, my love. Promise you'll think about it." I promised. He was such an operator.

We went downstairs to the kitchen. Sergei was sprawled out on one of the sofas in the large reception room watching television. There was fresh coffee in the French press and sandwiches on the counter: cheese and pickle and salmon spread. The Actor called out "Cheers, mate." Sergei grunted a reply. We gathered up everything, including a bottle of single malt Scotch, and retreated onto the small walled garden. The air wasn't quite as heavy as it had felt wafting off the upstairs balcony.

"I'm thinking about selling this house," The Actor said, absently as he poured out the coffee.

"Please don't. It just feels so right. You know?"

"That's exactly what Philippe said, ' . . . it feels so right.' Well, she can't live on her own, my mum, not anymore. The doctor said as much. That's one of the reasons we're down here. I've got to go and sign the papers, and produce a big fat check for the care home."

"What about a live-in nurse?"

"You've seen what she's capable of. I can't have the blood of some poor innocent nurse on my hands. Besides, when she's not terrorizing me, she's terrorizing the neighbors around here. I've had complaints."

"What's the matter with her again?"

"That depends on who you talk to, some kind of dementia — bipolar — schizophrenia — psychotic depression, who knows. The thing is, she's not getting better — she's getting worse. It's either a care home or Broadmoor. Fancy a walk?"

It was one of those marvelous blue-sky English summer days, with the smell of fresh-cut grass on the air, and an ominous mass of dark clouds hovering over the landscape, in the distance. The Actor was dressed much the same as he was when I first met him and mistook him for a DEA agent. The Yankees baseball cap and the sunglasses did provide enough disguise for him to go undetected, at first glance. I'd pulled my hair back and wore one of The Actor's T-shirts and my sloppiest jeans, hoping to blend in, but people stared at us nonetheless.

We walked as if we had somewhere to be, but no set time to be there. It was a twisty-turny walk. The Actor was clearly familiar with the terrain. We crossed Princess Victoria Street, proceeded up Clifton Down Road towards Clifton Down itself, where we walked up Ladies Mile, turned through some trees that emptied onto a clearing, about 150 feet from The Lookout: a place to view the magnificent Clifton Suspension Bridge and the Avon Gorge.

Exhausted from the walk, on what had turned out to be quite a hot day, we just couldn't make it to The Lookout without resting first. Luckily, I had the presence of mind to carry a couple bottles of water in my bag. The Actor spied a bench close by, under a shade tree, on a field populated by a couple having a picnic, a man walking his dog, and several middle-aged couples trouncing around. I was happy to sit down and sip some water. The Actor, feeling safe, took off his hat and sunglasses. Beads of perspiration, which he mopped away with his hand, were beginning to form on his forehead. He took a sip of water and released a contented sigh. We sat in silence for a moment, lost in the act of just being.

I could tell from the expression on his face, he was savoring a few good memories that served to offset the painful ones. I thought it best to let him have his moment. I was content to enjoy the sun on my face, the smell of the grass wafting on the breeze — but our individual-sized private times were cut to an abrupt halt.

She was rushing towards us like a locomotive, her floppy hat flopping, her oversized bosom and multiplicity of bulges heaving. As she mowed through the summer air, she shouted: "Jimmy! Jimmy Sykes! I would have known you anywhere!"

The Actor looked like a rabbit who's just spied an Airedale running its way. He was trying to figure out which way to run, but it was too late. There she was, in her huge red T-shirt and white elastic-waist cotton pants, standing over us gasping for air.

"Your hair's shorter . . . blonder . . . but . . . I knew it was you. My husband told me . . . don't bother . . . but I had to come over. *Our Neighbours* was my favorite show, never missed one, never. Now, did you ever go back and marry that girl, Vickie? She was such a lovely girl."

The Actor was squirming and looking at me for help. I had no idea what the hell was going on.

"I'm not really Jimmy Sykes. He was just a character I played."

A bespectacled man in his 60s, clad in a short-sleeved white dress shirt, open at the collar, black knee-length baggy shorts, sturdy black walking shoes, black socks and a tan panama hat with a black band, was walking his dog about fifty feet away. The man started to trot over to us. I thought, maybe it was the husband, come to retrieve the old bat and rescue us.

The large floppy-hatted woman, was rummaging through her purse, from which she retrieved a crumpled piece of paper and a pen.

"Jimmy. Could you just sign this, please. 'To Phyllis, your biggest fan?'"

The Actor looked at me, stifled a laugh and said, "Of course, Phyllis."

The man with the dog finally arrived. He was not Phyllis' husband, who I suspect had run off to the nearest pub. Phyllis turned to him and said: "It's Jimmy Sykes from *Our Neighbours!*"

"Don't be ridiculous," the man said, "this chap is an actor. Push off, you daft cow."

The Actor handed the crumpled paper back to Phyllis, who walked off in a huff.

"You forgot your pen, Phyllis," The Actor called after her, but she just kept on walking.

"Still daydreaming on the Down, eh, my young friend?"

"Hello, Mr. Gribble. How's Mrs. Gribble?"

"That Mrs. Gribble is no longer with us."

"I'm sorry to hear. I didn't know."

"Oh, she's not dead. Divorced me. Moved to Biggleswade. Married her sister, happier than any man has a right to be. Who's this you've got with you?"

"This is my fiancée, Felicia Lake. This is Mr. Cornelius Gribble, my former employer and benefactor."

"Felicia Lake. My word. *I'll Never Get to Heaven as Long as I Love a Devil Like You*. The way you sang that song. Played it over and over. Drove my first wife crazy. Thank you, my dear. Thank you, from the bottom of my heart."

Mr. Gribble gently took my right hand to his lips and kissed it, at which point, his dog jumped on me and started licking my face. Mr. Gribble took the dog in tow. I swabbed my face with a wilted tissue. "Tommy, try to control yourself! I apologize for Tommy, but when it comes to women, he does have good taste," Mr. Gribble laughed. "Well, it was a pleasure to meet you Miss Lake. Take care of our boy, will you?"

He turned to The Actor and asked: "Down to see your mum?" The Actor shook his head in the affirmative. Mr. Gribble walked off, with Tommy trotting in front of him.

"If the acting thing doesn't work out," he called over his shoulder, "you can always come back, do a bit of yard work for me. The Lion!"

"The Lion!" The Actor shouted.

"The Lion?" I asked in total confusion.

"We're going to the Lion Pub tonight. It'll be fun."

"That's what you said about this place. Oh Jesus, look over there. Look."

Off in the distance, the corpulent Mrs. Floppy Hat was grabbing anyone who passed by and pointing in our direction. A group of three adults, and a school-aged child started walking towards us, slowly at first, then picking up speed. The Actor yanked me off the bench.

"Let's find a cab and get the hell out of here," he said.

In the cab on the way back we managed to laugh about old floppy hat and the adoring fans of Jimmy Sykes. I wondered out loud about The Lion. The Actor assured me that it would be fine. The locals were used to him, and the barman would eject anyone who got out of hand.

"Besides, we'll take Sergei. I'd like to see old floppy hat try to get around him," The Actor said.

"What's the real deal with you and Sergei?"

"He's straight as an arrow. He's my cousin."

"You and Sergei are related? By blood?"

"He's my father's sister's kid. He's got two sisters, also my cousins. One lives in Australia the other in Pennsylvania. Don't look so surprised. I didn't hatch out of an egg, you know."

When we got back to the house Sergei was sleeping on the sofa, where we left him. Any errant thoughts about filling my lonely moments with Sergei when The Actor was off doing his thing had to be pushed way deep down inside me, with all the other junk I was trying not to deal with. Even I had to draw the line somewhere. It would practically be incest, or close to it.

"Earth to Babe, well, do you want something or not?" The Actor asked, as he brushed past me on the way to the downstairs toilet. The door was open. I could hear him peeing, "Want what, honey?" I asked loud enough so he could hear me.

"Something to eat, Babe," he answered.

With all of our shouting and The Actor's peeing, we managed to wake up the sleeping giant, who was grunting something I couldn't make out.

"With your back? You should sleep on the bed, mate," The Actor called out as he zipped up, flushed and washed his hands.

The garden doors were open. I wandered out and sat in one of the big chairs.

"How was your walk?" Sergei shouted.

The Actor was at the open refrigerator door, head stuck inside, "I saw Gribble," The Actor shouted back.

"The Lion?" Sergei hollered.

"The Lion indeed, mate."

The Actor announced he was making tea. Sergei said, "Cheers" and I said, "Thank you, baby," as my thoughts drifted to nursing homes, marriage, bondage and the finer points of Bristol, which wasn't a bad place at all. I wanted The Actor to keep this house as an escape pod for me, because in the back of my brain a thought — no it was more complex than just a mere thought — a concept was forming, about how radically my life was going to change, once I married The Actor.

It was one thing to bask in the reflected glory of a surgeon, an Academy Award-winning production designer, and an aging rock star, but with The Actor, there would be no basking — baking would be a better word. Baking in the glare of the spotlight.

The Actor was right: I had to sing again, if only to reclaim my own fifteen minutes, my own public persona, and my own reason not to end up sitting at the wives table.

His wrists were looking a whole lot better, as he carried a tray brimming with leftover sandwiches, a fresh pot of tea, cups, spoons and cream and sugar, into the large reception room, where Sergei had implanted himself. I brought up the rear with a plate of chocolate biscuits.

Sergei had brought along a stash of DVDs. He was really keen to watch *Mildred Pierce*, so we watched *Mildred Pierce*. We picked our favorite character in the film. Sergei liked Wally, the Jack Carson character. I liked Zachary Scott and, of course, Joan Crawford's wardrobe, which I argued was its own character.

The Actor surprised us. I thought he would have chosen Zachary Scott. Sergei thought, Eve Arden. But, The Actor chose the Bruce Bennett character, Bert Pierce, Mildred's loser husband, who, in the end, turns out to be a pretty heroic guy.

As the credits were rolling, I innocently asked: "So did you two grow up around here?" Sergei lowered his brow and gave The Actor a look.

"It's OK, she knows," The Actor said.

"Around here? You must be joking. We're the undesirable lot they used to chase out of here," Sergei said.

"We're two blokes from the 'hood, Babe. We grew up in the ghetto, Easton, Stapleton Road," The Actor laughed.

"St. Pauls," Sergei added.

"Where are you from, Babe? What's your 'hood?" The Actor asked.

"Well, I was born in Italy and raised in Bearsville, New York. It was kind of rural. It's near Woodstock. You've heard of Woodstock, right?"

The Actor bowed his head and chuckled, to himself.

"You were raised in Woodstock, New York, amongst the rich hippies. You don't know what the 'hood is, do you, girl?"

My father has his work on exhibition in the Museum of Modern Art, the Tate Modern, and countless other museums and public spaces, as well as in the homes and corporate headquarters of the rich and powerful. I make no apologies. The Actor was right. I had no idea what the ghetto was, and I wanted to keep it that way. The Actor had other plans. He wanted Sergei to drive us around to The Actor's old Council house in Easton. I could tell from the look on Sergei's face that he thought it was a bad idea.

The phone rang. Sergei was grateful. He jumped up and sprinted into the small reception room to answer it. Pickles was calling with news from the front. The Actor took the phone and drifted off into a corner by the stairs. Sergei and I began to clear away the dishes. I could see he was on edge. He wanted to say something — I could just feel it. He'd turned on the faucet over the sink, clearly planning to commence washing up. I leaned over and turned off the tap.

"Spit it out, Sergei," I said.

He grabbed the edge of the sink as if to steady himself.

"If you only knew what his mum did to him in that house . . . you wouldn't want him going anywhere near it, that's all. That's all, I'm saying."

It was at that point that I realized, I had gone way too long without a drink. Sergei said it was too early for him. But it was five, definitely the cocktail hour. Apparently, Sergei didn't do his drinking until the sun went down. I never understood that too early for alcohol jazz. I may be wrong, but I'm pretty sure humankind used to view liquor as breakfast food in the olden days, when people needed to fortify themselves against constant attack by large animals, disease and other people.

I remember reading that during the filming of The African Queen, on location in sub-Saharan Africa, Humphrey Bogart and director, John Huston, drank whiskey from the time they got up until the time they went to sleep. They were the only ones, of the cast and crew, who didn't get dysentery. I rest my case, and raise my glass. Mario had his nerve medicine, and so did I.

Like Mario, Sergei had been helped financially by The Actor. After leaving the army, Sergei had found it hard to adjust. Consequently, he returned to the thuggish behavior of his pre-army days, with enhanced skills in the grievous bodily harm department. This resulted in a three-year prison sentence. Without The Actor's help, the sentence would have been much longer, and there would have been nothing waiting for Sergei when he got out, but a life of more crime. Now, thanks to his cousin, Sergei was a successful businessman as co-owner of the personal security firm Tight Security.

"He's the closest thing to a brother I'll ever have, Miss. I'd lay down my life for him, I would. He's a strange one, I'll grant you that, but there's reason, legitimate reason," Sergei said, as he washed the dishes.

"You know, I thought you two were . . . well . . . you know . . . " "You're not the only one. Keep the punters guessing, I say. He's better with you around, Miss. I'm not crying no crocodile tears over that little shit Philippe. He didn't help the guv, just made him worse. Please stick with him, Miss. He needs you. You understand him."

"I'm committed, Sergei, just like you. I just want the best for him. Mind if I ask you a personal question? How come a nice guy like you isn't married?"

"I prefer prostitutes, Miss."

"Straightforward, no complications, you always know where you stand."

"Exactly."

"I can dig it."

"Dig what," The Actor asked as he entered the room.

"God, you have got hearing like a wolf or something."

"Sense of hearing and smell, just like an animal. You're right," Sergei laughed.

"The police found Philippe's car at London City Airport," The Actor said, with a slight tremor in his voice.

Sergei dropped the cup he was drying. I poured myself another drink, and one for The Actor and Sergei. Sergei was right. Philippe was a little shit, by all accounts and a kill-joy, to boot. Here we were bonding as a little family, enjoying ourselves in the beautiful wilds of Clifton Wood, and this fucking Philippe business again.

CHAPTER 20

Put me in the last fifteen minutes of a picture and I don't care what happened before. I don't even care if I was IN the rest of the damned thing - I'll take it in those fifteen minutes.

— **Barbara Stanwyck**

She wasn't drop-dead gorgeous. That never mattered, because when she was on screen you couldn't take your eyes off her. She was compelling in a way that's almost indefinable. She was raw. She was from the neighborhood. She knew more than she would ever tell. She was seductive. She knew that sometimes the straightest way to a man's heart was right through his chest. She was sublime, vivacious and tough as nails: she was Barbara Stanwyck.

Born into poverty on July 16, 1907 as Ruby Stevens in Brooklyn, New York, Barbara Stanwyck, by 1944, was earning more money than any woman in the USA.

One of my favorite Stanwyck films is the 1946 noir classic, *The Strange Loves of Martha Ivers*. It's an unrelenting, brutal tale of greed, deceit, perversion and murder. Stanwyck's character, Martha Ivers, who has a calculator where her heart should be, is at the pinnacle of a twisted love triangle, that includes a very young Kirk Douglas, in his first film role as Walter O' Neil, a weak alcoholic lawyer, who has forced Martha to marry him through blackmail. Then there's Van Heflin, as Sam Masterson, the hapless town bad boy, now war veteran-turned-drifter, for whom Martha has been carrying a torch so long her fingers are singed. Throw in Lizabeth Scott, as Toni Marachek, the down on her luck sultry blonde, add a cup of brilliant dialogue from Robert Rossen's flawless script, a heaping helping of Lewis Milestone's direction and Victor Milner's brilliant cinematography, and you have extraordinary film.

When I think about The Actor and me, I can't help thinking about the promotional tag line for *The Strange Loves of Martha Ivers*: "Fate drew them together . . . and only murder could part them!"

So, here's my take on the whole fucking Philippe business. This is what I think could have happened: Philippe and The Actor got into an argument about something, the argument escalated into a brawl, which by The Actor's own admission, was not uncommon. Maybe the two of them had been drinking, when things got out of hand, and somehow Philippe ends up dead. The Actor calls Sergei, who comes over and helps The Actor dispose of the body. Or, maybe The Actor and Philippe were into their who-can-take-more-pain sex thing, and that spun out of control and Philippe ended up dead, and The Actor calls Sergei; either way it's an accident pure and simple. The Actor could have called the cops instead of Sergei. But imagine the mess that would have been? Everything, and I mean the total truth, warts and all, would be up for endless public scrutiny and consumption.

There would be a trial, maybe jail time for involuntary manslaughter. I don't know much about Brit law and diminished capacity, but everyone who knew The Actor knew his capacity was diminished most of the time, especially when he wasn't working. What about The Actor's daughter? What about The Actor's career? Obviously, no one gave a toss about Philippe. No one had come forward to report him missing except The Actor's mum, which, in and of itself, was odd, to say the least.

A part of me wanted to believe that Philippe had disappeared of his own volition, for his own reasons. He wouldn't be the first person to just walk away from his current life to start a new one. God knows, I've done that at least a half-dozen times. Sometimes, the only cure when you feel your life is suffocating you is to cut and run — literally run for your life, shed the old one like a butterfly sheds the chrysalis or a snake sheds its skin. This is what I would like to think happened.

Or an even better scenario might be that Philippe had fallen ill or tripped and hit his head and was now a victim of amnesia. No, on second thought that was not better. He could regain his memory

THE ACTOR

and return to The Actor. My life would then turn into *The Strange Loves of Martha Ivers*, for real. Emphasis on the word strange.

Oh, hell, maybe The Actor's crazy mum pushed Philippe off the Clifton Suspension Bridge, into the Avon Gorge. All I really knew for sure was I didn't have all the facts, and The Actor was not going to give them to me. Merciful on his part, come to think of it, because plausible deniability is always a good thing.

The Actor and Sergei had retreated to the large reception room off the kitchen, where they spoke in hushed voices. I was chilling in the garden (I call it a patio) sipping my Scotch and longing for a nice big hit off a fatty spliff. I could only make out bits and pieces from their conversation, something about "a major cock-up," "that's the filth for you," and not "giving a right bloody toss."

For my part, I was reminiscing about another partially overheard hushed conversation, about five or six years ago, which occurred right after my second husband Nick was involved in a car accident outside of Rome, Italy, resulting in the death of the other driver.

Needless to say, Nick had been under the influence of alcohol and drugs while driving. I don't know how he did it, but he walked away with a suspended eight months prison sentence for vehicular manslaughter and a hefty fine. Thank God, I was in Rome shopping at the time. The rest of his European tour was sold out after the news of the accident broke.

After that, I hopped on a plane back to the States and met Pickles at my crib in New York. I never went back to Nick, although we did get together from time to time in the intervening years. It was hard for me to see him, and not think of him as a murderer. I'm pretty sure he felt the same way when he looked in the mirror, because the boozing, and the drugs, and the whore mongering just got worse.

Even if there was a lingering suspicion, I didn't feel that way about The Actor. Probably because there was no concrete and demonstrable proof that he had anything to do with Philippe's disappearance.

My mental meanderings were shattered by the sound of breaking glass. All at once, Sergei was standing over me.

"You'd better get in there, Miss," he said with some urgency.

I jumped to my feet and ran into the large reception room. There were the remaining shards of what had been a very nice bistro drinking glass scattered across the floor. Scotch was running down the wall opposite the large sofa. The Actor stood with his back to me guzzling what remained of the Scotch, straight from the bottle. There was that dark cloud over his head again and lightning in his eyes. This was going to be tricky. I had to be bold and decisive. I wasn't really sure how I was going to handle this, but whatever I did I had better do it with confidence, and fast.

Sergei was hanging back, waiting to see what happened next. The Actor felt my presence. He whirled around looking very much like the waiter who had shot me in my dream.

The Actor held the neck of the Scotch bottle tightly by his side. He was trembling with rage, every breath was audible. He stared at me as if he didn't know who I was. That's when I made my move.

In one swift motion, I stepped into him, kissed him passionately on the mouth, removed the bottle from his hand, then shoved him down on the sofa. This brought him to his senses.

"I think you've had enough to drink, don't you?"

"Why can't I have a moment's peace? That's all I ask. Just a moment's peace."

He bent over and held his head in his hands. I sat down beside him and rubbed his back. He let out a heavy sigh. The worst of it was over, for the moment anyway. Sergei tip-toed into the room with a dust pan, brush and paper towels, cautioning us to watch where we put our feet.

"Leave it, mate. I'm sorry, Serge. Just leave it, please."

"If it's all right with you, guv, I'll just pop out for some air, back in time for The Lion. We're still on for The Lion?"

"Yeah, Serge, we're still on."

"Nine-ish then?"

"Nine-ish is fine," The Actor said.

Sergei gave The Actor a reassuring pat on the shoulder, as he left. After the front door slammed shut, we sat in silence, holding hands, not really wanting to talk, but knowing we had to talk if we were ever going to get through the next few minutes in one piece.

The Actor produced a big fatty spliff from out of nowhere, like magic. We burned it and then the words came, unfortunately without intent or direction.

I wondered where Sergei had gone. The Actor said Sergei had

THE ACTOR

gone to get his knob polished. Well, a man's got to do what a man's got to do, and as often as he can, if I was reading Sergei right.

"He can't babysit me every fucking moment. He's been looking after me ever since we were lads, and I'm older than he is. Believe it? He's like a brother to me. I love him. I really do."

"I wish I had those dresses, the ones I bought and left at JD's. I had to throw out that white dress you liked. That was a great dress. Do we have any more Scotch?"

"Two or three bottles, I think. What we really need is champagne. That's what we really need."

"Weren't we supposed to be cutting down on the drinking and smoking more weed? By the way, the French make really sturdy champagne bottles, FYI."

We were getting pretty wasted, just drifting along with the tumbling tumbleweeds. I was determined to steer the conversation back on track.

"So, can I ask you a personal question?"

"Yes, you can stick a dildo up my bum."

"OK, but that's not the question."

"It's not? Sorry. Ask away, my love. Ask away."

"If Philippe comes back, will our twosome turn into a threesome?"

"You're asking me math questions now? Oh, I get it. This is a riddle."

"No, no. Listen to me, carefully — the sound of my voice, not the voice in your head. If Philippe returns, will I have to share you with him?"

"I'm not prepared to share you with any man, especially if I'm having sex with him."

"Let me understand this: I can't be shared with another man, but you can share yourself with the whole world?"

"Babe, I'm an actor . . . giving the illusion that my sexuality is universally available is part of my job."

"Except in your case, it's not an illusion."

"Ouch! What brought all this on? Philippe's not coming back."
"What makes you so sure?"

"Well, I just have a feeling's all. A very strong feeling." "Do you miss him, baby?"

"Not as much as I did, but I still think about him, remember things, times together. I met him for the first time in this house. The room we're in was his room, when he lived here with my mum. He said he was just renting a room. Can you imagine? All the money I sent that bitch, and she's renting out rooms. She tells me they're lovers. Philippe was not into women — at all. I think he was actually frightened by you lot. Yeah, sometimes I miss him. You miss Gordon. I've heard you say."

"I do, honey, but Gordon's dead. I know he's not coming back."

The Actor became strangely silent. Slowly stretching out on the sofa, he nestled his head in my lap and drew his knees up to his chest. My big baby man: complex and damaged, accomplished and insecure, talented and hapless. Mine to care for and love, as best I could. I found myself stroking his hair gently, as these thoughts and more drifted through my mind like . . . well . . . like tumbling tumbleweeds. He was making this low rumbling sound, almost as if he were a cat purring: momentary contentment in the eye of the storm.

It would be two whole days before The Actor would relay Pickles' disturbing news, but by that time I had already had a duologue with the distinguished Professor whose first words to me were, "Child, you are not going to believe what is going on up in here." I don't know what I found more disconcerting: Pickles channeling Bette Davis or Pickles channeling Florence from *The Jeffersons*.

I had a vision of Pickles on the other end of the phone frantically fanning himself, with one hand, as if he were having a menopausal hot flash. When he finally calmed down enough to give me the facts, I was the one fanning.

Apparently, both The Actor and I were in hot water with the cops for different reasons. Even though The Actor left a message for DS Crawford, that he was leaving town for a few days, it was not sufficient. When Crawford called the house after receiving the message, to find The Actor had already left, he was not a happy guy, especially since Philippe's car had been found at London City Airport, giving rise to more questions that needed answering.

Crawford had taken his unhappiness out on poor Pickles, wanting to know exactly where The Actor was, with whom and why. And didn't The Actor know what it meant when Crawford had told him to let the police know if he planned to leave the area, that

that meant don't leave the area? No wonder Pickles was hysterical. Pickles told Crawford that he had no idea exactly where The Actor was, only that The Actor was with me and his bodyguard and driver Sergei. Pickles was convinced Crawford thought he was lying. The upshot was Crawford wanted to see The Actor down at the nick within the next 24 hours. "You know when the police say some shit like that, honey, it's just an out and out threat," Pickles said.

As for me, I had left St. Mary's Hospital before the police had a chance to question me. Due to the fact that JD and I were both intoxicated, that trauma doctor, Dr. Kazuo who arrived with the paramedics, and who I thought was so cute, reported the situation to the cops, who were then obliged to question me. What an asshole. I take it back. He was not as cute as I thought, and I was intoxicated at the time I thought he was, so there.

Overnight we had turned into Bonnie and Clyde, and we hadn't done anything. Well, OK I had cold-cocked JD with a champagne bottle and almost killed him, but it was self-defense and nobody knew about that anyway, except me and The Actor and JD, maybe. As for The Actor, he probably did get drunk or have one of his blackouts and accidentally kill Philippe in self-defense or maybe not. It was something only The Actor and Sergei knew for sure. There was no body or forensic evidence, or was there? Pickles and I were both worried about what evidence Philippe's abandoned car would yield. There had been no word on the scrapings the police had taken from the stain on The Actor's cellar floor or the DNA samples taken from Philippe's hairbrush and toothbrush.

This is why people have lawyers. Pickles assured me that The Actor had been onto his lawyer straight away and his lawyer had gotten a law firm, experienced in these matters, to deal with the cops for both The Actor and his lovely fiancée. I knew the words experienced and law firm juxtaposed equaled a whole lot of money. Thank God, The Actor and I had a few bucks between us. We would definitely have to return to London.

On a brighter note, JD was all right. He didn't remember a damned thing – a prayer answered - but when they scanned his skull they found a tumor the size of a walnut. They had already gone in and removed it. It was benign; however, the pressure from it would have killed him if he hadn't had surgery. In a way, I had actually saved his life. "And what about my dresses, the ones I left at JD's place?" I asked Pickles.

Pickles had gone to the hospital to see JD, or so he said. Personally, I think it was to see that male nurse he was chatting up. Anyway, Pickles wasn't a relative, and JD was still in recovery. His nephew, however, was leaving the hospital, and as he passed the reception desk, he had heard Pickles ask about JD. The nephew and Pickles got to talking. Seems the nephew had gone to JD's to get some things for him while he was in the hospital and found my dresses.

The nephew thought it was odd, because they were brand new and still in the shopping bags and what with his Aunt Sylvia having been dead for some time . . . Pickles told the nephew they were mine and went back to JD's with the nephew to retrieve my dresses and my other cool purchases. Of course, I was thrilled. I promised Pickles I would take him out to dinner to that place in Hampstead Heath he liked so much, and buy him a new ensemble to boot.

What I found odd was why Pickles would go to the hospital to see about JD in the first place, especially after the way JD had treated Pickles. Then the penny dropped: The Actor had sent Pickles, and The Actor had told Pickles why.

"Let's just be thankful you don't have to add murderess to your CV," Pickles chuckled.

"Raymond, I fail to see the humor in this. You know, this makes you an accomplice after the fact, just like my future husband."

"Babe, The Actor was just trying to assess the situation to see what kind of damage control was needed, that's all."

"How did you get that kind of information from the hospital anyway?"

"I didn't get it from the hospital, I got it from his nephew — but you know me, sugar, I can get blood from a turnip."

"Don't let this go to your head, but I do miss you."

"I miss you, too, sweetness. Brace yourself. This next bit of business is going to be tough, but don't shoot the messenger."

"Go on. Spill it."

"You and your future husband are front page news, big time. There's a picture of the three of us leaving the hospital splashed all over the tabloids and the internet. So, I'd keep a low profile, if I were you. Buy a wig and some Jackie O sunglasses."

THE ACTOR

"What the hell? Who took a picture at three o'clock in the morning?"

"Remember that nurse I was talking to? Turns out he wasn't a nurse, he was a reporter. Sorry, Babe."

"Don't you be sorry, honey. Fucking vultures. How in the hell did he know we were there?

"I wish I knew, Babe. I wish I knew."

The Actor was right where I'd left him, on the sofa sleeping peacefully. I was standing there wondering if I should throw a blanket over him, when he awoke with a start and shook his head like a wet dog.

"What's going on?" he asked.

"Nothing. You were sleeping."

"Oh. Do we have any more of those Frazzles, I wonder?"

"I've got the munchies too, but the Frazzles are back at the house under Pickles' bed."

"Look in the cupboard," The Actor said as he sat up and stretched, "I think there's some crisps."

We sat on the sofa eating from a big bag of Bar-B-Que potato chips, still floating on a high, but a little more sober than we had been. We talked about The Lion and what we were going to wear.

"I've seen almost everything you've ever done. Before you were a star, I saw you on Broadway in the revival of *Look Back in Anger*. I saw you in that crazy gangster miniseries. I've even seen *Commando Brigade* and *The Reality of Desire*, twice. I went to the movies two times in the same week."

The Actor tilted his head to the side in that way of his and gave me his patented grin. He reeled back clapped his hands and let out a laugh.

"Want my autograph?" he said slyly, "Come on, you autographed my collection of your music. God, I couldn't be happier right now. You're a fan. No, I don't mean it the way it sounds. It's just that I thought you had no respect for what I do."

"I have nothing but respect for your work, baby. You are right now the undisputed Obi-Wan of what you do."

"Aren't I, though?" he sighed, "And I do my own stunts, well a good deal of them anyway."

I started to sing *Lovesong* by the Cure when The Actor leaned over, crushing the bag of crisps that lay between us, and whispered: "You're singing, Babe." As much as I hated to admit it, he did make me want to sing. The things love will make you do. At this point, I was willing to throw caution to the wind.

"You know, I do want your autograph, baby. Here's the deal, when we get back to London, I'll have your autograph tattooed on my butt."

"Please tell me you're not joking, because I can have the same bloke who did my tat come to the house. I can watch. I *can* watch, can't I?"

"I'm not joking, and yes you can watch. Now, please don't start running a mind movie about it, because we're supposed to meet Mr. Gribble at the Lion and I don't think I'll have time to tend to you, if you get all hot and bothered."

"I'm always hot and bothered. You know that."

"I'm not arguing with you, baby."

Sergei got back at around half past eight. We had to scramble when we heard the front door, because we were still in bed in a state of disarray. We had a quick shower together to save time. While we were dressing, I started to freak. I heard this faint buzzing in my head and after the JD brain tumor thing, well let's just say I have a tendency towards hypochondria.

"Do you hear that?" The Actor asked. He was shaking his head as if he expected something in there to start rattling.

"You mean that buzzing?"

"Yes. It's a definite buzzing sound."

"Thank God, you can hear it too."

The Actor opened the bedroom door and the mystery was solved. "It's Sergei, hoovering," The Actor said.

"Don't you mean hovering?"

"Hoovering, American translation, using the vacuum cleaner."

"Oh, vacuuming."

"Tomato, To-mah-to, what do think of this shirt?"

"I like. I like very much. I may have to borrow that shirt."

"Babe, I love you, but just keep your hands off my bloody shirts."

Sergei thought we looked a little too hip for the room, but it was too late to change. He also admonished us for leaving smashed up crisps all over the place, the kids these days. We apologized profusely, and hugged and kissed him until he turned red.

THE ACTOR

The Lion was a fairly ancient, imposing, and newly scrubbed-up triangular building that sat like a wedge of wedding cake, on the corner. Walking up Argyle Place, it had taken us just under ten minutes to get there. We entered to the sound of Madonna singing *Borderline* and an impromptu sing-along, while a few couples danced. Far off the beaten track, the place was crowded but not uncomfortably so. One of the waitresses tapped the busy barman on the shoulder. He looked up and waved to The Actor and Sergei, motioning towards the other room to our right. My fears were somewhat calmed when we spied Mr. Gribble waving us in from a table near the back. He was seated with a petite brown-skinned woman with wavy, chin-length black hair. She was tapping the table and bobbing up and down to the music. Behind me, I could hear Sergei singing along with Madonna.

"This is when Madonna was cool," I said over my shoulder to Sergei, "I lost interest after *Into the Groove*." "*Ray of Light* was good," Sergei countered. "Fair enough, *Ray of Light* was good, but..."

"Don't get Sergei started on Madonna or we'll be here all night," The Actor laughed.

Introductions were made all around. The woman was the second Mrs. Gribble, Sita. The first Mrs. Gribble, Lita, was the sister I'd heard about earlier that day. The Gribbles' food was served shortly after we were seated, which reminded The Actor, Sergei and me how hungry we were.

The Actor and Sergei ordered the New York Burger and chips and I ordered the smoked trout sandwich. Pints of Courage Best Bitter were delivered promptly. We all settled into the traditional atmosphere of a proper Clifton Wood community pub. That lasted for about ten minutes, when an inebriated jarhead stormed our table insisting The Actor take off his baseball cap so he could get a good look at him. Sita leaned over and whispered, "He's not from around here." Then Sergei stood up, and as he did the jarhead took a step back.

"Is there a problem, mate?" Sergei said calmly.

"Oh, you let this big gorilla do your fighting for you?" the jarhead said to The Actor.

The Actor looked at Sergei and then at the jarhead, then leaned forward and said: "Yeah, mate. I do." The jarhead backed off mumbling "ponce," under his breath. Sergei remained standing until the jarhead was across the room.

Returning to his table, I heard jarhead tell his mates, "No, that's not him." Meanwhile, The Actor had been clutching a fork in his right hand under the table the whole time.

"If they're local, they'll come by the table and say hello and that's it. Only the ones who aren't from around here get like that," Gribble said.

Sure enough, a few people did just what Gribble had predicted and then a new round for the whole table arrived courtesy of some people at the bar. There were also inquiries about the health of The Actor's mum, with visible relief when The Actor said she probably wouldn't be returning to the neighborhood. Sita Gribble told me that she and her husband lived just up Church Street, a stone's throw away.

"You can't miss it," she said, "the only house with a front yard. It's where Gribble grew up."

I told her I liked her haircut and asked where she got it done. She pulled a wallet out of her purse rifled through it and produced a business card. "It's a full-service salon. They're very good." I thanked her and wondered whether I could get a last-minute appointment.

That night, I learned Mr. Gribble had taught both Sergei and The Actor at Easton Comprehensive School. Sergei was fearsome even then, hanging with a crew from the Council flats in St. Pauls, eventually dropping out of school.

The Actor also got into trouble with shoplifting, graffiti and public drunkenness, but he was a loner. Mr. Gribble had caught The Actor nicking a VHS of Shakespeare's Julius Caesar, starring Marlon Brando, from a stall at the St. Nicholas Market. Gribble found out after he'd paid for the VHS, that The Actor didn't even have a VHS player at home. This was the way Gribble came to find out about The Actor's interest in acting. Having no children of his own, Gribble took The Actor under his wing.

"There was something there," Gribble said, "I could see it." Gribble went on, as The Actor and Sergei ate and drank, exchanging glances and pretending they weren't listening. Sita Gribble sipped her G&T demurely, as she gazed on her husband with admiration and affection.

THE ACTOR

When The Actor was thirteen, Gribble took The Actor's class to see *Midsummer Night's Dream* at the Bristol Old Vic Theatre. The Actor's curiosity extended beyond the classroom to such an extent that Gribble paid for The Actor to attend a summer session of the Old Vic's Young Company. In exchange, The Actor did yard work and odd jobs for Gribble.

This first foray into training as an actor was a clandestine operation. If The Actor's mum had found out, there would have been hell to pay. This is when the plan to move to London was hatched. There was no way The Actor's mum would have allowed him to go to the Bristol Old Vic Theatre School, even if Daniel Day-Lewis and Gene Wilder were alumni. As far as she was concerned, after the departure of The Actor's father, The Actor's duty was to get a job that would keep a roof over their heads and provide her with an endless supply of cigarettes and booze.

To swan off to some posh acting school was out of the question, and as far as she was concerned out of The Actor's depth entirely. Boy, was she wrong. In the end, Gribble did buy The Actor a VHS player, which was promptly nicked by Sergei.

"Mr. Gribble, bringing that up . . . I was out of control, man. The drugs had me."

"That was then, and this is now," The Actor said. "You turned your life around." We all drank a toast to Sergei.

The DJ, who had been doing a really decent job, put on *FM* by Steely Dan, and that just did it for me. I saw The Actor nudge Sergei and the next thing I knew Sergei had lifted me out of my seat and we were dancing. Let me tell you, that Sergei had some serious moves. The Actor grabbed Mrs. Gribble. The next thing I knew, the floor was crowded. The movements of the dancers were inspired by a power that only comes when you just abandon yourself to the music, full stop. It was glorious.

When the song was over and the applause and catcalls subsided, the joy of the dance remained like a shimmering afterglow on everyone in the pub — even the DJ and those who remained seated, like Mr. Gribble.

The Actor hugged Mrs. Gribble, who got the giggles. He moved with open arms towards Sergei, who said, "You're not hugging me," and everyone laughed. Mr. Gribble rose to kiss Mrs. Gribble on the cheek as she sat down beside him, still giggling. I complimented Sergei on his dancing, and he blushed. The barman came over to clear off the table, which I thought was a little odd. He and The Actor were chit-chatting when the barman leaned over and whispered something in The Actor's ear. The Actor's face drained of all color, and I could see his right hand start to tremble. I leaned over to Sergei and whispered, "Melt-down alert. Better get your cousin to the Men's Room, now."

"Well, George Bernard Shaw said 'If you can't get rid of the skeleton in your closet, you better teach it to dance.'" Mr. Gribble said to no one in particular.

The Actor was in better shape when he and Sergei returned to the table. They didn't sit down; instead, they gave their goodbyes to the Gribbles. The Actor pulled me to my feet and whispered, "We're leaving." I said my goodbyes to Sita and Cornelius Gribble and wished that I had the time to get to know them better. "You'll come back and have dinner with us," Sita said.

Sergei stopped us before we reached the door.

"Just hang back for a minute or two and then come out," Sergei said to The Actor. The Actor nodded and left me standing there while he went over to the bar. Some patrons seated there turned around and raised their glasses to me. I smiled back feebly, in a state of utter confusion. The Actor returned.

"I bought a round for the house and took care of the barman and the wait staff," The Actor said with a slight tremor in his voice.

"What's going on, baby?" I asked.

"We'd better go," he said, taking my arm and guiding me towards the door.

As the door opened, the music and the noise of the patrons enjoying their free drinks and shouting their farewells to us spilled out the door, muffling what sounded like a heated argument taking place on the pavement. When the door closed there was the unmistakable sound of an enraged woman venting at the top of her lungs.

"Baldie!" she yelled, "they're 'round here. Baldie!"

From around the opposite side of the building a short, gaunt man with long, stringy black hair came running. He was wearing a torn Iron Maiden T-shirt and dirty jeans.

"I didn't see them come out the other way, Jen," Baldie said.

THE ACTOR

Jen was backed against the building with Sergei acting as a human barrier.

"That's because they're here, you git," Jen hissed.

The Actor pushed me over to the side. Baldie and Jen looked like a couple of junkies to me. Jen was petite and pasty, dressed in cut-off jeans and a blue tank top, both of which looked as though they could use a good washing. Her bleached blond hair, held in place by a rubber band, looked as if it were exploding from the top of her head. She wore run-down flip-flops exposing her dirty feet.

"Just let them pass," Sergei said to Jen, "We're not looking for trouble."

"What should I do, Jen?" Baldie asked.

"If you know what's good for you, mate, you'll just stand where you are, and do nothing," Sergei growled.

"I ain't afraid of you," Jen said to Sergei. "My mate rang and told me you was down here. Oy! I'm talking to you pervert," Jen shouted in The Actor's direction. "Remember me? Danny's sister? Where's that freak boyfriend of yours? He's got Danny, I know it. You ruined our Danny, the two of you. Ruined him."

With that Jen broke down and cried hysterically. Sergei backed off and Baldie ran in to console her. Sergei pressed a wad of bills into Baldie's trembling hand.

The Actor, Sergei and I walked down Argyle Place with the sounds of Jen's sobs reverberating down the dark street.

"If I ever find that bastard, Philippe, I'll kill him. You hear me?" she screamed after us.

We walked on for a while in silence. I was seething.

"I don't believe you gave those junkies money," I said to Sergei.

"Don't be angry with Serge. I told him to do it. Look on the bright side, maybe they'll O.D.," The Actor said.

As we walked, I learned that Jen's brother, Danny, was Philippe's boy-toy before Philippe and The Actor hooked up. Philippe had been abusive to the deeply closeted and confused Danny. Danny had been an unwilling participant in Philippe's sadistic sex-games. Even after Philippe had moved in with The Actor, Philippe would not leave Danny alone, so Danny appealed to The Actor for help. The Actor gave Danny the money he needed to disappear. Danny was able to move out of the country, and only The Actor knew where he was.

"Danny's a good kid. He came from Stapleton Road . . . the old neighborhood . . . a lifetime of bad breaks. I wasn't about to let Philippe get at him. That's why we had the argument that night," The Actor said, at which point Sergei shot him such a look that The Actor stopped talking.

Apparently, Jen with her limited mental capacity, and truncated life experience, thought Philippe and The Actor had "turned" Danny. But Danny had known since he was twelve that he was gay. He also knew that there was no coming out, not where he lived, not with his family. They'd kill him themselves before they'd see him with a man. Then Philippe came along, and Philippe was a different animal altogether. He was a seriously scary guy who enjoyed inflicting pain. He was a predatory beast, intent singularly on his own gratification, and woe unto anyone who got in his way. Danny's family and the whole Stapleton Road lot backed off, engaged in empty posturing, and lip service, which salved their own egos, but did little to help seventeen-year-old Danny.

Philippe had thought he owned Danny. Philippe also thought he controlled The Actor, but as I was learning The Actor was nobody's fool.

CHAPTER 21

I wonder which is the sickest, the audience which seeks to escape its miseries by being transported into a land of make-believe, or the actor who is nurtured in his struggle for personal aggrandizement by the sickness of the audience.

— George Sanders, Actor

Every time I read this excerpt from George Sanders' letter to his friend and erstwhile biographer, actor Brian Aherne, I can't help but laugh — it's just so George Sanders. The paragraph that follows reveals much more about the man:

I think perhaps it is the actor, strutting and orating away his youth and his health, alienated from reality, disingenuous in his relationships, a muddle-headed peacock forever chasing after the rainbow of his pathetic narcissism. My love and best wishes for a happy New Year.
George

I get the feeling that despite his protestations, Sanders did have a love for the very thing he condemned: the acting profession. After all, it did provide him with a decent living for many years. I don't believe you can deplore something with such eloquent passion unless you've loved that something, then felt betrayed by it. This is all part and parcel of the human condition, isn't it? I mean, songs have been written about this.

We all are capable of loving, desiring something so strongly we feel repelled by our own attachment to it, our own weakness in the face of it. I think George Sanders was capable of seeing the ironic truth in all things, with such acuity that it must have made life profoundly painful. Maybe he should have tried to see the humor in his own cynicism. Who knows? What I do know is that thinking too much will give you a headache.

I already had a headache, so what difference did it make? As we entered the little house in Ambra Vale South, I remembered the bottle of painkillers The Actor had given me and wondered: if I took a couple with all the alcohol in my system, would I still be in a fit state for our usual sexploits? My thoughts were momentarily diverted as The Actor and I said our good-nights to Sergei and headed to our room. I lost the race for the ensuite bathroom, which meant I had to use the family bathroom down the hall. When I returned, The Actor was naked, standing at the foot of the bed holding the riding crop in one hand and four long strips of leather in the other. He held both hands out to me and said, "Please?" I never fully understood the true meaning of the phrase, "This is going to hurt me more than it's going to hurt you," until that moment.

I awoke to an empty bed and the smell of eggs, toast and coffee. I'd had a deep dreamless sleep. I remembered The Actor snuggling up to me and kissing me with wet cheeks. He thanked me for tying him face down spread eagle to the bed, and thrashing him with the riding crop. I had tied him really tight, as he had requested, so tight in fact, I had to cut the leather strips from his wrists and ankles. I couldn't remember actually beating him. I remember crying, but I couldn't remember if it was as I fell asleep or as I was sleeping; either way, I was glad he had his club, because I couldn't see myself doing this on a regular basis.

I peed, washed my face, brushed my teeth, threw a robe on and hurried downstairs. The bi-fold doors to the garden were open, and the boys were eating their breakfast out there. When The Actor saw me he put his coffee down and jumped up to greet me.

"There she is," he said, "sit down and let me get you something." I tried to tell him not to bother, to finish eating, but he kissed me, said it was better if he moved around. No one, including me, wanted to talk about the Jen and Baldie incident.

"You know, we haven't talked about the wedding yet, not that I want anything fancy," I said.

"Well, Serge, you'll be my best man, won't you?"

"Just name the time and place and I'll be there."

"We don't really have a time and place do we, Babe? I mean, it will have to be after the premiere and before the Press tour."

"Why can't we get married in Cornwall? We can go surfing."

Sergei laughed so hard, I thought he was choking.

"Surfing! Are you mad?" The Actor said, "Look, we'd have to wait almost a week after filling out all the paperwork, probably more because you're American. No luv, sorry can't get married in Cornwall. We need someplace relatively close, where we can get a quickie marriage and then hop off to someplace nearby for the honeymoon, someplace secluded where the Press won't doorstep us."

"Tuscany," Sergio said. "They do quickie weddings in a chapel and then you can take a short flight down to Hydra for the honeymoon. Hydra's secluded. Rent a house. They have really high walls from the days of blood feuds and vendettas. No cars. No scooters."

The Actor looked at me and I looked at him, then we both looked at Sergei with awe and disbelief.

"I was seeing this stripper. She told me about it," Sergei said, sheepishly.

"Tuscany and Hydra it is, then. Cheers, mate," The Actor said.

After The Actor finished talking to Maida, he called the house and spoke to someone, but it wasn't Pickles — the tone was much more formal than it would have been with Pickles. It was as if The Actor were speaking to an employee. Whomever it was, The Actor was giving instructions about booking a chartered flight to, and hotel rooms in Tuscany for a party of seven, the chapel and the wedding officiant, catering for a reception in our hotel suite, renting a secluded house in Hydra and booking a flight from Tuscany to Hydra for the bride and groom. The Actor told the mystery person, if they ran into trouble to ask Mario and Pickles to help. I was completely unprepared for The Actor's display of organizational skills.

"We have almost two whole weeks," The Actor said, with a grin as he hung up the phone.

He then invited Mark Fragile and Maida, who was disappointed to hear that Pickles was going to be the maid of honor, and of course Mario would be there. Since my father wasn't able to do it, I asked Maida to give me away. She was thrilled.

"Babe, we can fly your father out if you like."

"We can't. My father had a stroke and he's in a nursing home."

"I'm sorry," Sergei said, with genuine concern.

"Babe, I didn't know. You never said."

"I know, honey. I just don't like to think about it." The Actor hugged me. I started to cry, and I just couldn't stop. I guess it was joy and fear. You see, I'd forgotten how much real courage love takes.

"I'm such a coward," I sobbed, "I can't guarantee I'll always be there for you when you need me."

"Be there for me when you can, luv," The Actor said.

"I don't want to hurt you anymore, and I don't want you to want me to," I whispered.

The Actor's voice cracked as he said, "I'm sorry. It's not about want, Babe. You understand that, don't you?"

"I understand. We aren't going past your old house. We're just not doing that." From over The Actor's shoulder I saw Sergei, put his hand over his heart, then give me a thumbs up.

I did want to get my hair done, but the full-service salon Sita Gribble had recommended was booked. It would be another week before I could get an appointment. My hair was like a wild beast with a mind of its own. I decided best to just wash it and let it do its thing. I was doing my own personal beauty maintenance full time. It was exhausting. The Actor would have thought I was gorgeous if I walked around in a sack cloth and ashes; in fact, it would probably excite him to no end. God, he was so worth loving.

I really needed an extra emery board to do some emergency nail repairs before we headed out on the second leg of our journey. I thought I might find one in The Actor's mum's room, but the door was locked. Unfortunately, The Actor caught me examining the lock as he was coming up the stairs.

"What are you doing, Babe?"

"I was just looking for a nail file," I said backing away from the door.

The Actor grabbed my wrist as he passed me and pulled me into our room.

"So, is a nail file your tool of choice for lock picking?"

"No, no. I need a nail file to do my nails, well an emery board, really. I thought . . . you know . . . since your mother is a woman, allegedly, that she might have an emery board I could use."

The Actor shook his head, "I have to say, I find this streak of criminality in you fascinating. Breaking and entering, grievous bodily harm..."

"Although I may have a facility for those kinds of things, I don't make a habit out of them."

"So, you say," The Actor laughed as he threw me down on the bed. "Just remember," he went on as he straddled me, "when we're married you can't be forced to testify against me, and I can't be forced to testify against you."

CHAPTER 22

The key to acting is sincerity and if you can fake that, you've got it made.

— The Actor

Through cadence, diction, movement, intelligence, technical mastery and sheer force of personality, The Actor could hold the heart and soul of an audience hostage.

Many of his films focused on themes of betrayal, degradation, injustice and sexual revenge. He had chosen his vehicles carefully, but not conservatively. There was always an element of risk inherent in the project itself — and in his performance.

His films turned out to be unpretentiously important, crafted by writers and directors who were at the top of their game, yet working outside the mainstream. This allowed The Actor to explore some difficult emotional territory. I have to honestly admit, I was in awe of the command he had over his art — in awe, and on some level, terrified. You see, it was about process.

My father's process had been to lock himself in his studio, sometimes for weeks on end. This, for my brother and me, meant the loss of a playmate and protector from the violent mood swings of our crazy mother.

In the weeks before my father actually began the physical labor of sculpting a piece, there would be no talking to him unless you wanted to see the wrath of Zeus ready to throw down a thunderbolt. He was deep into himself during this incubation period. Drawing and discarding drawings for hours, then abruptly going out to walk in the woods, near our house, for even more hours. My mother, tense and fortified by drugs, would warn us to leave our father alone: "He's creating." She said this as if he were God, and for a long time I believed he was.

Now, I had a new God and he was a jealous God, which meant I had to behave myself. I needed something to absorb my mind and body, to the point of distraction, while The Actor was involved in his process. I was sure it was the only way for me to survive with my own persona intact. A sense of purpose never hurt anyone, except maybe Philippe.

Sergei, The Actor and I spent the rest of the morning packing our things and securing the house in Ambra Vale South. No one would be back for at least a month or more once we left, which meant we had to clean out the refrigerator, throw sheets over the furniture in the two reception rooms, close the curtains, put tarps on the garden furniture, arm the alarm and let the local constabulary and the next-door neighbors know that the house was going to be vacant for a while. The front door locks had already been changed.

I felt a slight twinge of sadness leaving the little house, because it reminded of the house Gordon and I had in San Francisco, the house where he lived his last days. I felt very comfortable in this neighborhood, close to the sea and the beauty of the Wood and the Gorge, but I was romanticizing. How long it would take before I became bored and restless? I had enjoyed playing house with the boys, though. Our little road show was travelling on to the Barchester Beaufort Grange Care Home, where The Actor's mum was to be ensconced for her health, and the public's safety. I really had no desire to trudge all the way down to Cornwall, so The Actor could further punish himself by engaging in some demented act of filial duty, but when I asked him why we had to go he said, "Because she's my mum." It only made him angry when I pointed out that she had a nurse and a doctor and a housekeeper, so I dropped the subject. But in Brit speak, I was not well pleased.

The closer we got to the care home, the bigger the knot in my stomach grew. We could have swung round onto Easton Way from the Newfoundland Circus road to visit The Actor's old 'hood, but thank God we didn't. Who knows what kind of traumatic shit would have risen to the surface from that stroll down memory lane.

I was having some sort of private freak out on the drive to thecare home, while The Actor slept blissfully with his head tilted back and his mouth open. My mother used to fall asleep on the sofa like that when she was watching TV. A fly flew in her mouth once. It was so funny, I pissed myself from laughing so hard. I wasn't laughing now, though — more on the verge of tears. The Actor would want me to go with him to sign the papers, deliver the check and make arrangements, but I couldn't dare step foot into the care home without going to pieces.

I guess it had to do with my father. My father was in just as nice a place as this Barchester Beaufort Grange joint, but no matter how you sliced it, when you walked into one of those places you were looking at the future, in some way shape or form. I found that thought way too much to bear, especially without any mood-altering substances in my system.

Naturally, we couldn't present ourselves to the care home administrators stinking of booze and weed; therefore, The Actor and I were stone cold sober. Sergei was his usual temperate self since it was still daylight, and he was still on duty.

"Sergei, what's over there?"

"That's Pond Field Wood."

"Well, didn't we just pass a Wood?"

"Yeah, Barn Wood and up ahead over there is Hermitage Wood."

"Jesus, enough with the Woods already . . . and how come you say Wood instead of Woods?"

"Because we're British."

"I'm sorry, Sergei. I'm so on edge. Look at his nibs, sleeping like he's six months old. Do you believe when I met him he wasn't sleeping at all?"

"You're like medicine to him," Sergei said.

"Am I? That's a sweet thing to say."

We drove on in silence. The big baby man slept on, and I thought about our telepathic dreams where he reached out to me to help him, when I had no idea how to, but now seemed to be helping him in spite of myself. We had gone through what seemed like a lifetime in a matter of weeks, settling into each other as if a groove had been carved out long ago. Two film noir characters: a woman with a past, a man with a dubious future, both unsure about the present, on a collision course with destiny. I was truly losing my mind, and I didn't give a shit.

THE ACTOR

Sergei pulled the sedan into a parking slot in front of the huge facility. I shrank down in my seat, trying to make myself invisible. The cessation of motion shook The Actor from his sleep. He pulled a handkerchief from his pants pocket to wipe away the drool that had accumulated on the side of his mouth, stretched and looked at me with that grin. Like a chirpy puppy dog, he was always happy to see me.

"I can't go in there," I said as calmly as I could.

The Actor's happy face melted into hurt and concern. "I don't understand, Babe. Why? What's the matter?"

"It's my father, he's in one of these places . . . I have such a hard time . . . I'm sorry. I know this must be hard enough for you as it is."

The Actor put his arms around me and whispered, "Serge will go with me. We won't be long. And next to the day we get married, this is the happiest day of my life, believe me."

I sat in the car, window rolled half down, and watched The Actor and Sergei approach the Barchester Beaufort Grange Care Home. I admired the fierce loyalty and love between them. There was so much love in The Actor: for his work, his daughter, Sergei, Pickles and Mario, music, his shirts, his deceased father and mental mother. It was astonishing he had any love left over, but he did, and I was happy to luxuriate in it even though I knew all that love in his heart shared its space with so much pain.

I must have dozed off because I was awoken by three taps, like in the Hitchcock film *Marnie,* but there was no super-hunky Sean Connery trying to help me recover from complex post-traumatic stress disorder; instead, a uniformed policeman was outside the car door asking me to "Please step out of the car, Miss."

I was still a little groggy and I guess part of me thought I was dreaming. There were two police cars parked in front of the Barchester Beaufort Grange Care Home. The Actor was being led out of the building by a uniformed cop, and a plain clothes officer. Sergei followed behind, looking angry and homicidal. The manager of the care home, a petite blond woman, ran after them shouting to The Actor, "Is there anyone you want me to call? Anything I can do?

Your mother is still coming, isn't she?" "I don't understand. Are we being arrested?" I asked as I was taken to one of the police cars by the officer who had awoken me. "No, Miss," was all he said.

The next thing I knew I was gently thrust into the back seat of a police car, on one side, and The Actor thrust in on the other. They weren't interested in Sergei, who reluctantly went back to the sedan and followed behind the two police cars. The plain clothes cop, who sat up front in the passenger seat, spoke to us. He told us not to talk to each other, that we were not under arrest, we were being taken in for questioning related to the disappearance of Philippe Noiret.

The Actor had retreated into acting mode. I had no idea who I was dealing with at the moment, but this time I was grateful for the skills his profession had given him. I only wished I had those same skills available to me. All I had was panic-induced bravado and the self-righteous indignation of a pissed-off, has-been, American diva, which would have to suffice. The Actor held my hand and gave me the grin: I knew we'd make it through whatever this was. I figured it must have been that Jen and Baldie who set the cops on us. How else would they know where we were?

"We have a right to know where you're taking us," I said.

"Avon and Somerset Constabulary Headquarters in Portishead, Miss," the plainclothes cop said.

I had no idea what the hell he was talking about, until up ahead I saw a huge modern brick, glass and steel building, with a swarm of reporters, photographers, news vans with satellite dishes, and local yokels waving autograph books and DVD covers. The Actor looked like someone had just punched him in the stomach. I heard him exhale, "Blimey."

"It's show time," I said pulling out my sunglasses, "Let's just show them why we're fabulous." The Actor had to laugh, in spite of himself. The two cops looked nervous and hesitated to exit the car for a moment. The Actor ran his fingers through his hair, took a deep breath and opened the door. He helped me out then, to my surprise, grabbed me and kissed me quite passionately, as the crowd cheered and cameras of every type known to mankind captured the moment. Then we briskly walked the gauntlet.

I flashed the peace sign while The Actor flipped it and gave them the patented grin. Attempts were made to stick microphones in our faces, but the police showed their training and prevented anyone from getting too close. As we entered the cavernous building, we were whisked down a corridor to a meeting room that was

THE ACTOR

enclosed in glass walls covered by mini-blinds. Thank God, I had my sunglasses, because the joint was ablaze with fluorescent lights. If I had to work in a place like this, I'd become a serial killer. At the far end of the room at the head of the table sat our old friend DS Crawford.

"Please sit down. I'm sorry about this, but I did ask you two to stay put whilst we were investigating Mr. Noiret's disappearance. Miss Lake, you left St. Mary's hospital before you could be questioned by the police in connection with Mr. DeLongo's accident."

"That wasn't my intention."

"Nevertheless," Crawford said.

"Perhaps you should introduce us, Crawford."

I was so unnerved by the fluorescent lights, I failed to notice the others at the table besides Crawford. I think The Actor had been oblivious as well, zeroing in on a familiar face the way I had, to cope with the apparent magnitude of the situation.

The man who asked for introductions was seated at Crawford's right. He was Detective Chief Inspector Leathersby, Crawford's boss; next to Leathersby; was a member of the local constabulary, Detective Chief Inspector Briggs; and at the far end of the table was a woman, in very well-tailored corporate drag, organizing a small mountain of papers. Crawford didn't introduce her, and tried to continue where he had left off, but was interrupted by The Actor.

"Are we under arrest? Shouldn't our briefs be present for this — whatever this is?"

DCI Leathersby spoke.

"Neither you nor Ms. Lake are under arrest. You're here because new information has come to light with regard to the disappearance of Philippe Noiret. We hope you'll both help us by answering a few questions."

"If we're not under arrest, then we can leave," I said.

"Would you rather we place you and your future husband under arrest, Ms. Lake? Because, we can do that," DCI Leathersby continued.

"What do you want to know?" The Actor asked.

"Well, if it's all right with you, sir," Crawford said to Leathersby, "I'd like to just go over recent events and bring everyone up to speed, so we're all reading from the same page."

Leathersby glanced down to the woman at the end of the table, who now sat with her hands folded, back straight in rapt attention. Crawford followed Leathersby's gaze, his eyes resting briefly on the woman, and then darting back to Leathersby, who nodded giving Crawford the go ahead.

"We've been down to see your mum in Cornwall hoping she might shed some light on Mr. Noiret's disappearance, but I have to say it was a waste of effort. She's pretty far gone, isn't she?"

"I could have saved you the time. That's why we're down here, to close up her house and make arrangements for her to enter the care home," The Actor said.

"How did you know about Cornwall? How did you know where to find us?" I asked.

"We're coppers, Miss," Briggs said flatly.

Crawford continued, "I did want to let you know before we go any further, that the blood sample from your basement was inconclusive; however, the hairs we were able to get from Mr. Noiret's brush gave us some interesting DNA evidence, but I'm getting ahead of myself."

"I'm going to take this opportunity to jump in Crawford, just so we can get this bit of business out of the way," Leathersby chimed in as he opened a folder in front of him.

"Ms. Lake, the trauma doctor who arrived at Mr. DeLongo's with the EMTs thought you were acting suspiciously, and reported the incident to the police. Also, there was the fact that both you and Mr. DeLongo were intoxicated at the time of his accident. Mr. DeLongo does not remember anything about that night, except that you and he were in a pub before going back to his flat. The trauma doctor thought there were some inconsistencies at the scene — nothing definitive, but nonetheless suspicious."

"I was just checking him out, God! I thought the doctor was cute and he turns me into some kind of prime suspect character on that basis, the asshole."

"You were checking him out?" The Actor said a little too loudly. "Yeah. So? I wasn't going to have sex with him or anything."

"Babe, we're going to be married and you're checking out some random doctor?"

"Like you don't check people out? Like you weren't checking out Leathersby over there? Come on. I was intoxicated at the time. OK?" "I love you, you daft cow. Does that not mean anything?" The

Actor shouted.

"And I love you too, baby. I'm weak, especially when I've had too much to drink, but I'd never . . . Did you just call me a cow?"

"That's enough!" Leathersby said, slapping his hand on the table. "I'm satisfied nothing went on at Mr. DeLongo's flat, the night of his accident, that need concern the police. Press on, Crawford."

"Thank you, sir. What exactly was the nature of your relationship with Mr. Noiret?"

The Actor's stomach contracted visibly. He looked at me, then back at Crawford.

"He was an employee, my personal assistant."

"And yet," Leathersby continued, "he lived in your house, and slept in a room that could only be accessed through your bedroom?"

"What's your point?" The Actor said.

"Were you and Philippe Noiret engaged in an intimate relationship?"

"I don't see what the hell that has to do with anything," I said.

"Ms. Lake, please. We don't like asking this question any more than your future husband likes having it asked, but we need to establish the exact nature of the relationship," Leathersby said.

"If you mean by intimate, we were lovers then yes, we had an intimate relationship, which by the way, is no longer illegal in this country."

"Was Mr. Noiret ever violent with you?" "Yes."

"Did he ever break your arm?" "Yes."

"And you never reported this to the police?"

"Have you seen the circus outside this building? How would you like that outside your house? I have a daughter. No, I did not report it to the police, when Philippe was violent. Where's this going?"

He was so good. He made no mention of his and Philippe's penchant for the rougher-the-better sex, all the S&M stuff — and the way his voice broke when he said, "I have a daughter" was brilliant. He was no longer a willing participant, but a hapless victim. Damn, he was good, like Lana Turner in the witness box.

Briggs asked, "Do you know Daniel Spigott?"

"Yeah, I know Danny."

"Did the man you know as Philippe Noiret," Briggs continued, "have an intimate relationship with Danny Spigott, and was Noiret violent with Danny Spigott in the same manner he was violent with you?"

"Yes, Philippe was fucking Danny, and yes Philippe would get violent with him. What has this got to do with anything?"

Briggs sighed and placed his palms flat on the table and stared at The Actor just long enough to make everyone uncomfortable. "Don't remember me, do you, son? I remember you. Good on you for making something of yourself. That cousin of yours, he's all right now, isn't he? Paid his debt to society, straightened himself out . . ."

Leathersby interjected, "If you haven't figured this out yet, I'm going to take the liberty of speaking for my colleagues: we're not interested in you, we're not interested in Ms. Lake. We're interested in the man you know as Philippe Noiret."

"What do you mean 'the man I know as Philippe'? Why do you keep saying that?"

The woman at the far end of the table gathered up her papers like a weary school teacher: "Gentlemen I'll take it from here."

I've never been a big fan of hard-tailoring, but I really liked the suit she was wearing, especially the cut of the pants. She either had it altered or hand-made, because she was tall, with long legs and arms and the jacket cuffs fell at exactly the right place, just a fraction below the wrist, always a problem when you're a tall woman with long arms. The suit was navy and her blouse was purple, which said to me she had a bit of a creative streak, but her perfume Chanel No. 5 was definitely the perfume of a traditionalist. I could smell it as she leaned in between The Actor and me to place two 8x10 photographs in front of us. One of the photos was a little out of focus. It was a head shot of a man with long dark wavy hair and a mustache. The other photo looked like a blown-up passport photo, the man was clean-shaven with short hair. The woman took a seat next to Briggs. She looked around furtively for a moment and then Leathersby handed her a Kenneth Cole leather briefcase. She thanked him.

"I am Cecile Jervay, special investigator from INTERPOL's Fugitive Unit. Can you tell me if either one of you recognize the man in those photographs?"

"It's Philippe," The Actor said. "What does INTERPOL want with Philippe?"

"This is getting way too James Bond for me," I said.

THE ACTOR

"Does the name Ray Jackson mean anything to either one of you?" Ms. Jervay went on.

She had a plain open face, that gave the impression you could trust her, but it was just an impression. You know what I mean? After The Actor and I dickered back and forth about Ray Jackson, only to realize we were confusing the name with Randy Jackson, the record producer and American Idol judge, did the exasperated INTERPOL investigator interrupt us. At least she was smooth about it, no hand smacking the table. She merely cleared her throat loudly.

"Philippe Noiret is in fact Ray Jackson from Perth, Australia, where he has an extensive criminal history, and is wanted for murder. Jackson is also wanted for murder in Thailand and for rape and extortion in Norway." For each country mentioned, Special Investigator Jervay shoved a wanted poster across the table at us.

"Ray Jackson is also a person of interest in several other crimes, which for reasons of National Security, I can't go into at this meeting." "About three years ago," she continued, "an elderly couple from Clifton, last seen in the company of a man fitting Jackson's description, went missing. We believe Jackson probably tortured them to obtain their pin numbers, killed them and then used ATMs to empty their bank accounts. This was the beginning of Jackson's activities in this area. We believe your mum was his next target, but when he found out who she was, he used her to move on to you."

You could have heard an ant digesting its food. The Actor's right hand started to tremble, and all of the color drained from his face. I felt nauseous. Briggs, for all his tight-assed façade, actually looked distressed at the effect the news was having on The Actor and me. He suggested we take a break and he departed to organize some tea. While Jervay and Leathersby conferred, Crawford came over and apologized. The police were unsure if The Actor knew Philippe's true identity. Due to the nature of the relationship The Actor had had with Philippe, the authorities suspected that The Actor may have been aiding and abetting Philippe, all along. As for me, I could have been helping The Actor shield Philippe, for all the police knew; thus the reason for our being brought in for questioning in such an abrupt manner. But, it was now clear, that neither The Actor nor I knew that Philippe was the infamous Ray Jackson.

During the break, The Actor stepped outside the meeting room to call Sergei. I visited the ladies' room and was appalled at how tired I looked. If The Actor still wanted to go down to Cornwall, we should spend one more night at his mum's house, because we'd be too knackered to make the long drive. I went back and told The Actor what I thought. He agreed. Too bad I'd left my flask in the car. The Actor hugged me and it felt good to hold onto each other for a moment.

When we went back into the meeting room, there was a tray with tea and sandwiches and bottled water, on a cabinet off to the side, to which we and the others helped ourselves. Leathersby leaned over and told The Actor that it wouldn't be much longer. Special Investigator Jervay dived back into it.

"DCI Briggs has been contacted by the Spigott family and they believe Ray Jackson, posing as Philippe Noiret, is responsible for the disappearance of Danny Spigott."

"Danny didn't disappear," The Actor said leaning forward, "well, not in the way you think. I gave him money to get away from Philippe. Danny's alive and well, working in a hotel in Miami. His family can't accept the fact that Danny's gay, so he was kind of getting away from them as well. Briggs, you know what the Spigotts are like. Danny's fine."

Special Investigator Jervay reached into her briefcase and pulled out a writing pad and a pen, which she shoved across the table to The Actor: "If you could just write down Danny's contact information." Jervay folded her hands on the table and took a deep breath: "There's no easy way to say this. Ray Jackson is an extremely dangerous individual. He may have fallen victim to foul play himself, he may have simply moved on to his next victim, or he may be lying low. We have no way of knowing, right now. Anyone who has come into contact with this man, and who is still alive, can consider themselves incredibly fortunate."

It was at this point that Leathersby addressed the elephant in the room, as if the atmosphere wasn't emotionally charged enough: "Do either one of you know the whereabouts of the man you know as Philippe Noiret?"

The Actor was not happy with this line of questioning.

"Why would we? Are Felicia and I under suspicion? I mean we could have met the same fate as Philippe . . . Ray Jackson's other victims. We still could if he's out there, somewhere. Nobody seems to be concerned about that."

"We are very much concerned about that," Special Investigator Jervay said flatly.

"Please answer the question," Leathersby said.

"No, we have not," I said, looking at The Actor for confirmation. He shook his head and said, "No."

We were then summarily warned by INTERPOL investigator Jervay to notify INTERPOL immediately if we were contacted by the man we knew as Philippe Noiret. She gave her card to The Actor and to me. The meeting ended as abruptly as it had begun.

DCI Briggs made a big show of his gratitude for our cooperation. We were on his patch, so he escorted us out. On the way a tall, balding man wearing a bespoke, dark blue suit and tinted glasses brushed past us in the corridor; as he did, I felt a chill. I looked back and he walked into the meeting room we had just exited.

"Have ghosts in the building, do you?" The Actor said to Briggs.

Briggs laughed a tense laugh, thanked us again, turned and scuttled off.

"Wanker," The Actor said, under his breath.

There were no signs of the Press when we emerged from the building. The Actor called Sergei, and in less than a minute the black sedan pulled up to the door. We got in and sped off, back to Clifton Wood and Ambra Vale South. We were followed by a black SUV.

"We've got a tail, Sergei," I said.

"I know, and we're going to have one from now on." Sergei said with disgust. "And I can guarantee the house has been bugged."

"What about our privacy?" I shouted.

"Simmer down, luv," The Actor said putting his arm around me, "The number one delusion of the 21st century isn't it . . . that there is such a thing as privacy. Once you get used to the fact that you're always naked, transparency becomes a weapon. Doesn't it Serge?"

The Actor started to laugh as he caught Sergei's eye in the rear-view mirror. Sergei joined in the laughter, which only served to annoy me, because I had no idea what they were laughing about. Whatever was going on between them, was definitely conspiratorial.

"Well, we can say and do as we please in the car for now. I've gone over it," Sergei stated.

"Good lad," The Actor said.

There was no way the SUV that was following us could squeeze its way down the narrow street, thank goodness. I half expected a swarm of Press there, in front of the house, door-stepping us, but the street was empty, except for a man walking his dog. Sergei dropped us off and backed out of the street, in search of a parking spot. As we entered the house, the man walking the dog took our picture with his cell phone.

The Actor took off his jacket and threw it on the floor: "Fucking filth!" He stood there for a moment, one hand on his hip, the other over his mouth. He spun around and grabbed me on my way to the kitchen.

"If you want to leave me, I wouldn't blame you. I don't know how I'd bear it . . ."

"It's not your fault, baby. It's Ray Philippe Noiret Jackson whoever the fuck's fault. I swear I'd kill him myself . . ."

The Actor kissed me tenderly, "That's my girl."

Sergei had taken a little longer than usual to get back, but he was on the case. There was no food or liquor in the house, and he had gone to get some Indian take-away and brought in a bottle from the boot/trunk of the car.

We ate outside, by candlelight, in the little garden where, presumably, we could talk without being overheard. "Briggs the prig," The Actor said, between bites.

"Bent as a dog's hind leg," Sergei added.

"What's up with the Bristol villainy, mate? You'd think somebody'd have a bullet with his name on it?"

"You'd think."

"I thought he was OK," I said.

"That's what he wants you to think. I give you three guesses who tipped off the Press," The Actor said.

"For all we know he's the one who set Jen and Baldie on us," Sergei said.

"They had Spooks, Special Branch, watching us on video. We bumped into one in the corridor."

"That's what the 'ghost in the building' remark was about."

"Yeah, and they're going over the car as we speak," Sergei said.

"And the man walking his dog, I think he's one. He took our picture when we walked through the front door," I added.

It was only seven in the evening, but it felt like it was much later. I guess because we had been up early and so much had happened, also we had gone without weed or liquor for what seemed like an eternity. The plan was to get some kip (rest) and head out at midnight for Cornwall. For my money, we could have gone straight back to London, and I would have been happy. I was missing Professor Pickles something awful. I had to fill him in on the haps. I knew he would find it totally thrilling that The Actor and I were being shadowed by MI5 . . . well maybe not, after his recent experience with the Feds.

I did the washing up. I felt I owed it to the boys since they'd been doing the cooking and washing up the whole of our stay in the little house. Sad, I had fallen in love with this little house and this part of the world; however, this last episode had put me right off it, even though I thought it might be fun to come back and have dinner with Cornelius and Sita Gribble.

"A penny for your thoughts," The Actor said, as he slipped behind me and wrapped his arms around my waist.

"I want to go back to London, get in bed with you, pull the covers over us and stay like that forever."

"Fancy burning one first?"

We left Sergei downstairs stretched out on the sofa watching Alfred Hitchcock's *Rebecca*. As we made our way upstairs I couldn't help but think the room we were about to get high in, sleep in, make love and dream in was where the man we knew as Philippe Noiret, had done the same things.

We were startled out of our sleep by a knock on the door. It was Sergei and it was now a little after 11:00 p.m. (23:00), time to get ourselves together and get back on the road. By the time we left the house it was midnight; not even the dog walker was about. We set the trash out and walked to the car without incident. Three and a half hours later we were just outside Penzance in Cornwall, where the English countryside wanders out into the Celtic Sea.

About a mile northwest of the town of Penzance, we pulled past an opened five-barred gate, into what looked like a large gravel corral, bounded on all sides by a low stone L-shaped building, which was actually a farmhouse and barn joined and converted into one house.

At about three-thirty in the morning it all looked pretty creepy. I was waiting for a wolf to howl and Peter Cushing to saunter out carrying a lantern. We could have used that lantern, because it was pitch-black save for the headlights. Sergei pulled up to what looked like a garage, fumbled through the glove box for what seemed like ages, until he found the remote device to open the garage door.

"I don't like this place," I said, grabbing The Actor's arm.

"Babe, it's only for a few hours," The Actor said.

"Well, won't we be waking everyone? Maybe we could just stay in the car until the sun comes up?"

"You'll be fine, Miss," Sergei said as he pulled into the garage.

"We're going in through the garage, we won't disturb anyone who isn't already disturbed," The Actor laughed.

Inside, the conjoined barn/farmhouse appeared surprisingly modern and cheerful, but there was a distinct vibe in the air that made my skin crawl. We walked from the garage past a utility room into the kitchen. There was an ample supply of liquor on a tray in the dining area. Sergei helped himself to a beer from the fridge. The Actor poured us each an Irish whiskey, and the three of us settled down on a sofa that sat before a fireplace in the huge kitchen. The fireplace came in handy. It was quite chilly in the house. Once The Actor and Sergei got the fire going, it was so nice and cozy sitting there between the two of them, I dozed off.

I was abruptly awoken by a loud crash. Still groggy, I couldn't tell from where the commotion came. The Actor and Sergei were nowhere to be found. The fire had gone out. I heard raised voices. I raced through a door at the opposite end of the kitchen that led to a narrow corridor illuminated by a light at its end. To my left, the doors were opened to an unoccupied bedroom, with adjoining bath. All at once, the voices stopped and someone screamed. I ran forward and found myself in what must have been the sitting room ablaze with lights and so huge I lost my bearings, for a second. It too was unoccupied. Then I heard a scuffling noise and a muffled scream. I was terrified. I found another door on the far side of the living room. There was a short narrow corridor, which opened onto a fairly large, four-cornered hallway, that had exits on either side, to whatever was outdoors. My God, this place was like a maze.

That hallway emptied into another narrow corridor with yet

another bedroom on the left and what must have been the master bedroom at the far end. The lights were on in the master bedroom. I could hear people speaking, but couldn't make out what they were saying. Without warning, The Actor appeared in the doorway.

"Babe, you shouldn't be here," he said. "I want to know what's going on."

As I approached the door, The Actor blocked my way. I peeked past him into the massive bedroom: there was his mum. She was in bed, tucked in tight, with her arms at her side outside the covers, lying flat and still like a doll. She was bathed in sweat and breathing shallowly. Her face was locked in a grimace, her eyes fixed on middle space.

Sergei was slumped in a chair by the window, looking as if the life had been drained out of him. A short, stocky man with a blond buzz-cut, dressed in a white T-shirt and black running pants, had a stethoscope around his neck. He was taking The Actor's mum's pulse. I was mesmerized by his forearms, which were covered in a Technicolor garden of tats.

"She's fine for now," he said without looking up, "may as well try to get some sleep. The sun will be up soon."

"Cheers, Colin," Sergei said, as he pulled himself up from the chair and rubbed his face, "Sleep tight, Auntie," he said as he stumbled past The Actor and me.

"Ta and all, Serge," The Actor said patting Sergei's shoulder.

"It never ceases to amaze me how strong that woman is," Sergei said as he made his way down the corridor towards the sitting room. "She flipped out and Colin there had to sedate her whilst me and Serge held her down," The Actor whispered.

"I can hear you," The Actor's mum said through clenched teeth. "That your whore you got with you. Let me tell you, dearie, he's nothing special."

The Actor turned his head sharply and bit down on his bottom lip. He took a deep breath, then calmly turned around and said:

"Colin, this is my fiancée, Felicia Lake. Felicia, this is Colin McCarty, my mother's nurse." Colin extended his hand, as he congratulated us. I told him I admired what he did for a living and he seemed surprised. The Actor looked over at his mother who had nodded out and was snoring loudly.

"Dr. Briganti will be here around eleven, she should be out until then," Colin said.

It was somewhere between five and six in the morning. Sergei had fallen asleep on one of the sofas in the sitting room. I decided to make some tea while The Actor got a blanket from the little bedroom next to the kitchen to throw over Sergei. The Actor entered the kitchen, distraught and full of manic energy: "I'll get the bags from the car. We'll all need a change of clothes."

After he had deposited our bags in the little bedroom and Sergei's in the sitting room, The Actor collapsed onto the sofa and was grateful for the cup of tea I handed him. There was no fire; still, we sat there, side by side, staring at the fireplace, in silence, for quite a while. I noticed it had gotten a little more comfortable in the house and The Actor said Colin had turned on the central heating.

As much to comfort himself as me, The Actor said when Dr. Briganti arrived, his mother would be examined, then transported by ambulance to Barchester Beaufort Grange Care Home. Colin would be discharged, the sprawling house closed and the keys returned to the owner who was a friend of The Actor's. Colin had packed his mother's things. It would be up to Sergei, The Actor and me to do pretty much what we had done at the house on Ambra Vale South.

I was curious about this house, in the middle of nowhere, with what had been sprawling farmland all around it. You could bury a body here and no one would ever find it, unless they knew where to look. Or, you could take a boat out and dump it in the sea.

We were awakened by Sergei at about ten in the morning. He was going to take a shower in the adjoining bathroom and wouldn't be long. The Actor told him to take his time, even though he knew he wouldn't. Sergei took very quick showers, a habit leftover from his prison days. He and The Actor made breakfast for everyone, including a grateful Colin, who took a tray into The Actor's mum.

I was straggling. I still felt tired. I'd slept uneasily because of the creepy feeling the house gave me. Also, The Actor, usually quite frisky when we got into bed, had rolled over and cried himself to sleep.

Dr. Briganti arrived with the ambulance not far behind. He was a tall, thin athletically built man with a very calm demeanor and soothing voice. After introductions and coffee, he and The Actor sat down at the dining table and conferred for a moment. Then the doctor. signed some papers and The Actor handed the doctor what looked like two checks, one of which the doctor gave to Colin, whose broad smile upon receiving it was testament to its generosity.

As The Actor's mum was wheeled out through the hallway exit, down the corridor from her bedroom strapped to a gurney, I watched from the corridor on the opposite side. Tears welled up and spilled down her cheeks. Our eyes met. There was something so soft and pleading in her face. It reminded me of the look my cat gave me, when I had to have her put down. It haunts me still.

Strange as it may seem, watching that ambulance carry away The Actor's mum also reminded me of my mother and somehow it gave me a new perspective on her suicide. Maybe she saw this thing that was happening to The Actor's mum happening to her and decided that was not the way she wanted to live out the rest of her life . . . like Virginia Woolf. I don't know for sure, but maybe in some way it was an act of courage, what she did: taking her own life, before it was taken from her. At any rate, it gave me a sense of peace to think that it was. I could not stop the tears from overpowering me with a sense of relief.

The Actor's arms were around me, pulling me close to his warm body. That familiar smell of his: whiskey, lemons and the sweat on his skin gave me such comfort. I felt the worst of everything was over. I looked into his eyes, red with his own tears, and I knew his tears were not for anyone present but for the absent among us. In my heart, I knew that this converted farm on the moor was the place where the man we knew as Philippe Noiret had probably come to rest. I had no proof about my mother's reasons for her suicide, just as I had no proof that the man we knew as Philippe Noiret was dead and buried. What I did have was *my* truth, even though I know the truth is not necessarily the facts, and the facts are not necessarily the truth. I was content to cling to my truth and let my truth be the facts, thus closing the chapters on my mother, Catherine Bannister Lake, George Sanders, and the man we knew as Philippe Noiret.

THE END

CPSIA information can be obtained
at www.ICGtesting.com
Printed in the USA
BVHW030815261120
594276BV00008B/27